Pamela Oldfield, born a Londoner, now enjoys life in the Kent countryside. She has a grown up son and daughter. As a primary school teacher, Pamela wrote her first books for children but was soon writing historical novels for adults. At that point, she says, her writing "hobby" became a way of life. With her husband Joe, she travels to research her books. She also helps aspiring writers by her talks and workshops here and abroad. Her books have been translated into seven different languages. *Lady of the Night* is her first novel for Piatkus.

Lady of the Night

Pamela Oldfield

PIATKUS

First published in Great Britain in 1998 by
Judy Piatkus (Publishers) Ltd of
5 Windmill Street, London, W1

First paperback edition 1998

**The moral right of the author
has been asserted**

*A catalogue record for this book is available
from the British Library*

ISBN 0 7499 3067 5

Set in Times by
Phoenix Photosetting, Chatham, Kent

Printed in Great Britain by
Mackays of Chatham PLC

Chapter One

July 1910

'Don't!' breathed Abby. 'Please don't!'

She clasped the wooden slats of the deck-chair, her small knuckles white with tension. As she stared through the slats her blue eyes were large and her mouth was tight with despair. From her hiding-place behind the stacked deck-chairs she ignored the crowd of excited people who thronged the liner's rail. She had made the voyage many times to visit her grandparents and remained unmoved by the hysteria of the moment. Unmoved, but not unaware. A perceptive seven-year-old, she could sense the heightened emotions as families prepared for partings; was aware of the heartbreak behind the thousands of coloured streamers tossed on to the waving crowds below them on the dockside.

The band on the *Mauretania's* foredeck was playing a selection of bracing sea-shanties as slowly but surely the vast ship was nudged from her berth at the 14th Street pier into the wide waters of Manhattan. Abby felt the increased motion and knew that the trip had begun in earnest. It was usually an exciting moment, but today she had other matters to distract her.

She whispered, '*Please* don't, Papa!'

She closed her eyes briefly but almost immediately opened them in alarm as a large, well-dressed woman collapsed giggling on to the deck-chairs. She wore a conical dunce's hat and waved an empty glass. To Abby's relief, a man with sleek blond hair and a moustache came in search of the woman,

1

dragged her to her feet and led her, still giggling, back to the rail.

Turning her attention once more to her father, Abby watched his hand carefully. The hand she adored. The gentle hand that tousled her own hair, that sometimes fondled her ears, pretending they were long and furry, calling her 'little rabbit'. The clever hand that made wonderful shadows behind the curtain – rabbits and foxes and a Halloween face. Now Abby watched, frozen-faced, as it moved to the waist of the woman beside him.

'No!' she insisted.

The hand moved up to the soft curls which hid the slim neck. Abby knew that neck so well: a fine smooth skin sprinkled with tiny freckles; a neck that smelled of cheap soap and talcum powder. Abby's fingers tightened on the wooden bars, unable to tear her gaze from the terrible sight. Now the long, well-shaped hand slid down the slim body and the woman offered no resistance. Abby was overwhelmed with jealous rage and a muffled groan escaped her.

Around her the noise of the ship's departure rose to a crescendo. There was a sudden, deafening blast from the *Mauretania's* siren. Cheers from the passengers mingled with farewells, tears with laughter, as the liner – nudged by half-a-dozen tugs – began to turn in mid-channel. People turned from the dwindling crowds below and stared upwards at the ship which would carry them across the Atlantic. Cunard's fastest liner, holder of the Blue Riband, was worth looking at. Her gleaming black hull supported a towering white superstructure topped by four angled funnels, each brick-red with a black band round the top.

Her father turned suddenly, looking for his daughter and, hardly knowing why, Abby slid down out of sight. When she thought it was safe she sat up again and, as she thought, her father had quickly lost interest in his missing daughter. His hand was again clasped around the woman's waist and the blonde head now rested against his shoulder. A slim red streamer had draped itself around them as though tying them together.

She whispered, 'I hate you, Papa! I hate you both!'

Her small body ached with anger and grief and the sweet, childish face was distorted by a scowl. She wanted something terrible to happen to him, to punish him for the betrayal. Scrambling from her hiding-place, she walked quickly away in the opposite direction.

Clive turned again from the rail. Around him people were beginning to disperse. The show was over. For the unemotional Americans, the last glimpse of the Statue of Liberty had broken the last ties with home. Thankfully, thought Clive, the only *emotional* American was below decks. He had been spared his wife's tears. Hopefully the dimenhydrinate had made her drowsy. With any luck she might even be asleep.

'Now where has that child got to?' he said. 'I told her not to wander off. Might as well talk to myself!'

Mary said, 'She'll be somewhere around. You know how Abby loves to tease.' Recognising his cue, Clive said, 'I know how *you* love to tease!' Smiling, he allowed his arm to tighten around her waist. Then he sighed. 'I'll have to go and find her. You'd better get down to the cabin and start unpacking in case "Her Ladyship" decides to check up on you.' He'd had enough of female company, he thought restlessly. The bars would be open. 'I could do with a drink.'

Mary said, 'So could I.' She angled her head provocatively. 'Do you *dare*?'

'Don't be ridiculous! Of course I don't dare. I'd have to be a complete fool to be seen buying my daughter's nanny a drink!' He made no attempt to hide his irritation.

'Oh dear!' She assumed a comic, childlike expression of disappointment. 'I'll have to find someone else then. A handsome sailor, perhaps!'

He felt a rush of annoyance. 'You stay away from the crew. You're paid to look after Abby and don't you forget it. I'll send her down to you when I find her.'

'Oh, *thank* you, Clive!'

His expression hardened. 'For God's sake, Mary! I've told you not to call me Clive unless we're alone. Anyone might overhear you, and it could be someone we know.'

She tugged down the jacket of her suit, her mouth set. 'You worry too much.'

'And you don't worry enough. Go on.' He jerked his head

3

towards the doorway. 'Get down to the cabin and make yourself useful.'

'Aye aye, sir!' Her right hand flew to her forehead in a mocking salute.

Some of Clive's pleasure faded. Damn her. Saucy little cow! She was already getting a sight too cocksure. They were all the same. He withdrew his hand from her waist, deliberately abrupt. Let her see that she had gone too far.

For a moment neither spoke. Mary sulked, albeit prettily. He ignored the reproach in the blue eyes, making a pretence of searching amongst the passing passengers for a glimpse of his daughter. Wretched little minx. Not that he was particularly worried about her. She'd come to no harm. Abby had travelled regularly; she knew her way around and the stewards knew her. Still, he couldn't return to the cabin without her. If Stella was awake she would ask awkward questions and he dare not risk a scene. This trip was going to be important to him in more ways than one and he didn't want to complicate it further.

Stella had loved him once, presumably, but now she knew him too well. And I know her, he thought bitterly. He knew he mustn't push her too far. Most of the time she managed to present an unruffled exterior, giving the rest of the world the appearance of a woman well in control of her feelings. Only he knew better; only he knew how fragile was that sense of control, and that the spectre of her unfortunate aunt haunted her. The doctor described Stella as 'of a nervous disposition'. Her mother insisted that she was 'highly strung'. Only her father had been more direct and *his* honesty had been inspired, Clive knew, by a desire to frighten off an unwanted suitor.

Clive admitted to himself that Stella had possibly inherited her aunt's instability. Just occasionally he had sensed a dark flash of anger which he had no desire to explore further. If he were honest, he would admit that at times he was wary of the woman who shared his bed. She was meek enough, always dutiful and she never refused him in bed. At least he couldn't fault her in that respect. Not that she was the liveliest of partners: she was submissive most of the time and appeared to find no pleasure in their love-making. When he was at his most despairing he reminded himself about her money.

He turned to Mary, vaguely aware that she had spoken to him.

She asked, 'Are you listening?'

'What did you say?' Clive worried constantly about Abby. Had she, too, been affected?

Mary said, 'You're miles away!'

Stella had also denied him the son he longed for, although he did not blame her for that. It seemed her body was not ideal for childbearing and Abby was the only child of three who had survived. For a moment the familiar bitterness surfaced and the despair gripped him. There were unresolved problems between himself and Stella for which he had no solutions. Better, therefore, never to speak of them. He discouraged her efforts to talk about their marriage. They managed a reasonably civilised relationship, and he could offer her nothing beyond that.

Mary said, 'I'll go, then.'

'Do that.' He didn't even glance at her. She could suffer his displeasure for a while. Do her good. He knew how *her* mind worked. Silly little thing. She was wondering whether she should let him into her bed during the voyage. It would be a first, and she would be committing herself. Agonising over the age-old question – would he respect her after her surrender? He smiled. Of course not. He didn't respect her *now*.

'What are you laughing at?' she demanded.

'None of your business, you hussy!' He winked and her face lightened. 'Now be off with you!' he told her.

Mary was useful. Available. A few stolen kisses and a snatched caress when they found themselves alone together provided a small frisson of excitement in an otherwise dull existence. She had known exactly where her duty lay since the interview nearly six months ago when he had refused the older, more experienced nanny in Mary Crisford's favour. While Stella dutifully checked the letters of reference, he and Mary had exchanged a conspiratorial look. Her eyes had promised payment in full, and he reckoned it was almost settlement day.

The last nanny had been a disaster: Nanny Payne of the large bosoms and wide hips. Too late he had discovered her religious principles and strict moral attitude. 'Nanny Pain' was more like it, he reflected ruefully. And to make matters worse, she had complained to Stella about his 'advances'. Damned nerve. Fortunately he had managed a convincing story, accusing the nanny of lying. Poor Stella, faced with the dilemma, had chosen to believe her husband and they had agreed that Miss Payne must go. Clive whistled under his breath at the memory. It had been too close for comfort.

As he watched Mary walk away, he smiled. He would have her before they reached port; they both knew it. If she played her cards right he would make it worth her while. If only her cabin had been further away. He had suggested it but, naturally enough, Stella had seen no reason to agree. Abby always shared with the nanny and their cabin was always next door. Clive gave a slight shrug. He and Mary would have to take their chance. He was pretty sure that his wife knew of his occasional flirtations and chose to look the other way.

As he turned to go in search of Abby he caught sight of a well-dressed man who was leaning on the rail nearby, admiring the receding skyline. He looked vaguely familiar, Clive thought, but couldn't place him. Probably nearing forty, he was hatless and the breeze blew brown curly hair that was already sprinkled with grey.

Clive's smile was courteous. 'I'm looking for my daughter, sir. I suppose you haven't seen a little girl wandering about on her own? Fair curly hair. She's wearing a sort of sailor dress. Blue. Lace collar. Little monkey's given me the slip.'

The man nodded. 'I did, actually Not two minutes ago. I thought it a bit precocious – a child of that age on her own – but I understand that some children are quite mature these days. She was talking to one of the deck stewards – your daughter, I mean.' He smiled. 'Quizzing the poor man about the lifeboats. Sixteen, he told her.' He pointed towards the bow of the ship, then added, 'Parr's the name.'

'Nicolson.' Their handshake was a perfunctory one. Clive indicated the fading shoreline and said, 'Quite a nostalgic moment for many people. My wife's American. Can't bear to see it go.'

'Understandable.' He ran fingers through his hair. 'Lost my hat overboard.'

Clive grinned. 'Probably a few fathoms under by now!'

'I daresay. I should think the sea-bed is lined with hats along this route!'

Clive nodded, then left the man to his musings and went in search of Abby. He would find the little minx, take her back to the cabin, then go for a drink. On second thoughts, he would buy her something first. A little trinket. Just in case she had seen him with Mary. Abigail was only seven, but if Clive had learned one thing in life it was never to underestimate a woman.

Below deck, Stella stood at the window of their suite and watched the land slip by – through The Narrows, past Sandy Hook and on towards the Ambrose Light. It was her last glimpse of home, and as always she felt a deep sense of loss as the country of her birth was left behind. She still loved America with a fierce passion so why, she asked herself for the hundredth time, had she married an Englishman? A marriage that had guaranteed her exile to a foreign land. She could never admit the extent of her regrets. Clive had long since given up trying to understand her bouts of homesickness which occasionally deepened into depression. With an Englishman's lack of sensitivity he would laugh it off. 'Pull yourself together, old girl!' was one of his favourite phrases.

Now tears filled her eyes and she blinked hard in an effort to discourage them. Clive hated any sign of weakness, especially in his wife. He said it made him nervous. Turning from the window, Stella breathed deeply several times. Clive had sent her below deck to rest on the bed, with instructions *not* to watch their departure. He seemed to believe that if she didn't actually *watch*, she would suffer less. It always astonished her that after so many years together he still made no effort to understand. To him her feelings were simply proof of the vulnerability of women; incontrovertible evidence of the superiority of men.

Aloud she said, 'Unpack, Stella. Do *anything*, but don't think about him.'

If she kept busy she might be able to ignore her feelings of increasing alienation. Opening the wardrobe, she stood staring into its emptiness. As empty as her life. Clive no longer loved her – if he ever *had*. Her daughter preferred her father's company. It was understandable since her mother was so frequently confined to her bed, but it hurt. She sat down on the edge of the bed, leaving the wardrobe doors to swing closed under their own weight.

She had made one crucial mistake, she reflected. By marrying Clive, she had moved away from her parents and lost Jerry who had been her champion for as long as she could remember. She closed her eyes, sick at heart. It was done and she must live with the consequences.

'Unpack, you fool!' she told herself angrily. Across the room she caught sight of her reflection in the mirror. 'Don't just sit there feeling sorry for yourself!'

When the stewardess came she would tell her it was all done, but would tip her anyway. That way Clive need never know. She opened the lid of the steamer trunk and began to draw out the clothes, removing the tissue paper, shaking them gently to dislodge the creases, then laying them in the drawers or hanging them in the wardrobe. The music from the band on the dockside had faded and the ship's orchestra had now relinquished the sea-shanties and was playing a selection of popular songs from the music halls. She recognised one and tried to hum it, but the sound dried in her tight throat and the tears pressed again at her eyelids.

Holding up the new grey silk, Stella held it against herself and studied her reflection. It picked up the colour of her eyes and made her look almost attractive, she thought wistfully. Maybe, just for once, Clive would look at her with something akin to admiration and even a little respect. He could do it if he wanted to. He was a consummate actor. When Abby was born, he had convinced the nurse with his impression of a devoted husband and father. Only Stella had known that he was pretending; that, in fact, he had been bitterly disappointed with his wife for failing to produce the longed-for son. The doctor's warning that she should never bear another child had added salt to the wound. She swallowed hard, her memories of that time tarnished by her husband's irresponsible behaviour. She had developed a fever following the birth and for several days her chances of survival had been slim. Clive's method of dealing with the anxiety had been to drink heavily.

Sighing, she turned from the mirror and reached for a hanger. 'Look on the bright side,' she thought. At least Clive had agreed to keep an eye on Abby while Nanny, in the next-door cabin, unpacked for herself and her young charge. It was good for the girl to spend time alone with her father. Stella was well aware that, in Abby's eyes, Clive could do no wrong. He was her hero. The child had put him on a pedestal and nobody else could challenge his position. Her own poor health meant that a reliable nanny was important. Abby had been devoted to Nanny Payne but after what happened . . . She had doubted her husband's word, but there was no way she dared support a nanny instead of her own husband. It had been a wretched decision to make and she still regretted it. Fortunately, after a few difficult weeks, Abby had become reconciled to Mary Crisford. Now she probably loved her *too* much, but that was her daughter's way. It was all or nothing with Abby. She smiled faintly.

Suddenly a fresh wave of despair gripped her as she thought about the nanny. *Was* there something between Mary Crisford and Clive, or was she imagining things? Since the débâcle with Nanny Payne she had watched her husband like a hawk, but had nothing definite to go on. An odd glance between them, perhaps, or Clive's expression on occasion when he spoke of her. And that half-smile which she once caught reflected in the mirror when he thought himself unobserved. She hoped with all her heart that she was wrong – that she was, as Clive had insisted, irrational on the subject of 'other women'. He had reproached her for her lack of trust, making her feel guilty, spiteful and unlovable. She had vowed never to put herself through a scene like that again – unless she was *certain*. And even then, what could she do? She would never survive the stigma of a divorce. Stella sat down suddenly, her legs weak, her heart thumping erratically. She had never before felt quite so alone.

Gussie Malone stepped out of the door on to the boat deck, feeling pleased with her appearance. Her nicely rounded figure was, she felt, set off to perfection in a jacket and skirt with a matching hat and shoes. Her satisfaction was shortlived, however, for she was almost winded as a small girl cannoned into her.

'Holy Mother of God!' she gasped, a faint hint of Irish in her voice. She caught the child's arm to prevent her escape. She was young, maybe six or seven with blonde curls. A heart-shaped face. Gussie closed her eyes and fought back the inevitable flash of longing.

'Let me *go!*' The little girl glowered up at her.

Gussie drew a long breath. 'Let you go, is it? Well, maybe I will when I've got a "Sorry" out of you. Has no one taught you any manners, child?'

'No!' The child wriggled furiously in an effort to free herself.

'Then I'll teach you some now.' Gussie glared down into the small face and tried to keep her own face straight. 'Rule one. When you almost knock someone down you apologise. That means you—'

'I *know* all that.'

'Oh, you do? Let's be hearing it then.'

'I don't want to. Let me go. I'll tell Papa and he'll—'

'Your papa, eh? And who may that be?'

The small girl's desire to show off overrode her caution. 'Clive Albert Nicolson, 31B, Clissold Avenue, London.'

Gussie was suddenly thoughtful. The child's information just *might* prove useful. Clissold Avenue was an expensive address. A well-designed terrace of large houses with elegant wrought-iron balconies and area steps which spoke of domestic staff. Clive Albert Nicolson obviously had plenty of money and, with luck, he might be persuaded to part with some of it. It all depended on his tastes.

She looked at his daughter. The face of an angel, she thought. She asked, 'So why the hurry – unless the blessed ship's on fire?'

'I'm counting the lifeboats, that's all. Now you've made me forget. I'll have to start again.'

'The lifeboats?'

'To see if he was telling the truth. He said there were sixteen and I—'

'Your father said there were sixteen?' She must keep the conversation going a little longer, she decided.

'Not Papa, silly! The steward.'

It appeared that Clive Albert Nicolson's daughter was a mite precocious. A pity – for the child's sake. Gussie decided to abandon her desire for an apology. 'Well, the steward was right,' she told her. 'There *are* sixteen.' In fact, she had no idea, but sixteen sounded reasonable. 'So you can count.'

'One, two, four, five – um—' She paused, then said doubtfully, 'I think that's right.'

Gussie smiled. 'Not quite. Something happened to three, but that's by the by. I think we'll go and find your father and tell him what a clever girl you are. What do they call you?'

'Abigail Violet Nicolson. After my grandmother. Abigail Violet Nicolson, 31B—'

'Yes, yes. We've been through all that.'

'—Clissold Avenue, London. But everyone calls me Abby. You can, if you like. Are you going to tell Papa?'

'That you bumped into me? No. Not if you walk properly beside me and don't go haring off again.' She relinquished her hold on the child's arm.

Abby regarded her warily for a moment and apparently decided against making a run for it. 'What's *your* name?' she asked.

'Augusta Maria Malone, but my friends call me Gussie.'

'Can I call you that?'

'Certainly not. You're just someone who came barging into me.' She looked down sternly. 'Someone who didn't even say "Sorry".'

There was a silence. The child stared down at her buttoned shoes. 'I'm – I'm sorry,' she said at last.

'Thank you. I accept your apology.'

'Can I call you Gussie now?'

'No, you can't. It's all about elders and betters. You can call me Mrs Malone.' She glanced around. 'Now, where will we find your father?'

'He was at the rail with—' Breaking off abruptly, Abby pointed back the way she had come and they started to walk back together.

'With who?' Gussie asked quickly.

'Nobody. Where's Mr Malone?'

'Dead and buried, God rest his soul.'

'*Dead*?'

'Haven't I just said so? I'm a widow.'

The child's eyes widened. 'But your dress is *red*. Mama says that when someone dies you have to wear black to show respect. And your hat is red, and so are the roses.'

Gussie sucked in her breath. Babes and sucklings and all that! She would have to be careful with this one. Red, indeed. Her *maroon* travelling suit always brought her luck, whereas black had never looked well on her. Men liked a bit of colour. Maybe the hat *was* rather flamboyant, even for a 'widow' whose husband had passed away twelve years earlier ... but then he hadn't passed away exactly. She had never been married *exactly*. The title simply gave her respectability. Still, she had done well for herself without a man of her own. She had clawed her way up to a small suite of elegant rooms, a wardrobe full of good clothes and a little money in the bank. After this voyage she expected to have a little more.

To Abby she said, 'It's not red, it's maroon, and it's a *suit*. And my husband died a long time ago and anyway, Miss Nosey Parker, it's no business of yours.'

'But Queen Victoria always wore black and Mama says—'

'I'm not Queen Victoria, thank goodness – she's long dead – and I'm not your mama.'

'Well, *Nanny* says—'

Gussie laid a heavy hand on her shoulder. 'Rule two, child. Learn when to stop. Like *now*.'

So the child had a nanny. A pity. They were often no better than they should be, and Clive Nicolson might be getting some womanly comforts from *her*. She wondered what the nanny was like. 'I had a nanny once,' she lied. 'She was horrible. I called her the old witch. She used to smack me and she had a long pointy nose.'

'Ugh!' Abby's face twisted in disgust. 'A pointy nose! *My* nanny is pretty and she smells lovely and—'

Gussie's mind was working fast. 'Was she with your papa at the ship's rail?' she asked, her tone casual.

There was no answer. The small girl's expression was suddenly thunderous.

Gussie's pulse quickened. So she *was*. 'And where was Mama?'

'Lying down. She gets upset when we leave New York, and she has to take a pill and sleep it off. Papa says it's ridiculous. I shan't be ridiculous when I'm a grown-up lady. It's because Mama's an American. Papa says they're very funny people. He's English and so am I. Papa says we have to be kind to Mama when she's poorly. He told Grandfather that she's teetering on the brink, whatever that means. I asked him what a brink was, but he said "I forget" and called me a snoop.' She frowned momentarily, then smiled as a new thought struck her. 'Papa wants to buy a motor car, but Mama says "No" because they're death-traps and he'll kill himself, but he'll buy one. I *know* he will. Papa says—'

'Papa says! Sounds as though the dear man never stops pontificating – and don't ask me what that word means because *I* forget.'

As Gussie strode along the deck, Abby hopped and skipped cheerfully beside her. A gust of wind tugged at the child's straw hat, dislodging it so that it hung down her back, releasing the full glory of the blonde curls. Gussie resisted the urge to touch them.

'Do they tong your hair?' Gussie asked her.

A nod.

'You should use curling rags. Tell your nanny. They're kinder than hot metal.'

Abby squinted up into the sun in an attempt to examine what she could see of Gussie's hair. 'I wish *I* had ginger hair,' she said wistfully.

'It's not ginger. It's light auburn.' Gussie always hoped this was true. She patted her frizzy hair which, drawn up, was hidden demurely beneath her hat. It was truly her crowning glory. Her gentlemen loved it. They took it up in handfuls and buried their faces in it. They spread it out across the pillow, murmuring with delight, or twined the bright curls around their fingers . . . or other parts. She shrugged mentally. Men! They were such children, most of them. A few were less than endearing. A very few were evil – but she had learned to obliterate the worst memories. She had been less selective in the old days. Careless, even. Now she prided herself that she could spot the men who hated women.

'Light auburn,' she repeated firmly. Once freed from the hairpins, the red halo exaggerated the green of her eyes and framed the soft sweep of her cheekbones. She might err on the side of plumpness and lack the stature of her taller sisters, but her red hair was her finest feature and Gussie knew it.

Suddenly Abby waved. 'Papa! Papa!' She raced towards a tall man who caught her and swung her round.

So this was Nicolson. Gussie's pulse quickened as it always did when she met a man with potential. Now her eyes widened with approval as she quickly assessed him. He was handsome in an aristocratic way, with smooth dark hair and fine features. His clothes had been well-tailored, his shoes hand-stitched, and

13

the smile he turned on her was lazily confident. 'If the nanny keeps her favours to herself I could do very well with this one,' she told herself, but still hesitated. Was it all just a little too easy? She was a trifle suspicious. There were five days before they docked in Liverpool, and it was important to get off to a flying start. She had to make the decision before midnight on the first day, or there would be scarcely time to bring the matter to a satisfactory conclusion. Men were a delight but money lasted longer. Seeing that he looked at her with interest, she hastily lowered her glance. A modest, discreet widow was how he must see her at first. He mustn't suspect the truth until it was too late. Once he was interested, the rest would follow in due course. She made up her mind. The collision with the girl had been a kindly act of Fate, and Gussie would make the most of the opportunity.

'You have a lovely daughter, Mr Nicolson,' she said, exaggerating the Irish lilt. For some reason men found it endearing. She smiled up at him. 'Abigail. Such a pretty name.'

The child whispered something to him and, with a light laugh, he lifted her up into his arms.

'Actually she's a bit of a minx at times!' he replied, as Abby twined her arms around his neck. 'A naughty little rabbit! But I see you already know my name.'

'Your address also. Your daughter is not backward in coming forward!'

They both laughed.

He said, 'No good having secrets with this one around. Little ears hear all. Little eyes see all. Hey! Abby! Don't strangle me!'

'A touch of the green-eyed monster!' said Gussie. 'I suppose I should introduce myself. I'm Augusta Malone.'

Abby said quickly, 'Her friends call her Gussie.'

He gave her a little shake. 'Abby! What is your mother always telling you? Don't interrupt your elders.' Turning to Gussie, he smiled and held out his hand.

They shook hands briefly. 'Do *you* have any children?' he asked.

Gussie had prepared herself long ago for this painful question. She gave a small, but convincing, sigh. 'Sadly, no. My dear man died soon after we were married.'

14

He raised his eyebrows fractionally. 'And you didn't remarry?' His voice softened. 'It can't be for want of suitors.'

Gussie wanted to cheer. The first compliment. Her hopes were rising. 'I'm rather an independent spirit,' she told him, aware that he was sizing her up, too. Not that it bothered her. Gussie knew she could survive the most severe scrutiny. But she had said enough. It would never do to appear too willing too early. She would simply make sure that 'Fate' brought them together again.

She could imagine his routine – dinner, a stroll on deck until his wife felt tired enough to retire, then off to the nearest bar for a few drinks and a late-night session in the casino. Not that she wanted her gentlemen to fritter their money away at the gaming tables, but it *did* give them a cast-iron alibi for a late return to the cabin. Oh, to be sure, they would meet again!

'You must excuse me,' she told him, allowing just a trace of reluctance in her tone. 'I've some unpacking to do. Boring but necessary. Will I be seeing you at the captain's table?' A reference to that particular privilege always impressed them. Not that she would be invited to share any such honour. Her face was already familiar to the crew, and they must have their suspicions about her. As long as she was never challenged outright or discovered *in flagrante*, she was safe.

He hesitated. 'The captain's table? I . . . well, anything's possible.'

She considered Nicolson, adjusting her first impression. So he was not rich or powerful enough to be included on that prestigious list. No matter. He was doubtless wealthy enough for her own purpose. It was a matter of some pride with her that she could often guess a man's line of business. In *her* line of work it was useful if not essential. Nicolson lacked the sharpness of a successful businessman. There was a certain intangible laziness about him . . . Languor. Was that the word? Maybe he had inherited money. She studied him, her head on one side.

Under her gaze he grew uncomfortable and said, 'A penny for them!'

She laughed. 'I'm enjoying the view,' she told him archly. A direct compliment could work wonders. So few compliments were paid to men that they had great impact.

He laughed, lost for a suitable rejoinder.

No, not inherited, she thought. Perhaps he was in the arts – an artist, a sculptor or a musician . . . No. His looks were too important to him for that. Hand-stitched shoes made a statement. An MP, then . . . a civil servant even. A judge? No, far too relaxed and probably too young . . . A doctor or a consultant of some kind? Not very likely. They had a committedness, an earnestness about them. She gave up with a shake of her head. Too early to tell, she consoled herself. You've only known him a few minutes. Wait for a few more clues.

He asked, 'Will *you* be on the captain's table, Mrs Malone?'

'Not if I can avoid it,' she replied in a low voice. 'It is usually very dull.' Before he could speak again she said, 'Enjoy the voyage, Mr Nicolson. I see that the weather forecast for tomorrow is good. Fair with sunny spells.'

A little too quickly he said, 'Ideal, then, for my morning stroll.'

So – he was already cooperating. 'Really? I had you marked down as a late riser! That shows how wrong a woman can be. Hasty judgements; my mother warned me against them.' Not that her mother could have been averse to them, thought Gussie, repressing a smile. If she *had* been, she would never have got herself pregnant by the master of the house. Not that Gussie blamed her. Life was too short.

Clive Nicolson's eyes held hers. 'I like the decks when they are half empty.'

'Me too. I try to manage a brisk mile after breakfast.' This was another lie, for Gussie loathed exercise of any kind. She felt that she had enough in bed without looking for more. But needs must, she thought. She would 'bump into' him tomorrow morning on deck. An early start, then.

He whispered to his daughter, who said, 'Goodbye, Mrs Malone,' without raising her head from her father's shoulder.

Gussie moved on, rustling expensively in her silks, the heels of her shoes tapping seductively across the wooden deck. Resisting the impulse to look back, she stepped carefully amongst the discarded streamers. A broad smile spread slowly across her face. What a piece of luck! The dear man was as good as hooked.

Later that night, just after ten, Gussie returned to her cabin. She had seen all she needed of Mr Nicolson's routine, which was as she had imagined it – except for the brief but very heated argument she had observed outside the smoking-room. Mr Nicolson had been accosted by Hemmings, one of the professional gamblers who also made a regular appearance on the Atlantic run. Gamblers did not waste their time or money on people like Gussie, but she had heard rumours that he had a nasty temper and his choleric appearance seemed to support this idea. So what had the altercation been about? Their voices had risen angrily and Hemmings had waved his fist in Nicolson's face before they had been interrupted by one of the stewards. They had gone their separate ways with grim expressions, leaving Gussie no wiser as to the cause of the argument. No doubt something to do with women or money, she reflected. It was always one or the other in her experience.

Still, as long as it didn't affect *her* plans, it was of no interest. Her present philosophy was to steer clear of other people's problems. In her youth she had been impetuous to a fault, but the passing of the years had taught her circumspection. There was no way, she now knew, that she could set the world to rights single-handed.

Closing and locking her door, Gussie went immediately to the large swing mirror and, turning to and fro, regarded herself with just a trace of anxiety. What she saw reassured her. No, she told herself. No need to worry. Clive Nicolson would have seen her as a handsome woman who carried her thirty-six years well. With a small, self-satisfied smile, she unbuttoned the grey dress she had worn to dinner, shook it and hung it in the wardrobe. Removing a few hairs from the shoulders of the dress, she examined them, frowning.

'Ginger, indeed! What a cheek!'

Tomorrow, for her stroll on deck, she would wear the navy-blue skirt with a matching blouse and the white jacket.

'Very nautical!' she muttered, closing the wardrobe doors with a satisfied smile. She had made a good start, she congratulated herself.

She sank on to the edge of the bed, bounced up and down a little and then gazed around cheerfully, enjoying the luxury of what Cunard liked to call their en-suite rooms. She always booked what *she* called a first-class cabin. Her gentlemen expected it. It also meant a little more space as well as quieter neighbours. It was expensive, but the profits from these trips would pay for it and leave a tidy sum to be invested for her old age.

Only once had her luck failed her – on the dear old *Olympic* when her elderly client had suffered a heart attack. Mr Pritty from Pennsylvania. A slow starter and very shy, but so eager to succeed. The first night had been a total failure, but he had explained that he was very 'out of practice'. The following night, Gussie had drawn on all her experience. When it was satisfactorily concluded, she was congratulating herself that he had finally managed it when she realised that he'd gone rather quiet. At first she'd thought he was asleep. Snoring – or so she assumed. Then she'd tried to wake him. In a 'penny dreadful' it would have been hilarious, but in fact it had been an ordeal for everyone except Mr Pritty who, barely conscious, was oblivious to everything and missed all the excitement.

'The poor man!' she murmured, smiling at the memory.

All very awkward at the time, but the captain had been as eager as she was to avoid a scandal and the crew had strict orders to keep silent about the whole sorry business on pain of instant dismissal. Not that there had been a wife to worry about for Mr Pritty was a confirmed bachelor, if he was to be believed. Certainly he was travelling alone, and when Gussie went to the hospital to take him some flowers the nurse had told her she was his only visitor. White Star line had written to her suggesting very firmly that Gussie might prefer to travel on another shipping line in future, and she had transferred to Cunard without any real regrets. Men were men wherever you found them, and one ship was very like another.

The *Mauretania* was an older ship, but faster than the *Olympic*, and her male passengers were just as rich and every bit as lusty. Her natural optimism suggested that such a disaster would only happen once and maybe she had been partly to blame. She had chosen unwisely. Poor Mr Pritty had been overweight and over seventy. Foolish of her to expect anything else, but she had learned from the experience. Not that he blamed her. Weeks later she had received a letter from him via the *Olympic* in which he thanked her for her kindness and apologised for his 'ungentlemanly behaviour'.

Now she eased off her grey satin shoes and regarded them with intense pleasure. They were expensive but worth every penny. She unfastened her corset and allowed it to fall to the floor. A heartfelt sigh escaped her. Her first night aboard ship was always spent alone, and she treasured the solitude. She would pamper herself with a hot toddy and a few chocolates. Lying on the pillow was Clara, a large rag doll. Its hair was yellow wool, the dress crumpled cotton. One of the black shoes was missing. Now Gussie picked up the doll and kissed it. As she hugged it to her, she remembered the woman who had made it for her all those years ago.

Sister Everistes of the sweet, young face and bright blue eyes, who had been the nearest thing to a mother she had ever had. Sometimes, lying restless in the deepest part of the night, Gussie fancied she could hear her laughter as she raced boisterously across the tennis court, her blue skirts tucked up into what Gussie imagined as the legs of her bloomers. If Gussie concentrated hard, she could even smell the astringent convent soap with which they had all washed.

The young nun's death – so unexpected . . . so unfair – had marked the end of innocence for Gussie. An older girl had recounted the sad details with great relish. An epileptic fit. They had found her lying on the floor of the chapel, her head damaged from the fall, blood oozing, eyes staring.

'Split her head right open!' the girl told Gussie, who was listening in a daze of misery and grief. There was no one to whom Gussie could turn for support and consolation. No mother to write to. No father to visit. The father whom she had never seen, who paid for her education, remained – as he always would – a shadowy figure somewhere on the fringes of her life. Only Clara remained and Gussie had transferred all her affection to her. Later, faced with yet another loss, the doll had offered consolation. Now, she was all that Gussie had to love.

With an effort Gussie turned her thoughts back to the present. To Clara, she said defiantly, 'His name's Clive Albert Nicolson. And not a bad looker. Not by half! It should be interesting.'

But the sombre mood persisted. For a moment she stared at Clara with an anguished look in her eyes, besieged by dark memories. Suddenly she pressed the doll fiercely to her heart, blinking back tears, refusing to be crushed by the past. After a long moment she laid Clara on the pillow and said shakily, 'You can tell me what you think of him tomorrow night!'

She began to remove her underclothes, tossing them into an untidy pile on the nearest chair. Anything to prevent thought. Then she took each garment from the pile and folded it. The shoes were carefully brushed and stuffed with tissue paper.

Ten minutes later, in her nightdress and dressing gown and feeling slightly better, she rang for the stewardess and ordered rum and hot milk. When it came she climbed into bed and turned her attention to the chocolates which waited on the bedside table, compliments of the shipping line. It always puzzled her why rich passengers should be treated to free chocolates when they could easily afford to buy them. The steerage passengers, hard up and careful with their money, would surely appreciate them more. Her fingers hovered over the small selection. Hmm? Tonight she would start with the strawberry cream and follow it with a cherry fondant. The almond cream topped with a nut would be saved until last.

When both the toddy and the chocolates were finished, she scrambled out of bed to kneel beside it and say her prayers.

'Sweet Mother of God, forgive me for all my sins and bless this ship and all who sail in her including me. Let Clive Albert Nicolson be an easy fish to hook, and no more heart attacks or the like. In four years I'll be forty, and I'm a bit long in the tooth for that sort of malarkey . . . Fine weather would be a help as always. I look so pasty when I'm seasick as well you know and the menfolk are less generous with their money and less inclined to do what they do best . . .'

She searched for any other favours she needed. 'And keep the nanny out of it if you can. Remember me to my darling Tess and to Sister Everistes. Well, good night, God bless!'

Back in bed, clutching the doll, she stared up at the ceiling, thrilled as always to see the moving pattern of the ship's white wake reflected there. She thought about Abigail and her father and then, drowsily, she wondered about the child's mother. American. Well, they *were* different, to be sure, but generous with it. She recalled a certain Hiram Wentworth. Noisy but very quick. He had been what the politicians like to call 'an American cousin'

20

and he'd been a big spender. She owed the hat to him. Half asleep, she began to think about the only man she had ever really loved, but this was dangerous and she knew it. Crying over spilt milk was for idiots – but losing him had broken her heart. He had come into her life eighteen months too late and nothing could change that. With an effort she forced his image from her mind and concentrated on the coming day. She would be up early, washed and spruced, to take an early breakfast. Then she would make a start, walking the deck, ready to 'bump into' Clive Albert Nicolson.

Chapter Two

Stella settled herself into the pink upholstered chair and drew it a little closer to the table. From their position in the Upper Dining Saloon they could look down into the lower one, and as always she drew a deep breath of contentment. The pale oak panelling gave the room a light, airy atmosphere and she found the elegant decor soothing. Crossing her fingers that breakfast would be a peaceful affair, she smiled nervously at Abby who was studying the menu, pretending she could read. Clive beside her was quiet, deliberately unapproachable. He was never very good in the morning, Stella reminded herself. There was really no need to feel anxious.

Abby asked, 'Can I have kedgeree, please, Mama?'

Clive said, 'You're holding that upside-down – and no, you don't like kedgeree.'

'I do now, Papa!' Unabashed, she reversed the menu. 'Really I do.' The large blue eyes widened seductively. 'Why can't I have it?'

Stella said, 'Please, Abby. Your father said "no" and that's the end of it.' She hoped that Clive had registered her support. He was always complaining that she didn't back him to the hilt.

'Smoked haddock, then?'

'You don't like fish, dear. Do be sensible.'

The beautiful face relapsed into a sulky pout which Stella ignored. Why was it that Abby pushed so hard, she wondered wearily. Abby could tell when her father was in a difficult mood and yet, perversely, she seemed determined to make things worse. It was almost as though she needed to test his forbearance; to know that she could reach the limits and still be loved. Lately she

23

seemed to be getting worse, constantly demanding attention and bored with her dolls. Stella sighed. At Abby's age *she* had been content with her nursery world and sure of her parents' love. Clive boasted, however, that he had been a restless demanding child, so maybe Abby took after her father.

Stella caught the eye of a woman at the next table and forced a smile just as the steward reached their table, notebook in hand. Trim in his uniform, with an immaculate jacket, he came sharply to attention and winked at Abby who promptly forgot her sulks and tried to return the wink.

'Good morning to you all,' he said.

'Good morning,' said Clive.

Abby beamed at the steward. 'I remember you. Are you married now?'

He looked at her in surprise. 'Why yes. Two weeks ago, to be exact.'

Stella gave her a warning look which she ignored. 'Did you have any bridesmaids?'

Clive said, 'That will do, Abby.' To the steward he said, 'She's got bridesmaids on the brain!'

Abby looked startled. 'On the *brain*?'

Stella smiled quickly and said, 'It's not polite to – to question people, Abby.'

Abby opened her mouth to protest further and the steward changed the subject adroitly.

'Bit of a swell before dawn, but it seems to have died down.' He treated them all to a bright smile. 'I hope you had a good night's sleep.'

Stella said, 'Oh yes, thank you,' while Clive said nothing, studying his menu.

Abby said, 'I did, because I had a special dream sweet. Nanny gave it to me. It's pink and it's all sweet and it makes you have lovely dreams!'

Stella said hastily, 'Now then, Abby! What did I tell you about stories?'

'It's *not* a story. She *does* give me one. Lots and lots of times. I dream about princesses and fairies and magic castles.' She frowned slightly. 'At least I think I do, but sometimes I can't remember. Nanny says that's because—'

Clive glanced up. 'Don't talk nonsense, please, Abby. There are no such things as dream sweets.'

Abby opened her mouth to argue but changed her mind. She smiled sweetly at the steward. 'Is Miss Emily still in the play-room? I liked her so much and she tells wonderful stories. Last time she told us about a goblin whose name was Lotto and he lived in the forest under the roots of a tree, and then one day a maiden came along with rare beauty – oh, did I say he was ugly? Did I say that?'

Stella said, 'Abby, the steward is waiting to take our order. Tell us—'

But Abby rushed on eagerly. 'And the goblin followed the maiden because she had a rare beauty and then he found the maiden crying and said don't cry pretty maiden, but she cried louder and louder because she was afraid of him because he was ugly and—'

Clive said, '*Abby*! Your mother told you to stop!'

Abby said, 'I'd like kippers for my breakfast. Please.'

Stella groaned inwardly. 'But you don't like fish. Why don't you choose something you know you will enjoy. Egg and bacon, maybe?'

Prompt on cue, the steward said, 'The bacon's especially good this trip. I recommend it.' He leaned down towards Abby and lowered his voice. 'Better choose it before it's all gone. They're going mad for it!'

Abby thought it over. 'I'll have bacon *and* kippers.'

Clive found his voice suddenly. 'You'll have eggs and bacon or you'll go without!' he snapped.

Stella felt her stomach tremble. The steward looked awkward.

Abby said, 'Pa*pa*!'

Stella said, 'I'll have egg and bacon, too. And some brown bread and butter and a tray of tea. And – and toast and honey.'

The steward scribbled dutifully then looked at Clive.

'A pair of kippers,' he told him.

Abby opened her mouth, but Clive silenced her with a look and Stella could breathe again. When the steward had gone Clive said, 'So where's Nanny? She can't be seasick in this weather. It's like a mill-pond.'

Abby began, 'She didn't sleep well and she isn't—'

'Abby! I asked your mother. Not you.'

Stella found herself stammering. 'She *is* a little under the weather actually. Dark under the eyes. But no, not seasick. I said she could miss breakfast.'

'Did you!'

It was not a question but a challenge. An unspoken criticism. Stella recognised the signs.

'Please, Clive, don't let's quarrel,' she begged, her voice low. 'Let's just enjoy the voyage. Let's be happy.' Her voice shook and she felt tears rise. She snatched a handkerchief from her purse and pressed it against her eyelids. Now he would despise her.

'For God's sake, Stella!' he hissed furiously. 'Do you have to make a spectacle of yourself? Pull yourself together and stop whining!'

The food came and they ate in a repressed silence. The salty smell of the kipper combined with the slight roll of the ship to make Stella slightly nauseous, but she said nothing and forced down the eggs and bacon without enjoyment. Abby toyed with hers, poking at the egg yolk until it ran and cutting the bacon into minute pieces. Catching her eye, Stella gave her a look which said, 'You'd better eat it!' and Abby finally began pushing reluctant forkfuls into her mouth. Among the other cheerful diners, their own silent table attracted curious glances. Why on earth had she given in to the nanny, she asked herself wearily. She knew Clive had no tolerance for weakness of any kind. It was her own stupid fault.

By way of conversation she asked 'How was the casino last night?'

Abby said eagerly, 'Did you win, Papa?'

To Stella's surprise he smiled at his daughter. 'Don't I always, little rabbit?' He rolled his eyes humorously. 'I won bundles and bundles of lovely money! Oodles and oodles of it!'

As Abby clapped her hands with excitement, Stella's relief was physical. It would be all right. Her husband would snap out of his sullen mood. She saw in her daughter's face an echo of the same relief and felt a moment's compunction. Was this repressed hostility between mother and father to be Abby's training for marriage? For a moment guilt flooded her, adding to her insecurity, but then she reassured herself. Even at seven years old her daughter was strong-willed and independent; there were times when Stella envied her bold spirit. Abby was, in fact, very like Clive and there were times when he was pleased to recognise this. When he was in this mood, however, her wilfulness grated on him and Stella found herself 'pig in the middle' – trying to keep the peace. She herself had been a willing child, wanting only to please 'the grown-ups' – grown-ups who protected her from the harsh realities of life. Marriage to Clive had done nothing to develop her independence.

She glanced past her daughter to a man who sat at a table about twenty yards away. He caught her eye and immediately looked away. In a level tone she said, 'Clive, I've just seen that man again! The one I noticed on the voyage out.'

Before she could warn him against turning round he did so. 'Where? Which man?'

She lowered her voice. 'Don't you remember when we travelled out? You thought I was imagining it but then *you* saw him, too. Nice-looking in a homely sort of way. Brown curly hair. About forty. He's sitting alone – to your right.'

'Yes, I see him. But he's not watching us.'

'He *was*, Clive. It's the same man. I'm sure of it. Are you sure you don't know him from somewhere?'

'Quite sure. There's nothing wrong with my memory, Stella. He looks vaguely familiar but I don't know him. I'll have another cup of tea.' He pushed the cup and saucer forward.

'Which man?' said Abby.

'Hush, dear!' Stella refilled Clive's cup and handed it back to him.

Abby asked, 'Is he a *spy*? I know about spies. A man spied on Nanny once when she was undressing. Spies are—'

Clive's mood swung again. He said grimly, 'This child's manners are deplorable. Children should be seen and not heard – or didn't you know that?' He turned towards his daughter. 'You will go straight to your cabin, Abby, and you will tell Nanny that you must both stay there until I come to you. I shall have a word with your precious nanny. Spies, indeed.'

Stella watched her tearful daughter depart. Looking at her husband, she clearly saw the malice in his eyes. With a sickening clarity she saw that he was enjoying himself, that he relished the power he had over them. With a look or a word he could make them miserable or happy. He held them in the palm of his hand and on a whim could crush them. The unwelcome thoughts were not new, but today they frightened her and she was touched by a growing panic. Once she had adored him; had actually *pitied* the women who could never be his wife. She had been so proud of him – his looks, his easy charm, his confidence. The sad truth was, however, that Clive Nicolson was two men – a great charmer and a bad-tempered bully. Gradually, over the past years, she had had fewer glimpses of the charm. He reserved that for their public engagements where she saw the way women looked at him, envying her the relationship. In private he too often allowed the mask to fall, revealing the cold, unsympathetic man she had married.

Stella drew in a long, ragged breath, unable to tear her eyes from his face. She had long since been forced to face the fact that the love match had existed only in her imagination and had gradually accepted the knowledge that he no longer loved her.

He glanced up as he finished his tea and dabbed his mouth with his napkin. As their eyes met, the realisation that she no longer loved *him* came as a searing shock.

Clive set off along the deck, leaning forward against the strong breeze. The sun was visible through a hazy cloud layer, but the July air had an unseasonal nip to it and he clutched the lapels of his blazer closer round his neck for extra warmth. As he walked he wondered uneasily about his wife. Several times on the outward voyage she had imagined that they were being watched, but he had tried to ignore it. Now, on the way back to England, it was happening again. Was this the way her aunt had started, he wondered. He could do without any extra worries with that bastard Hemmings whining for his money. He was refusing to wait another day, threatening to report him. Who to, for God's sake? The captain? The man was a fool. The police would never take action against a man for a private debt. It was a matter of honour to be resolved between the two of them and, if Hemmings would give him time, he would win enough to repay him. God Almighty! The previous night he had, as he had told Abby, won 'oodles' of money – though not enough. He had won seven hundred and twenty guineas to be exact. It was a good start, but he could do better. He owed nine and a half, and time was limited. Hemmings had an unsavoury reputation. If Clive hadn't paid him off by the time they reached port, he would be in serious trouble.

He raised his hat as two middle-aged ladies approached, arm in arm.

'Good morning, ladies.' He gave them a little bow. Women loved that sort of thing.

'Oh, good morning, sir.' They fluttered excitedly. 'Out for your constitutional?'

'Yes, indeed. Blow away the cobwebs.'

'Oh, yes. We do, too. And walk off the breakfast You see . . .' she giggled . . . 'we have *cream* on our porridge! Very naughty but we indulge ourselves. So now we must create a little space for lunch! We always have beef on the first day at sea. They do it so well on this ship. It wouldn't do to waste it.'

They both tittered at this little sally and Clive laughed with them. Two spinsters, he thought dismissively. Well, he had brightened their day. He said, 'You look as though the walk keeps you fit!'

'Oh, do we? How lovely! We do try, weather permitting.'

He smiled and moved on, aware that they watched him go. It occurred to him that Stella would have ended up like those two if he hadn't married her and given her a child. Not that he was her only suitor, but poor old Jerry was a bit long in the tooth. Getting on for fifty most likely. And the Yank was a poor loser to boot. He hadn't taken kindly to a younger, more handsome Englishman snatching his darling Stella from under his very nose! Clive sighed. Poor Stella. Rich and beautiful and possibly flawed. She'd been swept off her feet. Head over heels! He'd taken a chance. He knew that. Still . . . She hadn't blossomed as he had hoped; as he *deserved*. Instead she had grown nervous and morose. God knows why. He hoped she *wasn't* taking after the batty old aunt. Hester – or was it Esther? He shook his head. Five minutes later he turned and began to retrace his steps, his face darkened by a frown of annoyance. He would have to talk to Mary and Abby now, and was in no mood for it.

'Mr Nicolson!'

He turned to see Mrs Malone hurrying after him.

She said, 'A fine morning.'

Of course! He smiled with real pleasure. He had forgotten all about her. 'Mrs Malone. Good morning!'

She was a little breathless, he noticed. Had she been running after him? He was flattered. He said, 'You're looking very well this morning. Roses in your cheeks as well as your hat!'

She laughed delightedly. 'I'm giving you fair warning, Mr Nicolson. Flattery will get you a long way! I've a weakness for it.' She fell into step beside him. 'And where're your wife and your daughter? Not taking a little walk?'

'My wife is a little below par – the slightest swell upsets her. Abby . . .' He hesitated. A small white lie wouldn't come amiss. 'She's in the playroom with her nanny. Or *should* be. Stella constantly bewails the fact that nannies aren't what they used to be.'

'Stella. Such a pretty name. It means star. Did you know that, Mr Nicolson?'

Seeing that she hurried to keep pace with him, he slowed his steps a little, smiling down into her face. 'No. Is that so? Star. Hmm. And what does Augusta mean, if I may ask?'

'You may, Mr Nicolson. It means wise. A wise woman.'

'And are you?'

'Wise enough.' She put up a hand to hold her hat as the breeze quickened. 'I looked for you in the casino last night but you weren't there.'

She seemed a little embarrassed by the confession. 'I took you for a gambling man, you see. So maybe I'm not quite as wise as I like to think.'

She gave him a mischievous glance, her green eyes large behind long pale lashes. A long wisp of frizzy ginger hair had escaped from its hairpins and blew across her face. As she brushed it away with well-kept fingers, he could imagine it tousled across the pillow as she slept. Clive was intrigued, wondering how she lived. Then he remembered. She had said she was a widow. No doubt her husband had left her well provided for if she could cross the Atlantic at will and in style.

He said, 'I'm sorry I missed you. Your company would have been very welcome. My wife retires early to bed and it can be a little lonely.'

'Well now, there's a coincidence!' she exclaimed. 'I enjoy a quiet drink and a little conversation myself before I go to bed.

Last time I travelled I met a charming young priest: Father O'Malley from Donegal. Single, of course. We passed a very pleasant hour with the good book before going to bed.'

Something in her tone made him look at her, but her expression was all innocence. Her laugh rang out.

'Oh, Mr Nicolson! I do believe – did you misunderstand me now? That would never do. Going to our *separate* beds. Is that better?'

The 'something' in her voice was more pronounced and he stopped and stared at her.

'Mrs Malone! Such a thought never crossed my mind!' His eyes challenged hers. Was she playing with him? If so, it was a game he relished. His pulse quickened. Was she – could she *possibly* be one of *those* women? 'So you went your separate ways. I feel almost sorry for the young Father O'Malley.'

They walked on, laughing together.

She said, 'Did I say he was young? He was, as it happens. Young and foolish.' She sighed heavily.

Now what did the sigh mean?

'Young and foolish and very innocent.'

A virgin? Was that what she meant. He felt a surge of excitement as he saw the way the conversation was going. He said, 'I envy him. I can scarcely remember being young and innocent. The world has a way of seducing young men.'

'Indeed it has!'

As she tilted her face away from him, it was suddenly hidden by the brim of her hat so that he could no longer see her expression. There was a certain confidence in her manner that suggested a woman who knew her own mind. The sort of woman he admired. The sort of woman he should have married had circumstances allowed. He pursed his lips thoughtfully. Mustn't allow her to make all the running.

He pulled a watch from his pocket and glanced at it, tutting with annoyance. 'I must cut short my walk.' He hoped Mrs Malone was disappointed. 'I promised my wife I'd amuse Abby for an hour or so. She loves listening to stories.' Impulsively he added, 'If I'm lonely tonight, I just may come in search of you.'

Her smile was brilliant. 'I'll probably be in the Verandah Café,' she told him.

He tugged open the door and looked at her enquiringly.

'I'll walk a little further,' she said.

He raised his hat, smiled and stepped inside. Closing the door, he snapped his fingers and said, 'Bullseye!'

Gussie, familiar with the discomforts of the slatted wooden recliners, had covered hers with two thick towels before lying down. A handkerchief protected her face from the sun as she relaxed in its warmth aft of the boat deck. Footsteps paused beside her and she recognised the white shoes and trousers of one of the deck stewards.

'Can I get you anything – Mrs Malone?'

She stiffened slightly, then said, 'Nothing, thank you,' without removing the handkerchief. So he had recognised her, she thought; knew her, maybe, for what she was. So what? Why should she care? Women of her profession travelled all the great liners. They did no one any harm and were generally left to their own devices. Some of the crew themselves were no better than they should be, always with an eye on the main chance. Anything in skirts was suitable prey, but the young women were preferred. Many a pretty daughter had fallen in love for the first time during an Atlantic crossing. There was something about life at sea which set the heart racing romantically, not to mention the allure of naval dress. Even Gussie felt a mild thrill at the sight of an officer in his dark blue uniform and winking gold buttons.

More footsteps and then a childish squeal of recognition.

'Oh look, Mama. It's Mrs Malone!'

Before she could feign sleep, the handkerchief was plucked suddenly from her face and Abby stared down at her with undisguised delight.

'Oh, Abby! Hello there.' The child's obvious pleasure was a great compliment and Gussie forgave the interruption. She smiled up at Abby's companion. This was obviously the mother. Stella Nicolson was almost a beauty, she thought, surprised. Only her expression spoiled her. Tense and guarded, it hardened the lines of her face.

'I'm Stella Nicolson. Abby's mother – for my sins!' She spoke with a soft drawl and Gussie was reminded that she was American.

Stella Nicolson hesitated. 'May we join you for a few moments? I'd be real glad of some company right now.'

Gussie sat up, adjusting her chair. 'By all means.' She gave the mother a quick scrutiny by way of comparison, as she did every woman she met. To Gussie, her face was her fortune. To her, looks were of paramount importance and if her own were inferior in any way her self-confidence suffered. Stella Nicolson had dark hair under a smallish hat which bore an attractive arrangement of gold and green ribbon. Her features were fine but her face was thin and her complexion a little pasty. Was she *ill*, Gussie wondered. Her fashionable dress was striped in dark green and grey silk and had obviously cost a great deal of money. Better clothes but hardly blooming, Gussie decided, and was reassured. She smiled cheerfully.

Abby said, 'I told you, Mama. I said we might find her and here she is.' The child hopped excitedly from one leg to the other. 'Her friends call her Gussie, but we can call her Mrs Malone.'

Gussie asked, 'And how did you enjoy your time with your papa?' She explained to Stella, 'I met your husband earlier. He was on his way to collect Abby from the playroom.' They both regarded her blankly. 'He said he was going to take her . . .' Gussie stopped.

'Papa was cross with me,' Abby told her, her face suddenly resentful. '*And* with Nanny. He grumbled at Nanny and made her cry. Sometimes I hate Papa!'

Obviously embarrassed, her mother put a warning finger to her lips and her daughter fell silent.

'Oh dear!' Gussie laughed. 'Truth *will* out!'

Stella drew a deep breath. 'I guess so. We got off to a bad start this morning. A little stormy over breakfast! My husband *was* rather annoyed with them. Probably preferred not to mention it.'

'Papa was *horrid*! He said I was talking nonsense, and I wasn't.'

'Darling, *please*!'

'Well, he *was* horrid. He made *you* cry, too. He said—'

'*Stop*, Abby!' Stella Nicolson swallowed. 'I was *not* crying.' She smiled shakily at Gussie.

Perhaps not, thought Gussie, but she looked as though she might start at any moment. To avert a social disaster she said

33

quickly, 'Children! They put two and two together and make five!' She turned to Abby. 'They're having a tug o'war on the foredeck in about ten minutes. Don't you want to watch it? If Mama will let you.'

'Tug o' war's *boring*.'

'This one *won't* be,' Gussie told her.

The child hesitated. Perverse as they come, thought Gussie.

'Mama?'

'Of course you should go, darling.'

Gussie said, 'Why don't I take her? I'll leave her with one of the stewards. They're very good with children.'

Abby said, 'We might see Nanny.'

'We might, yes.' Gussie winked at the girl's mother. 'I'll be right back.'

She marched her small charge along at a brisk pace, taking time only to hear the real version of the morning's events. So that was the other side of the coin, she thought. Clive Nicolson could be bad-tempered. Well, we're all human. Still, it would be interesting to talk with the wife. Living the life she did, Gussie missed the company of women and the chance to talk was not to be missed.

She deposited Abby as promised, at the front of the small crowd waiting for the fun to begin. The two teams, busily rolling up their shirt-sleeves, mostly consisted of male passengers. They were all in high spirits, laughing and joking with the spectators and bandying good-natured insults with members of the opposing team. The entertainments officer was drawing a line across the deck with a piece of white chalk and a few bets were being surreptitiously placed. There was no sign of the nanny, so Gussie left Abby in the care of one of the stewards. She made the child promise not to wander away but to wait there for Gussie to collect her.

Returning to Stella Nicolson, Gussie settled herself down once more, eager for an exchange of confidences, but Stella Nicolson's pale face and haunted eyes suggested that a single kind word might break down the fragile composure. Agitated fingers fiddled with the smooth dark hair and she sat stiffly in the deck-chair. Gussie had no desire to cause her pain so, to start the ball rolling, she began a version of her own past that was part truth, part fiction.

34

'Men!' she began, with a light laugh. 'We can't live *with* them and we can't live *without* them.'

Stella Nicolson, tight-lipped, merely nodded.

Gussie decided to start with the fiction. 'I was married once but, to be truthful, it was not a wild success.' She shrugged. 'I sometimes think we expect too much and are doomed to disappointment. My husband was good to me in his own way, I suppose, but he never understood me. Never wanted to. He didn't seem to think it was at all important.'

Was she anywhere near the truth, she wondered. She had no experience of married life at all. In case she was wrong she added, 'But there. My husband was a sea-captain – away most of the time. I suppose sailors are a race apart in many ways. The sea is a kind of mistress.'

She let the ensuing silence continue, fussing with her handkerchief, arranging it carefully across her face. Perhaps the woman would feel safer if she remained 'hidden'. After a moment it seemed she was right.

'I married an Englishman, against my parents' wishes.' The voice quavered a little but it was a start.

Gussie said, 'Very stiff-upper-lip, Englishmen. Myself, I blame the boarding-schools.' She felt a tinge of guilt as she said this, and hoped Sister Everistes' ghost would forgive the small betrayal. Her own boarding-school had been a happy enough place. The nuns did their best and were never unkind. She smothered a feigned yawn. Mustn't sound too interested; she would try a little indifference. 'I suppose American men are more approachable. More relaxed in some ways,' she said eventually.

'I guess so.' A long sigh followed this remark. 'My folks are devastated. I hurt them both, but especially my father. He's so – so *caring*. I adore him. I wanted a man just like Father and, of course, there isn't one.'

Gussie was filled with an irrational envy. Her own father had had three legitimate sons by his wife, and was not at all thrilled to learn that the maid was expecting his fourth child. He had sent the maid and the unborn child back to her parents in Liverpool, but when she died in childbirth he had sent money on a regular basis for Gussie's keep. It seemed he was a wealthy man, for later, when her grandparents were dead, he had paid for a very decent convent education. Gussie understood that he had set eyes on his daughter only once when she was a week old, so she had no memory of him. She had no knowledge of him as a person, and had often wondered which of her parents she took after. A *caring* father would have been nice, but things could have been a lot worse. Gussie had never blamed him for the hole he had left in her life.

She was reconciled to the fact that they would never meet, for he had died suddenly when she was sixteen. The sheltered existence had been rudely interrupted by lack of funds and Gussie had been thrust into the outside world to look after herself.

Stella Nicolson turned her head slightly towards Gussie. 'They wanted me to marry a family friend. Jerry Land. Older than me, and a very kindly man. Poor Jerry adores me. My father insisted that Jerry would look after me *whatever happened*, and for a time I was willing to consider the idea. But there was no – no *excitement* between us. Of course I loved him, but I thought of him more as an uncle.'

Gussie thought he sounded wonderful and tried to imagine herself with an adoring, older man. She removed the handkerchief from her face and glanced at her companion.

'So how did you meet Abby's father?' she asked.

There was a long pause. 'We were invited to a picnic by friends of friends. Clive was there. He'd come to America in search of adventure. A fresh start, he called it. He'd worked his passage over. What I felt for him was different again. He was young, good-looking and so *British*. Different entirely, with his wonderful manners, and I just *loved* the way he spoke. Like listening to Shakespeare, I told my mother. Hah!' She pressed two fingers against her mouth. 'His *ideas*. They said English and Americans are "chalk and cheese"! I guess they were right in some ways. I don't blame anyone but myself. Certainly not Clive.'

Gussie heard the yearning. 'But if you'd married Jerry, it *could* have been wrong in other ways. That's what we never know. How it *might* have been.'

In a flat voice, Stella Nicolson said, 'Clive gave me Abby.'

'Yes. She's a lovely little girl.'

She was beginning to suspect that Stella Nicolson had already said too much and would later regret it. When the next question came, it took her by surprise.

'Was there ever another man in *your* life, Mrs Malone?'

She found herself answering it honestly. 'There was once. Years ago. Before I was married.' She wanted to stop there, but the temptation to go on was suddenly overwhelming. Talking about him brought him a little closer. 'He was a constable. Very new to the job. I was outside The Empire in Leicester Square – the music hall. You may know of it. I was just twenty years old.' She sighed. Better not to say what she was doing there; not watching the show, that's for sure! 'It was raining cats and dogs and not a taxi to be seen. There was a bit of a fight starting up along the pavement. Drunks at turning-out time.' She rolled her eyes. 'If there's one thing I do hate it's a man who can't hold his liquor . . . Anyway, these three men were going hammer and tongs – what the magistrate described later as "a mêlée". One of them had a knife. Someone whistled for a policeman and this young chappie came running. One against three it was, and in no time at all he was losing. There was a well-dressed couple next to me and the man said something about "going to help uphold the law." Good, I thought. The constable could do with some assistance. But the wife said, "Oh, don't interfere, dear. You'll only mess up your suit".'

'That's incredible!'

'Isn't it? Well, I couldn't just stand there and see the poor dear man beaten up so I waded in with my brolly. Whacking in all directions until . . .' She grinned at the memory '. . . until the blessed thing gave up the ghost. Broke right off. It was only a cheap little thing but it shouldn't have snapped like that.'

Her companion was sitting up, amused, a slight smile on her face. 'You were very brave!'

Gussie shrugged. 'One of them punched me in the eye – see this little scar – and I went down! I bled like the proverbial pig. When I got up, another one elbowed me in the ribs. Broke one of them, although I didn't know the half of it until the nurse told me later. Well, I lost my temper, didn't I? I picked up the policeman's truncheon – by this time his hat and his truncheon were both in the gutter – and I set about them.' She laughed at the memory. 'One of them staggered away and was never seen again. Another constable arrived and suddenly it was all over. The injured constable was in a bit of a mess and we were both carted off to the hospital. They kept me in, and next day he showed up with a bunch of violets. That's how it started . . .' Her voice trailed off as she remembered him walking towards her along the ward. Some of the older women whistled after him and he was pink with embarrassment by the time he reached her bed. Poor Harry. He was so shy. Hardly said a word, but before long they had started courting.

Gussie closed her eyes. 'I really loved that man,' she said, and wondered what reason she could give this woman for the abrupt end of the relationship. He died tragically? He was posted away? He met someone else, perhaps. She was spared the decision by the reappearance of Abby with a young woman in tow. Nice eyes. Face rather flat, but can't say the same for the chest. No prizes for guessing who chose the nanny, Gussie thought disparagingly.

She sat up abruptly and wagged a finger at Abby. 'Broken your promise, have you then? You were told to wait until I collected you.'

Abby pulled a face. 'I went to look for Nanny.'

'No toffee-apple for you then. I'll eat it myself.'

Abby stared. 'You haven't got a toffee-apple.'

'It's back in my cabin.'

Abby opened her mouth and shut it again.

Her mother intervened. 'Was it fun, honey – the tug o' war?'

'You're not supposed to call me "honey". Papa says—'

'Darling, then. Was it fun?'

Abby shrugged and Gussie felt an urge to shake her.

'They were all shouting and cheering and then the winning team pulled the others over the line and the steward blew his whistle, and then the losing team let go of the rope and the others fell down and everybody laughed and cheered again. They won a badge each with a picture of the ship on it. I knew it would be boring.' She threw a look of triumph in Gussie's direction, then looked at her mother. 'Nanny's got a young man,' she said.

The nanny gave her a look which might have killed a less resilient child. 'I haven't,' she said. 'What a fib!'

Abby voice was shrill. 'It's not a fib! You were talking to him. I saw you. He was laughing. He touched your hair. You were coming out of the elevator.'

The nanny said, 'You have to call it the lift. Your papa said so.'

'Lift, then. Anyway, I'm going to tell Papa about you and—'

The nanny's face was reddening. 'Abby! One of these days your tongue will split!'

Stella Nicolson looked helplessly at the nanny. 'Well, Mary?'

'It's not true. I swear it! He's not my young man. We just happened to be—'

Abby screamed, 'It *is* true! I *saw* them!'

Her mother help up a warning hand. 'That's enough, Abby. Both of you. If I hear another word on the subject I shall tell your father.' She looked at Gussie. 'Little wonder my nerves are so bad. All this bickering . . .' She drew a deep breath, closed her eyes and then opened them. To the nanny she said, 'Take Abby to the playroom and stay with her. You hear me? *Stay with her.*'

Gussie watched them go.

Stella Nicolson said wearily, 'She knows she's not allowed to have what Clive calls "followers". Nannies! They're such a problem.'

Gussie felt that the moment had come to extricate herself from the conversation. Stella Nicolson hadn't been the only one to say a little too much.

'Goodness gracious!' she said. 'It must be nearly twelve o'clock. Here we are chattering nineteen to the dozen and it will be time to eat again. I must spruce myself up.' She held out her hand. 'We may meet again some time.'

'Oh, I do hope so.'

With a quick smile Gussie turned and hurried away. Curious, she told herself. The child was obviously telling the truth about the nanny. And the mother knew it.

Usually, Abby loved the children's playroom, but this morning she stared round her with a jaundiced eye. The illustrated panels on the walls looked babyish and the rocking-horse, with his big brown eyes, was stupid. She could feel no enthusiasm for the doll's house, and the chest full of soft toys was definitely beneath the attention of someone of seven years. Miss Emily, the nursery nurse, was soothing a tearful toddler and had turned down Abby's suggestion that they should all play musical chairs.

But Abby was mainly unhappy because Nanny was being beastly and had refused to play Snakes and Ladders or read to her. Instead, she had decided to draw an outline of a rabbit for Abby to colour in. Since Nanny was no artist, the rabbit was looking decidedly odd and Abby found the other occupants of the playroom much more interesting.

Being an only child, she was fascinated by other children. She noticed a boy of about her own age and for a while she watched him surreptitiously. He was sitting in a corner, absorbed in a book. At last Abby sidled over to him.

'What's it about?' she asked.

He glanced up, startled. 'Trains. I'm going to drive one when I grow up.' He had nice brown eyes.

Abby said, 'Can you read, then?'

'Of course I can. Can't you?'

'No – but I could if I wanted to.' She felt affronted. Could he *really* read or was he pretending? She said, 'I bet you can't.'

'Bet I can!' He ran his finger slowly along the page. 'It – is – very – im – por – tant – to – stoke – the – fire . . .'

'My nanny reads faster than that,' Abby told him scornfully, 'and so does Papa!' She stalked back to Nanny with her head in the air.

Nanny glanced up. 'You don't have to be so rude, Abby,' she said. 'No wonder nobody likes you.'

Abby sat down beside her. 'I could read if I wanted to.'

'No, you couldn't. You have to *learn* how to read, and you don't even go to school.'

Abby felt like crying because she wanted people to like her. But she knew why Nanny was being so horrid. It was because Abby had told Papa about Nanny's young man. Now she wished that she *hadn't* told anyone, but it was too late.

Nanny held up the picture. 'How d'you like that?' She smiled at Abby. 'You can colour it in and then show it to your papa.'

Abby was surprised. *Now* Nanny was being nice again. She hesitated. Part of her wanted to be friends, but another part refused to abandon her mood. She looked at the rabbit.

'Rabbits don't look like that,' she said. 'Their ears stick up.'

'This is a lop-eared rabbit. I had one once, just like this one. Colour it grey and give it some whiskers, and then your papa will say what a clever girl you are.'

At that moment a small boy crawled past them, pushing a dog

on wheels. He was making little 'woofing' noises and Abby forgot all about the rabbit. She crouched down beside him and took the dog from him.

'Look! He's chasing a cat up a tree!' she told him, making the dog run up the table leg. 'Woof! Woof! Come down, you naughty dog!' She laughed with excitement, but the boy's eyes had filled with tears. She looked at him anxiously.

Nanny said, 'Leave him, Abby.'

The little boy held out his hands for the dog.

'Look!' Abby tried again. 'I can make the doggie jump over this chair – see! Over he goes! Woof! Woof!'

Two tears rolled down the boy's face and, seeing this, the nurse came over and picked him up. She said, 'Don't cry, Stevie.' She smiled at Abby, who handed over the dog without a word.

Nanny said, 'Come and colour in the rabbit, Abby.'

Abby sat down and picked up a grey pastel. 'But why is he crying?'

'You took his toy away. Look, it doesn't matter. Just get on with your colouring.'

'I don't like rabbits. I want to colour a clown.'

'I can't draw clowns.'

Nanny sounded exasperated and Abby felt a small gleam of triumph. If she herself felt miserable, then she wanted Nanny to be miserable too. She said, 'I *did* see you with your young man!'

She heard Nanny gasp. Then she said, 'But they didn't believe you, Abby. They believed me.'

Abby scribbled across the rabbit, then found a black pastel and drew in some thick, black whiskers. She was afraid to look at Nanny's face.

Nanny said, 'But I forgive you, Abby. I do.' Her voice sounded strange.

Abby found a green pastel and drew in some stalks of grass for the rabbit to eat. She was beginning to like the rabbit now that it was coloured in. Maybe Papa would let her have a rabbit of her own.

Nanny said, 'How would you like to be friends again? You forget about the young man and tonight I'll give you *two* dream sweets.'

Abby tried not to look too excited, but her inside felt funny when she thought about *two* of the special sweets. 'Why?' she asked. It was the question she always used to buy herself some time.

Nanny pressed her lips together, the way she did when she was not pleased.

'Because then you'll go to sleep for a long time and have *more* lovely dreams than usual. Twice as many. You'd like that, wouldn't you?'

Abby nodded. If only she could *remember* the wonderful dreams. What was the point of them if she could never remember them when she was awake? She gave Nanny a sideways glance and wondered if the young man really was going to come to their cabin. He had threatened to come knocking on the door and Nanny had given a funny little squeal and said, 'Oh, you *mustn't*! No, *really*? We can't!' If he *was* going to come to their cabin, then she would like to be awake to listen to what they said to each other. If she had two dream sweets she would miss it all.

'Is your young man coming this evening?' she asked.

Nanny gave a funny sort of gasp. 'Abby! You sly little baggage! No, of *course* he's not coming.' Her eyes were all sparkly. 'It's not even *allowed* for the crew to be in the passengers' quarters – unless that's their job, and John is on the entertainment staff. He's a singer; he's nothing to do with cabins. So he wouldn't *dare*.'

'John?' Abby asked. 'Is that his name?'

'John Donald Stamford. So if he married, his wife would be Mrs Stamford.' Suddenly she started to laugh and then clapped a hand over her mouth. 'And as for coming to visit us in our cabin – well, I simply wouldn't let him in.'

Abby was disappointed. 'Not even if he asked nicely?' She had learned early on that 'asking nicely' often produced results. 'If he said "*please*"?'

Nanny gave her a funny look. 'Not even if he asked nicely and said "please". But he wouldn't dare. And even if he *did* dare' – she looked at Abby – 'I wouldn't. I swear it. But you did like him, didn't you, Abby? He is rather handsome, isn't he?'

Abby thought about it. Did she like him? If she said 'yes' then maybe he *would* come. It would be quite exciting. She suddenly had such a brilliant idea that she felt dizzy. She would *pretend* to take the dream sweets, but then she would put them under her pillow and *pretend* to fall asleep and have dreams. Then if he did come to visit she would see him again.

'I liked him a lot,' she said. 'Is he going to marry you, because if he is? . . .' She was going to offer to be a bridesmaid but Nanny interrupted her.

'Marry me?' Nanny rolled her eyes. She was in a very odd mood. 'Of *course* not, you ninny! I hardly *know* the man.' She laughed again. 'But if he does want to marry me and you've been a good girl, you will be the first person to know and it will be a wonderful secret. How's that? Are we friends again?' She held up two crossed fingers and said, 'Pax?'

'Pax.' Abby nodded. She felt happy and began again on the rabbit, giving it a fluffy white tail and yellow eyes. Suddenly she made up her mind. She would *not* go to sleep like a good girl. She would stay awake like a *bad* girl!

Chapter Three

Stella stood at the ship's rail, staring down at the breaking waves which tumbled past the ship's dark hull. She had enjoyed a light lunch and was supposed to be resting. Clive had been in a surprisingly good mood during the meal and Abby behaved herself for once, exchanging smiles with Nanny, explaining that they were now 'best friends'. Clive had gone to the smoking room to enjoy a cigar and Nanny and Abby had set off in search of the entertainments officer. As always there would be a fancy-dress party, but usually there were a few unscheduled events organised by enterprising passengers and Abby hated to miss anything.

On her way to the cabin, Stella had changed her mind. She would stroll on the deck instead, alone and unencumbered by her family. She wanted to think – about Clive and about Mrs Malone. The latter she had found very good company and rather inspiring. Fancy fighting in the street! Obviously it had been done with the best intentions, but really! Hitting people with an umbrella and then a *truncheon*! Her mouth curved into a smile. The woman had spirit, that was obvious. She could never imagine herself behaving with such recklessness, not even in the same situation. Unless perhaps in self-defence although, even then, Stella suspected that she would be more inclined to run than fight. She might *faint* with fright.

Mrs Malone, it seemed, was always in control. She lived alone but that didn't prevent her from travelling to and fro across the Atlantic – a sea well known for its difficult, sometimes hazardous, conditions. Today the sky was blue with broken cloud, but the sea was rising and could get worse. Or an impenetrable fog would descend. How on earth did Mrs Malone manage if she was taken ill on the voyage? Presumably the stewardess would help. Stella had never been alone. She had always had someone to care for her; someone on hand to minister to her needs. It was hard to imagine ever being required to make decisions, pay the bills or do anything more demanding than arrange their holidays in Cornwall.

If anything happened to Clive – if he died or deserted her – would she be able to cope? The very thought sent a shiver of fear through her and she frowned uneasily as she considered her own limitations. Mrs Malone, on the other hand, had survived being widowed and had managed. Quite successfully, by all accounts. For a long moment Stella considered the possibility of being left to fend for herself and Abby. As always it filled her with dread – and yet ... This time she was aware of a very small flicker of determination; a new, still fragile desire to be strong. She would naturally go back to America where she belonged; back to her parents who would welcome her and Abby with open arms. They, however, would not live for ever. Already her father had a heart problem. There was always Jerry. He would look after them given half a chance. But he was much older than she was, and it was possible that she could find herself alone at some point.

Unconsciously she squared her shoulders. She would talk again with Mrs Malone in the hope that some of her courage would rub off. She straightened her back and whispered, 'Yes! I could do it!' and felt exhilarated. If she was ever left in financially difficult circumstances she would find employment of some kind. She wondered briefly what Mrs Malone did for a living – or had her husband left her with a comfortable annuity?

'Good afternoon, madam.'

She jumped at the voice and found one of the deck stewards beside her. He held an empty tray and asked, 'Can I get you anything? A drink from the bar? A pot of tea?'

'I don't think so, thank you.' She returned his smile. 'Lunch was a little more substantial than I intended!' Did he see her as the drink-from-the-bar or the pot-of-tea type? Probably the latter, whereas Mrs Malone would be the former.

'Glad to hear it, madam,' he told her. 'The *Mauretania* would hate to have any of her passengers go hungry.'

She laughed. 'No fear of that.'

'Your first trip?'

'No. We travel regularly. I'm an American and I get homesick.'

He tucked the tray under his arm and she groaned silently. He was settling in for a few of the 'revelations' that all the crew enjoyed so much. Already she knew the thickness of the steel plates which made up the hull and the number of turbines which powered the ship.

He said, 'I was with her when she first tied up in Manhattan. September 1907. Her first crossing. What a day that was! The launch, too. Another never-to-be-forgotten day.' He leaned beside her on the rail and Stella was suddenly aware of his nearness. She hoped nervously that Clive was still in the smoking room and wouldn't see them together. Then her eyes narrowed. Why *did* she hope that? They were doing no harm, just talking about the ship. Perhaps it would do Clive good if he caught them at their innocent tête-à-tête! Perhaps it would make him jealous. Maybe she should keep this young man talking for as long as possible.

She said, 'I read about the launch. The papers were full of it, naturally.' She turned her head, giving him her wholehearted attention. Perhaps Mrs Malone would find them together. She began to feel rather daring and smiled at him.

'Four million rivets,' he said, brightening with pleasure. 'And steel plates that weighed five tons apiece! The *Mauretania* can't be beaten. More than twenty-five knots an hour. That's an *average* speed!' He whistled his admiration. 'Men would give their eye-teeth to work on this ship. Even my cousin, and he's on the *Lucy*.'

Stella raised her eyebrows enquiringly and he grinned.

'The *Lusitania* to you, madam. Yes, our Steve's a trainee cook. Works in the galley. He won't hear a word against the *Lucy*, but he'd jump at the chance to be on this ship!'

Stella studied him carefully. Slim, almost girlish, with very pale blue eyes and sandy hair. Not exactly handsome but not ugly either. It was a long time since she had looked at another man.

He went on, 'The launch now. That was something, that was. It was raining cats and dogs. Well, it would. They say it rains nine days out of ten in Swan Hunter country.'

He chuckled, glancing at her face to see if he had made her laugh. She smiled obediently.

'But nobody cared, madam. Of course, you've only got the hull at that stage. No innards and no superstructure. That all comes later. But it's still an occasion. There were thousands to see her launched. The Duchess of Roxburghe was doing the honours. Bottle of champers wrapped in ribbons and stuff. Bandsmen playing their hearts out ...' He paused thoughtfully. 'Did I say Duchess? It was the *Dowager* Duchess of Roxburghe. And the promoters or whatever they're called – they had this idea – really just a bit of excitement but the crowd loved it. They laid three of the ship's funnels on the dock and the bigwigs' cars drove right through them! That got the press boys going. Bulbs popping all over the place.'

'I remember the pictures in all the newspapers!' Stella told him. 'So you were there. How wonderful.' She felt the freshening wind tug loose a strand of her hair and didn't bother to tuck it back under her hat. She wondered suddenly what she looked like to this very young man; he seemed around nineteen or twenty. At least he was prepared to stand and talk to her. Was she old enough to be his mother, she wondered, and hoped not. Maybe her hat would blow away. Then her hair would fall round her shoulders and she would look prettier. She straightened a little. This was decidedly more interesting than dutifully resting on the bed in her cabin. She laughed suddenly and for no good reason except that she felt good.

'What?' he asked.

'Nothing really.'

He smiled. 'It's the sea, madam. The freedom. It gets to people. They come on board with all the worries in the world and before long they've forgotten all about them. Nothing more to worry about than choosing what to eat. And it's a real tonic, the sea. People take a cruise for their health, it's so relaxing. And bracing. That too.'

Stella thought she could do with a little of both. Or better still, a great deal of both!

She turned, leaning back against the rail, feeling rather pleased with herself.

And then she saw him.

Her heart began to race. He was sitting about ten yards away, reading a newspaper. Or pretending to do so. She turned back to the steward. 'Don't turn round just yet, but there's a man reading. Squarish face. Grey eyes. Curly hair. I keep seeing him. He seems to . . . to dog my footsteps.'

After a suitable pause the steward turned, took a look and then turned back. 'Don't know him,' he said. 'He's not a regular. Mind you, he might have travelled out when I was on leave.'

As though aware that they were talking about him, the man folded the newspaper and stood up. Then he strolled away without glancing at either of them.

The steward said, 'If he's bothering you, I could have a word with him. Or maybe a senior officer . . .'

'Oh – I don't know.' She shook her head. If Clive found out he'd be furious. 'I couldn't say he was *bothering* me – not in that way – and I don't want any trouble. My husband thinks I'm imagining it, and maybe I am.' Familiar, frightening doubts crowded in. She clutched the rail, already chiding herself for her over-reaction. Forcing herself to appear calm, she wondered what Mrs Malone would do in her shoes. Probably beat the man over the head with her parasol. She gave a shaky laugh and drew a deep breath.

'Are you sure, madam?' The steward looked disappointed. His chat had been interrupted. 'If so, I'd better get along. Duty calls and all that. If you're sure you don't need any help?'

Stella hesitated. 'You couldn't find out who he is, could you?' she asked.

He pursed his lips. 'I could try,' he said dubiously.

'Oh, forget all about it. He doesn't look like a murderer, does he? Quite unassuming, really. I'm just being silly.'

He allowed himself to be persuaded and Stella watched him go with relief. Enough excitement for one day, she told herself ruefully. After a moment the thought occurred to her that perhaps Mrs Malone knew something about the man. She had said she was a frequent traveller. She straightened up, coming to a decision. She would say nothing more to Clive about him, but she would make a few enquiries of her own. And if she met with a brick wall? Stella tossed her head. She might even challenge the wretched man herself.

* * *

49

Later that night, in the Verandah Café, people who had dined well now relaxed in the comfortable armchairs, enjoying the warm night air. Staring out across the moonlit deck to the sea beyond, they drank coffee, nibbled petits fours and let the music flow over and around them. The pianist – a young, bespectacled man resplendent in tie and tails – seemed oblivious to their indifference. Gussie, half hidden by a large potted palm, hid a yawn and wondered what the time was. She had spent the past hour cursing Clive Nicolson and watching people come and go around her. The medley came to an end and, as though to compensate for their lack of interest, the audience applauded with exaggerated enthusiasm.

Damn Clive Nicolson! thought Gussie. If he was not going to appear, she had wasted the first two days of the trip and would have to start all over again with someone else. Where was the wretched man? A private poker game, perhaps. She bit her lip anxiously, trying to hide her impatience. She had been so sure of him. If he had changed his mind, she would like to know so that she could go back to her cabin and get to bed.

Ah! She sat up. There he was at last. At once her heart sank for he was tottering across the deck, making his way unsteadily into the room. She averted her eyes, pretending to flick dust from her skirt. Let him find her. It would look better.

'Am I late?'

He slumped heavily into the chair beside her and she feigned a start of surprise. There was a fatuous grin on his face. 'Dear Mrs Malone!' Breathing whisky fumes, he seized her hand and kissed it clumsily.

Uncomfortably aware of heads turning, Gussie withdrew her hand and said, 'Oh! It's Mr Nicolson, isn't it? Have you come to hear the music? I'm afraid you've missed most of it. We've had a wonderful programme. All my favourites.'

He leaned closer and said, 'I won, Mrs Malone! I won!' He stuffed a hand into the pocket of his jacket, pulled out a handful of five-pound notes and tossed them on to the table.

Appalled, she collected them and pushed them into his hand. 'Will you put them away, now! You'll be putting ideas into folks' heads!' It was putting ideas into *hers*!

Reluctantly he stowed the money away. 'You should have seen

their faces. So who's been a clever boy then? Eh?' His laugh turned into a cough.

Gussie, instantly the business-woman, mentally raised her prices. For two reasons. Firstly because she didn't like her gentlemen inebriated. It was so difficult to get rid of them afterwards. Secondly because he was loaded with money and probably wouldn't even remember tomorrow exactly how much he had won. She marshalled her thoughts. They hadn't actually discussed what would happen after they met, but he was far too tipsy to start a discussion. She would pretend they *had* agreed a price. The important thing was to get him out of the Verandah Café before he bought more whisky . . . and before he spoke indiscreetly to anyone else. She whispered the number of her cabin and made him repeat it. 'It's on the boat deck. Give me two minutes' start. Do you hear?'

'What's that?' He sought out the barman and tried to catch his eye, but Gussie caught it first. She shook her head and the man, understanding, busied himself with another customer.

Leaning closer she repeated the number of her cabin, adding, 'Now, have you got that?'

'I've got it.' He blinked, repeating it earnestly to prove that he had understood. After a moment he said loudly, 'What? . . . Why? Is it your cabin?'

To Gussie, the words seemed to reverberate around the room.

'Ssh! Holy Mother!' She lowered her voice. 'It is indeed, and you know well what that means. I'll be ready and waiting for you and we'll have ourselves some fun.' She stood up, eyeing him doubtfully. With her fingers crossed, Gussie walked out across the deck and hurried along to the stairs. As she waited for the lift she tapped her toes impatiently. He would be good for nothing, but he needn't know that. She smiled. She would let him sleep and then wake him and ask for the money. It worked every time. Men hated to think that they couldn't function. They loved to be told, 'I'm exhausted! I pity your poor wife!' She tutted. What children they were! Still, the good Lord had made them so and He must have had his reasons.

Back in her cabin she undressed swiftly and splashed herself with lavender water. She unfastened her hair and brushed it into a fiery mass. The small violet-flavoured cachou would make her breath smell sweet, and a floral-scented sachet had been in the bed since noon. She hesitated. Which should it be – her frilly black corset and the red garters, or the delicate peach nightdress with the gold ribbon?

'Come on, Gussie! Make up your mind!'

Frilly black won. She was barely ready when the knock came at the door. With a smile of welcome on her face Gussie threw open the door.

Then gasped. The man outside was not Nicolson but a complete stranger wearing a silk dressing-gown over striped pyjamas. He was short and bald and looked like a civil servant, and his eyes widened when he saw her.

'Glory be!' Gussie slammed the door. Through it she called, 'One moment, please.' Leaning back against the door she crossed herself and rushed for her decorous, 'everyday' dressing gown. Decently covered, she stood in a blind panic. Please God! *Please*! Not the ship's detective! Not another polite but humiliating chat with the captain! Opening the door a little less generously she said, 'Who is it? I'm preparing for my bed. What is it you want at this time of the night? Who are you?'

He said, 'I'm sorry to trouble you but a gentleman has collapsed against our door. I think he's been drinking. I wondered if perhaps he's your husband. All he will say is the number of this cabin.'

'My husband? Certainly not.'

'We were trying, the steward and I, to get him back on to his feet. The steward suggested I should come on ahead and try this number.'

Gussie's mind whirled. Holy Mother! She saw her first night's money slipping away from her and cursed her luck. But it could have been worse. At least this man was not a detective. Unless he was lying – and if he was, then he was a great actor. He sounded genuine.

'I'm a widow,' she told him, carefully omitting her name, 'so, thank the Lord, he doesn't belong to me. He must have confused the cabin numbers. Maybe he's on another deck. Maybe the promenade deck. I'm afraid I can't help you.'

She began to close the door but at that moment two figures shuffled awkwardly into sight. The steward was half dragging

Clive Nicolson, whose dead weight made their stumbling progress a slow one.

She heard him say, 'This way, sir. Soon have you safely home.'

Nicolson looked up and caught sight of her. 'Sorry I'm late—' he began.

Gussie thought frantically. At any moment he would say her name. She said, 'Good heavens! I do believe it's Mr Nicolson. I've noticed his family in the dining room. He has a wife and little girl.'

The steward said, 'So you do know him?'

'I know the wife and daughter,' she corrected him sharply. 'I have made the acquaintance of this man *briefly*. I can't tell you the number of their suite, but I'm sure you can track them down from the passenger list.'

Nicolson said, 'Mrs Malone!' and gave her a lopsided grin.

She gave him a withering look. 'What a sad sight, to be sure. I don't envy your poor wife,' she said. 'Now, if you'll excuse me—'

She closed and locked the door. Take the poor man away, she told them silently and rolled her eyes expressively. He's a liability. For a moment she listened to their erratic progress along the corridor. When she could no longer hear them she let out a deep sigh.

'Gussie Malone, you've picked a dud!' She wondered how it would all look in the cold light of morning.

Abby lay in bed with her eyes half closed. She had pretended to swallow the dream sweets and she had drunk the hot milk Nanny had given her. But the two pink pills were under her pillow and she was wide awake. Peering through her eyelashes she saw Nanny undressing, something she had never seen before. Usually she was fast asleep before this stage in the proceedings, and only in the morning did she see Nanny in her nightdress. She watched in silent fascination as first the blouse was unbuttoned and then carefully removed. Underneath she wore a cotton camisole with lace round the top of it. Much prettier than her own liberty bodice, Abby thought. It was all so unfair. But maybe when *she* was grown up she, too, would wear lacy things underneath.

Nanny glanced over at Abby's bed, then came across to make sure she was asleep. Abby closed her eyes properly and wondered whether to give a little snore but decided against it. It might come out like a *big* snore, and then she'd start to giggle and spoil everything.

'Sweet dreams!' said Nanny and laughed to herself.

After a while Abby peeped out again. Now Nanny was humming softly to herself and she had a little smile on her face. She unhooked her skirt and dropped it to the ground. Abby almost squealed with laughter. Nanny had long drawers on down to her knees – white, with more lace. What would happen, thought Abby, if John came knocking and Nanny was in her drawers and bodice? But, of course, he *wasn't* coming because Nanny said he wouldn't dare.

After the skirt, the lace camisole was pulled off over Nanny's head and Abby was astonished. The round lumps under Nanny's blouse were all soft and floppy. Cook had told Abby that they were called bosoms. Nanny was *stroking* them. How funny. She had closed her eyes and was smiling at nothing. Abby was enthralled. It was much more fun than the wonderful dreams she could never remember. Whatever would she look like underneath her drawers? This thought made her want to laugh, and she had to stuff the sheet into her mouth to keep herself quiet.

Nanny suddenly reached under her pillow and produced a nightdress that Abby had never seen before. It was pale green, and there were little white daisies sewn on to it round the neck. Abby thought it the most beautiful thing she had ever seen. Without removing her drawers, Nanny pulled it carefully over her head, tied the ribbons at the neck and looked at herself in the mirror. Abby was slightly disappointed. Now she would never know what Nanny looked like *under* her drawers.

Abby thought that even if John Donald Stamford *didn't* come to visit she had had some fun. And Nanny would *never* know. Unless Abby told her. Now Nanny was brushing her hair, and turning this way and that to get a better view of herself. Abby prayed silently: please God, let Nanny marry John so that I can be a bridesmaid. She imagined herself in a frilly white dress with a lace-edged camisole underneath and long white drawers. She was so wrapped up in this vision of herself that the knock on the door startled her.

For a moment Nanny did nothing. The knock was repeated and this time she hurried to the door and opened it.

'John!' she said. 'Oh, my goodness! You can't come in. I told you not to come.'

But somehow the door had opened wide enough to admit him and there he was, *standing in their bedroom*. Thin, pink-faced and handsome. He glanced her way and Abby held her breath.

Nanny said, 'She's out for the count!' and laughed.

He said, 'I've just come off stage. I couldn't wait to see you.' He took a step nearer to Nanny. 'You – oh God, Mary! You look wonderful!'

Nanny said, 'Wonderful? What? In this old nightdress?'

'Give us a kiss, Mary. You said you would. I'm on stage again in twenty minutes.'

'Give you a kiss? I never said that! Did I?'

Give him a kiss! thought Abby desperately. Once you had kissed them, they had to marry you. She could hardly breathe.

'Just one then.'

Abby held her breath as they came together briefly. One day a boy would kiss her! She wondered if Mary would have a baby now. Because they did. She knew.

'Gosh, Mary! You're a terrific girl. All the other chaps are ribbing me, but they're all jealous.'

'Jealous of me and you?'

Abby risked a better look and saw that Nanny's face had turned a pretty pink colour.

'So you've had your kiss,' Nanny said. 'Are you going now?'

'Mary!' he laughed. 'Have a heart! I'm only human. Can't I have a – little *tickle* before I go?'

'No, you can't, you cheeky thing!'

'Mary, *please*!'

Nanny slowly lifted the edge of her nightdress. 'You can have a little look. At my ankles – but that's all!'

He bent down and lifted the small foot, but somehow Mary overbalanced and fell on to the bed.

He stared down at her and gasped, 'Oh gosh, Mary! Let me!'

'Let you what?' She sat up, looking indignant.

'You know. Let me just look at it. Just something to remember.

I won't touch you, I swear I won't! Lift up your nightie. No, let me. Please!' He pulled off his jacket.

Abby was startled. Was he going to *sleep* in their room?

'John! No!'

Suddenly he threw himself on to the bed and Mary gave a little scream. Forgetting that she was supposed to be asleep, Abby sat up to get a better look. Nanny was giggling and John was trying – Abby stared, transfixed. *He was trying to undo his trousers with one hand!* His other hand had disappeared under Nanny's nightdress! Abby blinked in disbelief. That was rude, wasn't it? Then Nanny tried to push him away, still laughing, and he slipped off the bed with a crash. Abby began to giggle, and then Nanny and John both turned in her direction.

'You said she was asleep,' he cried, struggling now to button up his trousers.

Abby went on giggling because suddenly she couldn't stop. She could see from Nanny's face that there was trouble ahead.

Nanny said, 'Abby! You sly little baggage!'

'God, Mary! The kid's been *watching* us!'

Nanny slid from the bed and marched across the room. 'Abby, you are a hateful, disgusting child! I hate you! D'you hear me!' Her face was furious.

Abby wanted to stop laughing. She desperately wanted to say, 'Sorry, Nanny,' but now fear was playing a part and she was becoming hysterical.

He said, 'This is all your fault! I've got to get out of here.'

Nanny said, 'They'll see you – you'd better hide somewhere!' and grabbed his arm, but there was a knock at the door.

'What's going on in there?'

Abby recognised her mother's voice – and so did Nanny. She said, 'Oh Lord! That's done it!'

Terrified, Abby slid under the bedclothes, still giggling.

Stella had gone to bed earlier and had lain awake in the large double bed, trying to recapture some of the elation she had felt earlier in the day while talking to the deck steward. Then she had felt a small surge of confidence, but the appearance of the man with the newspaper had put an end to that. Her old doubts and insecurities had resurfaced Was she imagining things? If so, then was she going mad? The spectre of insanity hung over the family on her mother's side; but even before Stella became aware of this fact, she had been a nervous child. Easily frightened, overly cautious. She thanked God that Abby took after her father.

At the age of fourteen Stella had suffered what her mother described as 'a nasty turn'. It had been more than that, although no one would ever admit it. She had slipped into a deep depression which lasted for almost six months. During this time she wept frequently and couldn't eat; she lost weight and was confined to bed. It was about that time that Gerald had moved next door. A warm-hearted bachelor, old enough to be her father, he had quickly endeared himself to her. He brought her books to read and jigsaw-puzzles to amuse her. They played draughts and worked on cross-word puzzles. As soon as she was well enough to leave her bed, he accompanied her on walks. They remained close friends after she recovered. Years later, the knowledge that he was in love with her had come as an unwelcome shock. She was still coming to terms with the idea when she met Clive.

Now, sighing deeply, she whispered her mother's oft-repeated warning.

'Stay calm, Stella, and you will stay in control.'

It appeared that her Aunt Hester had *not* remained 'in control' and had been forced to spend most of her adult life in what her parents euphemistically called 'a home for unfortunates'. The 'unfortunates' were those who were unable to live in the real world for one reason or another. Stella had once accompanied her mother to visit Aunt Hester and the experience still haunted her.

Now Stella was beginning to fear the worst – that her own mind was playing tricks. At first she had thought she was imagining the man, but now Clive had seen him and today the deck steward had also seen him. What puzzled her was the fact that nobody thought it strange that he came into view so frequently. She wished quite desperately that she could confide in someone and suddenly admitted to herself that that 'someone' was Mrs Malone.

'*No*, Stella!' she told herself.

Discussing her innermost fears with a comparative stranger was out of the question. Unthinkable. But if she *were* able to do so, she felt sure that Mrs Malone would reassure her one way or the other – she would either agree that the Nicolsons *were* being watched or she would convince Stella to the contrary. The trouble was that Mrs Malone might not stop there. She might also feel obliged to offer a few home truths, one woman to another. 'Stop letting that husband of yours browbeat you,' she might say. And Stella would have no answer to that. Because he did, and because Stella knew that she must take some of the blame for that. She had allowed him to bully her.

She felt a rush of hopelessness. The holiday with her parents, from which they were returning, had been marred by several arguments between her father and Clive. Her father no longer made any attempt to hide his dislike of her husband and had commented adversely on the change in Stella. His daughter, he told Clive, had always been quiet but now she was positively timid. Stella had fled the scene which, demonstrating the truth of his allegations, had infuriated both him *and* Clive.

So why, thought Stella, didn't she do something? *Now*.

'Such as . . .?' She could dress and go in search of her husband. She could go to the casino and explain that she was worried about the lateness of his return. He would be astonished – and he would be very angry. She wondered whether she could deal with that.

Stella sat up and slid from the bed, longing for the courage to act but terrified of the consequences. She would compromise; she would be dressed when he came back and she would pretend she was just about to go in search of him. Pulling on her clothes with trembling fingers, she thought she heard a sound from next door. A bump . . . muffled laughter . . . She listened. Was that a *man's* voice? She felt a shiver of apprehension. Surely Nanny hadn't got a *man* in the bedroom with them?

She rushed out of the cabin and knocked on the next door. It opened and she found herself face to face with a young man. They stared at each other, shocked. The young man recovered first.

'John Stamford, madam,' he said. 'I'm a member of the entertainments staff. The singer.'

Stella looked at him, momentarily speechless.

'It's nothing to worry about, Mrs Nicolson,' he went on. 'Miss Crisford rang for the stewardess but she had – she was – er – busy with another passenger, so she asked me to pop along in her place. When we're not on stage we help out in other ways.'

'*Pop along*? What for?' Stella put a hand on his chest and pushed him back into the room. Abby, giggling, sat up, her cheeks flushed with excitement.

Mary said, 'She was hysterical. It was a nightmare. First she was frightened and then she was – I rang for the stewardess—' She eyed the young man.

He said, 'Well, no harm done.' He smiled nervously at Stella. 'Your daughter's still a bit shaky but she'll be fine.'

Stella crossed to the bed and stared down at her. Suddenly revealed were two small pink pills. 'What are these?' she demanded, turning to Mary.

'Just sweets.'

Abby said, 'They're my dream sweets.'

'Well, Mary?' Stella waited for an explanation.

Mary lowered her voice so that Abby shouldn't hear. 'I give her one each night. I pretend they will make her have lovely dreams. They help her to sleep. The power of suggestion. You know?'

'I'm afraid I don't.' Somehow she suppressed the tremor in her voice.

Abby said, 'I didn't want lovely dreams. I wanted to stay awake, and I did.'

'But this young man has just told me you had a nightmare and woke in a hysterical state!'

Abby looked at Mary.

Mary said, 'She was ages going to sleep and – and *then* she had the nightmare and she woke up screaming and laughing and crying and . . . and I was scared. She couldn't stop. I pressed the bell and this gentleman came and we—'

Abby gave a squeal and began to giggle again.

'Abby!' Stella lost patience with her and slapped her on her bare arm. 'Stop it, for heaven's sake! I can't think why you're being so stupid. *Did* you have a nightmare?'

Abby nodded; her face began to crumple.

'Don't nod at me, young lady. I want a yes or no.'

'Yes.' Tears rolled down her face. 'It's all Nanny's fault. I hate her! She made me promise—'

Nanny said quickly, 'Don't tell lies, Abby. We all know what a fibber you are.' She turned to Stella. 'I'm sorry. I should have come to you – instead of ringing for the stewardess. I didn't want to wake you. I thought Mr Nicolson would be cross.'

Stella stared down at Abby who, hearing this, began to giggle again.

The young man said hurriedly, 'Well, I'll have to leave you to it. I'm due on stage for the reprise.'

He looked uncomfortable – as well he might, Stella thought wearily. Dealing with hysterical children was hardly part of his duties. She wondered whether to tip him and decided against it. It might look like a bribe.

Stella said, 'Yes. Well, thank you for doing what you could.'

Abby gave a little scream and began to giggle again. The young man made good his escape and Stella bit her lip in frustration. A nice little anecdote for him to pass on to his colleagues. Now they'd all be sniggering about them. This trip was turning into a fiasco. She glanced at Mary who looked flushed and ill at ease. And something else that Stella couldn't quite pinpoint. Was it simply guilt?

Mary said, 'I shouldn't have let him in. It made things worse.'

Suddenly Stella wished Clive was at hand to deal with the matter, but he wasn't. She said, 'Go back to bed. Get some sleep, both of you, and not another sound.'

Abby stopped laughing. 'Don't tell Papa! We didn't mean to wake you up.' She glanced at Mary. 'Don't blame it on Nanny. She couldn't help it.'

Stella hesitated. 'Telling Papa' was her way of never dealing with unpleasant situations. But it was also a way of handing over the power. Maybe this time things would be different. She was surprised to realise that she had dealt with this matter with tact and firmness. In fact, she felt rather pleased with herself. Perhaps she *could* be strong. Perhaps it was *not* too late.

She drew herself up. 'We'll talk about it in the morning, Abby. I'll think it over, but I'm making no promises.'

The morning, however, brought further problems and the previous night's drama was temporarily overlooked. Stella had taken her bath and was already brushing her hair when Clive finally woke and rolled out of bed. He sat down heavily in one of the armchairs and clutched his stomach. His face was ashen and his eyes were dark with pain.

'Clive! What's the matter? You look terrible.'

'Thanks for the vote of confidence.'

'I didn't mean that and you know it.' Here we go again, she thought. 'All I meant was—'

'For Christ's sake, keep your voice down, can't you?' He glared at her and she felt her fragile courage draining away.

Somehow she must persevere though, she reminded herself with her new-found confidence. There was to be no more tiptoe-ing round this man.

'What happened to you last night?' she asked him. 'I was so frightened. Those men bringing you back in the middle of the night. Were you taken ill?'

'You could say that.' His tone was sarcastic.

'Was it drink or something worse? A seizure of some kind?' She stared down at the dark, bent head. 'They said they'd found you in a state of collapse. You wouldn't let me send for a doctor.'

He made no reply.

'*Clive!*' she insisted.

He groaned and muttered, 'God Almighty!' Then he looked up suddenly. 'My jacket! Where's my jacket? Oh God! That bloody little thug! If he's—'

Stella crossed to the wardrobe and pulled his jacket from the hanger. 'Here it is.'

What on earth was all *this* about, she wondered, with deepen-ing anxiety. Her husband had always been unwilling to confide in her. It seemed to be his desire to keep her in the dark about every-thing which didn't immediately apply to the running of the home or the care of their daughter. What she had come to see as a lack of trust was deeply hurtful to her. Equally so, however, was his lack of interest in *her* feelings. He disliked anything to do with emotions and would never discuss their problems without flying into a temper. When she attempted to understand his reasoning he called it 'prying'. Any suggestion she made with regard to the nature of their relationship was met with scorn.

Now she watched with apprehension as he plunged his right

hand into each pocket of his jacket. Then he threw down the jacket and swore.

'It's gone!' he groaned. 'It's all bloody gone! God! That bastard Hemmings! I'll kill him. I swear I will!'

She said, 'Hemmings? Who's he?'

He ignored her. 'He's taken every penny. How the hell does he expect me to get the rest of it if he—' He doubled up again, then glanced up at her and she saw the pain etched deep in his eyes. 'Well, don't just *stand* there, woman! Get me some milk of magnesia, for God's sake.'

Fuming inwardly at his rudeness, Stella obeyed. He snatched the glass from her and swallowed down the chalky liquid in two large gulps.

She said, 'You should let the doctor take a look at you. Let him find out what's wrong.'

He gave her a look of such dislike that she drew back. This was so like him, she reflected bitterly. He needed help but wouldn't even allow her to sympathise.

As though to prove her wrong, he said, 'I don't need a doctor. I *know* what's bloody wrong. Hemmings punched me in the gut. Half killed me, the blighter. I'm in agony. That's what's wrong. Satisfied?'

'Punched you? But *why*?' The thought of violence alarmed her. She took a deep breath. Keep calm, she told herself. Stay in control.

Clive glared at her, white-faced. 'So that while I was doubled up on the floor he could steal my winnings. That's why.'

'Winnings from a poker game?' So maybe he hadn't been drunk. Perhaps she had misjudged him.

'I had pockets full of money. I was on a roll for once. All I needed was one more night's play to double it. Then he could have had the lot. Stupid bastard!'

She thought rapidly. 'Did you owe him money?' He was in debt. Thank goodness her parents didn't know. She said, 'Maybe I could get hold of some money.'

'I don't want your damned money.' He tried to stand, but found it too painful and sat down heavily with a grunt of agony. 'I never have wanted it. Bloody father patronising me because I married his darling daughter. A money-grubber. That's what he thinks of me. A gold-digger.'

'That's not true. He's never said such a thing!' She tried to sound convincing although, in fact, her husband was absolutely right. Her father *did* consider him a 'gold-digger', but he had never made his opinion public. He had been more than generous to them since the marriage; he had made Clive a junior partner and had opened two shops in London. To be honest, Stella knew that Clive had worked hard. At the beginning he had shown considerable flair, but recently she suspected that profits had fallen. Her father was worried.

She said, 'Father wants what's best for us. You know he does.'

'Tell that to the marines!' he said petulantly. 'He wants what's best for *you*, and he doesn't give a damn about *me*. He wanted you to marry dear old Gerald, who follows you round like a faithful hound whenever we go over there.'

'There's no need to be rude. He's a decent man.'

'Oh, he's *decent*, is he? Then it's a pity you didn't marry him. Might have been better for both of us.'

Stella wanted to throttle him. He was now going to slide into an orgy of self-pity; she knew the signs. To change the subject she said, 'Why not report this Hemmings? He can't just go round attacking people and stealing their money – even if you *do* owe it to him. He ought to be arrested. At least detained. Or maybe the captain would caution him.'

He leaned back and his face was beaded with perspiration. 'Do try to use your brain, Stella. You're so stupid. Private gambling isn't exactly encouraged aboard the *Mauretania*. So who is going to care if I gamble and then lose my winnings? They're going to say—'

She said suddenly, 'What does Hemmings look like? Is he curly-haired? About our age? Thick-set with—'

'No, he isn't.' He stood up again, straightening up with an effort. 'God! Probably ruptured something. Bloody gorilla!'

Shella opened her mouth to protest at his language but thought better of it. Maybe, on this occasion, it was doing him good to express himself so violently. At least now his anger was directed at the absent Hemmings rather than at her.

She said, 'I just wondered if he was the man who keeps . . . the man I keep seeing.' She fell silent. After a long pause she asked,

'So how much money do you need to pay this Hemmings the rest? I'll try to see what I can do.'

He walked back to the bed and sat down carefully. Then, with a grunt of pain, he allowed himself to fall back on to it. 'A hell of a lot,' he said. 'But you'll be wasting your breath. I can tell you now that your beloved father won't even consider it.'

She was appalled. No, she thought; he certainly wouldn't lend that kind of money. 'But you'd like me to try?'

Seeing him suffer, she waited for the compassion to come welling up as she watched his laboured breathing. She invariably felt more for him in defeat because there was always the possibility that he needed her. To her surprise she felt nothing. The absence of pity troubled her. Was it true, perhaps, that she no longer cared for him? Was this indifference on her part all she had to look forward to for the rest of their lives? It was a bleak prospect for both of them.

She said, 'You rest, Clive. I'll see if I can send a wire. I don't quite know how it will be managed but I'll try.'

He said, 'Get someone to send me a tray of soup and bread. Maybe if I eat . . .'

'Soup? At this time? I might be able to get porridge. That would be comforting to your—'

'Porridge, then. You always have to fuss.'

'And you're sure you don't want me to call the doctor?'

'I don't want you to do anything else. Just go, will you, and leave me in peace.'

She hardened her heart against him and went out. Closing the door behind her, she said, 'You're a small-minded, arrogant, ungrateful, selfish, stupid *pig*, Clive Nicolson!'

And she felt marginally better.

After Stella had ordered the porridge, she went into the next room to deal with the problem of the previous night. Mary was looking defensive and Abby seemed nervous.

'I'll talk to Abby first,' she told them. 'You, Mary, please go to the shop and buy Mr Nicolson's newspaper. Take ten minutes over the errand and then come back. Do not speak to the young man who was here last night. Do you understand me?'

Mary nodded, but she looked disconcerted by the turn of events. She threw a look in Abby's direction and seemed about to protest at her banishment. Seeing the glint in Stella's eye, however, she finally nodded and left them reluctantly.

Stella smiled at Abby as she sat down near the window. 'I want you to tell me the truth, honey. I am hoping that I don't have to tell your father about what happened, but if you lie to me I shall have to.'

The small round face crumpled immediately. 'I can't!' she said. 'I mustn't.'

'Why not?'

'Nanny said so. She's going to buy me some sweets, and I can be a bridesmaid and everything.' She looked stricken.

Stella forced herself to continue the inquisition. 'Why did John Whatever-his-name-is come to this room, Abby?'

Abby shrugged. 'I don't know. He just came.'

'Nanny didn't ring for the stewardness?'

'I don't remember.'

'I think you should try, Abby. It's important . . . *Did* you have a nightmare? *Did* you wake up screaming? I didn't hear anything and I'm only next door.'

'I don't know. I think so . . .' She looked ill at ease. 'Yes, I did.'

'What was it about – this nightmare?' Stella decided that if Mary had invited the young man to her cabin she would have to go. There could be no second chance. Her spirits sank. She would have to tell Clive. Not that he could blame *her*. For once she could not be held responsible. It was her husband who had insisted on engaging Mary Crisford with the blonde curls and dimpled cheeks.

'I don't know.' The question had taken the child by surprise. 'I forget.'

She was beginning to sound like a parrot. The Nanny had primed her well, thought Stella. She decided to try a trick question. 'Did Nanny mind when he kissed her?'

Abby brightened. 'No. She laughed. *And* she kissed him back. She—' Realisation dawned and she clapped a hand to her mouth. 'I forget,' she amended, too late.

Stella pretended not to notice the slip. 'Did they think you were asleep?'

Abby nodded eagerly. 'I shut my eyes and Nanny looked at me and said, "She's out for the count," and they both laughed – but I wasn't.'

She looked at her mother's face to see if she was cross and Stella managed a reassuring smile. Inwardly she was furious.

'He kissed her, and Nanny said he could look at her ankles.' She looked uncertain.

Stella uttered a silent prayer but said nothing.

'It's a bit rude!' said Abby.

Stella said, 'Go on, Abby.'

'He tried to pull his trousers off!'

She began to giggle, stopped herself and glanced anxiously at her mother. Stella was horrified. How on earth had they ever thought the young woman trustworthy? And what sort of effect would the incident have on an impressionable child like Abby?

'And I started to giggle out loud and they both jumped up and John said, "I thought she was asleep" and—' She stopped suddenly, her expression stricken. 'Now I can't be a bridesmaid! Nanny said that if I told . . .' Her eyes filled with tears.

Stella drew a long breath. 'Then what happened?'

'I just kept laughing and I couldn't stop. He put his jacket on and Nanny said don't go, and I was still laughing, and then you came in and spoiled everything.'

'I spoiled everything. I see.' Stella's heart was thumping. Mary Crisford would have to be dismissed. She would leave their employ the moment they reached England. *And* she would go without a reference. How could she have been so reckless – to invite a strange man into their cabin? *Anything* might have happened. What *had* happened was bad enough.

Abby said, 'But it was so *funny*! Please don't be cross, Mama.'

Stella drew the child to stand beside her. Her own hands were shaking with shock and she was wondering how and when she dare tell Clive. Not in his present mood, she decided, but she was desperately in need of advice.

'Listen, honey,' she said gently. 'I'm not cross with you. I *am* sorry you tried to tell me lies, but I guess that's Nanny's fault. But I don't like lies and neither does God. When you say your prayers tonight you must ask Him to forgive you, and I'm sure He will.'

She wondered what to say to Mary when she returned. If the

nanny knew she was going to lose her job, she might cause some mischief out of spite. They could hardly lock her in her room for the rest of the trip. If only she could talk to Clive. But he'd been injured and robbed, and he was deeply in debt. This business with Mary would be the final straw. She came to an abrupt decision: she would confide in Mrs Malone.

At that moment Mary returned with the newspaper.

Abby cried, 'It's all your fault!' And she burst into tears.

Stella pulled her on to her lap and put her arms round her. To Mary she said, 'I think I know all there is to know. You have behaved very badly, but Mr Nicolson is unwell. We'll talk about it another time.'

Colour rushed into Mary's face. 'I'm really very sorry. I didn't think there was any harm—'

Stella's restraint deserted her suddenly. 'No harm? *No harm*! For heaven's sake, Mary. He might have murdered the pair of you. Don't you see how vulnerable you were? You're supposed to be responsible. *Responsible*! Instead, you were utterly reckless!'

'I didn't know – I didn't think . . .' Her tears began in earnest and she fumbled for a handkerchief. 'John wouldn't hurt a fly. I know he wouldn't.'

'You know nothing of the kind, you stupid girl. You've known him less than twenty-four hours by my reckoning. He flatters you and you think it's a big romance. Well, you're wrong, Mary. Men like that take advantage of women like you. You think yourself lucky that Abby *wasn't* asleep. God knows where it would have ended if she hadn't interrupted the . . . the proceedings.' She held up her hand. 'So stop crying and dry your eyes. And those so-called "dream sweets". I'll take those, if you don't mind.' She held out her hand. The ship's doctor would probably be able to tell her exactly what they were.

Mary went to the cabinet over the bath, took down a small pill-box and handed it to Stella without protest. There was a faded inscription on the label, but it was unreadable.

'You will stay here, Mary, until I send for you. Oh, don't worry. I shan't expect you to miss lunch. Abby will come with me to the playroom, where I shall ask one of the nurses to keep an eye on her. I have several things to attend to.'

Stella put Abby down and stood up. Her legs felt weak and her head was thumping painfully; she was probably about to get one of her sick headaches.

Five minutes later she had deposited Abby in the playroom under the watchful eye of Miss Emily, with whispered instructions that she must not be allowed to leave.

'Don't worry, Mrs Nicolson. We're just about to have a story. Abby will like that.' She smiled at Abby, who willingly went forward to sit on one of the small chairs with about a dozen other children.

Stella went out into the corridor. She took a deep breath and straightened up. Now where would she find Mrs Malone, she wondered eagerly. Having made her decision, she couldn't wait to talk to her.

Chapter Four

Harry Parr was sitting in a sheltered spot on deck when the steward found him. As he became aware of the man's shadow, he quickly closed the notebook in which he had been writing and glanced up.

'Good morning,' he said with a smile. 'I hope you're not going to tempt me with offers of bouillon. I always eat too much at breakfast and then again at lunch!'

The thin soup served on deck at mid-morning was welcomed by late risers who had missed breakfast.

The steward, the inevitable tray under his arm, shook his head as he leaned forward. 'No, sir. I'm not.' He hesitated. 'The truth is, I'd appreciate a word with you on a slightly delicate matter . . .'

Harry frowned. 'Slightly delicate?'

'Yes sir. I hope you'll forgive me—'

'I hope I will.' He laughed. 'I'm intrigued.'

'It's about a certain lady, sir.'

Harry said, 'Do I know this certain lady?' His conscience was clear.

'Well, yes and no, sir.' He looked uncomfortable. 'Her name's Nicolson.'

Damn! thought Harry, less than pleased. He hadn't been as clever as he thought.

The steward went on, 'She's probably a few years younger than you. A pretty woman, dark hair, well-dressed. She's travelling with her husband and a pretty little daughter. All curls and big blue eyes.'

Harry said, 'What's it all about, then?'

The steward glanced round, apparently to make sure that they were not in danger of being overheard. 'It seems that – well, how shall I put it? Mrs Nicolson spoke to me about you yesterday, and she has the idea that you're following her.'

'Good Lord!'

'It's probably her imagination, sir. Even *she* suggested that it might be, but she seemed so nervous. I tried to reassure her by saying I would speak to you, but that seemed to make her worse. I let it go, sir, but happening to see you I just thought I *would* mention it. You don't mind, sir, I hope?'

'Following her? Poor soul! Why on earth should she think that?'

The steward said quickly, 'I was sure it was *not* the case, but you know how some women are, sir. They get an idea in their heads – bee in the bonnet – and that's that.'

Harry shook his head incredulously. 'Oh dear! I'd hate to think I was worrying anyone. I'm afraid it must be her imagination. But if I see anybody who fits your description I'll look the other way!' He laughed, but he was wondering what to do. Perhaps he should have a quiet word with her himself.

The steward looked relieved. 'Then that's all right, sir. I felt sure you'd understand.'

'Of course. I'd hate to get a reputation for frightening pretty women!'

The steward changed the subject abruptly. 'Well, another fine day. Not that it's going to last, I'm afraid. We're in for a few squalls later. Might have a rough night. Still, ship's well up to speed. That's the main thing. Can't afford to lose our number one spot in the record books. Blue Riband and all that. We've got it and we mean to keep it.'

Harry said, '*Mauretania* rules the waves!'

'Exactly, sir.' He glanced down at the notebook. 'Keeping a diary, are we, sir?' He didn't wait for affirmation. 'You'd be surprised how many of our passengers do just that. Especially those who are only making the trip once. Adventure of a lifetime for them. For others it's a way of life. All the luxury of the best hotels and a sea journey thrown in.'

Harry nodded, impatient to be rid of him. Fortunately, at that moment another passenger caught the steward's eye and beckoned him over and Harry found himself alone again. He sighed heavily, annoyed with himself. So Stella thought she was being followed? Very perceptive. He'd underestimated her. Dammit! He thought he had been clever, but obviously not clever enough. His employer, if he got to hear of this, would not be too pleased and with good reason. He stared thoughtfully across at the horizon.

'Dammit!' he repeated. He ought to keep out of her way for the rest of the journey, but that would be rather difficult in the circumstances. Should he talk to her, try to reassure her? Just a lonely bachelor looking at a pretty woman. Play it very innocent; pretend to be attracted by her . . . He shook his head. The idea might flatter her, but suppose it alarmed her. She might suspect his motives and report him again. Worse, she might alert that wretch of a husband. In fact, she might already have done that. He frowned. But if she had, surely Nicolson himself would have come in search of him? Harry slipped the notebook into his pocket. A *diary*! Well, it was in a way.

'Think, Harry!' he told himself.

After a moment the answer came to him. If Stella Nicolson had confided her fears to her husband, he would have put it down to a fevered imagination. Harry would have to think it over carefully. Mustn't make any more mistakes. Perhaps it *would* be best to speak to Stella Nicolson directly. For Harry, honesty was always the best policy. He stood up, stretched and began to walk back along the deck.

Gussie lay on her bed, half-dressed, luxuriously propped against two pillows and a cushion. She was eating chocolates and trying to convince herself and Clara that she didn't give a damn if she got fat.

'They like us plump. Something to get hold of,' she insisted, selecting a pineapple cream and noisily sucking out the centre. 'Mmm! Lovely!' She turned the lid of the box so that she could read the name of the maker. Nestles. Well, she should have guessed; they were one of the best. She had bought this box for herself – an indulgence she now almost regretted since the disaster the previous night had drastically reduced her spending money.

Not that she ever seemed to get any fatter. She glanced down at her blue skirt approvingly. She could still get into it without discomfort, and all her blouses still fitted comfortably at the neck. She thought the amount of 'exercise' she took probably kept her slim.

'All that upping and downing,' she said to herself. 'It's very wearing.'

She glanced at the clock. Nearly lunch-time. Good. She might see the Nicolsons. If she could get the wife on her own, she might find out what had happened. If *she* knew . . . She sometimes wondered what it would be like to have a husband. The same man every time. Did it get boring? A trifle predictable, maybe? You'd have to pretend a lot, presumably. Not that she would object to predictable; it might be rather nice to know what to expect. No unpleasant surprises. No polite lies. And you could say 'No' when you didn't feel in the mood.

Thinking about Abby Nicolson, her face softened. She really wasn't such a monster. Probably just needed a firm hand. A few years in a convent school would work wonders. Or a decent governess. One who said 'No' and meant 'No'. The poor child had probably had a succession of awful nannies who gave in to her – anything for a quiet life. She was a bright child, that was certain.

Gussie closed her eyes, fighting against the sense of loss that would never leave her. Abby reminded her so vividly of her own daughter who had been snatched from her at such a tender age. Only the love and support of her friends had pulled her through that particular fire. When Tess died, Gussie had wanted to die too. Shock and grief had come close to breaking her spirit. Even now, when she pressed the doll to her heart, she yearned anew for her lost child.

'But life goes on!' she whispered. She had made what she could of the lonely years; had fought against bitterness and won. Slowly she had rebuilt her life. Now, only the memories remained. Tess at eleven months, taking her first, tottering steps; Tess aged four, blowing out the candles on her birthday cake; Tess tousled in sleep. Gussie took great comfort from the knowledge that her daughter's short life had been a happy one.

Gussie stared across the room with unfocused eyes as, uninvited, the past crowded in. A man and a child. Each in turn had enriched her life, but she had lost them both. When the man she loved rejected her, she'd known there would never be anyone else. No one to match him. She had decided to stay single rather than marry for security and status.

'He was one in a million,' she said, helping herself to a coconut crisp. It made a satisfying sound as she chewed it. Chocolates were a lot like men, she reflected with a smile. They each had their good points. The hard chocolates lasted longer, but the soft ones were less likely to damage a vulnerable tooth. The crisp chocolates felt better in the mouth than the sticky creams but usually lacked their sweetness.

'Men are just the same,' she told Clara. 'The eager ones are always ready. Crash! Bang!' It was all over before it had begun. She always felt guilty, then. Were they getting value for money? Then there were the slower ones, the *shy* ones like poor Mr Fiske. Always carried an empty briefcase. Trying to look important; to give himself courage. 'Now *they* take for ever to come. Have to be coaxed and babied along. By the time it's all over, bless them, they're so relieved they're willing to pay a bit more!' She sighed.

Her own special man had seemed so keen. So very much in love with her. They had spent a blissful summer, seeing each other once a week. They had reached the stage where she had visited his home and met his widowed mother.

She shook her head. 'And wasn't that a day, to be sure!'

Gussie had been so nervous. Women were so perceptive. Suppose his mother had guessed her secret? She had felt as though the word 'whore' was written large across her forehead! Somehow she got away with it. Oh, the blessed relief! Not that his mother had rolled out a red carpet. She had been quiet to the point of morose, but had treated her son's friend with courtesy.

And all the time Gussie was wondering whether or not it was safe to renounce her profession and settle for matrimony. If only he had asked her – she would have thrown herself into his arms!

'But it wasn't to be.' She picked up Clara and stared fiercely into the faded stitching of the face. 'Somebody told him what I was. One of his colleagues. Recognised me, you see. That was what I most dreaded, and it happened. If only I'd had the sense to get out sooner. He need never have known.'

She had been renting a room at Bette's place along with three others. A neat arrangement in its way, but a far cry from the convent.

When the nuns had been forced to send her out into the world, they had found her a good situation – housemaid to a family of Russians. Respectable people, except for the wayward nephew who visited from time to time. Gussie's face darkened at the thought of him. What a fool she had been!

She glanced at the clock. Ten minutes to one. Lunch-time already. She put the lid on the box of chocolates before she could be tempted further.

Poor Harry. He had found out the truth and had been appalled, which was natural enough. Not many men would want to marry a whore. She had let him down in the eyes of his colleagues; she could imagine the comments: 'Poor old Harry! Guess what! That woman he's been mooning over – she's a whore!' They must have split their sides laughing.

'The trouble was,' she told Clara, 'that Harry was such a *good* man. Integrity was his middle name. So many high ideals.' Discovering the truth about her had almost broken him. No man would forgive a woman for that amount of pain.

She sighed, gently smoothing the doll's woollen hair. Not that she hadn't had her own share of pain one way and another, she thought wearily. It had started badly when the Russian nephew denied all blame and she had been dismissed. No reference. Just a week's wages. She had met Meggie in the station buffet at Kings Cross and, through her, had been introduced to Bette. The idea of selling her body had shocked her but, thanks to the antics of the young Russian nephew, she was not a virgin and understood what it was all about. Nobody forced her against her will. She could never claim that. Meggie seemed happy enough with her lot, as did the other girl, a Londoner who had a baby and no husband. Looking back now, it seemed to Gussie that she had drifted into a way of life which soon felt perfectly natural. Acceptable, even. A waste of her education, maybe, but beggars can't be choosers and the lack of a reference was damning.

Slowly Gussie slid from the bed, carefully smoothing her skirt. She pulled on her ivory silk blouse, cursing silently. She had wasted a whole hour in useless reminiscences and was no nearer knowing what to do about Nicolson. Either she abandoned him – putting it down to an error of judgement – or she should make one last effort. In front of the mirror, she pinched her lips to redden them and added a little false colour just below her cheekbones. A couple of combs dotted with rhinestones were carefully arranged in her upswept hair.

'We'll see what comes up, Clara,' she said when at last her reflection satisfied her. 'It's about time the good Lord offered a helping hand.' At the last moment she brushed away some of the colour she had put on her cheeks. 'Mustn't look like a tart,' she murmured, 'even if I am one!'

Gussie enjoyed her lunch immensely. She had chosen the salmon mousse and had followed that with beef and oyster pie. For dessert she made do with an ice-cream sundae, and washed it all down with two glasses of white wine. In her present uncertain state she felt that she owed it to herself to be generous since nobody else was likely to treat her well. But she had not been idle. A few questions to the stewards had elicited the information that Mr Nicolson was not sharing luncheon with his family. In their cabin recovering from his hangover, she decided. What he needed was a good thick soup to line his stomach, but no doubt he was making do with patent remedies which did little except line the pockets of the makers.

When she had finished her meal she made her way towards the Nicolsons' table. It was obvious that all was not well with them. Abby was silently twisting her napkin into a crumpled mass. The mother looked very tense and woefully pale, with dark circles under her eyes. As she sipped from her cup, she held it with two hands as though afraid the weight might be too much for one hand. The nanny sat with her eyes downcast so that her expression was unreadable. The slump of her shoulders, however, indicated a certain amount of unhappiness. Gussie slowed her steps slightly and waited for Mrs Nicolson to recognise her.

'Mrs Malone!'

It hadn't taken her long, thank goodness. 'Mrs Nicolson!' cried Gussie. She assumed an expression of pleased surprise. 'How are you this morning? And you, Abby? And you, Miss—' The nanny glanced up and Gussie read the expression as sullen. A fruit salad languished untouched in the dish in front of her. 'I'm sorry. I forget your name.'

The wife said, 'It's Mary Crisford.'

She made the name sound like the anti-Christ, thought Gussie, intrigued.

'She's feeling a little . . . unwell.'

Gussie felt a rush of dismay. There was clearly something seriously wrong here. Had Nicolson been found *in flagrante* with the nanny? If that was so, then her own chances were ruined. She might as well give up now.

Abby said eagerly, 'Nanny and John Stamford were kissing and—'

To Gussie's surprise, the mother leaned across the table and slapped her daughter sharply on her bare arm. Abby began to cry.

'What did I tell you earlier?' her mother demanded. 'You know very well—' With an effort she bit back the rest of the sentence. 'Go to your cabin at once!' She picked up the room key from the table and thrust it into her daughter's unwilling hand.

Abby's sobs grew louder. 'Oh, Mama! I'm sorry. I forgot.'

'Do as you're told!' With a hand that trembled, the mother pointed to the door.

Spluttering noisily, Abby made her way slowly out of the dining room, watched by many of the other diners. Some of these murmured sympathetically and Gussie smiled faintly, aware that Abby was making as much of her small drama as possible. So like her own dear Tess. When Bette's cat had died, Tess had worked hard at her tears, revelling in the grief, reluctant to relinquish the emotions. Bette, amused, had christened her 'dramatic Anna'.

'Children!' said Gussie. 'They're all the same.'

She looked at the nanny who, red-faced, had fixed her gaze upon the dish of fruit salad. Gussie offered up a prayer of thanks. So it was John Stamford and not Nicolson with whom the nanny had erred. She said, 'Oh dear, Mrs Nicolson. I hope I haven't caused any trouble.'

'Please call me Stella. And no, it's nothing to do with you.' She looked at the nanny with exasperation. 'Aren't you going to eat *anything*?'

'I'm not hungry.'

Behind the sullen words Gussie heard resentment and something close to despair. So what had happened exactly, she wondered.

Stella's eyes flashed. 'Then you will please leave the table. Go to the Reading Room. Stay there for twenty minutes and then join Abby. I have had as much as I can bear from the pair of you.'

The nanny rose silently and walked towards the door. Gussie hesitated. She was sure that the mother – that *Stella* – was going to ask her to join her. No doubt she would offer confidences and Gussie, intensely curious about other people's lives, would enjoy them. Unfortunately, at this moment Gussie had other priorities. If she could talk to Nicolson, she would know where she stood. She needed an excuse to go to the Nicolsons' cabin while Stella was still drinking her coffee.

'Children can be so exhausting,' she said. 'If you don't mind me saying so, you look very tired.'

'Tired? You have no idea!' Stella put a hand to her forehead. 'I've had the most appalling time. I simply must—' She drew a sharp breath. 'Mrs Malone, I know this is a great presumption on my part, but could I talk to you? I'm badly in need of advice and don't know where to turn. My husband . . .' She swallowed hard. 'It's all so – so *impossible*. Mrs Malone—'

'Call me Gussie.'

'Gussie, then. Thank you. I'm wondering if you can spare a few minutes? We could take coffee together in the lounge.'

'Coffee in the lounge?' Gussie was playing for time. 'Why, that sounds delightful. I was feeling a little bored with my own company.' She leaned forward and lowered her voice. 'But first I must pay a little visit . . . the ladies' room.'

'Of course. Yes.'

She looked so grateful that Gussie felt a twinge of guilt. 'And then I must go back to my room for my tablets.' She tapped her chest. 'A small problem. Nothing serious. I could join you in, say, fifteen minutes.'

Stella smiled with relief. 'I'll find a table and order the coffee. It gets so crowded in there after lunch. Everyone has the same idea.'

As long as she didn't go back to *her* cabin. That would be very awkward. Gussie crossed her fingers and hurried away. At the reception desk she said that she had to take a message to Mr Nicolson but had forgotten their room number. Armed with this information she found the right one and, outside, paused briefly. Presumably Abby was in the adjoining room. Little pitchers have big ears, so she must remember to keep her voice down.

She tapped on the door. There was no response so she tapped a little louder.

'It's not locked, for God's sake!'

Charming man! Gussie opened the door and peeped in, a smile on her face. Nicolson was lying on the bed, fully dressed except for his shoes. He glanced up, expecting to see his wife. Abruptly he sat up, one hand clutching his stomach. 'What on earth—?'

She closed the door behind her, one finger to her lips.

'What the hell are you doing here?' he asked.

Ignoring his question, Gussie crossed the room towards him. 'Oh, you poor man!' she breathed. 'Are you in pain? What's been happening to you?'

'You may well ask!' His tone was non committal, but she saw that his interest had been aroused by her sudden appearance.

She said, 'I waited for you last night with my hopes high. A real man, I told myself. Oh, I can tell!' She laughed. 'But when I saw you with the steward . . .' She shrugged. 'Well, I couldn't be saying "Come on in now", could I? Tongues wag! It would have been all round the ship. But you looked so poorly.'

He had struggled into a sitting position and now patted the bed beside him. Obediently she sat down, examining him with a solicitous expression on her face. 'Are you ill?' she asked.

'You could say I'm under par!' he admitted. 'Some bully boy took a pot-shot at me yesterday.'

'Took a – you mean he *hit* you?' Her eyes widened. Did Stella know about this, she wondered. She asked, 'Now who'd hit a lovely man like yourself? Tell me that.' She put up a hand and smoothed his jaw where the stubble grew. He smelled unwashed, but she resisted the urge to wrinkle her nose.

He said, 'Bloody little blighter robbed me, too. Left me short, damn him.'

Aha! Don't fall for this! Gussie told herself. Never lend a man money. They're supposed to pay *you*! 'Robbed you? Well, that's disgusting. Did you report the theft? We have a detective on board. Oh, to be sure. A doctor, too. The *Mauretania's* prepared for every kind of emergency.' She recalled suddenly that time was short and that she had no right to be here. If the wife came back . . . She stood up abruptly but he pulled her back.

He said, 'Come here!' and gave her a firm kiss on the lips. 'You waited for me, did you? Disappointed, were you. Missed me, eh?'

She returned his kiss. He had pulled her half across the bed and seemed to be making a remarkable recovery. Wonderful what a good woman could do for a man! The doctors should prescribe them.

His hands slid down over her neck and shoulders. 'Damn blouse!' he muttered. 'Can't get a feel of you!'

'Last night you'd have had more than a feel,' she whispered. 'So what about tonight? Unless you're planning to be punched again?' She laughed.

One hand slid over her stomach and down to the tops of her legs.

'Mr Nicolson!' she murmured. 'You've got the strongest hands!' But there was no time for this nonsense. She wriggled free and stood up.

'Hands?' He laughed. 'If you think my hands are strong, you're in for a big surprise!'

'You mean you want to come tonight?'

He threw back his head and laughed. 'In more ways than one!'

Gussie thought she'd like a fiver for all the times she'd heard that particular joke. She feigned shock, however, and said, '*Mr Nicolson*! You're a very naughty man!'

'So I'm told.' He grabbed her again, holding her close with one arm while feeling her breasts with the other. 'What time tonight?' he demanded. 'And don't you dare deny me. I can't stand a tease.'

She said indignantly, 'I've never teased a man in my life! 'Tis the cruellest thing!'

Remembering that his wife was waiting for her in the lounge she drew back, smoothed down her dress and tidied her hair.

'My God, you're a lovely woman!' he told her. 'I'll give you something tonight that you'll never forget!'

His eyes were bright, his lips moist. She tried not to think about the rest of him. 'Is that a threat or a promise?' she asked wickedly.

'It's both!' This also struck him as a wonderful witticism.

She laughed with him, rolling her eyes. 'Mr *Nicolson*!' she gasped. 'You're a bit of a terror!'

As she moved towards the door she took a deep breath. This was the moment of truth, the moment she always dreaded. She said, 'I don't come cheap, Mr Nicolson, but you'll consider the money well spent.'

Fortunately he didn't flinch. Once or twice she'd had a man misunderstand her, and that had been awkward. A few cheapskates argued the toss, trying to persuade her to do it for less. 'If that's the sort of woman you want,' she told them, 'you'd do very well outside Kings Cross Station!' She knew she was class: experience mixed with sympathy, mixed with a certain tolerance for the funny ways some of them had.

One had wanted a good spanking before he could get started. Another demanded that she always wore a black veil. Some liked the light on, others liked it off. A few liked her to speak with a French accent. She did her best to oblige, making allowances, pitying them for their weaknesses and their need of her. Yes, she was good at what she did, but there was a price. You got what you paid for. She had always believed in clear speaking, especially where payment was concerned. A settled price and money upfront. It was business. There was no room for vague promises and broad hints.

He said, 'What do you charge? Twenty guineas? Fifty?'

'Mr *Nicolson*!' She looked affronted.

'What, then?' Before she could answer he said, 'A hundred?'

There was not a moment's hesitation and she liked that in a man. Especially in *this* man. Hiding her delight, she said quickly, 'It's agreed. What time?'

'A soon as possible after midnight.'

'So late?'

'I've got important things to settle first.'

She couldn't afford to argue. 'Midnight,' she repeated. 'The witching hour. After that I might turn into a pumpkin!'

'I'll risk it! Now you'd better go.'

Thank the Lord, she thought breathlessly, fixing him with a broad smile as she opened the door.

'You won't regret it,' she said and slipped out, closing the door behind her.

* * *

Harry found Stella Nicolson alone in the lounge with a tray of coffee for two.

'Mrs Nicolson?' He smiled, raising his hat briefly. 'Some time I would like to talk to you, but I see you are expecting company.'

She looked dismayed. 'You!' she whispered. She glanced around as though to reassure herself that other people were within hearing should she need to call for help.

'My name is Parr,' he said. 'Harry Parr. I wonder if I might . . .'

Stella swallowed hard. 'You've been following us. Spying on us. I simply asked the steward who you were. I don't want any trouble, Mr Parr.'

'The steward has spoken to me about your worries.' He gave her what he hoped was a reassuring smile. 'I wonder if we might go somewhere a little more private? I could explain.' He realised immediately by her expression that he had said the wrong thing.

'I don't want to go anywhere with you, Mr Parr. Certainly not anywhere "private".' Her small hands were tightly clenched. 'Please go away. I – I have a lot on my mind at the moment.'

'It would only take a few moments,' he said gently. 'I would feel much happier if I could set your mind at ease. If I could tell you exactly who I am . . '

'I know who you are. You're Mr Parr.' She picked up the coffee pot, hesitated, then replaced it on the tray. 'I have a friend coming. This really is most inconvenient. All I wish is for you to focus your attention on someone else.'

Harry sympathised with her predicament. In her shoes he would probably feel the same, but he had to put her mind at ease. 'Perhaps later we could talk privately—' he suggested. Five minutes was all he needed.

Her eyes flashed, suddenly cold. 'Talk *privately*? Certainly not. Now, if you don't leave me alone I'll call for the steward.'

This is becoming ridiculous, thought Harry, and he came to an abrupt decision. He would tell her. 'I'm here at the request of your father, Mrs Nicolson.'

Suddenly he had her full attention 'My father?' She stared at him. 'You know my father?' Her eyes widened. 'Oh, no! Something has happened to him!'

'Not at all. It's nothing like that. May I sit down just for a moment? I'll leave as soon as your friend comes.'

Stella nodded and he sat down, searching for the kindest way to explain the situation. She was still wary, he could see that, perched on the edge of the chair as though poised for instant flight if the need arose. Poor woman.

'Mrs Nicolson, your father has been very disturbed over the past six months by certain discrepancies in the firm's finances.' Deliberately, he kept his tone noncommittal, his expression neutral, in an effort to minimise the shock. 'Your father has reluctantly come to the conclusion that someone has been tampering with the accounts.' He saw her eyes narrow and the colour bleached from her face. Better to get it over with, he thought. 'I'm afraid it looks as though your husband may be responsible. Your father hired me seven weeks ago to watch him.'

She said faintly, 'You're a policeman! Dear God!' Her face was parchment white and her voice shook slightly.

'No, ma'am. I was in the force at one time, but for several years now I've been running my own private detective agency in London.' He took his authorisation from the pocket of his jacket and passed it to her.

She stared at it as though mesmerised. 'My father *hired* you?' She read it aloud: 'Authorisation . . . City of London . . . Third of August, 1906 . . . Harry James Parr . . .' She handed it back suddenly as though it were tainted. 'This is – it's *crazy*! Impossible!'

'I understand how you feel, Mrs Nicolson.' Harry waited, allowing her the time to recover. He knew from experience that, faced with unpleasant facts, no one wanted to be hurried on to something worse.

After a moment she said, 'My father would never do such a thing. A private detective? Never!'

Interesting. She had made no effort to support her husband. Harry met her flustered gaze with compassion. Now a faint colour was returning to her face.

'Your father didn't want to involve the police at this stage. He thought it best to be discreet. Naturally he doesn't—'

'My husband tampering with the accounts? That's impossible. No, *no*! He wouldn't . . . Not Clive!' The grey eyes were wide with shock. 'That's a terrible thing to suggest. I'm sure my father has misled you . . .' She stopped. 'I mean – I think my father has himself been misled.'

He could almost see her thoughts whirling from rejection of the idea to a possible, unwilling acceptance. She picked up a cup and saucer. Seeing that it was still empty, she bit her lip in confusion as her hand began to shake. With great gentleness Harry took the cup and saucer from her and set it back on the tray.

He said, 'I'm sorry that I frightened you. I was actually following your husband but frequently, of course, you were together. I thought I was being inconspicuous. Obviously I was not as subtle as I imagined, although your father also asked me to keep an eye on you and your daughter. He is a little concerned for your safety.'

'Our *safety*!' Her mouth tightened. 'My husband may be – well, he may be irresponsible but he is not *dangerous*. I'm afraid my father has allowed his dislike of Clive to colour his judgement.' She glanced towards the stairs. No doubt hoping that her friend would delay a little longer, Harry thought.

Stella gave him a challenging look. 'And what have you discovered, Mr Parr – if anything? Am I allowed to ask you that?'

He hesitated, unwilling to cause her further distress. 'It's rather inconclusive at the moment,' he told her. 'I shall be sending your father a written report, but not just yet. I think it is too early . . .'

Her eyes narrowed and she leaned forward impetuously. 'Do you know anything about a Mr Hemmings? Now he *is* dangerous. He attacked my husband last night and has caused him a lot of pain. Clive was on the way back from a private poker game – but you must know all this. If you've been following him, I mean.'

'I did know he was gambling. I didn't know he'd been attacked.' Black mark, Parr, he told himself. Slipped up there. He *had* seen Nicolson staggering along the corridor, clutching his stomach, but hadn't witnessed any violence.

Stella Nicolson rushed on as though glad to have changed the subject. 'This Hemmings person punched Clive in the stomach and stole all his winnings. He's in agony but refuses to let me call the doctor.' She put a hand to her head and sighed heavily. 'Disasters seem to be crowding thick and fast at the moment, Mr Parr. I'm rather at my wits' end this morning, to be truthful.'

'Isn't there anyone to whom you can turn?'

'There is, actually. I'm expecting her now.' She rubbed her eyes tiredly. 'Not that I shall tell her anything about this – this business about the accounts. I'm sure there is no truth in what you seem to suspect. Father meant well, I know. He would always have my best interests at heart.' She frowned. 'Seven weeks ago? Then – were you on the ship when we made the outward trip?'

'I was.'

'I saw you then!' Her eyes lit up briefly. 'So I was right all along and I'm not —' She bit off the word.

He smiled. 'No, Mrs Nicolson. You didn't imagine me. You are *not* taking after your aunt.'

His comment, intended to reassure her, had the opposite effect.

She said, 'You know about all that? From my father?' Her embarrassment was obvious.

'Your mother, actually,' Harry told her. 'You must understand, Mrs Nicolson, how worried they are about you. Your mother feels that you are under a great strain but won't confide in anyone.'

She repeated his words slowly 'Under a great strain? I would say that's an understatement, Mr Parr, but speaking with you has cleared up one of the mysteries.'

He shrugged. 'Now I've given you even more to worry about. I'm so sorry. But since I've had to inform you about my activities, I'd like you to look upon me as a friend. An ally, shall we say? Or just a broad shoulder to cry on if necessary.'

She stood, with an attempt at a smile which went straight to his heart. 'I dare not allow myself the luxury of tears, Mr Parr. If I did, I doubt I would ever stop.'

Stella held out her hand and he stood up to hold it briefly in his own.

'I'll say nothing to my husband about our meeting,' she said. 'If we pass and I ignore you, you'll understand why. But I will remember your kind offer and I'll call on you for help if I have to.'

He thought he should let it rest there; better leave before the ladyfriend arrived. With an encouraging nod he walked briskly away. So Hemmings had punched Nicolson in the stomach? His mouth turned up slightly in a half-smile. There must be some good in Hemmings after all!

Chapter Five

Harry, alone in his cabin, dipped his pen into the ink and wrote: *May 10th 1910*. He underlined the date and frowned. Then he flicked back through his notebook, found the appropriate entry and read it through. The facts were damning and would no doubt cause Stella Nicolson great dismay, if her father confided the results of his investigations to her. He had told her as little as possible, but there was much more. Intuitively Harry suspected that she would insist on knowing the truth. A pity, he thought. Stella Nicolson seemed a genuine person and her life would be totally changed by the investigative work he had been asked to undertake. No matter how much the changes hurt her, she would be forced to face up to them. Presumably her relationship with her husband would end. She could hardly continue living the lie that Nicolson had created for them.

He rapped his fingers on the table-top – an unconscious habit – then, with a shrug, he reminded himself that it was not his problem. His task was to search out the truth. His clients were the people who must live with his findings.

He said, 'So be it!' and began to convert the scribbled notes into a final report.

Inquiries at the Devizes Branch of the National Bank revealed an account in the name of Clive Albert Nicolson. This was overdrawn but the actual amount was not revealed. The manager said that no money had been paid in for seventeen months and that N. had not been seen in the bank since February 1903. Efforts to discover his whereabouts had been unsuccessful. They had also returned various cheques over the past year.

I assume that these recent cheques may be connected with gambling debts but cannot verify this. The manager was reluctant to reveal the above and flatly refuses to disclose any names. If this matter leads to criminal proceedings, the police may have more success in this last respect.

(Informant was Henry Wolfe, bank manager.)

He sighed. How had Stella come to marry this unscrupulous wretch? Her father, in a confiding mood, had explained that their daughter had married after a whirlwind romance and against their wishes. At the time her parents had been deeply upset but, for their daughter's sake, they had set aside their doubts. They had offered Nicolson a junior partnership in the firm, expecting him to stay in New York; in that way they hoped to remain in close touch with their daughter. Nicolson had accepted, but had then insisted that they return to England. The two branches they had opened in London had been a problem from the start because Nicolson had no experience. Money from the American stores had been needed to bolster those in London.

How much of this had Stella Nicolson understood, Harry wondered, and how long had the so-called love match lasted? He knew from bitter experience how easy it was to make a mistake in matters of the heart. In his youth he had turned away from the woman he really loved and later had married a woman who meant little to him. Two serious errors of judgement which had dictated the pattern of his present life in which work was the sole reason for being. There was no time for a private life. Catching himself in an uncharacteristic moment of self-pity, he shook his head with annoyance and returned to his report.

May 14th 1910. Stayed at the White Lion for two nights (receipts enclosed). An entry in the church register shows that N. was christened here. His parents are listed as Madelaine and John Nicolson.

Further inquiries elicited the information (from various people who knew the family) that they were impoverished landowners who had come down in the world. It was widely agreed that John Nicolson drank heavily and gambled away much of the family money.

(Informants were Joseph Pratten, Hilda and Edgar Townsend, a Miss Ellen Bradley and Steven Godwin, postmaster.)

Harry was aware of a vague sense of betrayal as he wrote and wished that it had not been necessary to alert Stella Nicolson to the approaching trouble. For her sake he would have preferred to speak more positively about her husband, but it was impossible. Nicolson was an imposter – a liar and a crook. Harry would not mince his words. He was being paid to do a job and he would do it as honestly as he could. His whole life was based on a concept of decency and a dread of deceit: he had made a vow all those years ago that never – that nothing . . .

Feeling the familiar sweat break out on his forehead, he took a deep breath.

'Calm down, you fool!' he muttered, struggling to repress the unwelcome memories, but they came anyway. As clearly as the day it had happened, Harry saw his father with half his head shot away, blood and brains spattered across the wall behind his chair. His mother's horrified screams rang again in his ears. He had been ten when his father killed himself. Harry recalled the shameful, hurried funeral; the headlines in the newspapers. 'Senior policeman takes own life.' Worst of all, he remembered the sad little grave in a deserted corner of the graveyard.

After all these years Harry still failed to understand why his father had done what he did. The family had certainly not been wealthy but were comfortably off. Harry, their only child, was bright and doing well at school. The Parrs paid their bills and put good food on the table. *They hadn't needed the money!* That was the stumbling block as far as Harry was concerned. He might have forgiven his father – he *wanted* to forgive him – if the crime had been perpetrated from dire need. A man hanged for stealing to feed his family was not a criminal in Harry's view. But in the note his father left, he said he did it *because it was so easy!* Shameful. Unforgivable. His mother had never recovered from the shock.

'Unconsecrated ground!' whispered Harry.

For years he had refused to visit the grave, and probably he never would. He had loved and admired his father so much. The betrayal of trust had been total.

* * *

87

May 20th 1910. Winchester. Staying at the Dog and Whistle four nights (receipts enclosed). Town Hall records show that one May Rose Tompkins married Clive Albert Nicolson on August 10th 1898. Witnesses were a husband and wife by the name of Catt. According to the information you gave me when you hired me for the case, you were unaware of this much earlier liaison. I will try to trace them further. Unless the marriage was annulled or there was a divorce (which is most unlikely), the marriage between your daughter and Nicolson may not be legal. (Informants were Derek T. Holden, town clerk at Winchester and Miss Iris Catt, sister of the female witness at the register office ceremony.)

Harry drew a long breath. The bald facts were totally unpalatable, but it was not his job to soften the blow. Not that he could if he wanted to, because 'the law is the law full stop'. No getting away from that. It was often the case that his clients regretted hiring him when it was too late. Digging around in the past frequently turned up unsavoury information which might have been best left buried.

'I just do my job,' he assured himself, knowing that he did it well and without cheating the clients. He was scrupulous about expenses, remembering to deduct the cost of a glass of beer or the occasional tot of whisky. He didn't expect the clients to pay for what he chose to drink; a meal was fair enough – he had to eat – but the extras were so carefully considered that he sometimes erred on the wrong side.

Frowning slightly, he reread his report. Not a pretty tale. It looked as though Stella Nicolson had married a bigamist. Later inquiries had established that the first wife had lost a child, a boy, when a baby, but that the wife was probably still alive. More heartache, he reflected grimly.

He took out the half-hunter watch that his grandfather had left him and saw that it was nearly time for dinner. Good. He had had enough. He would carry on after a meal and a stroll on the deck. *If* Nicolson was still confined to his cabin. If not, it would be another busy evening. He wiped the nib and replaced the pen on the inkstand, then stretched his arms and eased his back. The paperwork was the worst part of the job.

* * *

When Gussie finally joined Stella in the lounge, she sipped her coffee and listened intently and sympathetically to her new friend's troubles. After a few moments' consideration she thought she could see a way to deal with the problem.

'Firstly,' she said, 'you must see to your husband. If I were you, I'd pop along to the doctor and ask for some strong painkillers. He's probably bad-tempered because he's in pain. Men are such terrible patients.' Seeing that Stella looked dubious she hurried on. 'Now the nanny . . . Better to keep her away from Abby for a while. Send her to the Reading Room to improve her mind. Tell her to come back in time to change for dinner – if you intend to allow her dinner, that is.'

'Oh, but of course I do!' Stella looked shocked. 'We can't starve the wretched girl, however badly she has behaved.'

'You *could*,' said Gussie. 'Teach her a lesson. Still, it's your decision . . . You, I think, should go and lie down. Take a little nap. You look as weak as water, if you don't mind me saying so.'

Stella hesitated. 'I can't,' she said. 'My husband is on the bed. If I try to sleep beside him he'll – well –' She gave an embarrassed laugh. 'Doubtless you can imagine . . .'

'But he's in pain!'

'He'll do his best.' She flushed.

'Hmm! I have it! Sleep in my cabin. I'll wake you in plenty of time for dinner.' She thought rapidly. Had she left anything incriminating in her room that Stella might see? No. She felt fairly safe on that score.

'Oh no! I couldn't!' Stella was protesting. 'It's most dreadfully kind of you but – sleep in your cabin? Oh, no! That wouldn't be right at all – and anyway . . .' She looked relieved. 'There's Abby. I can't—'

'I'll look after Abby,' Gussie told her. She wondered immediately if she had made a mistake, but the words were out and Stella was looking thoughtful.

'Oh dear!' she said. 'I'm actually rather tempted. But—' Her face clouded over. 'Suppose Clive finds out? That I'm sleeping in your cabin? He'd be furious.'

Gussie said, 'I'm not going to tell him. Are you? Abby needn't know either. Then it's all settled. I'll deliver Abby to her own cabin about . . . six-thirty? By that time the nanny can take over her duties – it's what she's paid for, after all. If I see your husband about – *if* – I'll say I passed you taking a stroll around the deck.' She took a deep breath. 'How's that?' she asked with a smile. 'Oh, here's my key. Make yourself comfortable.'

'I don't know what I'd do without you,' Stella told her. 'It's so terribly kind of you to take all this trouble.'

'Think nothing of it. You'll find Clara on my pillow. She's a good listener!' She laughed. 'Give her a cuddle and get yourself a good rest. Sleep is nature's best healer, you know.'

Stella, giving in graciously, took the key and set off towards the medical room in search of the doctor. Gussie, watching her go, prepared to do battle with Abby.

Ten minutes later she and the child were hurrying towards the main area where the concerts were held.

'But *where* are we going?' Abby asked for the second time. 'I *want* to know!'

'All will be revealed!' Gussie told her, striding purposefully along. 'Now let me see . . . Blue perhaps—' She stopped abruptly to stare at Abby, then shook her head.

Abby asked 'Blue what?'

'Not blue. Green, maybe . . .' She stopped again and leaned down, staring into Abby's face.

'Green *what*?' cried Abby. 'What are you talking about? *What*?'

'Didn't your nanny tell you it's rude to keep saying "what"? You should say, "I beg your pardon".'

'Nanny says that's what you say when you make a rude noise.'

'Does she? Oh well, just "pardon" will do.'

Abby's mouth tightened. 'Anyway, I hate Nanny,' she said firmly.

'I expect she hates you. So that's "Snap!" Ah! Here we are.'

She led the way into a large room at the rear of the stage which was actually one of the dressing rooms. Abby's eyes widened. Various large boxes and trunks stood around and garments and lengths of fabric spilled from several trestle tables. There were two other children in the room in various stages of fancy dress. One, a girl in a yellow blouse, was being helped by her mother who was winding broad strips of brown velvet round the lower part of her body. The other, an older boy, was making a few tentative slashes with a cardboard sword covered in silver paper.

Gussie said, 'I'll wager my best hat that the girl's going as a bumble-bee.' She proceeded to rummage through the clothes on the nearest table.

Abby said, 'Oh, fancy dress! You needn't bother. I have my costume already. Mama bought it for me. It's a—'

Gussie swung round. '*Bought it* for you? Well now, there's a thing. That's not the idea at all. How can you win a prize with a costume that your mother *bought*? Where's the fun in that, child?'

Abby looked baffled. 'But we always do. I'm always Cleo Patcher and I—'

'Cleo Patcher? And who's she when she's at home?' Gussie held up a roll of grey velvet and said, straightfaced, 'How about going as a slug?'

Abby looked stricken. 'A *slug*? No, *please*, Mrs Malone. I hate slugs. Horrid slimy things. Grandpapa says they eat the tomato plants. He calls them little varmints. What are varmints?'

'You should ask your grandfather. Little nuisances, I should think.' She dived into one of the large trunks and pulled out a pair of cardboard wings. 'What about a fairy? We could make a wand with a star on the end of it so that you could do your magic.'

'I've told you, I go as Cleo Patcher. I have a black wig and a long dress with a gold belt. Well, it's not *real* gold. It's gold paint. And little gold sandals.'

'Have you won?'

'No.'

'There you are, then.'

Stubbornly, Abby persevered in the face of Gussie's discouraging comments. 'Mama says I can't always be the winner because other children want to win as well. She puts some black stuff around my eyes because she always wears black stuff and—'

'I've never seen your mama with black round her eyes.'

Abby squealed with laughter. 'Not Mama. Cleo Patcher. She was Egyptian and they always—'

Gussie had tossed the wings back into the box and now examined a wire crown. 'You mean Cleopatra. C-l-e-o-p-a-t-r-a.'

'What? I mean, pardon?'

'That's how you spell Cleopatra. C-l-e-o-p-a-t-r-a. You can spell, I suppose?'

'I don't know.'

'Spell cat.'

'I don't want to.'

Gussie frowned. 'Don't you go to school?'

'Not yet. I'm only seven and Mama thinks I should wait a while. She's going to teach me to read as soon as she feels up to it. I don't want to go to school. They're rough at school.'

'You're not exactly a shrinking violet yourself now, are you?'

'What is a shrinking violet?'

'It's someone who's very timid. Afraid to say boo to a goose. Take my word for it, Abby Nicolson, you're not one of them.' Gussie glanced across at the other girl who was now looking distinctly bee-like. Her mother was creating a pair of feelers from a small coil of thin copper wire. 'Would you look at that now!' she told Abby. To the mother she said, 'That's what I call creative.'

'Oh, thank you!'

The girl smiled shyly and said, 'Bzzz!' and flapped her arms about, watching for Gussie's approval.

Gussie said, 'Why, that's just amazing! If I didn't know better I'd think you were the real thing!'

Blushing with pleasure, the girl turned back to her mother.

Abby, jealous, muttered, 'A bee's silly!' She looked into the trunk and picked out a long black garment covered with silver stars. 'I could go as the sky.'

'That's a wizard's cloak,' said Gussie. She draped a feather boa round Abby's neck and laughed. 'Hardly!' Removing it, she wound it round her own neck and winked at Abby.

'Are *you* going in for the fancy dress?'

'Certainly not. I'm just having a bit of fun. Grown-ups are allowed to have fun, you know.' Seeing that the bee's mother was regarding her with amusement, Gussie reluctantly returned the feather boa to the box. 'So how did you like being in America?'

Abby draped herself in the wizard's cloak. 'America's lovely. I like it. And I like Uncle Jerry, because he's my mama's dearest friend in the whole darned world. He told me so and that means I am, too, and he calls me honey and he likes being an American. When Mama walked into a door and made her eye all blue, Uncle Jerry was very cross.'

Gussie stared at her small companion. 'She walked into a

door?' Was this what she thought it was? Sometimes people *did* walk into doors.

'Yes. She and Papa were having a bit of an argument and Mama wanted to stay another week, but Papa said he was sick to death of New York and everyone in it and he wanted to go back to London and civilisation, and Mama started to cry and Papa said it's that bloody Gerald isn't it and Mama said no and Papa said—'

Gussie sensed, rather than saw, that the bee's mother was listening. Putting a finger to her lips, she lowered her voice and asked, 'And where were you, Abby, while this argument was going on?'

'At the top of the stairs.'

If this was marriage, thought Gussie, then maybe she'd got the better bargain after all. Feeling only slightly guilty, she prompted Abby. 'And then your poor Mama walked into a door?'

Abby sighed. 'Grandpapa said tell the truth for crying out loud, the louse hit you. But Mama said no he didn't, at least he didn't mean it, it was an accident – and Grandmama said you can tell us the truth honey and Mama said I *am*, and Grandpapa said bullshit he hit you I'll kill the bastard and—'

Gussie coughed loudly. 'Perhaps that's enough about that, Abby.' She stared down at the child and began to revise her opinion. Perhaps she'd been too hasty in her judgement. Abby was seven years old and bright with it. She was largely untutored. She'd probably had a succession of unsuitable nannies, and her parents' relationship was unstable. The poor child was lonely and bored. Gussie drew a long breath. Even her own Tess had a happier childhood. Impulsively she tossed a tangle of ribbons back into the trunk.

'I'm beginning to think you were right all along,' she informed a startled Abby. 'Cleopatra *is* the best idea. So we needn't waste any more time here.' Taking Abby by the hand she hustled her out of the room, across the stage and through the auditorium.

'Where are we going now?' Abby ran to keep up with her.

'To Reception,' Gussie told her. 'Do you know any tables? Two times? Three times? Do you have the foggiest idea what I'm talking about?'

Abby shook her head.

'It's called schooling,' said Gussie, 'and it's the most wonderful fun! Would I lie to you now? I shall ask for some paper and a couple of pencils. Then you and I are going to have ourselves a good time. Think about this now. There's you and me. That's two people. There's your mama and your papa. That's two people.'

She suddenly saw Tess, her plump little fingers clutching a pencil. She was seated at the table in Bette's parlour, writing with great concentration on the back of an empty sugar bag. Gussie's eyes closed briefly. Oh, *Tess*!

She went on hurriedly while she still could. 'If we all sit together at a table, that's *four* people. One two is two, two two's are four. Now that's called arithmetic. You'll soon get the hang of it. And we'll talk about cat and dog and mat and bog.' She smiled down at Abby, who was looking intrigued. 'Just you and me,' she told her. 'Our secret, remember. It's going to be fun!'

Stella found the medical room without much difficulty and was relieved to find a doctor on duty. He welcomed her into his tiny surgery and indicated a chair. When they were both seated he smiled. He was short, with a nose like a small beak and small, pale blue eyes. His name was Rowse.

'My husband is such a difficult patient,' Stella explained nervously. 'He is in considerable pain, but he won't do anything about it except complain. He won't take anything – except alcohol which he insists dulls the pain.'

'It dulls the perception of pain,' he amended. 'What exactly is causing the pain? Do we know that? Is it indigestion, perhaps? Many of our passengers eat too well and then suffer for it.'

'No, no, doctor. It's not over-eating. My husband has a digestion like a . . . a horse! Or is that a constitution?'

He smiled patiently. 'Has he ever had his appendix out, or could it be a grumbling appendix? That would be a little more worrying. The ship is not equipped to perform major surgery – except in dire emergency. If it was a matter of life and death . . .'

'I'm sure it's not that bad.'

'We usually aim to help our patients survive until they can be attended to on shore.'

'No-o.' She hesitated, wondering about the Hippocratic oath.

'He hasn't but . . . to tell you the truth, doctor – I do know what's wrong with him, but he wouldn't like me to tell you. I could if he were never to know I'd told you.'

The doctor looked at her thoughtfully. 'Ah! I wonder if I'm jumping to the right conclusion, Mrs Nicolson.' He clasped his hands and peered at her over the top of them. 'Would this possibly have a . . . shall we say *sexual* connotation?'

For a moment Stella had no idea what he meant. Then she felt her face burn. 'Oh *no*, Doctor Rowse! Nothing like that. Oh, good heavens, no!' She felt sullied by the suggestion. 'My husband has never – he would *never* . . .' She drew a deep breath and let it out again.

He said, 'These things happen, Mrs Nicolson, even in the best regulated circles. It's a sign of the times, I fear. I intended no disrespect to Mr Nicolson, you understand.'

Stella gathered her courage. 'Last night my husband had an argument. A quarrel, really. Actually it was more a fight than anything. Somebody punched him. He was awake all night and is still complaining. He refuses to see you himself, so I thought perhaps I would talk to you. He's so bad-tempered and hasn't eaten today. He just lies on the bed . . .'

The doctor pursed his lips. 'He really should see me in person,' he said. 'There might be some internal damage. Some bleeding, maybe. Kidney damage or a ruptured spleen . . .'

Stella felt the first pricking of alarm. 'Do you really think so? Oh dear!'

'I'm not saying this *is* the case, you understand. I'm just trying to discover the exact nature of the problem. Without seeing the patient that's not easy. Was it a rabbit-punch? A blow to the lower back – the kidney region?'

Stella shook her head. 'He definitely said it was his stomach, and he's holding himself at the front – like this.' She demonstrated, clutching her lower abdomen and doubling over, her face screwed up.

He looked dubious. 'I could give you something mild to relieve a little of the discomfort,' he suggested. 'Pills that will make him drowsy and may help him to sleep. I daresay all the tension in his muscles is adding to the problem. Er – what happened to the other man?'

'I don't think he was hurt.' Had Clive said anything about Hemmings being hurt? She couldn't remember. 'I think he'd gone before Clive picked himself up. It was a callous attack.'

The doctor nodded and stood up. He crossed to a small recess which looked like a pharmacy.

Left to her thoughts, Stella finally acknowledged something she would rather have ignored – that secretly she was glad Mr Hemmings had punched her husband. Now he would know how *she* had suffered. Her father had wanted to horsewhip him and she had almost urged him on. The pain and humiliation of that blow to her face had been the final proof, if any were needed, that in choosing Clive she had made a disastrous mistake. He was irresponsible and, occasionally, a bully. The knowledge that even now her parents would be discussing the marriage and wondering what could be done made her cringe. She hadn't told Mrs Malone about *that*. There was also the wretched matter of the business affairs and the hiring of that private detective. That she had also kept to herself.

'Mrs Nicolson?'

She looked up, startled. 'I'm sorry. I was miles away.'

The doctor handed her a small pillbox and a folded paper. 'I said I've given you some pills for him. Fairly strong painkillers. They should do the trick. If not, *do* try to persuade him to come and see me personally. Prescribing for a patient unseen is never very satisfactory.'

She signed for the pills, and he saw her to the door. She said, 'And this is – confidential, isn't it?'

'You have my word on it.' He hesitated. 'There is the little matter of a fee. It's written on the paper; any time will do. The dosage is on the box itself. Two at six-hourly intervals. No more than six in a twenty-four-hour period.'

Stella made her way back to the cabin. She would *make* Clive take one. Anything to stop his grumbling and hopefully sweeten his mood. She found him lying flat on his back, holding a copy of *The Field* above him.

She asked, 'How are you, dear?'

'Bloody awful!' He lowered the magazine and she was suddenly struck by his appearance. His face was an unhealthy grey. His unshaven chin did nothing to help, and his eyes were dull.

She said, 'I do *wish* you'd go to the doctor. He said it's—'

He looked at her sharply. 'You've *seen* him?'

'Yes. Doctor Rowse. I asked his advice. He's given me some pills to take away the pain.' Unwrapping the doctor's bill, she began trying to decipher the writing on the box.

'Doctors have a lot to answer for, Stella. You know my views on the medical profession.'

'Of course I do.' It was one of Clive's pet themes.

'They killed my grandfather.'

'Surely not.' She knew she was asking for trouble, but somehow she couldn't stop herself. It was as though she was testing her new-found resolve; deliberately risking a confrontation. He had claimed, when they first met, to admire her mind. Now, however, he hated it when her own views were not his.

Clive went on and Stella groaned inwardly. She almost knew the story by heart.

'Poor old sod had trouble with pains in his bowels. He'd had it for years, on and off. The so-called consultants, at a considerable fee, diagnosed a probable malignant growth. *Probable*. Recommended an operation, but my father said, "No". Mother, however, talked him into it. Opened him up and found nothing. No growth. Nothing wrong. Fit as a fiddle.'

'Except for the pains in his bowels.'

He ignored her comment. 'Next thing we know we go to fetch him home, he's running a temperature and they won't let him out of hospital. Next morning it's a fever. He's got an infection and he dies. *Dies*, dammit! That's the medical profession for you!' He snorted contemptuously. 'Doctor Rowse! You won't get me in his surgery unless I'm at death's door.'

'Then you won't want one of these to ease the pain.' She looked at him enquiringly, keeping her tone neutral.

For a moment she thought he would refuse on principle, but he said, 'Oh, give them to me now you've got them!' He took the box grudgingly and glared at the label. 'Damned hieroglyphics!'

'Doctors' handwriting is notoriously bad,' she said. 'I'll get you some water. Then I'm going to take a walk around the deck.'

'That's right,' he said. 'Just leave me. Don't bother about me!'

'But, Clive, yesterday you said I should get more exercise. Now you're saying—'

'Yesterday I didn't need you. Now I'm sick –' He broke off. 'Can't read a word of this. It's criminal, the way these doctors get away with it. Didn't they ever go to school? Didn't they ever learn to write legibly?' He glanced at her. 'Where's Abby?'

'She's with Mrs Malone.'

'Mrs Malone?' His face darkened. 'I don't want you getting too thick with that woman. I don't approve of her. You stay away from Mrs Malone.'

'I thought you liked her.'

'Well, I don't. And she's not a fit person for you to know. You'll get yourself talked about if you're not careful.'

Stella said, 'Not a fit person? What on earth do you mean? She's a very kind, very interesting woman and I like her.'

'Interesting?' He gave a short laugh. 'Well, I daresay you could say that.'

Stella looked at him coldly. Here was Clive Nicolson, a thief, a liar and a bully, casting doubts on Mrs Malone. Damn him! She said, 'We shall have to disagree then. I find her quite charming. I don't think it's up to you to tell me who I can or can't take as a friend.' As soon as she said it, she felt sure she had gone too far and braced herself for his wrath. Instead of speaking, however, he shovelled several pills into his mouth and washed them down with a mouthful of water.

'Another one for luck!' he said, fitting action to words.

Stella asked, 'How many have you taken? What does it say on the box?'

He tossed it towards her. 'Can't read it.' He threw the magazine on the floor, turned on to his side and closed his eyes. 'Let's just hope they work!' he said.

When she hesitated, he opened his eyes and asked, 'Still here? Don't let a sick husband keep you from your exercise.'

Stella counted to ten. She looked at his lanky form stretched out on the bed and thought of Gerald and her parents and New York. She had given up her whole life for him and he cared nothing for her. Now it was mutual, she thought angrily. Suddenly it was easier to admit how she felt about him than to try hiding the truth from herself.

He said, 'Go if you're going!'

As the words hung in the air between him, Stella realised how much she loathed him. It wasn't so much falling out of love with someone you know – it was discovering that the man was a complete stranger to her. There was no way she could spend the rest of her life with him. The knowledge was frightening and she felt her stomach knot with apprehension. She waited for a moment's dizziness to pass and then her mind cleared. She would go to Mrs Malone's room and she would take her nap. Later there were things to be done, and she knew exactly where she would start.

The Reading Room was the one place on the ship where talking was discouraged. A notice on the wall appealed to the users of the room to respect other people's need for quiet and privacy. Generally speaking the rule was adhered to, but occasionally the odd whisper caused heads to turn in protest. The readers seemed to be mostly women – possibly mothers escaping for an hour from care of the children. Lonely women found company of a sort; the timid felt safe there. Comfortable chairs and sofas were flanked by walls lined with bookshelves. There were magazines on the tables, their subjects ranging from nature to child care, from home improvement to cycling. The sun brightened the room and the sea outside formed a moving reflection on the ceiling. Later there would be fog, according to the ship's captain who spoke at intervals to his passengers.

Mary Crisford was reading *Oliver Twist*, the first book she had taken from the shelves. She was not enjoying it; it depressed her, but she couldn't summon the energy or enthusiasm to change it for something livelier. To outward appearances she was no different from any of her fellow readers. She sat at one end of a sofa, dutifully ignoring the elderly matron at the other end. A stout man with a luxuriant moustache sat in the next chair, eyeing her surreptitiously from time to time. Her eyes scanned the page, but she had to read each paragraph several times because she couldn't concentrate.

Life was *so* unfair, she reflected bitterly. It was all Abby's fault – nasty, sly little cheat. Mary had taken a shine to John and she was sure he liked her in return. Mrs Nicolson was *so* selfish. All she thought about was her precious child, never a thought for her nanny's future happiness. Surely an employer should feel *some* responsibility for their employee's welfare? Mary thought about John, and in her imagination he was tremendously handsome and infinitely desirable. An eligible bachelor who had chosen her from all the other young women on the ship. That must mean *something*. The more she thought about it, the more likely it seemed to her that John might be the one man in the world who would want to marry her. Her only chance of a life of her own.

She had once had high hopes of a butcher's roundsman. Nathan Webb, his name was. He had visited the house regularly at her previous job with the Atkins family, and had flirted with her quite openly. 'I'm shy, Mary Ellen, I'm shy.' That's what he used to sing. She could never hear that now without thinking of him. Not that he *was* shy. Quite the opposite. He used to lift up the hem of her skirt and whistle at her ankles. Used to say the sight of them made him feel giddy. She smiled faintly. Kept offering to take her to the fair on Hampstead Heath, and she'd been longing for that. The Atkins would never have agreed to go to such a place. Too many 'undesirables'. They were such a nervous couple; they saw 'undesirables' all over the place. Then Mary had discovered that he was married already.

The Reading Room was filling up. A young woman stopped beside the sofa and whispered, 'May I sit here?'

Mary glanced at the space between her and the elderly matron and said, 'Please yourself,' in a discouraging tone of voice.

However, the older woman smiled. 'Of course. Join us. We're none of us very fat!'

Wonderful, thought Mary, shifting reluctantly to make room. Why couldn't it have been a good-looking young man? Didn't *they* read? Squashed on a beastly sofa with a beastly boring book when she could have been strolling on the deck with John. She hadn't had a chance to see him, let alone speak to him, since Mrs Nicolson had caught them. Her face burned at the memory. The most embarrassing moment of her life. And *she* had had to suffer the telling-off. John had waltzed off, scot-free. She sometimes wished she had been a man. Men had all the chances. Nathan Webb had made the most of his, too. She'd been a fool to trust him. Was John another one?

She got up, crossed to the shelves and banged the book back into place with as much noise as she could manage. She looked at the adjacent titles: *Nicholas Nickleby* . . . *Gulliver's Travels* . . . *The Collected Works of Shakespeare* . . . Worse and worse, she thought disparagingly.

'Boring!' she muttered and moved over to the magazines. Seeing that most of them were already in the hands of others, she sighed noisily and snatched down a book on gardening. Returning to her seat she sat down as awkwardly as she could, intent on causing as much irritation as possible. She sighed heavily, frowning. The future was grim. No job and no reference. And no husband.

Thanks for nothing, Mrs Nicolson! She wondered what her employer would say if she knew her precious Clive had been patting the nanny's bottom, stroking her breasts and angling to do a great deal more. There was one rule for the rich and one for the poor. Her stomach rumbled and she put a hand over it. It would be easy to hate men, she reflected bitterly. They'd tormented her all through her life, even at school. Her face darkened and she turned the page slowly: 'How To Get The Best Out Of Your Compost' . . . How fascinating! Was *anybody* interested in such a thing? The next page was not much better: 'How to make pot-pourri' . . . She had been nine years old when Dennis Biggs had pulled off her knickers. He had thrown them over a wall and she had been too ashamed to tell the teacher. She had spent the rest of the afternoon in a haze of misery, listening to the boys whispering and sniggering about her. When she found her knickers, they were all muddy, and when she got home her mother had smacked her. She told her mother what had happened and she had *laughed*. Mary could still remember the shame of it – and nobody had smacked Dennis Biggs . . .

She was staring at a picture of a dahlia when she became aware of someone bending over her.

'Mary, are you all right?'

She turned in astonishment. A smile lit up her face as a flood of relief coursed through her. It was John. He had not deserted her after all. He still cared!

'Not exactly,' she returned in a low voice. 'It was awful. She went absolutely mad!'

He didn't look quite as handsome as she remembered. His eyes were too close together and there was a small pimple on his chin. Still, she was in no mood to be choosy. He was better than nothing.

He whispered, 'I can't stay long. We're supposed to mingle with the passengers and promote the various entertainments. I'm sorry about . . . you know . . . What about tonight? Could we meet somewhere else?'

The stout man sitting opposite said, 'Can't you two read? This is a *quiet* area! If you must talk, please go outside.'

Mary wanted to murder him. Was the whole world conspiring to spoil her fun? She glared at him and said, 'Damn!' loudly and distinctly. She was beginning to feel a little light-headed. What did anything matter any more? She was in so much trouble that he could report her to the Nicolsons for all she cared. The colour rose in his face and she stood up, satisfied. John looked a little surprised, but he led the way to the door.

Outside Mary said, 'You might have stayed last night. Nipping off like that.'

'I didn't know how to get out of it,' he explained. 'We hadn't agreed a story. I thought you'd be better on your own. You know – one story. If we'd both tried we might have tripped each other up.'

'I shall be dismissed. I know I will. The minute we get back.'

'Oh Lord! That's a bit much!'

'They're like that.' She sighed, twisting her mouth at the thought of them. She waited for him to offer help of some kind but he was shaking his head helplessly.

Then he said, 'So there's no hope for tonight, then?'

Mary glared at him in disbelief. Was that all he could think about?

'Don't you *care*?' she demanded. 'Are you *listening*? No work and probably no reference. You were in it as much as I was, but nobody says a word to you.'

'It was your fault. You said the kid would be asleep, and she wasn't. Don't blame me. If Mrs Nicolson had reported me *I'd* have lost my job!'

'So what?'

They glared angrily at each other.

He said, 'So it was all up to you.'

'Thanks very much!' Disappointment was welling up inside her and she felt choked.

'Look,' he said, 'let's not get into an argument. I just wondered – did you tell her my name?'

'I said it was John, but I pretended that was all I knew.' He was *still* worrying about himself, she thought. Utterly selfish. Deciding to rattle him a little, she said, 'So what about when we get ashore? D'you want to meet me again? Finish where we left off?' She forced a smile. 'I think it would have been fun.'

He hesitated. 'Depends where you live. My family's in Southampton so—'

'I don't live anywhere now, do I? I *did* live in Clissold Avenue, London, but thanks to you I doubt I'll live there much longer. I could come to Southampton. Look for work there. Meet you somewhere.' She didn't hold out much hope; she just wanted to worry him. 'Unless you've already got a girl there. A girl in every port?'

He said, 'Course I haven't. Let me think about it. I might come up with something. Now I must dash or they'll have a search party out for me.' He pulled her quickly towards him and gave her a peck on the cheek. 'Be seeing you!' he told her and hurried away.

Mary stared after him, wanting to believe that he was in earnest. After all, he *had* come looking for her and he was right – in a way it *had* been partly her fault. She should have checked on Abby before he arrived. But meet him tonight? How in heaven's name was *that* going to be possible?

Chapter Six

Promptly at six o'clock, ship's time, the lights above the stage were switched on and the children's fancy-dress competition was under way. In twos and threes passengers began to wander in, eager to find the best seats from which to watch the show. By ten past six there were close to two hundred people in the audience. Some were simply passengers with an hour to fill, others were the parents, aunts and uncles, waiting for a glimpse of their children and praying that *this* year the son or daughter, the nephew or niece, would win a prize. All those participating would receive a medal as a souvenir of the occasion, but the winners would be given a small trophy to put on the mantelpiece.

Not only was it a chance for the young people to 'perform' on stage, but winning a prize meant being mentioned in the following day's newsletter and that was certainly something to be valued. It was difficult to know who were most excited – the relatives out front or the children back-stage.

Clive had insisted that he was well enough to attend his daughter's big moment as Cleopatra. He now sat next to his wife who had Mary Crisford on the other side of her, separated by an empty seat which he presumed was for Abby. He had rather hoped to be next to the nanny, but Stella was in a very strange mood and he dared not suggest it. A section of the ship's small orchestra was present, playing a medley of hits from the current West End shows and trying unsuccessfully to encourage the audience to 'sing along'. Clive was certainly in no mood to sing anything, for the pain below his ribs was no better. If anything, it was worse. However, he had decided to join the poker game later so needed to prove to Stella that he was fit enough. He didn't want her trotting off to the doctor again, saying God knows what to him. Women! They did love an invalid. Fuss, fuss, fuss. It was what they did best.

'I'm sorry,' he heard Stella saying to someone. 'We're keeping that place for a friend.'

Alarm bells rang in Clive's head. A 'friend', not 'my daughter'. That could only mean one thing: Gussie Malone. Damned awkward, her and Stella hitting it off like this. Of all the women on the ship, Stella had to pick Gussie. Incredible!

Sure enough, as the 'house lights' dimmed to the accompaniment of a roll on the drums, Gussie Malone appeared in the aisle. She looked extremely chic in a pale cream suit with an embroidered collar. Clive was aware of the many admiring glances she provoked and, despite his pain, he was conscious of an almost unbearable urge to pick her up and carry her off to the nearest bedroom. God, she was an attractive woman and tonight he would take her, if it was the last thing he did! From the corner of his eye he watched as, waving cheerfully to Stella, Gussie edged her way along the row to join the party. Making a dramatic entrance, he thought, amused. She caught his eye and made a brief but distant nod in his direction before settling herself next to Stella. By some strange quirk of fate, his wife and Gussie Malone were both sitting with him.

The humour of it was spoiled for him by the realisation that Stella still considered Gussie a friend in spite of his warning to the contrary. His wife was beginning to worry him. She had deliberately disobeyed him. When he felt better, he would tackle her on the subject; he wanted her back under his thumb where she had always been. He would spell it out for her eventually in no uncertain terms – but now might not be the best time.

His thoughts were interrupted by another short roll of drums and the spotlight focused on the Master of Ceremonies as he walked on to the stage. This splendid fellow sported a monocle in his left eye, a bow-tie at his neck and a red silk handkerchief in the top pocket of his dinner jacket. A roar of applause went up for him and he bowed in all directions. Smiling broadly, he cleared his throat and stepped to the footlights.

'Ladies and gentlemen,' he began. 'I'm sure you will agree

with me that this evening's show is, for all of us, the highlight of the voyage.'

Clive shouted, 'Hear, hear!' and there was some laughter.

'Tonight we have for you an amazing selection of fancy dress. Our children and their parents have been working diligently in order to make this an evening to remember. They have once again come up trumps with a dazzling display of ingenuity and have created a wonderful selection. Choosing a winner is going to be so *difficult*. That said, I for one can't wait to get started on the parade.' He scratched his chin and went on, 'Many of you know the form this competition will take, but those travelling on the *Mauretania* for the first time will not know the procedure. I ask the "old stagers" to be patient while I explain to the newcomers amongst us.' He then went on to list the different categories and the prizes.

Clive thought, Get on with it! He muttered, 'Stand some people on a stage and they can't stop talking!'

Stella glanced at him. 'He has to explain it, surely.'

She turned back to her conversation with Gussie Malone and Clive bit back an angry retort. His wife was giving him the cold shoulder and she would pay for it later. As a fresh cramp took hold, he clutched his stomach and drew long, slow breaths. Since his contretemps with Hemmings, he had spent most of the time lying flat on the bed and the pain had eased. Walking to the concert hall had been more painful than he had expected and he was becoming seriously alarmed. Could it be that Stella was right, and that Hemmings had done him a real injury with that spiteful upper-cut below the ribs? He wondered if there was internal bruising – or even *bleeding*? He felt faint with fright at the latter prospect. Weren't his kidneys some-where in the region of the blow? Could kidneys rupture? And the solar plexus, whatever that was. Not to mention a spleen and a liver. Or a gall-bladder . . . He dragged his attention back to the stage as the drums signalled the start of the fancy dress parade.

'So here's our first contestant in the under-sevens – Miss Amy Weller from Dunstable! Come along, Amy.' He beckoned furi-ously and a small girl walked hesitantly on to the stage, her first thrust firmly into her mouth, her eyes wide. She was dressed as

Miss Muffet and a velvet spider dangled from a string on the end of a short stick. There was a round of applause, and then a young woman appeared from the opposite side of the stage and led her into the wings.

'And now a big welcome for contestant number two – Master Robin Bell from St Ives in Cornwall.'

More applause. Clive took a quick look at Gussie, but her eyes were fixed firmly on the stage. He had promised her a large sum of money and he felt like death. Well, if he couldn't carry out *his* side of the contract, she would have to use those clever hands of hers to please him as best she could. In spite of his pain, the thought of it made him grow hot. Gussie Malone was a woman and a half!

Robin Bell was a knight in cardboard armour. Half-way across the stage, the visor on his helmet slipped down, obscuring his view, and he had to be prevented from falling off the edge of the stage. The audience loved it.

Clive looked at Mary, who was laughing with the rest of them. Her sullen expression had gone, thank goodness. A shame about the singer, he reflected. Stella had told him that she had heard the young man knocking on the door next to theirs and had quickly despatched him. Thank God for that, he thought. And for once Stella was right: Mary must go. A great pity, but these things happened. She had been warned about 'followers', so she had only herself to blame.

The audience applauded a brother and sister as witch and wizard, a boy as a soldier, another as a fisherman complete with rod, line and cardboard fish. Clive yawned and blinked. The tablets made him so drowsy. He closed his eyes and was sharply nudged awake by Stella's elbow.

'You'll miss Abby!' she reproached him.

A succession of disguises floated by him – Jack and Jill, Titania, pirates, elves and goblins. How much longer, he wondered irritably.

'And now let's have your applause for Cleopatra – Miss Abigail Nicolson from London!'

Clive stood up and shouted, 'Bravo!'

Stella pulled him back down on to his seat. She really was becoming very bossy, he reflected. Abby appeared in her dark, fringed wig and multicoloured tunic. She wore a gold belt and a heavy chunky necklace; a pair of gold sandals and an embroidered cloak completed the costume. She made an impressive entrance with no sign of nerves. As Clive stared, entranced, she stood centre stage and took her time, smiling at the audience, revelling in the applause. In a clear voice she said, 'Cleopatra – C-l-e-o-p-a-t-r-a!' Then she threw her arms wide and made a little bow. The audience roared with delight and Clive wanted to cry with pride. But who had taught her to spell, he wondered. She had always said 'Cleo Patcher'; the endearing mistake had been a family joke for the past few years.

He said to Stella, 'Did you teach her that?'

Stella shook her head. Damn! She was in an awkward mood; trying to say as little as possible to him. He couldn't remember what, if anything, he had done to upset her, but she could be moody on occasions. Normally her icy silences followed one of his drinking bouts, but this particular mood seemed to have come out of the blue. Still, he would pretend not to notice. There was the question of the money he needed for tonight's game. Hemmings would no doubt be thinking they had seen the last of him, but he would prove the bastard wrong. He would breeze in as large as life with a fistful of money and bluff his way back into the game. He had looked in Stella's purse and knew exactly how much she had. If she wouldn't give it to him, he would take it. He would pay her back from his winnings. The rest he must wheedle out of Gussie. He would promise her a bonus – or a percentage.

The last of the contenders had crossed the stage and now, to another roll on the drums, they all returned, jostling each other and waving to mothers and fathers in the audience. Clive opened his mouth to shout his congratulations to Abby, but was gripped by a severe cramp which effectively silenced him.

'God Almighty!' he spluttered, waiting for his wife to show some interest. Instead she gave him a curt glance and turned to speak to Gussie. Bitch! He'd make her pay for – 'Oh God!' He thought he might pass out.

Stella said, 'I told you to go to the doctor, but you always know best.'

On stage, the Master of Ceremonies was reading out the names of the winners in the reverse order. The bumble-bee had come third. The knight was second, and Abby was first! It should have been Clive's proudest moment, but pain and fright had distracted him and he was hardly aware of his daughter's triumph.

'I need a drink!' he muttered through clenched teeth and, ignoring Stella's protests, he pushed his way along the row and stumbled out. As he went, he thought he saw the man Stella kept complaining about. Odd. *Had* the wretch been watching them? Another spasm shook him and chased the idea from his head. He made his way to the nearest bar and dragged himself up on to a stool.

'A brandy!' he told the barman. 'No! Make that a double. And hurry it along!'

Gussie, almost running, returned to her cabin and closed the door thankfully behind her. As she did so the ship's horn sounded mournfully, signalling the fog which had been forecast since early that morning. Gussie barely registered the sound. She felt as though she had seen a ghost. Shocked, she leaned back against the door, her hands over her face. The last person in the world she had expected to see on the *Mauretania* was Harry!

'Harry Parr! By all that's holy!'

She would have recognised him anywhere. The man she had loved for so many years had been sitting in the back row of the audience, watching the fancy-dress competition. Presumably he had a child taking part. *A child*. Oh, Harry! Could she bear it? Her heart beat so rapidly and with such force that she thought she might not reach the bed, and she allowed herself to slide into a sitting position behind the door instead. Harry! Mother of God! And looking exactly the same, only older – but weren't they all?

Gussie didn't know whether to laugh or cry. The thought that he was on the same ship was wonderful, but he was obviously with his family and how was she going to be nice to his wife?

'Harry!' she whispered, sick with longing after all these years. Then, 'Stop it, you *eejit*!' she told herself. 'It was all over a long time ago. And you've no one to blame but yourself. There's no going back – ever.' And suppose he had seen *her*? She went hot and then cold at the very thought. Suppose he sought her out, out of curiosity. Once a policeman, always a policeman! Probably a superintendent by now. Sweet Jesus! He must *never* know that

110

she was still . . . must never guess how she earned her living. *Never*! If they *did* meet she must remember her story. She was a respectable widow who had been left comfortably off and who added to her pension by . . . by doing *what*? What could she do?

She swallowed hard. By travelling to and fro on ocean liners and entertaining men in her cabin for a hundred guineas a night! Oh yes! That would impress him for sure!

'Harry!' she said again and tears pressed at her eyelids. 'Oh, my dear Harry.' She struggled to her feet and crossed to the bed, where she sat down and picked up Clara. Whatever would he think of her? She had *promised* to turn her back on her profession and start a new life. She had sworn there would never be another man in her life *or* her bed. And she had meant every word. The trouble was that Harry hadn't believed her. He had stormed off into the night with tears in his eyes and she had never seen him again. He had never given her a chance to be what they both wanted her to be. 'Once a whore, always a whore!' he had shouted. And she had proved him right. She pressed her face into the doll's soft body. Look at her now. Almost past her prime, and still depending on her looks to sell her body. She was disgusted with herself. Suppose he asked her outright. That would be like Harry. He would go straight to the heart of the matter. 'Gussie, have you married?' She could lie.

'Gussie, have you slept with other men?' She could lie.

'Gussie, are you truly a respectable widow?' She could lie – couldn't she?

'No!' she whispered, as the tears began to fall. She could lie with the best of them, but could she lie to Harry? For Harry only the truth would do. He was that sort of man. A great sadness settled within her. It weighed on her plump shoulders and darkened the world around her. This might have been a second chance sent from God in answer to all her prayers.

She crossed herself slowly.

'I'm sorry, Harry,' she said, mopping her tears with Clara's soft body. 'And thank you, Holy Mother, for giving me this chance. But the truth is, I don't deserve it and I can't take advantage of it.'

After a moment she drew in a breath, deep and slow. Then another. She dropped the doll, crossed to the small chest of drawers and took a folded paper from its hiding-place. It was

Harry's first and only letter to her: the one he had written to thank her for her intervention at the fight. The paper was fragile and brittle, the folds worn with age.

Dear Miss Malone,

A few lines in haste to thank you for your timely appearance last night and for your courageous action. I shall call in at the hospital to see you as soon as I come off duty. Hoping you are on the mend.

Respectfully yours, Harry Parr.

'Respectfully!' That one little word. After his colleagues' revelations, Harry had felt no such respect for her. His superiors had warned him to end the unsuitable association. How could Harry know that she had refused all men from the moment she met him and had almost starved in the process? Without references, Gussie had searched in vain for a job – *any* job. Even Bette had understood her passionate need. She had even fed Gussie once or twice, but time had run out. Harry had discovered the truth before Gussie could find a respectable way to earn her living. He had asked her outright: 'Is it true?' She wanted to lie but she couldn't. He such an honourable man. She understood how he felt and had never blamed him for his rejection of her. Later, Bette urged her to contact him again. 'Circumstances have changed,' she told Gussie. 'Give him another chance. It's only fair.' Fair? Life was never fair. Or maybe it was. Maybe people got what they deserved.

She'd stayed with Bette and her 'girls'. If she couldn't have Harry, she didn't want any other man. Not permanently. She'd had another offer, a few years later, from a handsome young artist. Leo. A young Italian with dark hair and a dazzling smile and a way with words that could melt a woman's heart. He knew what she was; had been one of her regular clients ever since he landed in England. He begged her to marry him. No one in Italy would have known the truth about her, he'd argued, and she could start a new life in Venice where they would be rich and respectable. Gussie was tempted for a while and Bette and the other girls had said, 'Do it!'

Only it wasn't as simple as that because by then Gussie had a child, a fact she had kept from the Italian. Bette had said, 'Leave

Tess with me. She's happy enough here. He needn't know.' But Gussie couldn't bear to part with Tess. She had plans for her daughter, was saving up to send her to a convent. When she was old enough to understand things, Gussie meant to try for a post as a housekeeper. There was no way her daughter would follow in her mother's footsteps. So she'd taken a gamble. 'If you'll have us both, Leo, I'm yours,' she told him. She could still remember the look on his face. Shock. And something else she recognised as betrayal. He had looked at her the way Harry had done years before. The expression in his eyes had hurt her more than the loss of dazzling prospects. Like Harry, he had said, 'No.'

Gussie had come to terms with her way of life. She had convinced herself that she had a part to play in the lives of others. Especially the men. Having no one of her own to love, she took a pride in satisfying others' needs. For the short time each was with her, he gave her a kind of love and she was grateful for it. For that same short time, the man was hers to love and cherish. No man, she told herself, was all bad. They had their strengths and their weaknesses, their joys and woes. Some were single and needed a woman simply to satisfy a normal urge. Others were unhappy, with or without a wife, and came to her for comfort. A few came to celebrate a promotion or a legacy or the birth of a child. Whatever the reason, Gussie loved being needed; loved *giving*. Most of the time she managed *not* to be ashamed of what she did for them, and rarely allowed herself to think about the wives she was helping to betray. A very few men had mistreated her. One, mean with drink, had tried to strangle her with her own stocking. She had fought back and survived.

But now Harry Parr was on board the *Mauretania* and they must *never* meet. Somehow she must make sure of that. She felt cold with fright as she realised how near she had come to bumping into him without the slightest warning. Where was his cabin? Where was he seated in the dining room? At least she could be on her guard. He was at a disadvantage because he had no idea that she was on board. If she met him walking with his family, she would pretend not to recognise him. If he recognised her, she would pretend it was a case of mistaken identity. She would call herself Mrs da Silva and pretend she was married to her Italian admirer.

'Mother of God, Harry!' she said helplessly.

May be it would be safer to pretend she was unwell and stay in her cabin – but then Stella would come fussing. And then she wouldn't see him again and she couldn't bear that. She drew a long sigh. It was all so foolish, she reflected sadly. Here she was, making all these plans to avoid him when all she wanted was to be held tightly in his arms, close to his heart.

Just once more.

Harry sat at the table, which was too small for him. His knees were crushed and his back ached. The basic cabin was meagre but he was not complaining. The Nicolson assignment had been very interesting – a real challenge – and the remuneration generous. He had done a good job and was certain that he had given value for money. That knowledge pleased him. He stretched his back, turning his head gently from side to side to ease the crick in his neck. He preferred to write on deck in the comfort of a deck-chair, but that was impossible at the moment because of the fog. And when the fog lifted, a breeze would flutter the pages. The ship was not designed to help those who wished to achieve written work.

He wrote carefully, but the detailed and damning report no longer gave him the satisfaction he was accustomed to. Now he had met 'the injured party', he was fully aware of the distress his revelations would cause her and it troubled him. It was the only aspect of his work that Harry did not enjoy. He glanced at his watch which lay beside him on the table. Another half an hour until dinner. He tried to rearrange his legs and smiled at the sound of the fog-horn. There was something about its lugubrious note which struck a chord in his own soul. He wanted to say, 'Yes, I know. Life's like that!'

May 24th 1910. I can now verify the fact that May Rose Tompkins is still alive and the marriage with N. is still in effect. A male child was born to the marriage on October 2nd the same year, but died shortly after birth. May Tompkins now lives with a man by the name of Archie Blain. They claim to be a married couple and are employed by a wealthy family in Bath as cook and gardener. Their employers are Sir Joseph and Lady Croft – a couple in their late seventies. They have handed the manor house over to their son and now live in one wing of it.

(Informants were local P.C. Arthur Hewison; Mrs Annie Long, housekeeper to the Crofts, and Mr Albert Spiers, proprietor of the Hay Wain).

Harry was re-reading this when he was interrupted by a knock at the door.

'Just a moment!' He laid a newspaper across the report and opened the door.

Stella Nicolson was outside. She stood very straight, trying to hide her agitation. Dismayed, Harry said, 'Mrs Nicolson. How nice to—'

'It won't be,' she promised him. 'You see, I've been tracking *you*, Mr Parr. I hope you don't mind. You said I could call on you.'

'Please come in.'

She hesitated, then stepped quickly inside.

It felt strange, having a woman in his room after so long. He said, 'If you sit on the chair and I perch on the edge of the bed, I think we will have observed the proprieties!'

'I have more to worry about than the proprieties, Mr Parr,' she told him.

Poor, unfortunate lady. How right you are, he thought. They seated themselves and she allowed herself a brief but disparaging glance round the cabin. 'Is this the best my father could offer?' she asked. 'It seems rather cramped.'

'I chose this as less conspicuous, ma'am.' He thought he knew why she had come, but hoped he was wrong. 'Part of my disguise, if you like.' He smiled, trying to put her at ease.

Stella Nicolson was outwardly composed, but a slight tremor in her clasped hands betrayed the inner turmoil as she said, 'Mr Parr, I want to know what is in the report. I want to read it.'

He was right. 'No, Mrs Nicolson. I cannot allow it. I thought I had made that clear.'

'You did, Mr Parr, but I am here to insist that I have a *right* to know.'

'Your father will tell you in his own time, I'm sure.'

'He may not choose to do so. He may want to protect me and I – I don't *want* to be protected. I'm not a child.'

Harry was silent. So much for hoping.

She said, 'Suppose I offer to pay for the report? You send the bill to me instead of to him.'

'The answer's still "No", I'm afraid. It wouldn't be ethical to disclose to a second person—'

'Ethical, Mr Parr?' His remark appeared to have touched a nerve. Her eyes flashed. 'Do private detectives have ethics? Don't they spy and snoop on people and dig into their secrets? Is that ethical?'

Harry gazed at her in astonishment. 'I only meant that—'

'I don't *care* what you meant or didn't mean.' She had raised her voice and the colour was creeping into her face. 'I want to know everything there is to know about my husband. About his past. About his involvement with – with the finances – about—'

'And I can't tell you!' He felt annoyed with her. Hurt by her criticism. Of *course* he had ethics. He didn't lie or cheat. He did a difficult job as well as he could.

They glared at each other.

She said, 'Or *won't*!'

'I'm sorry.'

'Save your platitudes, Mr Parr. I shan't leave here until I know.'

He shrugged his shoulders. Two could play at that game. The minutes ticked away. It would soon be time for dinner and she would have to go. There was the child and the nanny to think of. And surely her husband would be looking for her?

Stella said, 'I mean what I say, Mr Parr. You won't deter me.' As she glanced round, Harry noticed that a few sheets of his report were sticking out from beneath the newspaper on the table.

He saw her eyes go to them and jumped forward just as she also made a snatch at them. For a long, undignified moment they struggled and Harry won. Mrs Nicolson sat down again, flushed and angry.

'How very unchivalrous!' she snapped.

'Unladylike, too!'

'Go to hell!' His surprise must have been obvious because she added, 'Oh yes! I can swear when the need arises, Mr Parr. My husband has a lively vocabulary and is a good teacher! Why don't you put *that* in your report?'

Another silence descended, and Harry began to wonder how it would end. She would surely admit defeat and go; he could hardly throw her bodily into the corridor. He glanced at her quickly. She was fiddling with a button on the front of her blouse.

'Look, Mrs Nicolson,' he began, in a conciliatory tone. 'Don't you think your father has your best interests at heart?'

'Of course he has, but he doesn't know the whole truth. Oh, he may know more about the . . . the swindling and the gambling debts, but does he know how precarious Clive's temper is? He knows that Clive struck me while we were in New York. Did he tell you that, I wonder? He thinks that's the first time it happened. But he's wrong, Mr Parr. It wasn't the first time!' Her mouth trembled and she was struggling for composure. 'My husband is a large man, and he frequently drinks too much and just as frequently loses his temper. Not with Abby. Not ever with her, I'm pleased to say. But I have been a disappointment for him, you see. Like most men he wanted a son, and I cannot give him one. So he has a grudge against me. Maybe I'm in *danger*, Mr Parr? How about that? Still determined to refuse me access to that report? Perhaps you should think about it.'

With her words, the first doubt crept into Harry's mind. He had been instructed *not* to show the contents to the daughter *on any account*. That was his brief, and he was loyally carrying out his employer's wishes. But she had a point. *If* she should suffer an attack, her father would probably blame him for not using his common sense. Harry closed his eyes so that Stella Nicolson shouldn't recognise the fact that he was wavering. Making the decisions was the worst part of the job, and it had taken him some time to get used to the responsibility. In the police force there had been rules and regulations; there had been procedures to abide by, and someone higher up to tell you what to do.

'The answer's still "No",' he told her.

'I don't accept your answer. I want to see that report *now*. I must know the worst. I need to understand my position, no matter how bad it is.' Seeing that he didn't immediately refuse, she pressed on. 'Will my husband be arrested, for instance? Will he go to prison? For this whatever-it-is? Embezzlement?'

'Possibly. If your father decides to prosecute.'

'It's true, then? You're sure there's no mistake?'

'I very much regret it but – no.'

'A lot of money?'

'Your father didn't tell me that, but he spoke as though the sums were considerable.'

Harry knew it was thousands rather than hundreds but didn't want to add to her worries. Some information should be left mercifully vague.

She sighed heavily. 'I have Abby to think about,' she said. 'How will I tell her that her father is in prison?'

Harry didn't know. *His* mother hadn't needed to tell Harry anything because he had seen it for himself when he ran into the study after hearing the shot; he had never heard a gun go off before and yet he recognised the sound. Next day his mother had sent him to school. 'Best thing for him to carry on as normal,' she had told the neighbour who had offered to look after him for a few days. To carry on as normal! Even at ten years old Harry had realised the stupidity of his mother's words. At school the other children were curious, asking over and over again, 'What did it *look* like?' when all Harry wanted to do was forget it. Benny Marsh had been the worst. He had tormented Harry, laughing, calling his father a coward. Harry had fought him and lost. When he ran home crying, his mother had said, 'Look at the state of you, Harry Parr!', too upset to pay him much attention. Harry pushed the memory to the back of his mind.

Now he said, 'Need she know? She's so young. Pretend he's had to go abroad.'

He didn't feel qualified to give advice. Normally he didn't need to know what the outcome of his investigations would be. He did his part and left them to it. The trouble was, he knew exactly how Abby would feel with a shameful family secret hanging over her life. The disillusionment and the pain and the loss of an idol – the hurt never ended. The terrible fact was, of course, that Nicolson being sent to prison was only part of the final picture. Harry knew it all. Abby would grow up with the knowledge that she was born out of wedlock; that her wonderful father was not only a thief but a bigamist; that he had lost a legitimate son and still had a legal wife.

'What is it?' she exclaimed. 'I can see it in your eyes. Mr Parr, you must tell me the truth. Is there *more*?'

He nodded and she gave a little cry of shock and fear. Harry hated what was happening to her. Perhaps he should tell her? He felt for the woman, understood her argument and saw the logic in it. He made one last effort.

'I think you should leave now, Mrs Nicolson.' He stood up. 'You are placing me in an impossible position. I have signed a contract with your father and he specifically instructed—'

'You can sit down again.'

He remained standing.

Stella swallowed hard, her eyes large and dark with confusion. How she must be dreading the truth, he thought with a rush of compassion.

She said, 'Don't worry about me, Mr Parr. I am stronger than you think, and I am not friendless. I have recently met a woman who has been a source of strength. I can trust her, I can talk to her. About you. About my husband. I intend to confide fully in her.'

'Is that wise?'

'Would you rather I dealt with this alone?'

'This lady—'

'Her name is Malone. She's the widow of a sea-captain. Quite fearless and very down-to-earth. Abby seems very taken with her, and she appears to like the child. Not that my husband approves, but then he doesn't want me to have a friend.' Her tone hardened. 'As soon as he knew, he began trying to poison my mind against her – telling me how unsuitable she was as a companion. He knows nothing about her, but he tried to infer that she was not a lady. "No better than she should be" – that was how he put it. But for once I ignored him. Gussie and I are friends, whether he likes it or not. Oh yes, we are on first-name terms.' She looked at him, frowning slightly. 'Are you all right, Mr Parr? Have I said something?'

Harry sat down slowly. 'Gussie Malone?' It couldn't be. Malone was Gussie's maiden name.

'Do you know her?' She was startled.

'No, no!' He was telling himself not to be a fool. That this Gussie Malone was not *his* Gussie Malone; not the young woman who had come to his aid so many years ago and been knocked unconscious for her trouble. The name was hardly uncommon. *It couldn't be Gussie!* If it was, she had married a sea-captain. *And was now a widow*! His heart was racing and he felt giddy with excitement. For God's sake, Harry! Stop this! How could the sound of her name do this to him? It was ridiculous. Gussie was long gone from his life. Water under the bridge. This must be another Gussie Malone. But what had Stella Nicolson said? 'Quite fearless and down-to-earth.' That sounded like Gussie . . .

'Mr *Parr*! Are you deaf?' Stella Nicolson was staring at him angrily. 'I said, "Show me the report!" Now!'

'I can't do that.' He made a big effort to concentrate. Nearly lost it, Harry, he told himself. Deal with one thing at a time.

The woman opposite narrowed her eyes. 'Suppose you were to glance away and I happened to catch sight of it and . . .'

Women! They could be very devious. He shook his head. ' "No" means "No".'

She thought about it. 'So my father forbids you to show me the report. Did he forbid you to answer my questions?'

Harry wished she would go away. He hated this scene and wanted it to end. Suddenly he had something else to think about. 'No,' he admitted. 'Not in so many words.'

'Then I'll ask you specific questions and you can say "Yes" or "No". Or nod or shake your head, depending how silly you want this to become. And don't look at me in that way, please, Mr Parr. You are forcing me to adopt this hectoring tone.' She took a deep breath. 'Have you discovered anything in my husband's past that I should know? That he should have told me about before we married? Information that I was entitled to hear?'

Harry rolled his eyes. 'Yes, Mrs Nicolson.' He wanted her to leave him to his thoughts. He needed to think about Gussie.

'So what is it?' she insisted. 'Something immoral? Criminal?'

He came to a sudden decision: he would tell her some of it. 'Your husband spent a month in prison when he was twenty for injuring a man in a drunken brawl. Did you know that?'

She looked shaken. Well, she had asked for it. Had *insisted*. But he wished she wasn't quite so pale. He didn't want her to faint on him.

'No. Anything else?'

'You're asking specific questions, remember.'

amaze me how on board a ship they always manage to have fresh flowers.'

The rest of her table agreed heartily. Gussie had gone out of her way to be nice to them all, having long ago developed a strategy for the dining room which had served her well. It was important, she knew, to be extra kind to any woman less attractive than herself who might otherwise take against her out of jealousy. Necessary, also, not to flirt with any attached man since this would antagonise the wife. On this trip she had had no problems. She shared a table with an elderly couple – Mr and Mrs Dewitt from Ohio – and with a single woman, Miss Green from somewhere in Kent. Miss Green was a forthright woman in her forties who was obsessed with the idea of votes for women. The Dewitts were quiet, very nervous people who described themselves as 'regular home bodies'. But they had won a competition and were 'doing the Grand Tour – before we're too old to travel.' Privately Gussie thought they had already left it too late. Europe, she thought, was likely to be too great a culture shock for them.

Mrs Dewitt said, 'We're having the beef.' She smiled at Gussie.

'The beef? Oh, splendid idea. The *Mauretania* does an excellent roast beef. Very traditional.'

'Very *British*,' said Mr Dewitt.

'Very.' Gussie picked up her menu and studied it carefully.

Miss Green was telling the Dewitts about a meeting she would be attending in London.

'So stay away from Number Ten,' she warned them with a wolfish grin, 'because there might be some action. We might give the papers a headline.'

The Dewitts looked puzzled. The wife said, 'Votes for women?'

'Why not?'

Mr Dewitt asked, 'Where is this Number Ten?'

'Where the prime minister lives. It's in Downing Street.'

'Oh, sure! We'll stay right away! Thank you kindly.'

Gussie beckoned the steward. 'I'll have the egg mornay, please, and then the halibut, and then I'll decide on a dessert. Oh, and the rest of my wine. I only drank half of it yesterday.'

He consulted his notebook. 'Ah yes. The Beaujolais. Certainly.'

Miss Green gave Gussie a challenging look and asked, 'Will you be there, Mrs Malone?'

'Will I be where?'

'At Downing Street.'

'I'm afraid not,' Gussie told her. She was tempted to add that she might well be entertaining one of the MPs, but thought better of the idea. Did she want the vote, she wondered. It might be a good idea to try to put right the mess the men were making of the country, but she certainly didn't fancy manning the barricades with Miss Green and her friends. And who would she vote for? She didn't think much of any of them.

The food began to arrive and there was less time to talk. Gussie allowed her gaze to roam the dining room in search of Harry Parr, but couldn't see him. Just as well. If she couldn't see him, he couldn't see her. She relaxed. The egg mornay was delicious and the halibut fresh and tasty.

'I think someone must have thrown a line overboard!' she remarked. 'Fresh off the hook!'

Mr Dewitt said, 'You'd like the beef. Wouldn't she, honey?'

'She would, yes.'

Miss Green persevered with her chef's salad with Scottish salmon and said nothing. No doubt her mind was on higher things, thought Gussie – like the banner she would carry or the slogan they would chant. She had told them she taught the pianoforte at a small private school. It seemed a strange combination, but maybe the boredom of those daily scales had finally inspired rebellion.

Gussie cleared her plate and anticipated the dessert trolley. She had decided that, if she *should* bump into Harry, she would stick to the story about the sea-captain's widow – but she would have to make it convincing. Where had she lived with her imaginary sea-captain? How long had they been together, and how exactly had he died? And had they been happy, and had they had any children? It was going to be tricky. Probably impossible. She *must* make sure that they didn't meet.

Mrs Dewitt asked, 'Do you like animals, Mrs Malone? We have a yard dog and a parrot and a couple of horses. Our neighbour's looking after them while we're on our trip.'

Miss Green said, 'There's no room in my life for pets at the moment. They're such a tie.' Discreetly, she removed a small bone from her mouth and placed it on the edge of her plate. 'They're a luxury I can't afford.'

Gussie said, 'I have a tabby cat who goes by the name of Tom after Dick Whittington.' Seeing that the Dewitts looked baffled, she finished her Beaujolais and launched into the unlikely tale of the Lord Mayor of London and his redoubtable cat. Half-way through it she was interrupted by an apologetic cough.

The steward was setting down a bottle of champagne. They all regarded him blankly, and Gussie said, 'Champagne?' It always went to her head.

'From a gentleman, Mrs Malone.' The steward handed her a note and withdrew.

Gussie said, 'For *me*?' but he had gone.

Mrs Dewitt looked thrilled. 'How exciting!'

'Well now! Isn't that something!' said her husband.

Miss Green said, 'God! Men! They're so transparent!'

She looked piqued, Gussie thought as she read the message:

Gussie,

Please share the bottle with your companions with my compliments. I would so like to talk with you. I shall be in the Verandah Café at eight-thirty. Harry.

They were all looking at her expectantly as very carefully she folded the note and slipped it into her purse. She looked up and met three pairs of enquiring eyes. 'It's from an old friend,' she explained shakily. 'For us to share.'

Genie-like, the steward had reappeared with four champagne flutes and prepared to uncork the bottle. As he poured the liquid into the glasses, Gussie took a quick look around the dining room. There was no sign of Harry. But he had found her, and she didn't know whether to be pleased or sorry. She didn't know whether to accept the invitation to meet him or to avoid the meeting. If they had drunk his champagne, it would be surly to ignore his invitation. When she asked Mr Dewitt the time, it was five minutes past eight. Gussie began to panic. Everything was happening too quickly. She wasn't ready for Harry Parr. Her cover story was still unwritten. And was he travelling alone? He had said, '*I* shall be in the Verandah Café', not *we*.

Miss Green asked, 'But where is this old friend of yours?'

They all looked at Gussie.

'He's very shy,' she said. 'Bit of a recluse, if you take my meaning.' She raised her glass and they all followed suit. 'To old friends!' toasted Gussie.

She took a sip or two and came to a decision. She wouldn't go; she wouldn't meet him. Let him think whatever he liked. He had broken her heart, and he needn't think that a bottle of champagne would put things right between them. She took another sip, and then a mouthful; then she drained the glass. Gallantly, Mr Dewitt poured the remaining champagne into her empty flute. She drank it and the bubbles went up her nose and she thought that maybe she *would* meet him. But could she bear to hear about the life he had made without her? No. So she wouldn't go. Definitely not.

'This way I still have my memories!' They were all staring at her. So had she spoken *aloud*?

Miss Green asked, 'Memories?'

'Nothing,' said Gussie. Was she lightheaded already? Had Harry done this on purpose, or had he forgotten? His twenty-second birthday. They had spent a day at the Crystal Palace to celebrate the occasion. Gussie had taken the picnic, Harry had brought the wine. Only he had brought champagne. She had made a complete fool of herself, talking too loudly, giggling and flirting with him. People had laughed at her and he had been so embarrassed. She had recognised the expression on his face, but she couldn't stop herself. They had ended up quarrelling over nothing and the special day had been ruined.

She said, 'Just an old friend.' Her voice trembled.

Mrs Dewitt exchanged a meaningful look with her husband, then laid a gentle hand on Gussie's arm. 'Finish telling us about the cat, honey.'

Gussie stood up. Her legs felt weak and she thought she might cry. 'If you'll excuse me. I – I don't feel too well.'

Miss Green smirked openly, but Mrs Dewitt said, 'You do look a little pale, honey. My husband will walk you to your room, won't you, Hector?'

Despite her protest, Gussie was grateful for his help as he took her arm and led her slowly out of the dining room. He delivered her safely to her cabin and told her to 'take a little nap'. Gussie closed the door and lay down on the bed. Had she decided to go to the Verandah Café or not?

'Holy Mother!' she whispered. She got up again and poured herself a glass of water which she gulped down. Then she sat, waiting for her head to stop spinning. She would close her eyes for just ten minutes and then she would decide . . .

Chapter Seven

Gussie opened her eyes half an hour later and sat up with a start. Her head felt a little better. 'Harry!' she cried – but what was the time?

'Twenty to nine! God Almighty!'

She slid from the bed and rushed into the bathroom, where she grabbed a flannel, ran some cold water and splashed her face. She looked terrible. But what did it matter? She was late and he had probably gone by now.

'Oh, Harry, *please* wait!' she muttered. It would take her five minutes to reach the Verandah Café on the next deck, and the pianist was due to play at nine. How could they talk there? She snatched up a silk shawl and flung it round her shoulders. At least she still had her beautiful auburn hair. He had loved that.

She flew along the corridor and went up in the lift. 'Be there,' she told him.

The room was already full, but she saw him almost immediately. He was slumped in a chair with a glass on the table in front of him. For a moment she paused to take in the look of him. Harry Parr: he looked very much the way she remembered. Gussie drew a deep breath. Stay calm, she told herself. It's only Harry. At that moment he caught sight of her and she thought she saw relief in his eyes. Resisting the urge to hurl herself into his arms, she crossed the room with her hand outstretched in an elegant greeting. Let him see that a handshake was all that was on offer.

'Harry Parr!' she said. 'Lovely to see you after all these years.'

He seized her hand, smiling the way she remembered. 'Gussie! I thought you weren't coming. Thank you . . . Oh!' He looked as though he wanted to eat her. 'Do please sit down. Can I get you a drink?'

'Coffee would be wonderful.'

They sat down and he stared at her. 'You're looking so – so *good*!' he said, forgetting to order the coffee. 'You haven't changed a bit.' He leaned back in his chair, then leaned forward again.

He wants to be as close to me as possible, Gussie thought, exhilarated. 'Thank you for the champagne. It was a kind thought.' She wouldn't remind him of his twenty-second birthday all those years ago. She asked, 'How did you find me? I mean, did you just notice me?' She had forgotten just how wonderfully grey his eyes were. With tiny flecks of gold. Hastily she looked down at her hands.

'Mrs Nicolson mentioned you in passing and I thought the name – well, naturally I didn't expect you to be *Mrs* Malone. But then I saw you at dinner.'

Astonished she said, 'You know Stella Nicolson?'

'Not exactly. I can't explain but –' He stopped.

Gussie's heart contracted. Surely they weren't having an affair? No! That was nonsense. What on earth was the matter with her?

He said, 'I'm employed by her father. In connection with the family's business interests.'

She risked another look at his face. 'But – aren't you in the police force any more? You were so ambitious.'

'No, no. I'm a businessman.'

'A *businessman*!' She couldn't imagine it.

He smiled. 'A private detective. I have my own agency. I do inquiries for people. I don't answer to any man, and I like that. The money's enough, and business is on the increase.'

'But why? You lived for the police force. You were determined to be a detective, if I remember.' And I do remember, she thought, pressing a hand against her chest. I remember all that I can bear to remember.

He leaned back suddenly, clasping his hands and pressing them against his chin. Gussie thought, he doesn't want to tell me. She let the question fade, then changed the subject. 'So do you have a family, Harry?'

'My mother died.'

130

His mother! Gussie recalled the miserable, withdrawn widow who obviously hadn't wanted a daughter-in-law. Didn't want to share her precious son.

She said, 'I'm sorry – not that she liked me, and I hardly knew her, but—'

Harry said, 'You never knew the whole story, Gussie. It wasn't you. That's just the way she was then. Something had happened—'

'Then she hadn't guessed about me? I thought afterwards that maybe she had.'

'It wasn't that, Gussie.'

'Did you ever tell her – what I was?'

'Of course not.'

So he had protected her. Gussie felt ridiculously pleased.

He said, 'We had a family tragedy, long before you and I met. It broke her heart.' He looked down, then up again. 'It doesn't matter now, but at the time . . .'

A family tragedy? She said, 'You needn't tell me, Harry,' although she was wildly curious. How naïve she had been all those years ago, she reflected, to think she knew him. And how unkind she had been – how *hasty* – to judge his mother.

'My father was a policeman; a very senior detective. They were investigating a big robbery and they recovered a lot of money. A suitcase full of banknotes. My father stole some of them – quite a lot, in fact – and put them in the bank.'

'*Stole* some?' The words slipped out and her tone was accusing. She regretted them immediately, but it was too late. Harry flinched. To cover the moment she said, 'Didn't anyone suspect anything?'

'Apparently not. He paid it in over a longish period; he didn't spend it. But he left a letter admitting everything . . .' He shook his head. 'In his last letter, he said that he regretted it immediately but daren't tell anyone and didn't know how to give it back. He said that the best he could do was to never spend it. Time went by until eventually, out of the blue, something came to light and it looked as though he had been discovered and – well, you know what they say about crooked policemen. He couldn't face the disgrace. Blew his brains out.'

'Oh, the poor man!' Gussie could almost feel the man's pain.

She understood the agony of something unalterable. The useless regret of past mistakes and the feeling of utter helplessness.

Harry shrugged. 'It was a great scandal, naturally, and my poor mother just shut herself away from the world. Except to visit his grave. She used to go along after dark to lay flowers on the plot. No proper headstone. I never saw it, but she told me.'

'You never saw it? Never saw his grave?' She was astonished.

'I couldn't. My mother wanted to be buried with him, but they wouldn't allow it.'

Gussie said, 'He made a mistake, Harry. Can't you forgive him? You, too, made a mistake – with me. What you did to me—'

'Leaving you, you mean?'

'No, Harry. What you did to me that day *before* you left me. That was a mistake, but I've forgiven you. You should forgive your father. We're all human, Harry.'

He didn't answer, but she could see that her words had affected him. She looked at him with sudden understanding. 'So you became a policeman in your turn. Trying to right the wrong?'

He gave a short laugh. 'Something like that. I think I hoped that by being a strong upholder of the law I could balance out the damage he had done to the reputation of the force – and to the family.'

'And you never told me.'

'I think I would have done eventually.'

'Poor Harry . . .' She wanted to take him in her arms and comfort him, but instead reached out and touched his hand briefly in a gesture of sympathy. 'So why did you give it up?'

'Partly because my wife hated it—'

Oh God! she thought. He's got himself a wife. The disappointment was acute, but she tried not to let it show in her face.

'She hated being a policeman's wife,' he went on. 'She was always fearful for me and always claimed that I'd joined for the wrong reasons. She was right. Leaving wasn't such a great wrench, in fact. At first I was carried along by my own enthusiasm, determined to make my mark. But the truth is I wasn't cut out for the job, really.' He grinned. 'No team spirit, that's my trouble. And I hated taking orders. I prefer what I do now. I'm the boss.' He tapped his chest and grinned suddenly.

There were touches of silver in his hair, but it was as thick and unruly as ever. She said, 'So you found yourself a wife.' It was all she could think about.

The grin disappeared. 'Yes. Poor Edie. I married her shortly after you and I went our separate ways.' He looked at her steadily. 'I missed you so much. I think all I wanted was to fill the gap you left in my life.'

So he had missed her. Her heart leaped. Gussie couldn't speak, couldn't take her eyes from his face. He had missed her, but how much? By all accounts he hadn't wasted much time finding Edie. She wanted to think badly of him, but it was difficult with him so close and practically breaking her heart.

'Her name was Edith Brooks. She loved me, Gussie.'

Gussie could believe it. Hadn't she been head over heels in love with him herself! And still was. She asked, 'What was she like?' She wanted Edie to be unlovely. She felt mean about it, but there it was.

Reading her mind, Harry smiled and said, 'Not as lovely as you, Gussie,' and she felt worse.

He put his head on one side, considering. 'She was taller than you, with smooth brown hair and a sweet mouth. But she lacked your – your *fire*, Gussie. She was quiet and rather shy. Her father was a dentist and a pillar of the local church, so my super approved of her, of course. I think he thought – that is . . .' He broke off suddenly.

At his words, Gussie had stiffened involuntarily. Her delight faded and she said, 'He thought anyone would be better than an Irish trollop like me?'

She waited, feeling the old resentments, opening the old wounds. Hurting, but hating herself, she was unable to hold back. 'Isn't that the truth of it?' She could see by his expression that it was.

'Gussie!'

Abruptly her anger faded. 'I'm sorry, Harry.' It wasn't fair to make him suffer. 'Go on.'

After an awkward silence he went on. 'I truly tried to love her in return, but it was impossible. I regretted marrying her because I felt that I didn't make her happy. The moment I saw her walking down the aisle towards me, I knew I was living a lie. I felt so guilty because she looked so trusting and her smile was—' He shook his head. 'She looked so beautiful. She was *radiant* with joy.'

Gussie felt a stab of jealousy. *She* would have looked radiant, given half a chance. Walking down the aisle towards Harry would make any woman beautiful and radiant.

He said, 'Just before she was taken ill she said she knew I didn't love her, but that it wasn't my fault.'

'Did she know about me?'

'She knew there'd been another woman, but I wouldn't talk about it.'

There was another silence. Gussie reminded herself that it was all in the past. How could it still have the power to wound?

Harry said, 'Poor Edie.'

He was talking about her in the past tense, Gussie noticed suddenly, and he'd also said that Edie had been taken ill. 'Where is she now?' she asked casually.

'She died. Meningitis. We'd only been married six years.' His expression was suddenly bleak.

The relief was like a weight being lifted from her shoulders. She was so *glad*. Later she would say a few Hail Marys, she promised herself. Contrite, she said, 'I've upset you, Harry. I'm sorry. I shouldn't be asking all these questions but ...' She shrugged. 'I can't help being curious about the way your life turned out. I've often – sometimes – thought about you.' So was he *still* unmarried? She dared not ask.

For a long time neither spoke. Gussie wanted to tear her eyes from his face, but couldn't do it. She felt like a starving man who is suddenly offered food.

At last he said, 'I was out one night on foot patrol. Breaking in a new recruit. Showing him the ropes. What to look for, what to listen for ... His name was Sidney Sparke. Very keen, but not what you'd call robust. Tall but skinny. We got on well enough. We were approaching a corner off the Old Kent Road and we heard a scream. We rushed to the house and there was a woman leaning out of her window, trying to attract attention. She said there was a man in the back garden – a prowler, she called him.' He broke off, frowning at the memory.

Gussie waited. Let him tell it in his own time, she thought.

'Sidney was thrilled. His first experience of action. I knew exactly how he felt. The longing to prove yourself – but I wasn't sure how he would react under fire, so to speak. I wanted to keep him where he would see the least action. I said, "Wait here. I'll go round the back." There was an alleyway between the houses. I ran down and there he was. The prowler – a burly sort of man, ugly expression. Looked half mad, with staring eyes. I wasn't too keen to tackle him myself, to be honest, but as soon as he caught sight of me he rushed towards me. I jumped on to him, but somehow he sidestepped and I went straight into the wall.'

'Harry!' Her hands flew to her face.

He smiled. 'You weren't there to rush up with your brolly and save me, so there I was in a right pickle!'

They both laughed.

He went on, 'For a moment I was stunned. Then I tried to get up, but I staggered and fell again. By now the man had run back through the alley and Sparkes had tackled him. By the time I got back to the front garden they were on the grass and this bastard had picked up a rock: the sort people use to edge the lawn; they paint them white.'

Gussie nodded.

'I screamed, "Don't!" but he brought it down with such a thud. I heard Sparkes' skull crack. I *heard* it! I've never forgotten that sound. I knew then; I didn't need the hospital to tell me.'

'He was *dead*? Oh, Jesus!' Shocked, Gussie crossed herself.

'I didn't know whether to go after the man or stay with poor old Sparkes.'

'You stayed with him,' said Gussie. 'He might have been just conscious and frightened, and he needed you.'

Harry nodded. 'He was still alive then. Just. He kept mumbling something I couldn't catch.' He shrugged. 'We never caught the man who killed him. Afterwards I felt sure I'd made the wrong decision. Whichever way I'd done it, it could have been wrong. But if I'd gone after the bastard I might have caught him. Arrested him and seen him go down for murder. Because that's what it was ... I lost my confidence for a while after that – what with losing Edie and then that. I had to see Sparkes' parents. They were totally broken up. Their only son ...'

She rushed to reassure him. 'But you weren't to blame, Harry. No one could have blamed you.'

He shrugged. 'A few months later I was knocked down by a runaway carriage. My left arm's still not quite right. A bit stiff and painful at times. They offered me clerical work, but I thought it was time to get out.' His attempt at a smile went straight to her heart.

'So you set up on your own.'

He nodded. 'It worked out better than I hoped. The police sent me clients – people they couldn't help. And I advertised. Things went well. Recommendations. Word of mouth.' He smiled. 'It pays the bills and there's money in the bank. Funny old world!'

After a long silence he looked round. 'What happened to our coffee?' he asked.

'You didn't order any!'

He slapped his forehead, grinning. 'I'm going mad! It's you, Gussie! I can't believe you're actually sitting beside me.'

Gussie watched him as he went to the bar to order the coffee. So her presence was distracting him. Driving him mad. What did *that* mean? That he still found her attractive? So had he remarried?

He came back, followed by the barman with a tray of coffee and a plate of biscuits.

'I'm starving!' he confessed. 'I hardly ate any dinner.'

'The sea's certainly getting rougher.'

'It wasn't the sea,' he confessed. 'I was too nervous about meeting you again. Sent back a nice piece of steak, and you know how the stewards are. They take it personally.'

Gussie didn't know; she was a strong eater. 'They do. Yes.' The way she was feeling, she would have agreed the moon was made of green cheese if Harry had suggested it. Just to hear his voice again, to share his laughter, after so long. He was staring at her, too. In books they would have said 'devouring her with his eyes', thought Gussie. To hide her emotion, she picked up her coffee and sipped it.

He said, 'Now, tell me all about your life, Gussie. I've talked about myself long enough.'

Gussie froze. 'About me?' Her hand trembled so much that she hastily put the coffee cup back on the table. 'Well now, I've nothing to tell.'

'Of course you have,' he smiled. 'Mrs Nicolson said you were married to a sea-captain but that now you're a widow. I'm so sorry.'

'Oh, that.' She swallowed hard, trying to remember what she had decided to say. What exactly had she told Stella – if anything? 'Yes. I was, that's true. But it wasn't a wild success.'

'Why do you call yourself Malone?'

'Oh!' She thought desperately. 'His family didn't like me. He'd already been married before but she'd – she'd died. They thought he married again too quickly, and they resented me. Natural, I suppose.' She was rather pleased with that; she could almost believe it herself. 'I thought, I'll be Malone again.'

'So what *was* your husband's name?'

She stifled a gasp of dismay. 'Dewitt!' It was the first name that came into her head. 'Hector Dewitt.'

'Merchant Navy?'

She stared at him, uncomprehending.

'Or Royal Navy?'

'Oh yes! Sorry. Merchant.' Please don't let him know anything about the Merchant Navy, she prayed.

'And?' He watched her over the rim of his coffee-cup. She remembered that he was trained to observe people; trained to root out falsehoods or inconsistencies. He was a *detective*, wasn't he!

'And he died,' she said firmly. 'At sea – washed overboard in a storm.'

'Good heavens!' He shook his head, appalled. 'How dreadful for you. Poor Gussie.'

Abby's words about the colour of her clothes came back to Gussie, and she added, 'I did wear black, for a while.'

'I'm sure you did. Even though you said it wasn't very successful. I mean, you must have cared a little for him – unless you married for the security.'

Gussie thought he probably hoped that was the reason. No one liked to feel that they could be easily replaced. 'That's exactly it,' she told him. 'And it was the same for him. He wanted a home to come back to; slippers by the fire and a nourishing stew on the hob. Sailors dream of these things.' She laughed, gaining

137

confidence in the story. 'Like you, I married in haste, and he was never there, and when he was I didn't like him as much as I'd thought I did. In fact, I didn't care much for married life. It's very over-rated in my opinion. I don't know what you think about it, but I was disappointed. Just for the sake of a "Mrs" in front of my name and the tradesmen showing respect . . .' She trailed into an awkward silence, wondering if she had said too much. Always a fault, she knew. Her tongue ran away with her when she was nervous. 'But I felt guilty when he died,' she added, hoping to redress the balance. 'Buried at sea – but I was glad in a way. Graveyards are dismal places.'

Harry was looking at her intently. Oh Jesus! What have I said, she thought, panic-stricken.

He said, 'I thought he was washed overboard.'

'Yes.'

'So how could he be buried at sea?'

Hell and damnation! Gussie felt a frisson of fear. I've done it, she thought. I've been a sight too clever. 'I mean, he's under the sea – not under the earth. I mean, there's no body and no grave.' She felt exhausted and irritable. He was making her tell so many lies! Maybe she would pluck up courage when she got home and go to confession. Not that God would recognise her – it had been so long.

But he seemed to accept her explanation. He looked at her for a long time and then he put out his hand and touched hers.

'I went back after Edie's death,' he said. 'To look for you. Back to Bette's place.'

Gussie's heart somersaulted. 'You did?' She was pleased that he had wanted to have news of her but fearful of what Bette might have told him. Gussie had made her *promise* on the Holy Bible, but Bette was unreliable when she'd had a drop too much.

'I saw Bette,' he said carefully.

Suddenly Gussie's joy evaporated. The tone of his voice said it all. He *knew* about Tess! Bette had betrayed her. Gussie felt choked with rage. Bette of all people had let her down. She couldn't speak, waiting for the worst. Her rage cooled as quickly as it had boiled, to be replaced by the conviction that he would blame her. She knew it.

138

He said, 'Bette said you were going to marry an Italian artist. Very rich. Young. I was so – so pleased for you.'

Gussie faltered in her condemnation of Bette. So she hadn't mentioned Tess? Was that *all* Bette had told him? She clutched at the faint hope. 'Leo? Yes, he wanted me to marry him. He was a dear man but then . . .' She looked at him steadily. 'And he knew exactly what I was, you know.' That was true, anyway.

Harry had the grace to look embarrassed. 'He was no fool then. Not like me.'

'He was a gentleman.'

'Not like me,' he repeated.

She had hurt him and now she was sorry. Why did she say these dreadful things?

'You were a policeman, Harry,' she told him. 'An artist is more – more *bohemian*. Not so precise and – he had no rules and regulations. No superintendent looking over his shoulder. He was a free spirit.'

Oh yes, he was all those things, but she had said 'No' when he refused to accept Tess. Poor Leo. Bette had said she was mad to let him go, but what did Bette know about the workings of Gussie's heart? Gussie hardly understood them herself. She had only known that the one man for her was Harry Parr. If she couldn't have Harry, at least she could keep his child.

She said, 'I don't think I would have liked Venice. All those waterways; it could be damp. He understood. We parted as friends.'

'So – you are alone again – a widow. How do you manage – or shouldn't I ask? It's really none of my business. It's just so exciting. Seeing you again, and you looking so well and happy.'

Gussie said, 'I should never have let you fall in love with me, Harry. It wasn't fair. I could see how it would end. Whenever we got too excited at school, Sister Everistes used to say, "It will all end in tears." And I knew with us that it would.'

'Don't reproach yourself. It's over and done with, and we've both survived.'

Gussie sighed deeply.

He asked, 'So how do you earn your living – or is a sea-captain's pension enough?'

Gussie cursed silently. Just as she thought they were over the worst ... She heard herself say, 'I teach the piano. Private lessons. Mostly children but a few adults.'

'The piano! Good heavens, Gussie, you're full of surprises!' he laughed. 'I didn't know you could play ... Another cup of coffee?' He looked at the tray. 'I say, the biscuits are rather on the dull side. Perhaps we—' He broke off, catching the eye of a passing steward. 'Could we have a few petits fours?'

'Certainly, sir. I'll fetch you some.'

He brought them a plateful of marzipan fondants and chocolate leaves, and while they enjoyed the little feast Harry asked, 'So you have a home of your own?'

Gussie's fondant went down the wrong way and she prolonged the cough while she considered her answer. In fact, she had some good rooms in an expensive part of town.

'A nice little place,' she agreed. 'And you?'

'I live in a room adjacent to my office. Snug as a bug, as they say.'

She noted the 'I' with a sense of relief. A companionable silence developed and Gussie began to relax. They had talked about the past without recrimination and were still friends. It had all been very civilised.

Suddenly Harry said, 'I didn't realise Bette had a child. You never told me. A nice little thing. Pretty hair.'

Holy Mother of God! Stricken, Gussie looked at him, her confidence shattered. He *knew* about Tess – or else he was making an informed guess. He had seen the likeness: her father's curls and her mother's green eyes. Panic edged closer. Had Harry known all along? Had he been playing games with her? Letting her think her secret was safe until he played his trump card? Damn him, then! Gussie rallied quickly. Wasn't defence the best form of attack? She leaned forward.

'If you think you're going to upset me, Harry Parr, let me tell you you're wrong. I've been through too much for you to hurt me again. Tess was—'

He looked astonished. 'What have I said?' he protested.

'Tess was my child and well you know it. Bette told you, didn't she? Isn't she the blabbermouth! Your child and mine, Harry. Oh yes! Didn't you see it in her lovely little face? Those curls everyone admired? You recognised her. So she was *our* daughter. Now that's what you wanted to hear, isn't it – but if – if you think—'

She faltered to a stop. Harry's expression had undergone a dramatic change. His eyes widened. 'That child was *our* daughter? But Bette said . . . *our* child? But we didn't – except that one time – oh my God, Gussie! After *that*!'

Gussie drew back, shocked in her turn. She had made a terrible mistake. 'Oh, Harry!' she faltered. He *hadn't* known . . . The phrase rang in her head. He hadn't recognised his own child.

Harry was very pale. She looked at him anxiously

He said, 'You had my child, Gussie, after I forced myself on you. God Almighty!' He stared at her, white-faced. 'There hasn't been a day since when I haven't hated myself for what I did. I've wanted to ask your forgiveness but—'

'I forgave you, Harry. I understood.'

'You *forgave* me?' His grey eyes were dark with shame. 'Maybe you did – but I could never forgive myself. I treated you no better than those men I so despised. And I *hurt* you, Gussie.'

'You loved me, but I'd humiliated you. And you'd fallen from that pedestal of yours. You couldn't deal with any of that.' Her voice was low as she said, 'I understand men, Harry. Have you forgotten?'

'I'm so sorry,' he whispered.

'You needn't be. How could either of us be sorry it happened when it turned out so beautifully? Tess was a darling child. The light of my life.'

'But you didn't *tell* me.'

'Would you have wanted to know? How would you have explained a *daughter* to that superintendent of yours? I thought you were in enough trouble. I didn't want to make you the laughing-stock of the entire force.'

'But Bette said . . .'

'Bette lied because I told her to. "If he ever comes back, tell him she's your daughter," I said, and that's exactly what she did.'

Gussie felt breathless, suddenly tearful. So now he knew. Was she pleased or sorry? He looked shocked, as well he might. Put that in your pipe and smoke it, Harry Parr.

His expression changed. 'You said "*was*" . . . Gussie?'

Gussie leaned forward and took his hand. He had to know the

141

rest, she thought, and that would be the worst. 'Now, Harry darling, I have to tell you this. Tess was *killed*, Harry. She's dead. She died just before her sixth birthday. I was with her in the hospital and – oh, Harry!' Her composure deserted her and tears began to flow down her cheeks. 'I wasn't to blame, Harry. I loved her more than anything in the world, and I was saving up to take her away from there – and you mustn't blame Bette because she looked after Tess and loved her. She was a happy child, Harry. Always laughing. Don't ever think otherwise.'

She was vaguely aware that Harry had left his chair to crouch on the floor beside her. He was holding her hands. She looked down into his face and in it saw the face of her daughter as she lay in the hospital bed. The lovely grey eyes had been wide open, but Tess was hardly breathing.

Gussie forced herself to continue. 'I got there about an hour before she died. Bette was with her. White as a sheet, she was, and shaking like a leaf. But Harry, Tess knew that we were there. I held her hand, and the doctor came and told us there was no hope at all. He said that her head was so badly damaged, but she was in no pain. He didn't want to put her through any surgery. "Let her die in peace". That was what he said. They were so kind, Harry. Her head was bandaged but they hadn't shaved her hair. I was glad of that.' Her lips trembled. Harry had a right to hear how it had ended for the daughter he would never know. 'It was a horse-bus, Harry, that knocked her down – but don't blame the driver, the poor man. He was beside himself with grief and shaking something terrible. It was an accident. Tess was walking with Bette and a cat ran out into the road. She snatched her hand away from Bette's and ran after it and . . .' She stopped.

Harry was kissing her hands, she noticed, and the room had gone very quiet. Peering over his shoulder, she saw that the sad little scene had attracted attention from the other passengers. Poor Harry, she thought. She'd embarrassed him again.

A steward materialised beside them. 'If madam is a little upset, sir, may I suggest a small brandy?'

Harry said, 'Make it two – and thanks.'

Gussie felt a large handkerchief being thrust into her hand and she began to wipe her tears. She said, 'I must tell you now. I was shopping when it happened – fetching the pie and mash for our

142

evening meal. I wasn't . . . with a man, if that's what you're thinking.' He began to protest but she rushed on, 'I wasn't neglecting her, Harry. I was at work. I had a proper job in a laundry. As soon as I knew that I was in the family way I gave up – the other. I was shopping.'

The brandy arrived and Gussie sipped it gratefully. Seeing that she was recovering, Harry sat back in his chair and drank his in one gulp. Around them, people resumed their conversations.

'I don't blame you at all, Gussie,' he said. 'You were marvellous. Bringing up a child on your own.' He leaned forward. 'Brave and wonderful, Gussie. I wish I'd been there to help you through it all. I've properly messed things up, haven't I, one way or another? But at least you've made a new life for yourself. I'm full of admiration.'

Gussie winced inwardly and took another sip of brandy.

He said, 'It's never too late to make a fresh start, is it? It shouldn't be.'

Gussie blinked. 'A fresh start?' What was he talking about?

'You and me, Gussie. We could at least *think* about it, couldn't we? We've both been through difficult times. Maybe we're wiser than we were then. We could take things a day at a time. We could help each other, couldn't we, Gussie?'

She couldn't breathe. A fresh start? After all the *lies* she'd just told him about her sea-faring husband? But just suppose he never knew they were lies. Maybe she could confess in church and be given absolution – and then if God had forgiven her maybe the lies wouldn't count for so much . . . Suppose she *could* carry it off? Just suppose she let things happen as Harry suggested, a day at a time . . . But that was what she had done last time, and where had it got her?

'Gussie?'

She stared at him, speechless. What were her alternatives? She either stood by her false story of respectability, or she admitted that she had spent much of the past hour lying to him again.

He said, 'Please, Gussie, just think about it. We made mistakes last time, but this time we could get it right. Say you'll think about it.'

'I will, Harry.' She dabbed her eyes one last time and returned his handkerchief. She mustn't be asked any more questions, she decided. Then she couldn't tell any more lies. She longed for the seclusion of her own cabin. While she was wondering how to leave him, a shadow fell across the table. She saw Harry's expression change as he looked up. A heavy hand descended on her shoulder and Gussie's heart sank.

She knew without looking up that it was Clive Nicolson.

He said, 'Ah! Mrs Malone!'

She glanced up. 'Good evening, Mr Nicolson. I think we're in for a squall later tonight.'

'According to the captain's report we are, yes.' He looked at Harry with an enquiring lift of his eyebrows.

Gussie detected a hint of disapproval. 'Mr Parr, Mr Nicolson,' she said, keeping her tone neutral. 'Mr Parr is an old friend of mine.' She looked at Harry and was surprised to see that he, in his turn, was looking unfriendly.

Harry said, 'A pleasant surprise for us to meet in this way.'

Gussie willed Clive Nicolson to leave them but, as though reading her mind, he looked her straight in the eye and said, 'I'm at a loose end this evening. My wife is feeling a little unwell.'

Neither of them invited him to join them, and the omission was very obvious. Instead of taking the hint, however, he said, 'Perhaps I could buy us all a drink.'

Damn you! thought Gussie. He was deliberately frustrating them. They must either suffer his intrusion or be discourteous. She was terrified that if he spent any time with them he would say something, deliberately or accidentally, that would arouse Harry's suspicions. She stood up, smiling.

'I must refuse your kind offer. I was just saying to Mr Parr that the sea is making me feel a little queasy. Bed is the answer, I think.' She threw Harry an imploring look.

Harry was forced to say, 'Well, just one then, Mr Nicolson. Then I have a report to finish before I go to sleep.'

Clive Nicolson said, 'Fine with me, old chap. What's it to be then?'

'A whisky, please. No ice.'

'Couldn't agree more. Nasty American habit, ice. Kills the flavour.' He smiled at Gussie. 'I hope you sleep well.'

He put the slightest emphasis on the word 'sleep' and the hair on the back of her neck rose. She said, 'Thank you, Mr Nicolson,' and crossed her fingers.

They watched him walk to the bar.

Gussie said, 'I'm sorry to desert you, Harry. I just can't bear the man!'

'Don't worry about me. I'll get rid of him right away.' He stood, holding out his hand for hers. 'Shall we meet again? I don't want to lose you again, and it's a big ship.'

Gussie told him the number of her cabin. 'Just in case,' she said, then blushed. 'Not for – that is, I don't mean – what I mean is, if we *shouldn't* happen to meet.'

He asked, 'What about having breakfast together? There's a permanently spare chair at my table.'

'I'd love that. I'll look for you. Good night, Harry.'

With a final anxious look towards the bar, she hurried out on deck. She needed air, she told herself. That had been too close for comfort. And now she had had to leave the two of them together. Harry would be discreet, she knew, but would Nicolson? The deck was damp with windborne spray and smelled of wood and whatever the deck-hands cleaned it with. There was nobody else about as she made her way unsteadily towards the rail, which felt cold and damp. In the glow of one of the lights, the nearest lifeboat creaked in its davits, and she heard jazz music tinkling faintly from somewhere within the ship. Beyond the rail the sea loomed darkly and the rising wind howled. The ship heaved and she clutched at the rail to steady herself, grateful for the cool but bracing air that blew across her face. Below her in the gloom the white foam raced by.

She frowned. Why had Harry been so hostile towards Nicolson? Was it jealousy? She shrugged. The adrenalin which had carried her through the ordeal now waned, leaving her deeply fatigued. But she clung to the memory of Harry's reaction. He hadn't said a word against her; he had called her brave and won-derful. Marvellous, too. Was she all those things? If so, it was news to her. If only Nicolson had kept away. Then she could still have been with Harry. Through all the lonely years she had for-bidden herself to hope that they would ever see each other again. Now they had done so, and all she wanted was to be near him. He had kissed her hands, but only because she was crying. There was no way she must pretend that it meant anything more. She swallowed hard.

'Pull yourself together, Gussie!' she told herself. She craved her own bed and the privacy that went with it. She wanted to be able to think about Harry without interruption, but she couldn't go back to her cabin because Nicolson would come to her. Money or no money, she wouldn't entertain him . . . And why on earth had she given Harry her cabin number? She cringed with embarrassment. She had meant it innocently enough, but he would think the worst! Suppose he came to her cabin – could she refuse him? She braced herself again as the ship struck a larger wave than usual and a shudder ran the length of her hull. She shook her head.

She said, 'Damn you, Nicolson!' and then crossed herself.

'I hope you're not talking about me?'

Horribly startled, she turned to find him standing at the rail beside her. 'You frightened me!' she protested. 'Creeping up on me like that. I thought the two of you were having a drink.'

He shrugged. 'Your friend is a quick drinker. Or else he didn't like me.'

Gussie said nothing.

He put an arm round her waist, but she moved away.

'What's the matter with you?' he asked. 'New boyfriend, is that it? Throwing me over, are you, before we've even started?'

Gussie drew herself up. 'He's not my boyfriend. I told you, he's an old friend. Of the family.'

'You're such a bad liar, Gussie Malone!'

'And you aren't, I suppose?'

He didn't answer. Instead he winced and put a hand to his stomach. A small groan escaped him.

Serve you right, she thought uncharitably. Or was he faking it? Perhaps he saw her as a soft touch.

He closed his eyes, breathing heavily. 'Stella says I should see the doctor. Maybe she's right. It gets worse, not better.'

'Probably indigestion.'

'You're all heart, Gussie!'

She listened to herself, appalled. How on earth had they descended to this level? He did seem to be in pain. Bette's words rang in her ears. 'It doesn't pay to upset the clients.' She bit back

146

further insults. She had to persuade him to abandon their arrangement without alienating him.

Another couple passed them, swaying and staggering on the tilting deck, laughing at their own antics. The man said, 'I wouldn't stay at the rail too long!'

Gussie said, 'We're just going inside.'

She would tell Nicolson that she was feeling seasick and couldn't see him as planned. She searched her mind for a conciliatory way to say so, but before she could speak Nicolson changed *his* tone.

'Forgive me, Gussie. Bit of the old green-eyed monster, I suppose.'

She hid her surprise.

'The truth is, I want to ask you a favour. I'm a bit short of the old readies at the moment—'

'I never lend money!' she said sharply.

He held up his hand and went straight on, '—and I wondered if you could see your way to – well, to lending me some. Please, Gussie.' He grinned. 'For old times' sake!'

She was outraged. 'Old times' sake? Heavens above, you've the cheek of the devil! We only met yesterday! Lend you some *money*! Do I look like the Bank of England or something? I have to *earn* my money, or had you forgotten? I have to pay for my passage and it doesn't come cheap.'

'I know, Gussie. I wouldn't ask—'

'*No*, Mr Nicolson. Is that plain enough for you? I will not lend you any money.' Oh, *why* was her life so complicated, she wondered ruefully.

For a moment he regarded her in silence until she became nervous.

At last, he said, 'I thought to myself, if I were desperate there's no one on the ship who'd lend me so much as a farthing – except Mrs Malone! You're my only hope. I've got a game tonight and I'm on a winning streak.'

Oh God! thought Gussie. Does he take me for an *eejit*? If he's on a winning streak, he'd be winning and would *have* money. He wouldn't be needing me. She was thinking fast. It didn't appear likely that she'd ever see her money back, but his request might be useful. If she could agree to lend him some money, maybe he'd agree to forget the assignation they had made for later tonight. But her own situation was hardly rosy, and she had been relying on the night's transaction to put some money in her bank account. Think, Gussie! she told herself. The most important thing was that Harry should never guess that she was still a whore. If there was to be the slightest chance that the two of them might yet make a go of it, she had to be what she pretended – respectable. She must not allow Nicolson to drop the smallest hint about her reason for being aboard.

The ship gave another lurch and she tightened her grip on the rail.

'I haven't got much,' she told him.

'How much?' Seeing that she remained unconvinced, he said, 'I'll give you a share of the winnings, Gussie. How's that? Not just the original stake.'

She asked, 'How much?' and felt ashamed.

He hesitated. 'Ten per cent of my winnings on top of the loan.'

'It's not enough.' She was amazed at her impudence.

'Fifteen, then. I'll give you fifteen per cent on top of the original loan. I can't say fairer than that, dammit!'

Gussie agreed with him. But suppose he lost it all? She'd get fifteen per cent of nothing, and she'd lose her stake money. She longed to say 'No.' She longed to have nothing further to do with him, but she couldn't afford to do anything rash.

She said, 'Double or quits! If you lose, I don't see my money again. If you win, you double it.'

His laugh was genuine. 'Double or quits? God, Gussie, you really are the limit! D'you know that?' He thrust his hands into his pockets and shook his head as though in despair.

'I mean it.'

'Done!' he said.

She said, 'But if I lend you money you must stay away from me. I don't want you turning up at my cabin. Our earlier arrangement is cancelled. Definitely cancelled. D'you understand that, Mr Nicolson?'

He looked at her in surprise. 'Oh, it's like that, is it? It's Mr Parr! Who are you kidding, Gussie? I see your game. What is it? Richer than me, is he? Better between the sheets?'

'Don't talk like that!' she said angrily. Not about Harry, she added silently. 'You're not fit to polish his boots!'

'And you are? Come over all "holier than thou", have we?'

'Mind your own business!' She turned to move away, but he caught hold of her arm.

'Suppose I was to tell this fancy man of yours—'

Before she knew what she was doing, Gussie had lashed out at him. The ship rolled as she did so and her fist passed close to his ear. Gussie stumbled.

He said, 'Oops-a-daisy!' and saved her from a fall.

She jerked free from his grasp, furious and frightened. 'Don't you dare threaten me, Nicolson! Just don't try it! If you say a word to—'

'Now, now! Don't get cross.' He looked at her with amusement, which made her even angrier. 'Let's not declare war, Gussie. I'm an understanding sort of chap. If I have to choose between a woman and a win at cards I'd choose the win, any time. I'm a realist, you see. A woman is like a bus. If you miss one, there'll be another along shortly.' He laughed. 'So what d'you say, eh? Come on, Gussie! My lips are sealed. I swear on my mother's grave.' He grinned. 'Be a dear. Double or quits. I agree.'

Gussie wavered. She could not risk making an enemy of him. 'All right, Mr Nicolson. I'll lend you what I can, but I need my train fare and a cab home. I can let you have fifty guineas, that's all.'

'Oh, Christ!' He shook his head.

Her anger flared again. 'Take it or leave it!'

'I'll take it.'

'Don't bother to thank me,' she said caustically. At that moment the ship's movement threw her against him and she found his arms around her. His face was close to her ear and he whispered, 'If I win, we could celebrate, couldn't we? You and me. Forget lover-boy!'

She struggled to free herself. 'No, we bloody can't!' she told him. 'I don't want you anywhere near my cabin. If you win, you give me my money. That's it.' She glared at him, trying unsuccessfully to judge his mood. She hoped he was just tormenting her, but if he meant it . . . oh, damn the man! She pulled away from him, finding her footing unsteadily. The approaching squall was almost on them. 'Wait here. I'll bring you the money.'

'I'll come with you to your cabin.'

'*No*! Are you *deaf*?' She struggled to keep her balance. 'Wait right here.'

He shrugged and she staggered back to the door and stepped through it, tugging it to behind her. The wind had tousled her hair and she pushed the loose strands back into place. Making her way back to her cabin, she kept a wary eye out for Harry Parr. Fate was on her side for once, however, and she reached the cabin without meeting anyone she knew. She took the money from its hiding-place in her hatbox, wrote an IOU for Nicolson to sign, then set out again to find him.

'What's this?' He stared at the slip of paper she offered him. 'An IOU? You've got a damned nerve!'

'Just sign it before I change my mind,' she told him.

He signed it, muttering under his breath, and Gussie slipped it into her pocket. As she finally walked away from him, she felt a distinct lightening of her anxieties. She might never see her money again, but it was a good investment. If it meant that Harry remained ignorant of her true profession, it was money well spent.

Chapter Eight

Stella approached the bartender with a fixed smile. 'A bottle of whisky, please,' she said, busying herself with her purse.

The bartender said, 'I'm sorry, ma'am. We're only allowed to sell individual drinks.'

'But my husband wants a bottle. He's confined to his cabin and—'

'I'm sorry, ma'am. Maybe the shop?'

'It's closed,' she said. 'You must know that.'

He shrugged. 'Sorry I can't help you out.'

She looked at him, frowning. Was it her imagination, or was he trying to tell her something else? She asked, 'How much would a whole bottle cost?'

He named a figure.

'And suppose someone was prepared to pay a little more?'

He looked shocked. 'I don't know what you mean but . . .' He smiled and tapped the side of his nose. 'You're tempting me, ma'am, and I've always been open to temptation. Just to help a lady, then.'

Without further ado, he reached below the counter and produced a bottle which he wrapped in paper. She paid a little extra for it and hurried away.

When Stella reached the medical room, she knocked and went straight in. She found the same doctor on duty as on the previous time she called. Now he had his feet up on the desk, reading a thriller. Sheepishly, he put down the novel and moved his feet.

'Doctor Rowse, you'll remember me?'

'Of course. It's Mrs – um. . .'

'Mrs Nicolson. I'm afraid my husband is no better. I was wondering if you could prescribe some more of those painkillers for him? They do help him, poor soul.'

'I don't see why not. Let me see, how many did I give you last time?'

'Twenty,' she said, doubling it. 'They gave him some relief.'

He busied himself at the dispensary, then handed her a small pillbox. 'Twenty. There we are.' He pushed forward a form and, with a stubby finger, indicated where she was to sign for them.

'You've been a great help,' she told him.

Back in her cabin, Stella set to work. In the bathroom, she broke up the pills. In the lounge she opened the whisky, poured a generous helping into a large tumbler and sniffed it.

'Ugh!'

She set it down beside the bed and crossed to the little writing desk. Then she drew a sheet of the ship's notepaper towards her and wrote the date.

Dear Mrs Malone,

By the time you find this letter I shall be at peace. Information has recently come to me about my husband which makes it impossible for me to go on. Soon he will be arrested and no doubt sent to prison for reasons I need not explain. Cowardly though it is, I cannot face living through all that this means. My daughter Abby is my only concern. This letter is to ask you – to beg you – to take care of my little one when I am gone. Please take her back to her grandparents in New York. Mr Harry Parr will give you the address and any information you require. He has all the sordid facts in a report he is writing for my father. He seems very trustworthy and a gentleman. You can rely on him, I'm sure. My parents will reimburse you fully for all your costs – travelling etc. You have been the only real friend I have ever had, and I thank you for that. I also know that you will agree to my last request.

Yours in great tribulation,

Stella Nicolson.

She reread the note, folded it carefully and slipped it into the waiting envelope. Then she took the first large gulp of the whisky. It made her cough and her eyes ran, and it was a moment or two before she could control her breathing. When she was calm she rang for the steward. While she was waiting, she took another drink. It burned her throat but warmed her stomach, and it felt good. She began to feel slightly more in control, more certain that what she was doing was the wisest thing.

She opened the door to the knock and smiled a little shakily at the young stewardess.

'I'd like you to deliver this to Mrs Malone's cabin,' she said.

Was that *her* voice, she wondered, startled. It sounded very unsteady. She blinked at the girl, who took the letter but gave Stella a worried look.

'Are you all right, Mrs Nicolson?'

'Of course.' She put out a hand to steady herself against the door jamb. Her legs were suddenly unwilling to support her. 'It's – it's the sea,' she said.

'Oh, I see. Feeling a bit groggy. Yes, it is getting up a bit, I'm afraid. Let me know if I can help in any way.'

Stella wanted to say 'Thank you' but her mouth refused to function properly, so she simply nodded and closed the door. She took a few deep breaths and thought that feeling light-headed was not as bad as she'd expected. Or maybe she was drunk already? She wasn't used to spirits, but she had to admit that the whisky was making her feel more cheerful. It seemed to blur the edges of her misery and blunt the anger.

Back in the bathroom, she picked up the crushed pills and looked at them. They looked surprisingly innocuous. Rather dry and dusty, she thought, so she would have to swallow it with water. Or whisky. She could not face them now; she was too sober. Later, when she was really drunk. She wondered how quickly they would work. In her present relaxed state she didn't want to go too soon.

First she must finish the whisky and think about her life, and she must try to remember exactly why she was going to die and what would happen next, if anything. She giggled. Not to *her*. Nothing would happen to *her* because it would all be over. No terrible rows, no police arresting Clive, no trial. And her parents

153

wouldn't be able to say, 'We told you so!' Not that she could blame them. They had tried so hard to persuade her that Jerry would make a much better husband than Clive; that Jerry's love for her was no longer brotherly. He had told her the same thing. Why hadn't she listened to them, she wondered for the hundredth time. She groaned, knowing the answer. Gerald had been the familiar face. Clive had been the exciting newcomer. *The unknown quantity*. Life before Clive had been safe and predictable. And more than that, she had been at the age where she was tired of taking parental advice.

A timid, dutiful child, always aiming to please, she had growm into a timid woman. Clive had mocked her gently, calling her 'Papa's little poodle'. He had encouraged her to think for herself, to climb out of the rut. She was excited by the prospect of what he called freedom. Finally Clive urged her to take a risk. Marrying him had been the ultimate risk. Then, of course, his attitude towards her had changed.

She sat down at the writing table and put her head in her hands. Her thoughts were becoming elusive . . . vague . . . almost *pleasant*.

Gerald would miss her and so would her parents, but they would get over it in time. Abby – she mustn't think about Abby. She had made provision for her daughter, and that was all she could do. She had ensured that Abby would grow up in a decent environment where the news of her father's treachery might be kept from her until she was older.

Stella poured herself another glass of whisky and collapsed on to the bed. Now, perhaps, she should take the pills. Breathing heavily, she stared across the room toward the bathroom which now seemed a long way away. She began to sip the whisky, then she leaned back against the pillows and began to smile. She would get thoroughly drunk before she took the pills because that way she would hardly notice what she was doing. That way she could die peacefully. That way she could slip away in . . . in a warm . . . in a warm . . . hazy sleep . . .

Half an hour later the bottle was empty and Stella gazed at it with something of relief. Now she could do it . . . whatever it was . . . Oh . . . yes . . .

She muttered, 'In the bathroom.'

With maddening slowness, she slid from the bed and stood up. Her knees buckled and she fell against the bed. What on earth was she doing?

After a moment it came back to her. 'Bathroom,' she whispered. She persevered. With a superhuman effort she stood up again. Slowly and erratically she made her way towards the bathroom.

Clive drew a deep breath and waited for the pain to subside. When it did, he assumed what he hoped was a confident expression and rapped sharply on the door. Hearing a shout from within, he entered. Five faces turned towards him in obvious surprise. Clive recognised Hemmings, Brett and Cressey. The latter was landed gentry, larded with family money. Brett was new money; owned a racing stable somewhere near Littlehampton. Two of the men were strangers. Hemmings scowled.

Clive said, 'Clive Nicolson.'

The strangers said 'Waverly' and 'Price' respectively. They looked at him with suspicion.

Clive smiled. 'Sorry I'm late.'

There was a short silence while Clive held his breath. They *must* allow him to play. And he *must* win or else he was in serious trouble. The five men were already seated round the table. Brett was holding the cards, with the spare set to his left. A pile of wooden 'chips' waited on a card table behind Cressey. So, he was banker.

Hemmings flushed an angry red. 'You're too late.'

Clive pretended surprise. 'But Brett hasn't dealt yet.' If he ever met Hemmings alone in a dark alley . . .

Hemmings said, 'You're got a nerve, Nicolson, coming here.'

'And your conscience is clear, I suppose!'

Brett, unsure, looked at his companions. No one volunteered an opinion and he hesitated.

Clive knew it was now or never. He crossed to the sixth chair and picked it up. There was room for him beside Hemmings, but nothing would persuade him to sit next to *that* thug. None of the players moved to accommodate him.

Clive said, 'Well?'

Brett looked anxious. 'Well, gentlemen?'

Another player meant more money in the pot, and they were all greedy.

Clive allowed his gaze to linger on each of them in a way that was distinctly challenging. He asked, 'Do you want my money or don't you?'

Suddenly Price moved his chair along. Clive set his down in the space and sat, hiding his relief. Now he was opposite Hemmings. He could keep an eye on the man.

Brett said, 'We didn't expect you. Hemmings thought—'

Hemmings said, 'I heard you were indisposed.' His mouth twitched.

'Not me.' Clive smiled cheerfully. 'Perhaps you *hoped* I was.'

'I heard someone had given you a bit of a pasting. Give that man a cigar! I thought.' Hemmings' tone was scornful.

Clive fought down an urge to throttle his tormentor. He had decided that not so much as a groan would pass his lips, no matter how severe the pain. He would not give Hemmings the satisfaction of knowing that he'd inflicted such an injury.

He forced a careless laugh. 'Well, the money's burning a hole in my pocket.'

Hemmings said, 'I'm surprised you've got any!'

Clive thought, 'No thanks to you! You thieving bastard' and mentally blessed Gussie. It would never do to let them know just how little he had. If his luck didn't hold in the early stages, he'd be out with a flea in his ear.

He asked, 'So, are we going to play or sit here trading insults?'

Brett said, 'Fine by me!' and shuffled the pack with quick, expert movements. He handed the cards to Clive who now sat on his right. Clive cut them and returned the pack. Brett made a final shuffle.

'Here we go!' he said and dealt swiftly, flicking the cards deftly at each player.

Clive gathered his and spread them into a fan. Please, God! he thought. He picked up his cards one at a time – the queen of hearts was followed by the eight of hearts. Could make a straight flush, but he'd need the three hearts between them and that meant *serious* luck. He willed his hand not to tremble as he reached for his third card. Another queen, this time of spades – so the straight flush was out, but with two more queens he would have four of a kind.

Oh, God! His luck was surely going to run with him. He kept his face expressionless while his stomach churned with disappointment. There was still a chance. It all depended on which cards the others received. *Please*, God. Another card – the ace of clubs. Damn. But at least he had two queens. A third would give him three of a kind. Not brilliant, but he'd go with it. He glanced round at the other players but their faces, too, registered no emotion. One last card: it was the queen of diamonds! God Almighty! He had three of a kind! A cramp in his stomach grew in intensity, but Clive steeled himself to ignore the pain. Forget everything except the game. There could be no distractions. Hiding his excitement behind an impassive expression, he glanced enquiringly at Brett.

Brett caught the look and said, 'Jokers are wild.'

One of the highlights of the ship's entertainment programme was the concert in the main saloon. The ship's orchestra supplied the music, but the various acts were provided by the more talented among the passengers. People from all walks of life including show business travelled to and from America on the ocean liners and the *Mauretania*, as the fastest of them, carried more than her fair share of celebrities. These illustrious beings occupied many of the first-class suites and could occasionally be seen in the dining room or taking brisk exercise along the deck. They were never averse to going on stage, were generous with their time and, without exception, performed without payment. For the talented amateurs among the passengers, it was simply the chance for a moment's glory or their contribution to the success of the voyage.

As usual, details of the night's programme had been circulated well in advance and the saloon was filled almost to capacity. Harry Parr entered quietly and sat down near the back. He had seen Nicolson enter Brett's cabin for what he assumed was another poker game so, for the moment, Harry considered his time his own. He clapped dutifully as an elderly man finished a monologue about duty and honour. As the man left the stage, the Master of Ceremonies reappeared.

'Our next item is one we will all enjoy. Miss Charity Holness is well known in the north of England for her spirited renditions of the latest and most popular ballards. She is currently returning after a successful debut in New York. Let's give a very beautiful lady a very warm welcome!'

He led the applause as a slim young woman in a dark green gown made her way on to the stage and into the spotlight. She caught the eye of the conductor of the orchestra and they struck up the introductory bars.

Harry listened distractedly, his mind still on Nicolson. Hemmings was no doubt one of the party, so there might be further trouble later. And where, he wondered, had Nicolson's stake come from? According to his wife, Hemmings stole it all when he attacked him. Curious.

He searched the audience, expecting to find Stella Nicolson and Gussie. To his surprise there was no sign of either of them. He frowned. Then he spotted Mary Crisford with Abby, who was no doubt being allowed to stay up as a special treat. Perhaps Gussie and Stella Nicolson would come in later. Presumably they were together somewhere. He would wait a little longer, and then if they didn't appear he would go in search of them. At the back of his mind Stella Nicolson's last remark buzzed intermittently like a warning bell but, for once, he ignored his intuition and pushed the doubts away.

He wanted time to think about his daughter, Tess. The knowledge that he had had a child brought into focus yearnings he had long ignored: the desire for a wife and family and all that it meant. A shared life; other people to consider; the giving and receiving of affection. A solitary life had its advantages and he had managed to convince himself that being alone suited him. But it didn't. Harry was often lonely, and immersing himself in his work did nothing to solve that particular problem. He had visited his mother regularly until her premature death had left a gap in his life. He sighed.

The song ended and the applause was tumultuous. The singer was followed by a magician, who was in turn followed by an American comedian headed for stardom on the West End stage. Still Harry saw no sign of Gussie or Stella Nicolson, and he began to wonder if perhaps he should go in search of them. But *why*, he reasoned? He had no right to intrude on their privacy. They were probably having a womanly heart-to-heart somewhere quiet and might resent an interruption.

'And now, ladies and gentlemen, another high-spot of the evening. A selection of seaside songs from our resident vocalist Mr John Stamford, who will be supported by our very own delightfully talented dance team, the Mavis Trant Steppers! So – a roll on the drums and . . . here they *are*!' He withdrew once more into the wings as the singer moved forward and six young ladies ran on to the stage to form a semi-circle round him. They were dressed in knee-length bathing suits and saucy matching hats.

Stamford's voice was surprisingly good and the dancers well rehearsed and professional. Harry was surprised to find himself enjoying the number. When it ended he was astonished to see Mary Crisford jump to her feet shouting, 'Bravo! Well done, John!' Abby also stood and waved her hand and the singer, grinning broadly, gave them a special bow.

Harry thought, 'I wonder if Stella Nicolson knows about that' and was immediately reminded once again about Stella Nicolson. He had just decided to go in search of her when Gussie appeared at the top of the main staircase, looking round. She caught his eye, and Harry's heart raced at the sight of her, but he realised suddenly that she was looking distinctly flustered. She was waving an envelope and mouthing something, and her expression made him leap to his feet and hurry up the stairs two at a time.

As the orchestra came into its own and began to play a selection of 'Tales From The Vienna Woods', Gussie handed him a letter. She talked while he tried to concentrate on the wording.

'A stewardess gave this to me. It can only mean one thing, Harry. I rushed to Stella's cabin but the door's locked, of course, and she won't open it – assuming that she's in there. Nicolson might be there—'

'He's playing poker. They're certainly not together. Wait here.'

'But Harry, where—'

He ran to his cabin and let himself in. Rushing to his briefcase, he opened it and pulled out a bunch of skeleton keys and wires which he thrust into his pocket. Then he ran back to Gussie and together they hurried to the Nicolsons' cabin.

Gussie stared at the keys.

'What every private detective should have!' Harry told her. He hoped no one would come along while he was breaking in. If the cabin was empty, it was going to look very bad. He tried several keys without success while Gussie stood by, almost wringing her hands with impatience. He muttered, 'Come on, you little blighter! Open up!'

After what seemed a long time, the door opened and he stepped into the room.

Harry exclaimed, 'Jesus Christ!'

Gussie crossed herself, her lips moving soundlessly in a prayer. Stella lay on the floor, face up, one arm thrown out, one leg bent beneath her. Fearfully, they knelt beside her.

Gussie asked, 'Is she—'

'No. Not yet.'

Stella was breathing noisily and seemed to be murmuring something. Her hair was dishevelled and her face was flushed; there was a sheen of perspiration on her forehead. Harry cursed under his breath. Subconsciously he had *known* something like this would happen. He should never have parted with that unpleasant information.

Gussie snatched up Stella's hand and shook her. 'Stella! Will you wake up now? It's me, Gussie. And Harry Parr. Stella! Open your eyes now, there's a good girl. *Stella*!' She stepped back to allow Harry to look at her. 'At least she's alive,' she said.

Harry said, 'She's drunk! She reeks of whisky.' He glanced around and saw the bottle. 'There. It must have dropped out of her hand.'

'Then she hasn't – I mean, in the note she says she's going to end it all.'

'She's half-way there!' Harry said grimly. 'I think we should call for the doctor.' He looked at Gussie for confirmation, but she hesitated.

'If she's only drunk, maybe we could walk it off. They did that with me, when Tess died. I wanted to drink myself to death; I drank a whole bottle of brandy.'

Harry hid his dismay at the picture her words conjured up. He shook Stella gently, but she didn't react. 'I suppose we should notify her husband. If she dies . . .' But how would Nicolson react if he knew what Stella had attempted? Not with compassion, he thought.

Gussie said, 'If she lives, she'll feel guilty for wanting to die and angry because we've prevented it. With a husband like Nicolson, she's going to feel a whole lot worse.'

Harry nodded. There was an ache in his chest at the thought of Gussie's sufferings after the death of their child. If only he had been there . . . Guilt and regret settled within him.

Gussie was saying, 'Let's give it a try first. I'll see if I can get her on her feet. You fetch some coffee from the bar.'

'Suppose she's taken something else?'

They both looked round, but saw nothing suspicious.

Stella's eyes fluttered and she murmured, 'Mama?'

Gussie said, 'It's Gussie, dear, and Mr Parr. You're going to be fine.'

Harry said, 'OK. We'll do what you suggest. Are you sure you can manage her?'

But Gussie was already lifting the semi-conscious woman from the bed, raising her head, slipping an arm under her shoulders, talking to her sharply. She gave Harry a quick glance. 'I can manage,' she told him, then returned to her task.

Harry left her to it and headed down the corridor at a steady run. With unwonted clarity he remembered the night Tess had been conceived; the night he had abandoned Gussie; the only night when he and Gussie had been lovers. No! He closed his eyes briefly. 'Being lovers' was hardly an appropriate description of the cruel way he had forced himself upon her, mad with self-pity and wanting only to punish her for the humiliation he had sustained.

Earlier that day, his superintendent had been coldly supercilious. '. . . I find it incredible that one of my officers could be duped so easily. Doesn't say much for your intelligence, Parr, does it? A common street-walker! Made a proper fool out of you, didn't she! Pathetic, women like her. Wanton. The dregs of humanity . . . Brings the force into disrepute . . . You've let down your fellow officers . . .' To the young Harry, the tirade had seemed interminable.

He had stood through it all without uttering a single word in his own defence. All he could have said was, 'I didn't know, sir.' With hindsight he *had* thought the houseful of women rather odd, but they'd made him welcome and had been friendly enough. The few men he had encountered had been explained away as

'Lottie's brother' or 'Delia's cousin'. He had never doubted Gussie's word. He had enjoyed the relaxed friendship of the other women. None of them had propositioned him, and Gussie herself had remained chaste throughout their friendship. He had imagined her a virgin, for God's sake!

His superintendent's words, however, had driven out all that. Learning the dreadful truth had been traumatic. The next day he went to his sergeant and offered to resign. He had been refused. 'Learn by your mistakes, lad!' he had said.

A cold sweat broke out on Harry's forehead as he relived the ordeal. It had left him disillusioned, anguished and burning for revenge. When he found Gussie he had refused to listen to anything she tried to say in her own defence. He had struck her across the face; had called her filthy whore. Dragging her into a dark alley, he had slammed her against the wall . . . Oh God, did she still remember? If so, how could she have forgiven him?

At the bar he leaned against the counter, momentarily disorientated. Poor, sweet Gussie. Tearing at her clothes he had forced himself upon her, ignoring her anguished pleas – and, in a deliberate insult, had then thrust money into her trembling hand. In a blind fury he had run from her, terrified that he would kill her if he stayed a moment longer.

'What can I get you, sir?'

Harry swallowed hard. Out of that brutal encounter little Tess had been conceived. He stared around him, adjusting hastily to the present.

The steward asked, 'You all right, sir? You look a bit pale. Choppy sea has that effect.'

'What?' Harry remembered Stella Nicolson! 'I'm fine. I need a large jug of coffee, please, as quickly as possible. Black and strong.'

The barman looked doubtful. 'Dimenhydrinate does the trick quicker, sir,' he began but, seeing the look on Harry's face, he decided not to argue and prepared a tray as requested.

Harry carried the tray with some difficulty, staggering occasionally, intent on reaching the Nicolsons' cabin without mishap. He found Stella sitting unsteadily on the edge of the bed, propped against Gussie's arm. Her neck appeared too weak for the weight of her head, but from time to time she opened her eyes and groaned.

He said, 'Well done, Gussie! She looks a lot better already. Let's see if she can drink anything.'

Harry poured a half cup of coffee and now handed it to Gussie. She held it to Stella's lips. 'Stella, I want you to drink some of this coffee. It'll make you feel better. Open your mouth, Mrs Nicolson. Just take a sip.' She glanced up at Harry. 'It's to be hoped that "His Lordship" doesn't come strolling in.'

Harry said, 'I don't think we'll be seeing him this side of midnight.'

'Well, that's a mercy!'

He hoped Gussie wouldn't wonder how he knew. The fewer people who were aware that he was investigating Nicolson the better. Unless Stella had told Gussie the whole miserable story. He poured some more coffee and handed the cup to Gussie.

Gussie gave him a rueful smile. 'We'd be hard put to explain what we're doing here – oh! Good girl, Stella. She's taken a mouthful.'

Stella began to cough as the hot liquid went down. 'I don't want—' she muttered weakly.

Gussie tutted. 'Don't want it? Now what sort of talk is that, may I ask? Of course you want it, Stella. A nice cup of coffee will make a world of difference. Just you take another little sip . . . Now doesn't that taste just wonderfully reviving? It's going to help that poor head of yours . . .' She smiled at Harry conspiratorially and whispered, 'I think the poor soul is going to be all right!'

Harry, watching them, could imagine Gussie with her young daughter, soothing, coaxing, *cherishing* her. How she must have loved the child! How she must have grieved when Tess was taken from her in that one careless moment. No wonder she married her sea-captain, he thought. Probably yearning for someone to fill the gap in her life. Strange, though, that she was so unwilling to talk about her husband. Probably the sad memories were best kept at bay.

Fifteen minutes later Stella could sit up unaided. At first she found it difficult to focus, but eventually she said, 'Mr Parr?'

'That's me,' he said, smiling encouragement. 'You take it easy, Mrs Nicolson. You – you've had a nasty turn.' The phrase struck him as absurd. He caught Gussie's eye and she was smiling, too.

Stella remained unsmiling. They could see that she was weighing up the situation, remembering. The future she had tried so hard to banish was still ahead of her, with all the events she most dreaded. She stared from one to the other, eyes filled with a dark desperation that Harry could only begin to imagine. When she was finally able to think coherently she stammered, '*Why*, Gussie? I trusted you. You know what I wanted. I don't want to live.'

Gussie took both hands in hers. 'Now, Stella Nicolson, we have some talking to do, but not now. Not tonight.'

'I *want* to die!'

'So you do, you poor dear soul, but that's *now*. Tomorrow or next week you'll be seeing things differently. You'll be thanking me and Mr Parr for saving you from yourself.'

Stella shook her head weakly. 'You can't know what I feel,' she insisted.

Gussie's expression changed. 'Oh, but I *do*, Stella. I've also suffered, and *my* friends pulled *me* through, thank the Lord. Life may look black right now, but it'll get brighter and you'll wonder at yourself for ever thinking such a thing. Sister Everistes used to say "There's light at the end of the darkest tunnel," and she never spoke a truer word.'

Stella began to protest, but Gussie laid a finger across her lips.

'Should I stay, Harry, for a while? She may want to talk. I don't think she's up to it, but it may help her. We daren't just leave her.'

He nodded. 'I'll be in the Verandah Café if you need me.'

Gussie said, 'If Nicolson comes in, I'll say she felt unwell and sent the steward to fetch me. And Harry – thanks for your help. I don't think I could have managed without you.'

Harry thought of all the years when she had done exactly that.

'You'd have managed it, Gussie,' he said. 'You're stronger than you think.'

The concert came to an end with a grand finale. The dancers and the performers formed two semi-circles on the stage and accepted the rapturous applause with modest bows. Then someone waved a hand towards the orchestra and they all stood up with their instruments, and there was more applause. Abby clapped so hard she made her hands ache. Chattering excitedly, the audience began to drift away.

Abby said, 'John was wonderful, wasn't he, Nanny? I do hope you are going to marry him.'

Nanny smiled at her. 'I didn't think he could sing like that – and didn't he look handsome! I think a bow-tie does something for a man, don't you?'

'Yes, I do. It makes them look *manly*.'

Nanny laughed. The seats were emptying fast but Abby remained sitting. She wanted to make the evening last. Just a few more minutes. After the trouble they'd been in, it had been a lovely surprise when Mama said they were forgiven, and that Abby could stay up late for a special treat and they could go to the concert together. For some reason it had to be a secret from Papa, but Abby could keep secrets. She knew hundreds of secrets already. One more would be easy as pie. She knew that Grandpapa had told Grandmama that Papa was a scoundrel and a crook, and had said he would break him if it was the last thing he did. Abby hadn't told anyone that. It had worried her, though, but then they had left for England and Papa was as good as new and hadn't been broken so that was all right. She knew that Uncle Jerry had cried when they left for the dock because she had seen the tears in his eyes. She had seen him try to kiss Mama and she had said, 'Oh, please don't, darling. I couldn't bear it. If you only knew.' Uncle Jerry had said, 'I'll wait for you for ever, Stella. I'll always be here if you need me.' Abby had never told a soul.

Now Nanny said, 'We'll be left here on our own soon! Never mind. John might come round to look for us. We'll wait a few more minutes in case he does.' She smiled at Abby. Nanny was doing a lot of smiling all of a sudden; it made her look very pretty. Abby did wish that she could be as pretty as Nanny, but her nose was too pointed and there was something wrong with her mouth. Papa said it looked like a rosebud, which was worrying.

She swung her legs. At least her hair was the same colour as Nanny's. The lights were coming up again, and already some of the magic of the show was fading.

Abby said, 'I think I'll be a dancer when I grow up. Or else a lady singer. Did you like the lady singer's dress, Nanny? Wasn't it pretty!' Blue, she remembered, with a frill round the collar and another one round the hem. She had had a blue flower in her hair and little blue shoes with sparkly bits.

'Very pretty,' said Nanny, but Abby knew she wasn't really listening.

Suddenly the curtains parted and John walked through. He saw them and his face was transformed by a broad grin. He rushed towards them and Nanny went to meet him. Then he *kissed* her! Abby was astounded. Right out here where *anybody* could see! She pushed herself off the seat and went after Nanny.

John smiled. 'Well, Abby, did you enjoy the concert? Did you like my song?'

Abby nodded. She said, 'You were ever so good. *Ever* so!' This evening he had been transformed in her eyes from a funny little man with his trousers falling down into a kind of god. The kind who can stand on a stage in front of millions and millions of people and sing a song. She had been so proud. She had wanted to stand up and shout, 'I know him! He's going to marry my Nanny!' but of course she couldn't because it wasn't nice to make an exhibition of oneself. Mama had told her that. Still, it was a good feeling. She felt happy and bubbly inside, as though all the bad things were over and the good things were going to happen from now on.

Nanny said, 'Honestly, John, you've got a wonderful voice. Much better than all the others.' She laughed and her face was all pink and glowing. 'And that song! It's one of my favourites.'

'I sang it just for you, Mary. Did you realise that?' He took her hand.

'For me? Oh, *John*!' She looked down at Abby. 'Did you hear that, Abby? He sang it just for me.'

Abby said, 'You are lucky, Nanny,' and wondered if one day a man would sing a song just for *her*. If he did she would certainly marry him – but *not* if he was a scoundrel and a crook. What *was* a crook, she wondered. It was impossible to ask anyone, because then they would know she'd heard and it wouldn't be a secret any more.

John asked, 'So when do you have to be back?'

Nanny said, 'Mrs Nicolson didn't say. She was in a funny mood. She said, "Have a good time. I'm sorry about everything."'

I think she'd been c-r-y-i-n-g.' Nanny glanced at Abby. 'Then she said, "Be good, Mary".'

'Meaning what?'

Nanny shrugged. 'Who knows? It doesn't matter.'

Abby said, 'It means don't do naughty things like tell lies and interrupt your elders.'

For some reason both adults laughed.

'It *does*!' Abby insisted. Sometimes grown-ups could be very silly.

Nanny glanced round at the deserted auditorium. 'What's the time now?'

'Must be after midnight. The show usually runs for a couple of hours. Give or take a few minutes.' He pulled a folded paper from his pocket. 'Mary, I want you to take this.'

Abby felt dizzy. *A love letter*! It must be.

'It's my address in Southampton,' he said. 'My parents' address, I should say. I live at home when I'm not at sea. I'd like you to come to Southampton and meet my mother and father. My pa drives a tram. And my brother Anthony; he's a lot younger than me. And my elder sister Marion. She's married with twin boys; her husband, Dennis, is a good bloke, too. He's just finished his apprenticeship. Shipwright. They'll all love you, I know. As much as I do.' He hesitated. 'And I do, Mary. I love you.'

There was a breathless silence. Abby thought she would burst. He said he *loved* Nanny!

Nanny said, 'Oh, John!' Abby saw her mouth go all wobbly. 'You *love* me? How can you say such a thing? We hardly know each other.'

He kissed Nanny again and said, 'Ever heard of love at first sight? It does happen.'

His eyes are *sparkling*, thought Abby. He looked like a prince and Nanny was the princess, and they would live happily ever after.

Nanny said, 'You really do mean it? It's not a joke? I mean, you're not just saying it. You don't say it to all the girls?'

'Of course I don't! Would I give you my address if I didn't mean it? I – honestly, Mary, I can't stop thinking about you, and I talk about you to the others and they pull my leg about you. "He's

167

smitten!" they laugh, and I don't give a damn – oh, sorry – I don't care because it's true. I *am* smitten!'

Abby watched as they clung together. Smitten. She would remember that ... They were kissing for such a long time that Abby began to think they had forgotten her.

She said loudly, 'So will I be a bridesmaid?' She thought she would wear a blue dress with a frill top and bottom, and a flower in her hair and sparkly shoes.

Nanny and John both thought that terribly funny and they all three laughed and laughed. Laughing was such *fun*.

Abby said, 'But can I?'

Nanny said, 'Possibly' and John said 'Probably' and then he found a toffee in his pocket and gave it to Abby, and while she was unwrapping it he kissed Mary again. Abby popped the toffee in her mouth; it had chocolate on the outside and as her teeth crunched through the chocolate she knew suddenly that this was the best day of her whole life.

Chapter Nine

By half-past one the ship was quiet. The corridors were empty, the lights were dimmed. The liner chugged relentlessly through the dark seas, slicing into the huge waves, rolling with the strong wind. The massive hull reverberated and shuddered and the superstructure creaked and groaned. Vases of flowers had been removed from every ledge and table to avoid the inevitable spills. The passengers slept only fitfully, some not at all. It seemed as though the night would never end.

In the Nicolsons' cabin, Gussie waited for Stella's husband to return. Stella, pale and exhausted, was sleeping restlessly, but Gussie was reluctant to leave her. She felt she should at least pass her into other hands, even if those hands were Clive Nicolson's. At last she lay down on the other side of the bed and dozed.

'What the hell are you doing—'

She sat up immediately, a finger to her lips. She had prepared a story for him and Harry had removed the empty whisky bottle.

Gussie said, 'Mr Nicolson, Stella was taken ill earlier. Very sick. She sent a steward to fetch me. I thought if I—' She stopped. What was he grinning about?

He said, 'Didn't I tell you I was on a winning streak? Eh? Didn't I?' His smile was bleary, but his delight was obvious. With a start Gussie remembered the money she had lent him.

'You *won*?'

'And how!' he said, grinning like the Cheshire cat. 'I scooped myself a cool seven hundred guineas. It was like taking candy from a baby.' To prove it, he pulled banknotes from every pocket and tossed them into the air. 'Oodles of the stuff!' He sat down heavily in the chair beside the writing desk. He couldn't stop smiling and Gussie was pleased for him. She was pleased for herself, too, but it was important for him to understand the seriousness of his wife's condition.

She said, 'The doctor says Stella must have rest and quiet, Mr Nicolson, so when she wakes up please don't start to – to *question* her about it. He was most insistent. She was sick on the stairs, you see, and was very embarrassed about it. So please don't refer to it. Just treat her gently. Probably a chicken sandwich and a—'

He said, 'Now what was our little arrangement? What do I owe your ladyship?'

'It was double or quits, as well you know!'

He said, 'I paid old Hemmings every cent I owed him and then the bastard lost it all again!' He laughed. 'God! I've had a wonderful evening, Gussie. Never better! Started with three of a kind and I thought, "This looks promising." And so it was. So what's the damage, Gussie, eh?'

'Fifty guineas and my fifty-guinea stake. Don't play games with me, Mr Nicolson.'

He winked. 'Oh, but that's what you're good at it, Gussie. Isn't it? Playing games with the boys? Eh?'

'That's enough of that!' she snapped, suddenly fearful. He could still do her a great deal of harm if he so chose. To change the subject she said, 'So please be very kind to Stella when she wakes up. She'll be feeling very delicate.'

'Stella's the delicate type,' he said. 'She was born to be delicate. Like ruddy porcelain. One wrong word and it's tears and wringing of hands!'

Gussie could see that his euphoric mood was soon going to give way to ill-temper. She decided to get out while the going was good. 'I'll take my winnings, please.' She held out her hand.

He indicated the money on the floor. 'Help yourself. You won't cheat me.' His face creased with pain again. 'Oh, that bloody Hemmings!' he muttered.

'Are you still hurting?' she asked. 'You really should see the doctor. I knew a man once who—'

'You've known *dozens* of men!' His grin was wolfish.

Gussie pursed her lips. The man had a one-track mind. 'You should take better care of yourself,' she said.

She collected notes and coins until she had a hundred guineas. 'Well, I'll be off then.'

He nodded, clutching his stomach.

'And you will remember what I said about Stella?'

There was perspiration on his forehead. He muttered, 'Go if you're going!'

She bit back an angry reply and stuffed the money down the front of her dress. Then she went out quietly, closing the door behind her, and reached her own cabin without meeting anyone. Weary beyond belief, she was longing for a few hours' sleep. When she opened the door and stepped inside, it took a moment for her to realise that the light was on.

Then – 'Holy Mother of God!' she whispered.

A pair of men's brogues showed beneath the bedspread and Harry Parr, in his stockinged feet, was sleeping on her bed.

For five long minutes Gussie watched him in his sleep. A luxury, she thought, seated quietly nearby. A rare treat from God. Whatever had she done to deserve this, she wondered, a faint smile on her face. She allowed herself to speculate on the purpose for the intrusion – there was no need to wonder *how* he had entered her cabin; his expertise with the Nicolsons' lock supplied that answer. His face was different in repose. Less controlled, somehow. More approachable. Not that he was *stern* in any way, but Gussie felt he kept himself on a tight rein. There was a softness in the lines of his face which was not evident while he was awake.

'Oh, Harry!' she whispered. 'Tess had your hair!'

But he knew that. He had seen her briefly. Gussie wondered what might have happened if Bette had broken her promise and had *told* Harry the truth about Tess. Would he have come in search of Tess's mother? Would the child have worked the magic? They would never know now.

She looked at his shoes, which had moulded themselves to the shape of his feet. She wanted to pick them up and hug them. His grey socks had been clumsily darned around the heel. By whom, she wondered, with a stab of jealousy. Did he have a housekeeper, perhaps? If so, she was a poor needlewoman. Gussie wondered if she dare offer to tackle any 'holey' socks he had with him. She would enjoy that. But no doubt he would think it forward. Not as forward as selling herself to strange men, but unsuitable nonetheless. Maybe over-eager would be a better way of putting it.

She hoped Harry had come to her cabin to tell her that he loved her; that his earlier behaviour had been a mistake and that he had always regretted not marrying her. He might also say that she was not too old for a child. That would make her the happiest woman alive. So far he had said nothing along those lines; they had merely compared notes, filling in the intervening years. His version would be the whole truth and nothing but the truth, so help him God! Her own version of events had been a pack of lies . . . most of it anyway. What was she going to say to him if he *did* want to marry her? The choice was a difficult one. She either kept her past to herself, or she confessed that once again she had hidden her true self in a tangle of half-truths and omissions. If she told the truth, he would almost certainly abandon her again. If she tried to live a lie, the truth would almost certainly emerge later – and then he would leave her.

'Holy Mother? What am I to do?' she whispered. She closed her eyes, knowing even while she agonised that she had no choice at all. Harry had to know the truth. If he then wanted her, she would throw herself at his feet! If, as seemed more likely, he turned away from her, she would somehow live the rest of her life without him. Crushed perhaps, heartbroken certainly, she would be a mere shadow of her former self. But she would go on. No suicide for *her*. No man, not even *Harry*, was going to break Gussie Malone.

He stirred suddenly and she jumped to her feet, pretending that she had just entered.

'Harry Parr!' she cried. 'This *is* a surprise and no mistake. What on earth are you doing on my bed?'

He sat up and swung his feet to the floor, groping for his shoes.

'Gussie, I had to come. We have to talk.'

Her hand flew to her throat. His tone was serious, but she couldn't see his expression as he was still fiddling with the shoe laces.

'Talk?' She sat down again, waiting. If it was a proposal, she

172

must insist that he heard the truth before she gave him an answer. She must *not* withhold the truth.

He said, 'I've given this a lot of thought, and I think I've made a bad mistake. This whole mess has been my fault. Well, partly – Damm! Look at that!'

Gussie stared at the broken lace. Her heart was beating so fast that she felt ill. He *was* going to ask her! 'It doesn't matter,' she said.

Grumbling, Harry began to adjust what remained of the lace. 'It might just be long enough,' he muttered.

Gussie wanted to shake him. Fussing with his shoelace at a time like this? To prompt him, she said, 'This whole mess—'

'What?'

'You were saying?' She would close her eyes, she decided, when she told him. Then she needn't see his face. Needn't see the hurt look of disbelief in his eyes. But how, in God's name, was she going to say it? Maybe the words would just come.

He said, 'Oh yes. I was a little too hasty, you see. I didn't think it through, and now I can see the harm I've done. I have to put things right if I can. I blame myself.'

She blurted out the words before she lost her courage. 'Harry, I've told you some – I haven't been entirely—'

He wasn't listening. It was going to be harder than she thought.

He said, 'I thought if I tell you the whole story – take you into my confidence – well, you might help me out here.' He was looking at her earnestly, his face troubled.

Gussie closed her eyes. 'Harry, before you say another word I want you to know that I'm still – that what I said about . . .'

'Stella needs to know the truth,' he said. 'I just don't feel she should hear it from me.'

Gussie opened her eyes again. 'Stella?' She stared at him. *Stella*? How could it concern Stella?

The silence lengthened between them. Harry was watching her face anxiously. 'You must realise that there is such a thing as client confidentiality, and I'd be breaking that.'

'Client confidentiality?' Confused, she waited, no longer able to look at him. A strange deflation set in as the truth dawned. This was not about them, it was about Stella Nicolson.

He went on, 'I told you I'm employed by her father as a private detective. I learned a lot about Nicolson, and when his wife found out, she insisted that I tell her what I had learned – and, foolishly, I did. At least, some of it. That's why she tried to kill herself, because she knows now what an utter swine her husband is. I mean a really bad lot. Prison. Gambling debts. Swindling.'

Furiously, Gussie blinked back tears. Crushed by the disappointment, she rushed into the bathroom and pressed a damp flannel against her eyes.

'Stop it, you *eejit*!' she whispered. 'So you made a mistake? You nearly made a *worse* one, but you didn't. Now get back in there and listen to Harry. He needs to talk to you, though God knows why!'

When she returned, Harry gave her a quizzical look but said nothing.

Gussie sat down. 'Sorry. Go on, Harry.'

'Nicolson's very likely to end up in prison, and naturally Mrs Nicolson can't bear the thought of the disgrace.' His frown deepened. 'Now I happen to know that they aren't actually married.'

'Aren't—? Mother of God!' Gussie was shocked out of her disappointment. 'Not *married*?'

'He was already married when they first met, so his marriage to a second woman was bigamous. Now the point is, if Stella Nicolson knew this, she might feel a whole lot better.'

Gussie gasped. 'Better? She'll feel *worse*!'

'Not necessarily. It would mean that she has no legal connection with the man; she'll owe him no loyalty. No need for messy and sensational divorce proceedings. No need to be dragged through the mud with him; no need to be pilloried by the press. She could go back to America, to her family, and leave Nicolson to his fate. Don't you see? She could simply walk away from him. She could tell their friends in America that he had died suddenly. End of story. She could play the grieving widow for a while—'

Gussie felt herself grow hot.

'—and then marry Gerald . . . I've seen him. He seems a thoroughly decent chap. She could still have a happy life and Abby would have a charming stepfather.'

As they stared at one another, Gussie felt a moment's bitterness. Here was Harry – *her* Harry – busily arranging a glittering future for someone else. Waving his magic wand and putting the world to rights. For Stella. *Not* for Gussie Malone. It felt almost like a betrayal. Fate could be very unkind at times.

'Wonderful! Good idea,' she said, her voice bleak.

'What is it?' he asked. 'You don't sound too convinced. Have I got it wrong? Tell me, Gussie.'

'No. Not at all.' She shook her head a little too vigorously. 'It's clever. It could work. You should tell her.'

'The point is that if she still thinks she's tied to him, she could well make another attempt at suicide. And this time she might not warn us. She might succeed.'

Gussie tried to think clearly through the tangle of her own emotions. 'But what about Abby?' she asked at last. 'The poor child—'

'Exactly.'

Gussie rubbed her chin thoughtfully. She was trying to imagine how she would feel in Stella's shoes. An illegitimate daughter. Like Tess, really.

Harry said, 'I wish now that I'd kept my mouth shut. I was a fool.'

'You did what you thought best at the time.'

'But I was wrong. It's up to me to put it right if I can. With your help, of course. You're her friend, Gussie. She'll take the news better—'

Gussie looked at him, startled. '*Me? Me* tell her? Oh, no!'

'You, Gussie.' His eyes were eloquent. 'You are the only person who can tell her the truth. She'll be badly shocked – hysterical, even – but she'll accept it from you. I won't have the right words, but you can do it woman to woman. And you can convince her that she's better off *not* married to him.' Seeing that she had made no further protest, he hurried on, 'You could meet her tomorrow some time.'

'She'll probably have Abby with her. The nanny was in disgrace—' Gussie fought against the idea.

'Abby will be with the nanny. I saw them together at the concert earlier this evening. I think that little spot of bother has blown over.'

Gussie said, 'Suppose it all goes wrong. Suppose when she knows she's even *more* determined to kill herself?' Then I'll have her on *my* conscience, she thought uneasily.

Harry hesitated. 'Do you think that will happen? Seriously? This is someone's life we're playing with. If I thought for a moment . . .' He drew a long, deep breath. 'Oh, damn! I don't know what to do. I was so sure—'

Gussie said slowly, 'No, Harry, I think you're right. I was just trying to wriggle out of it. Now that you've told her half of it, she ought to know the rest. In Stella's shoes I'd be glad to know the wretch was *not* my husband. I'll do it, Harry. But you'll have to give me a few more details. I must be able to convince her.'

He nodded. 'I'll copy out the details from my report and slip it to you over breakfast. We are still having breakfast together, I hope?'

'We are, Harry,' she told him.

He stood up. 'Better be going. Can't have you compromised now, can we?'

'Harry—' She stopped. She didn't want him to go, but she couldn't ask him to stay. 'Nothing,' she said.

He turned from the door. 'Gussie, look, there's something else—'

'Don't say anything!' she begged. She was too tired, too confused, to make sense of anything else he might want to say to her. One step at a time. Impulsively she reached for his hand and pressed it fiercely to her lips. Then she opened the door, pushed him gently outside and closed it behind him.

'Not yet, my dearest Harry!' she whispered. 'Not yet.'

Clive woke next morning, and before he had even opened his eyes the memory of his win the previous night brought a smile to his lips. So much for Hemmings. Bloody bully! He had put *him* in his place – and watching the man lose heavily had been the icing on the cake. So much for Stella and her constant barbs on the subject of his gambling. She wouldn't be able to moan now. He would buy her something nice: a present. Flowers, maybe, if he could find the florist which was tucked away on board somewhere. Or an enormous box of chocolates. Or both! He would have them delivered with a note. Cheer the woman up – she needed something.

Last night he'd been secretly appalled at her condition. And as for sending for Gussie Malone because she was seasick –! She was more trouble than Abby in that respect. His daughter had never had a day's illness in her life. She was a tough little thing – took after her father, thank God! Two delicate females would be more than he could bear.

He turned, propping himself on his elbow, and studied his wife. Stella lay on her back with her mouth partly open, breathing noisily. She was very pale still, and her hair clung damply around her face and shoulders. He remembered when he first met her. He had gone to America, desperate for a new start. Friends had given a party and had invited the Nicolsons, among others. He had first seen Stella in a flimsy gown, blown by the wind – a slim, waiflike figure. He had wanted to pick her up and cradle her in his arms, the way one would a baby. It was her helplessness which had first moved him. So why did that same frailty now irritate him half to death?

'Oh, Stella!' he muttered, overcome by something very like regret. She was basically a sweet-natured woman, but so damned passive. So lacklustre nowadays – except when that bloody Gerald was around. Then she relaxed a bit; came out of her shell, so to speak. She ventured the occasional opinion and she *laughed*; she allowed herself to be happy when she was in America surrounded by kith and kin. Gerald's jokes she found funny, while she considered her husband's crude. Well, he was that sort of man and Stella had known it when she accepted his proposal. He'd never claimed to be a gentleman. Soon after he met her, they had spent a weekend at a horse farm in Virginia. Clive, Stella, her parents – and bloody Gerald, who always seemed to tag along. Friends had joined them there, and they had all ridden up into the Blue Ridge mountains with a lunchtime picnic. He and Stella had wandered off on their own after the meal and, unexpectedly, Clive had felt strangely at peace – in tune with his surroundings for the first time since he'd arrived in the States. Suddenly he had believed that, if only he were free, he could make Stella happy.

Until then he'd felt like the family exhibit: 'This is Clive Nicolson. He's a friend from England.' And he'd been studied and marvelled over and no doubt whispered over, because everyone knew that Stella was supposed to marry dear, devoted Gerald.

Who, incidentally, had loathed Clive on sight. Not that he'd said so, but Clive knew.

And one evening, after a little too much to drink, Clive had proposed. Bad move. But she accepted and, unable to wriggle out of it, he'd made the best of it. Which wasn't difficult. She was rich. He smiled faintly, remembering how he had gone down on one knee and clasped his hands together, mocking the proposal, half in fun. She'd said, 'Yes' in that breathless way she had. Women adored him. They always had: they fell into his lap like ripe plums! Once they were engaged he'd set about changing her – encouraging her to be more outgoing. He had seen her blossom, had watched Gerald fume. And her parents had observed from the sidelines, hiding their unease.

Stella moved suddenly, opened her eyes and closed them again. He waited, wanting to say something pleasant to her; maybe enquire how she felt after a night's rest. Not that it had been a restful night, for the squall had developed into a full-scale gale which was only just beginning to diminish.

Looking at her, Clive was moved to pity. He saw her on their wedding day, floating down the aisle towards him, as insubstantial as a shadow in her white gown, her face hidden by her veil. Had he loved her? Or was he simply thrilled by the chase and his own power? A lump came into his throat. He shouldn't have married her. They weren't suited; it was as simple as that. Not that he *had* married her in actual fact, but that was a technicality. They lived together as man and wife and she had given him a daughter. If she ever discovered that . . .

'Oh, God!' A long sigh escaped him and he fell back on to the pillow, frowning. He sometimes wondered about his real wife, and then the guilt began to eat into him. Was she alone and struggling? Did she ever wonder about *him*? He thought of the baby boy she had given him, and their despair when he died. Clive had held the pathetic bundle in his arms for a short time. But they had been unable to save the baby. A small part of Clive had died with him.

Poor May. She had been a jolly, *spunky* girl, and she had worshipped him. She knew he had been to prison, but she said all that was in the past and they'd make a new start. He swore he would never drink heavily again and would give up gambling. They'd had a lot of fun at first, but later it had turned sour. He had taken to drinking with his friends; there were debts and rows; she had accused him of neglect and they had started to quarrel. It had been downhill from then on.

'A bloody, *bloody* mess!' he muttered.

Clive had walked out on her with few regrets. And then, later, he had met Stella. He grabbed at his chance with both hands. A junior partner *with prospects*! The trouble was that Stella's father had been so tightfisted. So *pleased* when Clive had made mistakes; so determined to show him up in Stella's eyes. Mean, small-minded bastard! Clive had sometimes been tempted to tell him that his daughter was living in sin and his grand-daughter had been born on the wrong side of the blanket – just to see the look of horror on his face.

Eventually Clive could see the problems ahead. He could foresee a time at some point in the future when he would walk away from Stella. Against such a time, he had begun to salt away some of the money. If her father had been more supportive, Clive told himself now, that wouldn't have been necessary. But he wasn't, and the money in Clive's secret account was mounting nicely. Serve the old bugger right!

Still, that was before his win. Now he mustn't let dark thoughts spoil his day. He sat up carefully and slid his feet out of bed, trying not to wake his wife. Poor Stella. He glanced back at her and the unfamiliar feelings of goodwill still lingered. Maybe there was still time. Perhaps the win was a good omen. He would make it all up to her; he would make her happy. He would make her *so* happy that Gerald and her parents would be forced to eat their miserable words.

As he groped for his slippers he heard her moving behind him and turned to smile at her. His mind formed a pleasantry, but the expression in her eyes shocked him, chilling him into silence. There was loathing there, disgust and – was it *hatred*? He stared at her fearfully.

'What is it?' he stammered. 'Stella?' His sense of well-being faded. He felt cold as ice.

Stella said slowly, 'I know it all, Clive. Everything.' She struggled to sit up, pushing her hair from her face, never taking her eyes from his.

'What d'you mean – everything?' How could she know *any-thing*?

'The money. You've cheated my father. And you've broken my heart.'

Clive struggled for words without success. The surprise was total.

She went on, 'This is the end, Clive. I can't live like this any longer. I can't bear it.'

Inexplicably he began to tremble. 'Stella!' he whispered. 'You wouldn't leave me. You don't know what you're saying.'

'Oh, but I do.' Her voice held a dreadful finality. 'I'm not sure yet what my plans are, but you and I have no future together. It's over, Clive. It's all over.'

An hour later Stella was washed and dressed and had done her hair. She felt faint and ill from the excesses of the night before, but she did not intend to give in to weakness. She had made up her mind to end her life, and interference from well-meaning friends was not going to stop her. Yesterday's note to Gussie Malone had been a mistake, but she was learning. Next time she would not signal her intentions. Next time she would organise things a little better. She could see that drinking the whisky first had been another mistake. Never mind. There would be another chance; she would wait and watch.

Clive had left the cabin without another word, and Stella had watched him go with relief. Now she hurried into the next cabin where she found Mary still in her dressing gown, languidly brushing her hair. To her surprise Abby was still in bed, her head bent over a notebook and pencil. Stella stiffened her resolve.

'Nanny, what is the meaning of this? Don't you know the time?'

Mary smiled. She looked quite at ease, thought Stella, surprised. Perhaps sending them to the concert had been a mistake, but it had been necessary to make sure that they were occupied and unlikely to come into her cabin on some pretext.

'I'm sorry, Mrs Nicolson, but she won't get up until she's finished her homework.'

Abby looked up. 'I can't think when you talk,' she complained.

To her mother she said, 'It's the two-times table. Mrs Malone says I must know them before we meet again.' She smiled. 'I *nearly* know them. Shall I say them for you?' Without waiting for an answer she began, 'One two is two, two twos are four, three twos are six, five twos are ten—'

Stella said, '*Four* twos are eight. You missed that one.' She stared at her daughter. Was she really ready for this? Her own education had begun very late because her parents had been afraid of overtaxing her brain. Her aunt's condition, the doctors thought, might have been exacerbated by too much study at an early age.

Abby said, 'Sorry. Four twos are eight, five twos are ten, six twos are twelve—' She stopped, screwing up her face in a frown of concentration. 'I forget the rest. But I know cat is c-a-t and dog is d-o-g and ant is a-n-t.'

Stella said, 'My word! You are a clever girl.'

'Mrs Malone says I should have a governess or else I should go to school, because I've got a good brain and I'm not using it properly.'

'I see.' Stella felt a rush of guilt. Of course, Mrs Malone was right. She *had* delayed Abby's schooling. Well, it would be someone else's responsibility soon. All her failures and mistakes would be of no importance. All forgotten. She asked, 'Did you enjoy the concert?'

Abby's face lit up. 'Oh yes, Mama. It was wonderful. Better than the pantomime. There was a man who told funny stories and another who did magic tricks and a lady who could bend in half—'

'A contortionist,' Mary put in.

'—and John was in the concert. He sang a song and everyone clapped, and we did too and afterwards—' She stopped, looking towards the nanny.

Mary said, 'John is my young man. You met him the other night.'

There was a glint of something in the girl's eyes, thought Stella. Was it *triumph*?

Mary went on 'As soon as I can get away I'm going down to Southampton. He wants me to meet his family. He thinks I'll be able to find a position down there.'

Abby clasped her hands excitedly. 'I'm going to be a brides-maid! I can, Mama, can't I? I want a blue dress with sparkly shoes and—'

Stella said, 'We'll see.' Let someone else worry about that, she thought. She turned to Mary. 'Isn't it a bit early to be talking about weddings?'

'John doesn't think so.' She blushed. 'He's very – keen.'

Stella was aware of her own cynicism. Another young hopeful with rose-coloured glasses. But mixed with the cynicism was a certain amount of envy. Mary was at the threshold of her life while Stella herself was bowing out.

The nanny, eyes glowing, said, 'He says it was love at first sight.'

Stella wanted to say, 'Don't be such a fool!' But what did she know about matters of the heart? She was hardly a good example. Her own marriage was over, her life ruined. Perhaps this rash young woman would make a better choice of husband and would somehow survive the rigours of married life.

'It sounds as though congratulations are in order,' she said. She would ignore the little jibe implicit in that 'as soon as I can get away'. Let the girl go. She was finished with all of them; they would all manage without her.

'Thank you.' Mary sounded smug, but who could blame her?

Stella said, 'But I would like you to dress now, Nanny, and you too, Abby.'

'But Mama!' Abby protested. 'Mrs Malone says I'm to learn the two-times. I'm too old to be playing in the play-room with rocking-horses and suchlike. Mrs Malone is going to tell me about—'

Stella put a hand to her head which was beginning to throb. Although the sea had eased since dawn the motion was still enough to make her feel queasy, and she thought that some dry toast might do the trick.

She said, 'That's enough, Abby. Put away your – your home-work and get out of bed – *now!*'

'But Mama! It's not fair!' Her daughter's voice was shrill.

Stella thought, Not now, Abby. I haven't the strength to argue. 'I shall be back in fifteen minutes,' she said as firmly as she could, 'to take you down to breakfast, and I shall expect you to be ready.

Both of you.' She smiled coldly at Mary. 'Although your employment with this family is soon to be terminated, I shall expect you to carry on as usual in the meantime – which doesn't include mooning about over John!'

Outside in the corridor, Stella regretted the last remark. No doubt it smacked of sour grapes. She sighed. The waspish matron jealous of the young pretty girl. They had sometimes spoken of her Aunt Hester as 'waspish'. Perhaps that was why. In the past few weeks Stella had begun to understand things about her unfortunate aunt which had eluded her before. Unwilling to return to the cabin and unable to go on deck in case she encountered Clive, she wandered along to the shops, staring with unseeing eyes at the souvenirs on sale there: model ships, picture postcards, brooches, purses and a variety of boxed games for the children.

Aunt Hester, living with her parents in New Jersey, had suddenly fallen hopelessly in love with one of the tellers at her local bank – a happily married man who wanted nothing to do with her. The unrequited love had turned into an obsession and Hester had pestered the man with her attentions. At the time Stella had been ten years old and very curious. Aunt Hester, her mother had told her, was 'highly strung', that was all. Perhaps at times she was 'a little unstable'.

To help wean Hester from the unsuitable passion, she had been invited to spend the summer with Stella and her parents in New York, so that several hundred miles separated her from the object of her affection. Stella had dreaded her arrival, expecting some kind of crazy woman with wildly rolling eyes, but her aunt had been very normal, quietly spoken and with a gentle sense of humour.

Stella resembled her aunt physically with a slight frame, the same smooth dark hair and a strikingly similar laugh. This likeness had made the young Stella uneasy, but Hester's vulnerability touched her and they became friends. Hester had been with them barely two weeks when she first attempted to kill herself.

Now Stella recalled the occasion in stark detail. The picnic at the lake, feeding the squirrels, chasing butterflies and identifying the wild flowers. The peace of the afternoon had been abruptly shattered when Hester was sighted wading, fully clothed, into deep water. Her white skirts floated round her like a huge waterlily but, unable to swim, she soon floundered, weighed down by her sodden clothes. As Stella's father tugged off his boots and shed his new striped blazer, Hester's arms went up and she disappeared without a sound beneath the still surface of the water.

Stella could still recall her father's desperate swim and her mother's hysterical screams. The sight of the apparently lifeless, dripping form in her father's arms haunted her dreams for years. As her father staggered out of the water and laid Hester on the ground, Stella's mother had collapsed in a dead faint. Stella had found the sal volatile bottle and had brought her mother back to consciousness. The day had been etched indelibly on her memory.

A month later Hester had tried again, throwing herself in front of a four-horse omnibus. On this occasion she had been alone, but a graphic account of the incident had been given by a bystander. It was a miracle, the woman told them, that the horses' flailing hooves had not killed her. She had escaped with multiple bruises and a fractured rib. Stella, feeling guilty and disloyal, had been relieved when her unhappy aunt was returned to her own parents.

Now Stella stared fixedly at a small wooden pencil-box with *Mauretania* carved into the lid, realising that she and her aunt had more in common than anyone had guessed. Except in one respect. There was no way that Stella would allow herself to be locked away. Hester had made an obvious mistake – she had attempted suicide within sight of other people who then felt obliged to save her from her own destructive urges. Stella had made the mistake of leaving a note. Next time she would be more careful. Poor Hester! They should have let her die. Poor Stella, they would say after her own death; she was highly-strung, a little unstable. Please God Abby had taken after Clive!

She was about to return to the cabin when a familiar voice called her name and she saw Gussie hurrying towards her. Marginally her mood lightened. Here was the one person whom she could trust.

Smiling, she said, 'Gussie! Good morning. I've been listening to the two-times tables. What a surprise!'

Gussie said, 'Stella! I'm so pleased to see you. But should you be up and about? You look desperately – tired. I was planning to look in and see you later.'

Stella hesitated. 'I'm fine. I suppose – that is, I *must* thank you for all you did last night – you and Mr Parr. I must apologise—'

Gussie took hold of her hands. 'We won't speak of it again. Please. It's in the past.'

'That's very kind but – it was hardly fair on you—'

'That's what friends are for, Stella.'

'If you see Mr Parr—'

'We're having breakfast together actually.'

'Please pass on my gratitude.'

'I will. And may we talk later?'

Stella detected something in her friend's voice. 'Talk? What about?'

'Oh, just talk. This and that.'

'About last night?'

'No-o. Not really. Please, Stella?'

'We'll talk then. Now you must excuse me.' Cold with anxiety, she turned abruptly and hurried away. Stella's senses, highly tuned, perceived the lie.

Gussie had something to say and she, Stella, was not going to like it.

Chapter Ten

It was nearly eleven o'clock by the time Gussie found Stella, who had hidden herself away in a secluded corner of the deck where the sun still lingered. Gussie suspected that her friend had been avoiding her, but she understood. At least Abby was nowhere in sight.

'Clive is teaching Abby to play deck quoits,' Stella told her as Gussie sat down beside her.

Gussie and Harry had been lucky. The other passengers on his table were absent from breakfast, so the two of them had been able to talk confidentially without interruption. Gussie knew exactly what she had to say but not how to say it.

Now she took a deep breath. 'I hope you don't mind,' she began, 'but Mr Parr has told me about your problems with regard to Mr Nicolson. He was actually trying to explain to me why you – about what happened last night.'

'I'm truly sorry to have dragged you and Mr Parr—'

'No! That's not it. I just want you to know that this isn't mere curiosity on my part. Far be it for me to go poking my nose where it's not wanted – but there's something else Mr Parr felt you should know. He's actually very sorry that he told you anything about his job and his assignment. The poor man blames himself, to some extent.'

'It's not his fault,' Stella said wearily. 'Why does everyone treat me like a child? I can see what's happening as clearly as the next person.'

Gussie doubted that, but didn't labour the point. 'The thing is this, Stella.' She paused, disconcerted by the look on the other woman's face.

Stella said, 'Whatever it is, it won't change things. You don't know everything, you see, Gussie, and there's no reason why you should but I'm – my aunt, you see . . .' She swallowed and her mouth trembled. 'I have no future, Gussie. No real future. Nothing I can look forward to. I know what's best. I don't want you and Mr Parr to worry about me any more. I know you think you're helping me, but in fact you're not. I need to be left alone, Gussie. I don't mean that unkindly but—'

Gussie said, 'Listen to me. You will not be dragged through the courts. I expect you thought that *would* happen, but it won't. You will not be associated with any of your husband's crimes. You can go home to—'

'You don't *understand*!' cried Stella. She had taken a handkerchief from her purse and was twisting it unhappily in her lap. 'It's not just my husband.'

Gussie said, 'But surely he's your biggest problem?'

'Is he? I wonder.'

Her words startled Gussie and threw her off-course. 'What else could there be?' she asked.

'My aunt,' said Stella. 'I don't want to talk about her, but she *is* one of my worries. I don't expect you to understand.'

Gussie hesitated, then decided to revert to her original argument. 'Suppose you weren't married to your husband?' she suggested. 'What then?'

'But I am, Gussie,' Stella replied with a hint of impatience. 'Please, can't we leave this?'

Gussie ploughed on. 'But suppose you *weren't* married to Clive? Now wouldn't that be a whole lot better?'

'Suppose the moon were made of green cheese! You're being ridiculous.' Stella, obviously irritated, made as though to rise but Gussie caught hold of her sleeve.

She would have to say it straight out now, she decided. 'You're *not* married!' she declared.

Stella pulled herself free and stood up. 'That's enough!' she said sharply. 'I know you mean well, Gussie, but—'

Gussie caught her arm. 'Sit down, Stella. I won't have you walking out on me. Please.'

Reluctantly, Stella resumed her seat. 'It's nonsense,' she said.

'It's a fact, Stella.' Gussie swallowed hard, her throat dry with

188

apprehension. 'Clive Nicolson had a wife before he met you. *You are not his wife, Stella*!'

Stella stared at Gussie. 'Another wife? That's impossible.'

Taking Stella's hands in hers, Gussie shook her head, cursing Harry for talking her into this. 'It's the truth, so help me God! Why would I lie to you? Harry discovered that—'

Stella had gone very pale. She looked as though she might faint, and her eyes were glazed with shock. 'But the wedding?' she whispered. 'The church? Of course we're married.'

'No. He was already married.'

'I don't believe it.' Now flushed and trembling, Stella snatched her hands away, pressing them against her heart. She said, 'But Abby? She's his daughter, isn't she? Oh God! You mean that Abby is – is not his legal daughter? *No*! I'll kill him! He couldn't *do* this! He *wouldn't*!' Her eyes were wild, her breathing erratic. '*No*!' she gasped. '*No*! Tell me it isn't true!'

'Stella, dear, I'm afraid it *is* true, but you must see what this means? It means you're free of the miserable, lying wretch! Free! You can leave him to face the music on his own. Take the next ship back to America and let your father deal with him. Your husband can't take Abby from you because he's not legally her father!' She shook Stella gently by the shoulders, willing her to see the advantages. 'You don't need him, Stella,' she told her. 'You can make a new life for yourself and Abby.'

Stella covered her face with her hands and Gussie could see that, so far, her encouragement was falling on deaf ears. But that was understandable. It would take time for anyone to absorb and accept such dramatic information.

Stella glanced up sharply. 'Who did he marry?'

'A woman called May Tompkins. She's still alive, but she's living with another man.' Don't ask me about the children, thought Gussie.

'Were there any children?' Stella was watching her closely now.

'A boy. He died.'

'I'm glad.' She looked tearfully at Gussie. 'Is that very unkind of me? To wish a poor child dead?'

'Not in the circumstances.'

'I wish they were all dead. Him, her – what was her name?'

'May Rose Tompkins.'

'I wonder if she loved him? I wonder why he left her – or did she leave him?'

'That's not known. Stella, will you promise me you'll think about the situation calmly? I know what a shock it must be, but Harry is only telling you this to make things *better* for you. You do see that, don't you?'

'I suppose so.' She shook her head. 'Did you know Clive was in prison once?'

Gussie nodded.

'And he will be again. Oh God, how I hate him!' She pressed her fingers against her mouth. 'How could he stand there at the altar smiling down into my eyes, knowing how much I loved him, and all the time knowing that it was all false.' She stared at Gussie incredulously. 'We had such a wonderful wedding. Papa spared no expense. All our friends, all his business associates, neighbours, family. A huge marquee. The best florist. The finest caterers. And my dress – cream satin with five hundred tiny pearls sewn on by hand! Oh God! And all for a wedding that was what – illegal?' Her expression changed. 'Did we break the law?'

'*You* didn't. Your husband did. Not that he is your husband. Isn't it a relief to know that you are *not* married to him?'

'I suppose so.'

She didn't sound very sure, thought Gussie, but it would take time to adjust to being single again.

Stella went on, 'A hundred and twenty people sat down for the wedding breakfast and—' She stopped.

'What is it?'

'We did wonder why Clive had nobody. No names to add to the guest list. Papa passed comment, but Clive said they couldn't come to America. It was too far. Papa offered to pay for his parents to come over, but he made some excuse. Now I see it. How could Clive even *invite* them when they knew he was already married? What did they think when they received the invitations?'

Gussie shrugged. 'Maybe they didn't. Maybe Clive gave fictitious addresses so that they would never be delivered.' She frowned. 'Haven't you ever met any of his family?'

Stella shook her head. 'Never. It never seemed to happen. We would arrange something – or rather Clive would. And then there would be a letter cancelling – illness or a death.' She frowned. 'He must have written the letters himself! I began to think that his parents didn't approve of him marrying an American. I was hurt, naturally, but I didn't say anything. Then time passes and you lose interest. Oh! What about the marriage certificate?'

'Worthless.'

'Yes, it must be, mustn't it? And the Reverend Skarpe who married us was an old friend of Papa's from way back: fourth grade or somesuch. Thank goodness he's not still alive to hear what a farce it all was.' She sighed, then smiled suddenly. 'We had four little bridesmaids. The youngest was three. Pale pink dresses with tiny roses in a little circlet for their hair. There was to have been a little pageboy, but at the last moment he refused to take part. Perhaps he *knew*!' She laughed shakily.

But it *was* a laugh, thought Gussie, which was surely a good sign.

'Abby loves that photograph. It's the reason she's always wanted to be a bridesmaid,' said Stella. 'It seems that the nanny has found herself a young man – yes, *that* young man – and a wedding might be imminent.'

'Marry in haste . . .' said Gussie, smothering feelings of envy.

'Exactly.'

For a moment they sat without speaking. Gussie watched Stella's face, but she seemed to be lost somewhere in the past.

At last she looked up. 'How could he take me to bed – say that he *loved* me – when all the time he knew how I trusted him. Knew that he had betrayed me – *and* his first . . . his *only* wife. I'd given up so much to be with him.' She gulped. 'I think I feel faint.'

'Take a few deep breaths.'

Stella obeyed and was soon recovered. Gussie put an arm around the slim, trembling shoulders. Nothing she could say would help. Stella whispered, 'I can't even cry. He'll notice, and so will Abby.'

'Won't you tell him that you know?'

'Oh, no! I daren't. He can be very unpredictable. Very rough. I'll keep it to myself until I know what I'm going to do . . .' Her face crumpled. 'Oh, Gussie! I don't suppose he ever loved me, then. He just wanted to marry money. Oh God! I feel as though I could strangle him with my bare hands! Isn't that terrible?'

191

'Of course it's not. Quite moderate for the circumstances, I'd say!'

'I have to go away to think. To decide what to do. But you won't abandon me, will you?' Suddenly she laid her head against Gussie's shoulder.

'Now why would I be leaving you? And at a time like this!' Gussie smiled reassuringly as she smoothed the dark hair with steady strokes. 'Just tell me before you go that you're starting to feel better.'

'I think I am.'

Gussie stood and helped Stella to her feet. 'Remember, nothing he does can taint you or Abby. Cling on to that thought, Stella, because it's all that matters.' She gave her a final hug and then straightened up. 'And now, before you go off to have your big think we'll go to my cabin and I'll send out for a tray of tea and biscuits. We'll fortify ourselves, Stella,' she said, hoping that she sounded more confident than she felt. Smiling, she added, 'With a strong cup of tea we'll be ready for anything!'

Clive took one look inside the medical room and almost changed his mind. Waiting ahead of him was a mother with a bawling infant and a middle-aged man who was clutching his left wrist. Clive hesitated, poised for flight, but at that moment the door opened and a middle-aged woman came out, thanking the doctor profusely for his help. The doctor, a small plump man, gave Clive a quick nod and ushered the mother and baby into his surgery. Clive sat down unhappily. He had a deep dread of the medical profession and was fond of telling people that he 'avoided quacks like the plague'.

He had been telling himself that the pain in his gut would ease, but it never had. In fact it had grown worse. He was suffering severe cramps in the area below his ribs and it was beginning to frighten him.

'Morning!' The other man smiled at him. 'Trump's the name.' He was short and tubby with thin, greasy hair. Bulbous blue eyes were obscured by thick-lensed spectacles and his boots needed some polish. He was exactly the type of man Clive loathed.

Just his luck, he thought. If there was one thing he hated almost as much as doctors, it was their ghastly patients.

'Morning!' Clive mumbled the words in a vain hope that this would deter further conversation. Staring at the floor, he resisted the urge to clutch at his stomach as a fresh spasm sent waves of pain up to his brain. He didn't want to provoke a discussion of ailments.

The man held up his wrist. 'You'll never believe this,' he began cheerfully, 'but I've done my bally wrist in playing deck quoits! My wife loves the game. Potty about it, she is. So Silly Willy here has to play along. Every morning, sharp at eight, there we are on deck, leaping about like a pair of gazelles. Come to think of it, weren't you on deck this morning?'

'I was teaching my daughter Abby to play.'

'Thought so. I never forget a face. Nor a name. Funny, isn't it? Blooming elephant, that's what my wife calls me.' He laughed. 'Anyway, this morning I'd just got into my bally stride when wham! Something went. I felt it give. Strained a muscle or something, so my wife said, "Off to the doctor, Henry," and here I am.'

Clive said, 'Mmm!' and tried to suggest total disinterest. The pain increased and, in spite of his good intentions, he uttered a slight groan.

'I say, old chap, you all right?' The man peered at him.

Clive gritted his teeth. 'Of course I'm not all right! I wouldn't be here if I was – goddamn it!' He closed his eyes.

From the next room the baby's howls reached a new pitch.

'Dear oh dear!' said Clive's companion. 'Sounds as though *everyone's* got the grumps this morning!'

The *grumps*? For God's sake! Clive ignored the little dig. He felt humiliated and longed to escape, but the pain kept him pinned down. Panic nudged in a corner of his brain. He was losing control of the situation, and that always troubled him. Hating school, resenting the power the teachers had over their pupils, he had been 'a disruptive pupil', the bane of his headmaster and the despair of his parents. He had hated living in the same house as his dissolute father, whom he had never been able to admire in the way other boys admired their fathers. Often drunk and always gambling, John Nicolson had thrown away what remained of the family fortune. Clive had never forgiven him for that.

Clive had hated having to stand by helplessly and watch his mother grieve and worry as their standard of living fell year by year. As soon as he was old enough to leave school, he found a job and moved away. If he didn't know about them, then he needn't care. Then there was May. Would she marry him or wouldn't she? She had plenty of admirers, and Clive was by no means her first choice. Finding himself on the losing side irked him. He fought the boy she wanted to marry and put him in the hospital. They sent him down for that.

However, the young man offered his attentions elsewhere, when he came out of hospital and May had accepted Clive. Poor May Rose. When the boy died she went to pieces. Lost interest in herself and the home – and *him*. The doctor said it was only a matter of time, but he couldn't bear to be around her. He had to get away . . .

He glanced up as the surgery door opened, the mother and ailing child came out and then Trump went in. Thank God for small mercies, thought Clive, finding himself alone. He thought about the money he'd won the night before, and that made him feel better. He thought about Gussie Malone, and that helped. Shame about her change of heart. That could have been fun. There was a *gutsy* air about her which he liked.

Then he thought about Stella, and his smile faded abruptly. What in God's name was she up to, he wondered. What did she mean by 'I know *everything*'? That was impossible. She couldn't begin to know the half of it, poor woman! He had covered his tracks too well for that. She couldn't possibly know about May. So was she talking about the gambling (which he hadn't tried to hide) or about his assignation with Gussie Malone?

He doubled up, gasping with pain. Those tablets had been worse than useless. This was all that bastard Hemmings' fault.

Minutes later Trump appeared with a heavy bandage round his hand and wrist, but Clive was not about to renew the conversation. Without being asked, he hurried past the doctor into the surgery and sat down. It was a small room, swamped by a large desk. Folders lay in a pile at one end and at the other there were two medical textbooks. In the centre was a large blotter, a pen and ink-stand and a notepad. On the wall were several glass-fronted cabinets, and a small table in one corner held several metal trays containing instruments. There was a high, narrow, padded table covered with a white sheet. The very sight of it all increased Clive's unease.

When the doctor returned Clive said, 'I expect my wife's told you all about this bloody pain I'm getting?'

The doctor gave him a frosty smile, moved at a leisurely pace to his own chair behind the desk and sat down. He then moved a file or two and said, 'Name?' '

Nicolson. My wife—'

'I don't recognise the name, Mr Nicolson. Your wife probably saw my partner, Dr Rowse. I'm Dr Mawle. How can I help you?' He drew a pad towards him and began to write.

'I'm having terrible pains in my stomach or whatever – here. They seem to be getting worse. Your partner sent along some pills, but they're useless. I'd like—'

'Suppose you take off your shirt and—'

'Take off my shirt?' The idea was abhorrent. His fingers hovered nervously around the top shirt button.

'—and loosen the top of your trousers. Then lie on the table. I'll take a look at you.'

Surrender to this silly little man's probing fingers? Clive said, 'There's no need for all that. I'm telling you, all I need is—'

'Mr Nicolson, I have to examine you. I need to know what is causing the pain. Have you had your appendix out? Do you suffer from indigestion? Flatulence?'

'I only want something stronger to kill the pain. Just until I reach home. Then I'll see my own doctor.'

'If you'll just undress and lie down on the table?' Dr Mawle's expression was steely.

Damned if I will, thought Clive. Tell him the truth and be done with it. He said, 'If you must know, I got into a bit of a – an argument. It got rather physical and the other chap punched me – here. An upper-cut. Bloody painful.'

To his dismay the doctor's expression changed from annoyance to concern. 'To the solar plexus? Now that could be very nasty, Mr Nicolson. Kidney damage maybe, or a damaged spleen. That would hurt like the very devil.' His tone softened slightly. 'Look, the examination won't take more than a minute or two. You might be more seriously hurt than you imagine. A ruptured spleen could mean internal bleeding. As for the kidneys – have you noticed any blood when you pass water?'

Clive had made a point of not looking. 'No, doctor.' He was beginning to wish he had stayed away.

'Internal bleeding is very insidious. It leaks into the abdominal cavity and can go unnoticed. It is potentially dangerous, and you would be very unwise to ignore it. Have you felt faint at all? Dizzy, perhaps? Any coldness around the abdomen?'

Clive was beginning to feel *both*. He could feel a cold sweat breaking out on his skin too. Damn the old fool! He was trying to frighten him. He tossed up: would he walk out or be examined?

The doctor repeated, 'It will only take a few moments.'

Another wave of pain settled the question. A minute later Clive lay on the table while the doctor's fingers pressed here and there and Clive screwed up his face in agony as the extent of the pain was revealed.

'You can sit up now, Mr Nicolson. That's right. Get down and put your things on . . . I'm afraid there could be quite a lot of damage, and I'd like to have you in the infirmary for the rest of the day to keep an eye on you.'

Clive stood up, wincing. 'That won't be necessary,' he said firmly. 'A note to my own doctor will be enough, thank you, and some stronger painkillers.'

'But, Mr Nicolson, you don't seem to understand the risks. Internal bleeding—'

Fear heightened Clive's anxiety. He brought his fist down so heavily on the desk that the doctor jumped visibly.

'For Christ's sake, give me the bloody pills!' Clive demanded.

They glowered at each other as Clive pushed his shirt-tails back inside his trousers, buttoned the fly and pulled on his blazer.

The doctor shrugged. 'As you wish,' he said. Opening one of the wall cupboards, he filled a box with pills, and Clive saw with satisfaction that his plump hands trembled.

It was mid-afternoon and the weather was once more fine and warm. Gussie had found herself a sheltered spot out of the sun – no point in ruining her complexion. She was also protected from the prevailing breeze. Having once suffered an inflamed eye because of a speck of soot from a ship's funnel, she had no wish to repeat the experience. Stretched out on one of the long deck-chairs with her ankles crossed and her head resting comfortably on a cushion, she had hoped that Harry Parr might come in search of her, but so far that hadn't happened. Instead, she had seen Abby with Mary Crisford and her young man, and was musing on the folly of young love and immoderate haste.

At Mary's age, where had she herself been, Gussie wondered? When she had left the convent at sixteen she had gone into ser-vice as a housemaid with the Russian family. Nothing so lordly as a nanny. Long hours and precious little money to show for it, but they had been kind to her; she had never claimed otherwise. The elderly husband with his beard and spectacles, so hunched from his work as a watch repairer. His wife, Anna, much younger, always singing under her breath. Russian hymns, perhaps. No children. An English cook who drank the vodka on the sly. Oh, she was a tartar, that one, but fun in the evenings when her work was done and the drink was in her. She had a store of dubious jokes, most of which had gone over Gussie's head. Convent girls were notoriously ill-prepared for the rigours of the life outside the convent.

And then the nephew Alexis had arrived from France with his bohemian ways, his tales of life in Paris and his easy laughter. The same age as her, he had taught Gussie what little French she knew – and much more besides. He talked about politics and world affairs and she was impressed. Flattered by his inter-est, she had put the cook's dire warnings down to envy. Gussie knew she was beautiful with her bright hair, green eyes and the pale complexion she still strived to maintain. Slim, eager and so vulnerable. She had wanted him to fall in love with her. One night Alexis had come to her room with a bottle of wine. He had brought some of his poetry, he told her, and would like her honest opinion of his work. She had protested that she knew very little about poetry.

'What is this you are telling me?' he had demanded. 'The nuns – they taught you nothing of poetry? I don't believe!' He said 'nossink' and 'tellink' and Gussie thought him the most wonder-ful man in the world. When, an hour or so later, he suggested they sleep together, she was too drunk to protest. At the time, it had seemed a thoroughly good idea; what happened next had not been unpleasant. The unpleasantness had started the following morning when they both slept heavily and were discovered together. He was sent back to Paris and Gussie was dismissed. By some miracle she did not conceive, and she had always been grateful that she was spared that particular problem. Now she sighed. It all seemed a long time ago.

She stretched luxuriously and declined a tray of tea offered by a passing steward. Why was she wasting time on the past, she rebuked herself. She had more than enough to worry about in the here and now! The voyage was drawing to a close and Harry might easily disappear from her life when they reached England. Events on board the *Mauretania* had thrown them together, but he had a life without her and perhaps on reflection he would prefer to keep it that way. Alternatively, he *might* be considering asking Gussie to join him. If he did, what could she say? Somehow she needed to tell him the truth *before* he made any rash declaration of affection.

A shadow fell across her face and her heart leaped. But it was Stella.

'Gussie! You look so comfortable, I hardly dare to intrude.'

'Please! I enjoy your company.' Gussie indicated another chair and Stella tugged it into position beside her. There were dark circles under her eyes, but a little of her normal colour had returned.

'I have something to ask you,' she said, seating herself sideways on the deck-chair and clasping her hands on her knees. 'But first I have to thank you again for helping me through that – well, for being there when I needed you. Both of you. In the light of what I now know, I've made certain plans.'

Gussie regarded her with growing admiration. This delicate woman, so recently ready to kill herself, was now discovering a strength of purpose no one could have expected. Stella's predicament made her own problems fade into insignificance.

'When we get back to London, I am going to contact my father and ask for the name of his English lawyer. With his support, I shall ask Clive to leave the house. It was bought in my name with my father's money, and I don't think he can protest too much. Eventually I shall take Abby and go back to America, but there will be things to do and it will take time, during which I shall be alone and very anxious. I wonder, would you come to us as Abby's governess for that period? I would pay you, of course, and could give you a reference.'

Gussie listened with growing astonishment. A governess! She said, 'Oh, I don't think I could be a *governess*, Stella. I'm not qualified. I don't—'

'Of course you are,' Stella smiled. 'You've been teaching Abby her tables and how to spell. It won't be for long: six months at the most. You've had an education and you won't need to teach her anything complicated. Some arithmetic, the tables, maybe addition and subtraction at an easy level. Some more sounds and letters. Teach her to write her name. Maybe some needlework? Oh – and I'd like you to give her piano lessons, too, as an extra, of course.'

Gussie closed her eyes despairingly. *Piano lessons*! She hadn't the faintest idea how to play the piano. She was a fraud and was about to be shown up. But the chance to be a governess was tempting and she longed to say 'Yes' but hung back. She said, 'I'd have to say "No" to the piano lessons.'

'Oh! What a shame.' Stella shook her head slightly. 'I don't know where I got the idea that you taught the piano. Still, never mind. Maybe singing lessons?'

Gussie said, 'I don't think I know any songs.' But as she spoke, the words of one of them came into her mind, and she sang hesitantly, '. . . Oh, a little bit of bread and no cheese is better than an empty dish . . . And a happy little nest is something . . . Oh dear!' She frowned. 'Oh yes! A happy little nest is something, When you can't have all you wish.' She laughed. 'The convent songs were very moralistic, as you can hear.' And a fat lot of good they had done *her*, she reflected.

'But you remembered the tune.'

'Yes, I did.' She said cautiously, 'I suppose I *might* find it in me to be a governess.'

'Oh, Gussie, I wish you would! It would be such a relief to have you with me, and it would solve one of my problems. Not only would it be good for Abby – you get along so well – it would be company for me. In fact' – her eyes gleamed suddenly – 'you could come back to America with us if you wished.'

Once again Gussie's conscience was beginning to prick her. If she went as a governess to Stella's child, she would be taking the position under false pretences; she was far from being a suitable companion for either Abby or her mother. She frowned unhappily. Clive Nicolson was the stumbling-block. There was no way he would allow himself to be ousted from the house without retaliation if he knew that Gussie was going to move in and replace him! He would never approve of her appointment and would almost certainly betray her.

'Your husband would almost certainly object,' she suggested.

'He's not my husband!'

'But he's Abby's father.'

'He tricked his way into that position! In law, I suspect he has no rights in the matter of whom I employ as governess. Stop worrying about his reaction, Gussie. When my father's lawyer gets to work on him, he'll be only too glad to escape all his responsibilities in our direction. Just say you'll agree.'

Gussie said, 'It's a very kind offer, Stella, but it needs some careful thought. May I give you my answer later?'

'Of course.' Stella smiled with relief. 'I thought at first you were going to turn me down at once!'

'I wouldn't know what to charge.'

'I'd find out the proper sum from an agency. That wouldn't be a problem.'

Gussie thought it certain that a high-class whore earned more than a governess, but a few months' regular money would be a nice addition to her small savings. And the reference would be invaluable. She could also hear herself mentioning it casually to Harry. 'Oh yes, didn't I tell you? I'm going as governess to Stella's daughter. Just to help her through the next few months . . .' It would sound convincingly respectable. She smiled. 'If it's humanly possible, I'll say "Yes".'

As soon as Stella returned to the cabin she sensed trouble. Clive was lying on the bed, his narrowed eyes glittering unpleasantly; his face was set in grim lines and his hands clenched into fists. He had had time to think and he obviously had a lot to say. He was going to say it now, and Stella steeled herself. She had known that he would have questions to put to her. It had only been a matter of time. Resolving to take the initiative, she said, 'I've decided to hire a governess for Abby and I think—'

'I want to know what all this is about,' he said, sitting upright with an effort. 'All this "I know everything" stuff. If you think that's all it takes to get rid of me, you'd better think again. I'm entitled to an explanation. What exactly do you think you know, Stella?'

She wanted to sit down but decided against it; she felt slightly less vulnerable standing up. Taking a long breath to steady her nerves, she told him. 'I know that you have been taking money from the firm.'

His expression changing from anger to caution, Clive said, 'That's a damned lie!'

Stella eyed him carefully, wondering how much to tell him. Perhaps for the moment she would leave Harry Parr out of it. She said, 'Papa has been suspicious for some time now.' Bringing her father into it made her feel stronger. 'Do you really mean to deny it?'

'Of course I do. God!' He tossed his head. 'If the business is failing he's looking for someone to blame. He would choose me, wouldn't he? The outsider. The man who stole his daughter. Let's pin it all on poor old Clive! You must see that if you have eyes in your head.'

'So you know it's failing? You've never mentioned it to me.'

'Business is hardly your forte, my dear. You have money, not brains.'

She hated the 'endearments' he used during their arguments. 'I'm not as stupid as you would like to think I am.'

'You're not as *stable* as I'd like you to be, but there's nothing to be done about that. I bear with it. You don't always see things clearly, Stella. Not always clear in your mind. You make errors of judgement and you twist things. A touch of the Hesters, if you see what I mean. You get yourself into a panic, and you're doing it now.'

'I'm not getting in a panic.' Although God knows it would be understandable if she was. 'I'm very calm, Clive. Very collected.'

'The devil you are!'

She ignored the challenging look in his eyes. Don't let him rile you, she told herself. He's good at upsetting you, but don't let it happen today. Keep your temper in check, Stella. You hold all the winning cards.

He said, 'In another ten years they'll be putting you away. Tucking you up in a nice little home and throwing away the key. You won't see Abby; you won't see anybody.'

She managed to keep her expression steady. She wouldn't let him know how much those words had frightened her; how terrifying the spectre he had conjured up.

'I know you've run up huge gambling debts,' she said quietly, 'and presumably that's why you've been taking the money.'

Something flashed in his eyes – was it *fear*? The thought gave her courage to carry on. 'My father is going to take action against you, Clive. You will have to stand trial.'

Watching him, she felt little compassion as the flash of fear settled into something more permanent.

He began to bluster as she had known he would. 'Take action? *Take action*? Against me? The man's mad. I've done nothing actionable. Nothing at all. I've had expenses of one kind and another, but as for *actionable*. Your darling Papa won't see me in court, I'll tell you that for nothing!' He blinked rapidly. 'In fact I'll probably drag *him* through the courts – for slander. See how the bugger likes that.' He drew a quick breath. 'If he thinks he's going to nail me, he's wrong. Nobody's going to put me away. And what' – he clutched his stomach, screwing up his face – 'what sort of wife are you, eh? Siding with your father against me. They won't let you testify – you know that, don't you? And if they did I'd have you discredited. Taking after Aunt Hester. Oh yes! Take a good look at yourself, Stella. Your parents ought to be grateful to me for taking you off their hands! You're quite a responsibility, you know that? "Treat her gently, Clive. She's highly-strung." Highly-strung, my arse!'

'Clive!' For a moment she almost lost her temper. He knew how she hated coarseness of speech and he only did it to annoy her.

His expression changed to one of leering contempt. 'Oh dear! Miss Prim doesn't like nasty rough Clive's language. Then why didn't you stick with the saintly Gerald? He never says rude words, does he? Probably the poor sod doesn't *know* any!'

202

'He doesn't use foul language in front of—'

'He's a mother's boy.'

'He's a gentleman.' She took several slow breaths. 'I also know that you have a prison record.'

That *did* shake him. His face went white and then red. He stammered, 'That was years ago. And could hardly be classed as a *record*.'

'An assault, Clive. A month in prison for assault. You kept that pretty quiet.'

He was silent. She could almost hear his mind turning. Then he said slowly, 'How the hell did you dig that up?'

'Does it matter how I know, Clive? I do know you injured a man.'

He seemed to sag against the pillows as though all the stuffing had been knocked out of him, looking at her with an expression which defied interpretation. When he spoke it was slowly, as though dredging up the memories exhausted him. 'It was nothing – a bit of a dust-up. The man had it coming.'

'You hit him.'

Clive appeared not to hear her. 'He went for me first, but he lived to regret it. I gave him a pasting. Knocked out a couple of teeth and bloodied his nose.'

Stella watched, sickened, as her husband's expression revealed the satisfaction the fight had given him.

Clive shook his head. 'The fool didn't raise a finger to help himself. Just kept screaming for help until they came rushing out to drag me away.' He was breathing rapidly, agitated by the memories, and a muscle jumped in his right cheek. 'I knocked a few manners into the little sod, and I didn't regret it. It was worth a month inside, if you must know.'

She was suddenly trembling. 'Violence appalls me, you know that. I would never have married you if I had been aware of that fact. We might almost agree you married me under false pretences.' Somehow she managed to look him straight in the eye although she knew his rage was mounting, fuelled no doubt by fear of discovery.

He said, 'I wish to God I'd never married you, and that's the truth.'

'Did you, Clive? *Did* you marry me?'

He glanced up, trying to control his agitation. 'Did I marry you? What sort of question is that?'

'Did you marry me, Clive? Or were you already married?'

A shocked silence fell between them. Then Stella went on, 'Bigamy's a criminal offence, Clive. They can put you in prison for that.' At last she had beaten him. She saw the fight go out of him.

'Christ, Stella! Where – I mean how on earth . . .' His face crumpled.

Stella hardened her heart. 'My father hired a private detective. He's apparently been following you: digging into your past. Not a very pretty past, either, from all accounts. So it seems I am not Mrs Clive Nicolson after all. Nor is Abby your legal daughter. It's all a bit of a mess, Clive, wouldn't you say?' Still he said nothing. Stella became unnerved by the silence and she went on, 'We have lived together in sin all these years, and you knew it. Your wife is still alive, Clive. Oh yes, we know all about May Rose Tompkins. It seems that my father's money was well spent. His original instincts have been proved sound. I only wish—'

'You will never take Abby from me. *Never!*' His voice was a hoarse whisper.

'I intend to go back to America, Clive, and I'll challenge you in court if I have to. Abby will—'

'No!' His voice had risen.

Too late Stella recognised the signs. He moved from the bed in one swift movement to seize her wrist in a fiercely painful grip. 'Promise me that, Stella. Promise me. You mustn't take my daughter away.' When she didn't answer, he twisted her arm so that she cried out. 'You will never take my daughter!'

'You want her to stay in England and be shamed? Is that fair to her?' Stella gasped.

'She's as much mine as yours!' he shouted. He bent her arm so far that tears sprang into her eyes and she thought she might faint from the pain.

'Let go of me!' she begged. 'You'll break my arm!'

'I'll break your head – I'll wring your bloody neck – if you try to take my daughter!' Suddenly he released her and she fell to her knees, sobbing, nursing her arm.

'You *won't* take her!' he told her, his voice shaking with emotion. 'If you try – I warn you – you'll regret it.'

'Are you threatening *us* now?'

'I'd rather see you both dead!'

'For God's sake, Clive! Are you crazy?'

He sat down heavily on the bed, doubled up, and Stella thought what a pair they made, so much rage and pain.

She said slowly, 'I want her to forget you, Clive. If she thinks you're dead, she need never know that she is illegitimate. She can still think of you as an honourable man. Don't you want that for her? I want us all to forget you and the wrong you've done us. I've asked Mrs Malone to come as governess for a few—'

'Mrs Malone?' He came back to life. '*Mrs Malone*? You can't ask her to – Stella, she's not suitable. Haven't I told you? She's a – a whore.'

Stella rolled her eyes in disgust. Did he really think she was that stupid? 'You know nothing about her,' she said firmly. 'She is my friend, and we've talked. For your information, Mrs Malone is a respectable widow. She's been well educated in a convent school and she has a way with children. I'm not asking your permission, Clive, I'm telling you. Mrs Malone—'

His forefinger was pointed at her face and his expression was triumphant. 'She's a high-class whore, Stella. A courtesan. A prostitute.' He laughed. 'Lady of the night. Street-walker! Whatever you like to call her.'

He looked as though he had just won at poker, Stella thought incredulously. She stared at him. 'She's the widow of a sea-captain.'

'Gussie Malone propositioned me the first day we came aboard! I'm telling you!'

'I don't believe a word of it. You'd have said something to me before now. You'd have found it a great joke.'

'The joke's on you, Stella! I'm telling you – she was all over me with hints and winks. Ask *her* if you don't believe *me*.'

'Ask my friend if she's a – a *prostitute*? I shall do no such thing. It's a disgusting suggestion. She would be mortally offended.'

'She'd be taken aback, I grant you that. But hardly offended. Your Mrs Malone was going to charge me a hundred guineas!

That's how she earns her living, Stella. Women like her travel these liners looking for so-called clients. There's another one on board – you may have noticed her. Very Italian-looking, dark hair and wears an ermine collar whatever the weather. A so-called contessa. They pick on a rich gentleman and offer their favours. In a way, they're like the professional card-sharps. They trawl the big liners in search of rich pickings.' His face broke into a broad grin. 'If you don't believe me, ask Hemmings. He knows her.'

Stella stared at him, aware of the smallest flicker of unease. He seemed so *sure*.

'You mean the man who punched you – the professional gambler?'

'Exactly. He knows all the ladies of easy virtue. He recognised her; they met on the *Lusitania* a few years ago. You ask him what he knows about Gussie Malone.'

'I prefer not to ask him anything at all.' Her heart was thudding. 'A man like that. A gambler and a – a thug. He hit you, I recall.'

'Hemmings says she's well worth every penny. Lively, imaginative, willing to go along with fancy ideas—'

Stella shouted, 'Stop this! You're lying and I won't listen to it.'

His face darkened. 'But you'll believe all your father says about *me*, won't you.' He laughed mirthlessly.

Stella felt herself shiver with apprehension. He seemed so *certain*. But it was impossible. Ridiculous. He was just trying to upset her. For a few moments she was speechless. Her confidence had been shaken, but she felt that it was disloyal to Gussie even to *wonder* about the truth of such a terrible accusation.

He said, 'She's fooled you, Stella. I bet she's laughing herself to sleep at night.' He cocked his head, enjoying her discomfiture. 'Are you really fit to be a mother, Stella? Will the courts think so when they hear how gullible you are? That you want to employ a street-walker to educate our daughter? You'll be a laughing-stock! And when I tell them that you are taking after your crazy aunt; that you're becoming deranged; that you have days when you can't remember your own name or which month it is . . .'

She stared at him. 'That's utter nonsense!'

'Ah, but they might believe me! Who knows?' He shrugged. 'Suppose the courts find in my favour, eh? Have you thought about that? You see, dearest Stella, I meant what I said about

Abby. If you try to take her away you'll be sorry. Both of you.'

'*Both of us*?' She could hardly speak.

'Oh yes! I can be a bastard when I want to. You have no idea.'

'You'll *kill* us? That's what you're saying, is it?' Even as she spoke the words rang in her ears with a terrible finality. Victory had somehow slipped away from her. Clive was devious, totally unprincipled, and would willingly perjure himself to separate her from her daughter. If she took him to court he would claim that she was insane, unfit to be a mother. He would take control of Abby.

If, however, she *won* the case he would kill them both.

Chapter Eleven

Gussie dipped her pen into the ink and wrote the date. Then she wrote:

My dear Harry,
  It has been the most wonderful thing, meeting you again like this. You cannot imagine how much it means to me to know we are friends again . . .

She took a coffee cream from the box beside her and chewed it thoughtfully. First she must tell him how much he meant to her. Later she would confess. Then it was up to him. Somewhere in the letter she would say that she had given up her profession to become a governess to the Nicolsons' child. That would impress him.

  . . . I am so pleased that you know the truth about our little girl and so happy that you saw her with your own eyes, thinking it was another woman's child, but not to worry. You saw how beautiful she was. My deep regret is that she never knew her papa and that you were never able to share those few precious years . . .

Gussie wondered if that would sound like a reproach. She didn't want to punish him; she rewrote it:

  . . . My deep regret is that you were unable to spend more time with her, but at least she saw her papa on that one occasion . . .

Perhaps she should mention his own disastrous marriage and spare a kind word for his wife. That would let him know that she was bearing no grudges and could be as generous as the next person. She sipped her port and lemon, frowning a little.

. . . I am sorry your marriage did not bring you the happiness you deserve. Mine was hardly the—

'Holy Mother!'

She mustn't talk about her own marriage, for there never was one – and wasn't that the whole point of the letter? Realising that she would have to write a fair copy, she crossed out the last four words, put down the pen and picked up a pencil. Then she looked for a Turkish delight and ate the last one. The chocolates were disappearing fast, but at least they provided her with a little sustenance for this delicate and demoralising task.

. . . I shall be taking up a position with Stella Nicolson on my return to London – as governess to Abby, who is a bright child whose education has been sadly neglected. I will return to America with them when the London house has been sold.
Now, my dearest Harry . . .

Was that a little too amorous? Over-affectionate? She thought about him in those terms, but he might not appreciate the fact. By the time he had finished reading the letter he might well feel like diving overboard! She changed it:

. . . Now, Harry, I am coming to the most difficult part of this letter and the whole purpose of it. As God is my witness, I would rather confess to a priest than to you . . .

'Oh, Harry,' she whispered. 'My dearest Harry, don't turn away from me. Forgive me, *please*, and give me another chance.'

. . . but I now need to unburden myself. I have lied, Harry. Whatever else I may have been, I have never thought of myself as a liar and cannot let it continue. The truth is that I never have been married and have no right to call myself Mrs. That is the half

210

of it, Harry. The rest is that I have no right to claim respectability,
for I am still . . .

Still *what?* Still an immoral woman.

'Say it then, Gussie. If you've an ounce of honesty in you.' The pencil hovered wordlessly. Gussie picked up a sharpener and improved the point. Then she took a large mouthful of her drink and ate another chocolate. Picking up the pencil, she wrote: *. . . I am still an immoral woman.*

Drawing a deep breath, she wrote:

> *. . . Now I have the chance to become truly respectable in the eyes of the world and I mean to seize my chance with both hands. But I make no excuses for my past. Maybe I ought to be deeply ashamed, but it would be another lie to pretend that I am. I have survived by selling myself. I have charged for my services. A business arrangement. It is a profession as old as the hills, and has never felt dishonourable to me.*
>
> *Knowing how strong your sentiments are on the matter I doubt if you will even begin to understand, and I won't blame you for that. However, it is your decision, Harry, and you must deal with it as best you can. I think we are both lonely people and if we could forget the past we might be able to start again. I love you and I know I could make you happy, but it is up to you. If you cannot love me, Harry, for what I am and have been then we must part, this time for ever.*
>
> *Your loving friend,*
> *Gussie.*

Once again the pencil hovered. Maybe one kiss? She sighed. She wished that he had kissed her just once. It would have been something to cling to if the worst happened. Closing her eyes, she tried to imagine how it would be if he put his arms around her and pulled her close. She could almost feel his lips against her mouth . . .

Yes, she would add a kiss. But as she wrote it the newly sharpened pencil point snapped and Gussie stared at it, disconcerted. For anyone with a superstitious nature, it might look like a bad omen.

* * *

That evening, after dinner, Harry was writing the last page of his report. He had just signed his name and was blotting it when there was a knock on the door and a steward handed him a letter. Harry closed the door and for a moment or two stood where he was, eyeing the envelope. *Please*! he thought. Not another suicide note from Stella Nicolson. He already felt badly about what had happened and longed for the voyage to end without further incident. Stella Nicolson's father was going to be very displeased with him, but there was nothing he could do.

He sat down and slid the letter opener through the envelope flap with a sense of deepening unease. Then he unfolded the letter, which started with the words '*Dear Harry . . .*' He was swamped with relief, for Stella Nicolson would never address him in that way. He glanced at the signature; it was from Gussie! Suddenly his relief melted away and he didn't want to read whatever she had written. He knew from experience that anything palatable could be *told*. Only the unpalatable facts were consigned to paper, to be read alone.

'Oh, Gussie!' he murmured. Was it possible . . . No. She wouldn't lie to him a second time. Hardly knowing why, he refolded the letter and pushed it back into the envelope. He would pretend it had never been delivered; that he had never learned the contents. He had decided to ask Gussie to be his wife, and she must remain the respectable widow of a sea-captain; she must be Mrs Hector Dewitt who called herself Mrs Malone. It was all that he asked. Her earlier life no longer existed, and he had made up his mind never to refer to it again. So why did this letter terrify him?

'Open it, you fool!' he told himself.

It was that swine Nicolson who had first raised the doubt in his mind by the way he allowed his hand to rest on Gussie's shoulder. To Harry's trained eye that had been suspicious, hinting at a closer acquaintance than circumstances merited. It was that small gesture and an indefinable something in his voice when he said, 'Sleep well', as though it had some other meaning that only the two of them would understand. At the time, he had refused to consider the possibility of any kind of liaison because he knew so much about Nicolson that was bad.

Now he took the letter from his pocket. During his time in

212

the police force he had learned that in all situations he should expect the worst to happen. So what was the worst he could expect from Gussie's letter? The admission that she was – whoring.

'Whoring!' he said aloud. The thought of a succession of men lying above her, troubled him deeply, but he needed to know the worst before he could decide if he could live with it. There was no way he could marry her and then reproach her. Marriage meant a total commitment, an acceptance of the real Gussie. He unfolded the letter.

As he read it his hopes first rose, then plummeted.

'Oh *God*!' he whispered, crumpling the letter in his hand and hurling it from him. How could she call her way of life 'a profession'? 'A business arrangement'? Well, that much was true, anyway.

'Two lonely people.' Yes, he was lonely, but what he wanted to ease his loneliness was a loving wife. He thought of all the men who had used her and shuddered. No doubt there wasn't much Gussie didn't know about pleasing a man in bed. For a moment he tried to imagine it. She would be cheerful, solicitous, kindly even – never crude or spiteful. This realisation came as a surprise, and he was shocked to feel a flash of jealousy where he had expected to feel disgust.

'My dearest Gussie, how *could* you?' he exclaimed.

Edie had been a virgin when they married. His idea of a marriage was for a husband to initiate his bride into the mysteries of love-making. That would be impossible with Gussie.

A knock at the door startled him horribly. No doubt this was Gussie coming to see how he had reacted to the revelations in her letter. What would he say? How should he treat her? With politeness, certainly, but—

'Just a moment!' He retrieved the crumpled letter and pushed it with the envelope under his pillow.

As he opened the door his pulse was racing.

Stella Nicolson said, 'May I come in? It's rather important.' She stepped into the cabin without waiting for permission and turned to face him. She looked agitated and her eyes moved restlessly around.

Harry's relief was strangely tinged with disappointment. He

said, 'Please sit down,' and indicated the chair by his table, wondering impatiently what she could want.

She said, 'I'd rather stand, actually,' but then sat down. 'I've had a terrible argument with my husband, and it seems he is determined to thwart me at every turn. I won't have it, Mr Parr. I cannot live with him, yet he refuses to leave me. He says he will fight me in the courts to gain custody of Abby. I can't allow it, and I want you to understand that. I may need your help. That's what I'm trying to say.' She stood up abruptly, swallowed hard and made a sudden move towards the door.

Harry put out a hand to detain her. 'Mrs Nicolson, I don't think I do quite understand,' he began. 'What exactly can I do? Surely your father is the right person to advise you.'

She swung round to face him. 'My father is a thousand and more miles away, Mr Parr. He can't help me. I have to deal with this myself, and I will, but I cannot manage alone.' She pressed her lips together in a way that struck Harry as odd. 'It's the end of the line. You do understand that?'

'I think so. What I don't understand—'

She interrupted him. 'There was something else. What was it?'

'Mrs Nicolson, I do wish—'

'Oh, yes. Of course.' She clasped and unclasped her hands. 'I have decided to engage Mrs Malone as a governess for Abby, but she will also act as a companion to me. She is a strong woman, Mr Parr, and I shall need someone like that. I am learning from her. I need her friendship. You may argue that our relationship has been a short one, and I agree, but I *know* Gussie Malone is good for me.' She hesitated, pressing two fingers against her lips. 'My husband is furious. He would obviously like to think of me as friendless and alone. He has made some – has made a frightful accusation against Mrs Malone. I know he is lying, but I cannot prove it. To ask her would be insulting, and I understand you have known her a long time. Mr Parr, would you say her credentials are genuine?'

Harry was caught off-guard. Still attempting to come to terms with the contents of Gussie's letter, he was quite unprepared for Stella's challenge and thought rapidly, hating to tell a direct lie. 'Certainly I've known her a long time, but we did lose touch for many years.' He was desperately trying to think. 'Mrs Nicolson, what exactly are you implying?'

If he told her the truth, he would shatter Gussie's hopes of decent employment, which was probably the best chance she had ever had in her life. He couldn't do that.

She said, 'Clive has called her a – a *whore*, Mr Parr. I know it must sound quite bizarre, but that is the way of my husband. He will say anything to besmirch her reputation simply because I value her as a friend.'

'Mrs Nicolson—' She was watching him closely; he mustn't put a foot wrong. 'Mrs Nicolson, if Mrs Malone says she is a widow, then I think you should accept that she is telling the truth.'

It *was* a lie but he didn't regret it. Gussie's future was at stake. He might decide not to marry her, but he would never betray her. He had done her a great wrong in the past; this was his chance to redress that wrong.

'So she is not a loose woman?'

'Of course not.' As he confirmed the lie his self-image blurred for the first time in his life. Loyalty to the woman he loved had knocked him from the path he had trodden with such pride and determination since his father's death.

'I would expect her to give every satisfaction as a governess,' he went on firmly. 'She was educated at a very good convent, that I do know. She is also very fond of your daughter.'

Stella Nicolson gave him a long look. 'Would you employ her, Mr Parr?'

He dare not hesitate. 'Certainly I would.' But would I marry her, he wondered.

Her smile was bleak. 'Then it's as I thought. My husband lied about her; he had the audacity to suggest that she had propositioned him.' She seemed to be thinking. 'Well, I'll bid you good-day, Mr Parr. For now.'

'Mrs Nicolson—' He was becoming a little alarmed by her manner. She spoke normally, but underlying her composure he was aware of something else – something darker. He hoped she wasn't intending to make another attempt on her life. He said, 'If it would help you, I could call on you at your home in Clissold Park. There may be something I can do to help. Your father would, I'm sure, want me to be of service to you. A little moral support if nothing else.' Her answer could be illuminating, he thought.

'A little moral support.' She gave him a strange look. 'So are you saying you *will* help me?'

'Of course I will.'

'That's most kind. I shall look forward to seeing you again. I'm grateful to you for your promise of help, Mr Parr.'

So she was expecting to be there, he thought with relief. No more suicide attempts. He stared at the door after she had gone, trying to take stock of the situation. He had deliberately misled her about Gussie Malone. Highly unethical behaviour on his part, and probably actionable. He had broken one of his own strictest rules and felt no regrets. And he really wasn't sure why.

Gussie, wide-awake and sick at heart, clutched Clara to her. It was gone midnight and she hadn't slept a wink. Her letter to Harry had brought no response, which surely could mean only one thing: that he was no longer interested. As she had feared, her confession had disgusted him. Probably he would now make strenuous efforts to avoid seeing her again, and when they docked they would leave the ship separately and that would be the end. She tried hard not to care. She had known it was a gamble and it had failed. No one to blame but herself. Sighing deeply, she longed to give way to the luxury of tears but her pride forbade it. She still had her life, for better or worse. So long as she had her looks, she need never starve.

If only she could sleep, Gussie thought wearily. The day's events had exhausted her, and she longed for an escape from the thoughts that tormented her. She looked at the little clock. Nearly one o'clock. She sat up and tossed the doll aside, deciding she could not bear to lie there another moment. She would go for a walk. There was no law against roaming the ship in the early hours of the morning. Having slipped out of her nightclothes and into a blouse, skirt and light coat, she let herself out into the gloom of the half-lit corridor, closing the door quietly behind her. She had only taken a few steps, however, when she saw Stella Nicolson hurrying towards her. Gussie's heart sank at the sight of her friend. Stella wore only a nightdress and dressing-gown and her hair was dishevelled.

'My dear!' Gussie exclaimed, as the distraught figure reached her. 'Whatever is—'

'You must come quickly!' Stella told her breathlessly. 'I need your help. Yours and Mr Parr's. It's my husband. He's dead.'

Wrapped up in her own personal crisis, Gussie took a moment to understand what she was being told.

'Dead?' she echoed. '*Dead*? Are you sure? I mean, how on earth—'

'Am I sure?' Stella tossed her head. 'He's lying lifeless on the floor. He was trying to reach the bathroom. Staggering about. Maybe he felt sick. Maybe he needed to – you know what I mean . . . He spoke to me. Called for me to help him, but I did nothing but watch. There was nothing to say. He clutched his stomach and then he collapsed.' She swayed suddenly and leaned against the wall for support.

Gussie, shocked, was speechless. She had a sharp image of Clive Nicolson spreadeagled on the floor of the cabin. Holy Mother of God! The poor man!

'A heart attack maybe,' she said.

Stella smiled wanly. 'It was no heart attack, Gussie. The fact is that I've killed him. I had to.' Her eyes closed and she swayed again.

'You've – you've *what*?' Gussie clutched her to save her from falling. 'You've *killed* him? Oh no, Stella! For the love of God, don't say such a terrible thing.'

Stella nodded almost eagerly. 'I decided to kill him before he killed us. I told Mr Parr and he said he'd help.'

'Mr *Parr*?' Gussie stared at her. 'Mr Parr said he'd *help* you to kill your husband?'

'Not to kill him. I could manage that. To help us dispose of him now that he's dead. It will take all three of us to get him to the rail.'

Gussie looked around her, terrified that someone would appear and overhear the conversation. 'Look, let's go into my cabin,' she suggested. 'You can tell me about it there.'

'There's no time and there's nothing to tell.' Stella looked at her with an artificial brightness that made Gussie's flesh creep. 'It was easy. I mixed up all the tablets I could find – dream sweets, everything – and added them to his whisky. He was half drunk by then and didn't notice the taste. He drank it all. I waited and waited until I was sure. Now he hasn't moved for nearly an hour, and he's not breathing. I'm not sorry, Gussie. You must understand that it was necessary. He would have killed us, you see; he made that quite clear. He was going to persuade them to put me in a home and then he meant to take Abby.' Her voice was rising hysterically.

Gussie put a warning finger to her lips. 'Keep your voice down or someone will hear you.' She was normally sensible in a crisis, but Stella's words and the way in which they were uttered had given her a cold feeling of dread. 'You said Mr Parr was going to help you?'

Stella nodded. 'He said he would be glad to be of service, and that my father would want him to help me.'

'But I'm sure he didn't know you meant to—' Better not use the word 'murder', she thought, saying instead '—to do away with your husband.' It was impossible. Harry would never even lie. He would certainly not agree to help cover up a murder. Would he? If he would, then she had seriously misjudged him all these years.

Stella seemed disinterested in Gussie's protests. She caught hold of Gussie's hand and said, 'If we can get Clive to the rail and push him overboard, I can go back to bed. Then I simply report him missing in the morning. There'll be plenty of people to say that he frequently over-indulged. Others to say that he played poker most of the night. How am I supposed to know where he is?'

Gussie said, 'But Stella, you can't—'

'But Clive's no light weight and we *shall* need Mr Parr's help.'

Gussie wondered briefly if she was living through a nightmare and would shortly wake up. A look at Stella's wild eyes, however, convinced her that the situation was real enough. Poor Stella had obviously endured more than she could deal with, and her mind had collapsed under the strain. The discovery that they were not legally married and the threats her husband had made against her had tipped her over the edge, but would the courts see it like that,

Gussie wondered? If so, they would be lenient. If not – it didn't bear thinking about.

She put an arm round her friend's shoulders and gave her a reassuring hug. 'Let's go to my cabin,' she suggested again. 'While you have a nice drop of brandy to calm your nerves, I'll go and fetch Mr Parr. 'But there was absolutely no question, she decided, that she would help to tip Clive's body over the side. That was conspiracy to murder, and she wanted none of it. She might not be a model citizen by any stretch of the imagination, but neither was she a criminal.

Stella resisted her efforts to edge her into the cabin. 'I don't want a brandy, Gussie, thank you. I'm quite calm. We must get rid of Clive's body while it's still dark. I shall say he'd been drinking and must have stumbled. Missed his footing. I shall say I warned him about going on deck in his state, but he wouldn't listen.'

In spite of her reservations, Gussie felt a brief flash of admiration for the woman. It *would* sound very feasible. Stella might have become temporarily unbalanced, but she was still thinking clearly. She said, 'I don't think we should bother Mr Parr, Stella.'

Stella frowned. 'But we can't carry him on our own.'

'I don't think we should actually – that is, I think we could . . .' She searched her brain for inspiration. 'Why can't you just say you woke up and found him dead in the bed beside you? You could say he'd taken an overdose of the tablets – by mistake. An accident! Now wouldn't that be better?'

But Stella didn't think so. She had only one clear thought in her head, and that was the disposal of her husband's body. For one wonderful irrational moment Gussie thought of ringing for a steward and handing the entire problem over to him. But Stella was relying on her and she couldn't bring herself to betray her. Maybe Harry would know what to do. The trouble was that after her letter, Gussie had no desire to face him. Knowing what he must now think of her and seeing the disappointment in his eyes would be more than she could bear.

She said, 'Why don't you go along to Mr Parr's cabin and explain what's happened? He'll know what to do.' She was ashamed of herself but Stella, knowing nothing of the confessional letter, could have no inkling of the awkwardness of Gussie's situation. She wasn't really backing out, she argued silently, simply leaving the next move to Harry. Harry had apparently, *unbelievably*, offered to help, so he must have had some idea of what was likely to happen. Perhaps he already had a plan. He would probably persuade Stella to 'find' the body in the morning. That certainly made more sense than anything else. If he decided to involve Gussie, that would be his decision.

A fresh and unwelcome thought suddenly struck her. If Stella felt that Gussie had been less supportive than she might have been, she could well change her mind about the position of governess. Gussie, half-supporting Stella, was still agonising over what she should do when they heard footsteps approaching.

'Quick!' cried Gussie. 'Into my cabin! Don't argue.'

She dragged a protesting Stella into her cabin and shut the door behind them. They stood breathlessly regarding one another as the footsteps approached and then stopped outside. Gussie's heart was thumping uncomfortably in her chest. Had somebody discovered Clive Nicolson's body?

She whispered, 'Did you close your cabin door?'

Stella nodded.

'You're sure?' Maybe in her present state she had left it open and a wandering steward had noticed the body.

'Quite sure!'

Someone knocked sharply on the door. Stella whispered, 'Don't answer it.'

Gussie had a terrifying thought which left her weak at the knees. Suppose after all Clive was *not* dead? Suppose he understood what Stella had attempted, had recovered and had now come looking for her. She imagined him forcing his way in, grabbing hold of Stella and trying to strangle her. He was a big man and powerful, and Gussie knew that if it came to a struggle their combined chances against him would be slim indeed.

She muttered a quick prayer as they clung together, watching the door as though hypnotised by it.

The knock was repeated.

They waited. Surely whoever it was would give up and go away? Now that it was too late, Gussie wished that she had gone with Stella to Harry's cabin. At least they would have been safe there.

A low voice from outside called, 'Gussie! *Gussie!*'

Stella said, 'It sounds like Mr Parr.'

'Who is it? I'm in bed,' Gussie said.

'It's me – Harry. I need to talk to you.'

Gussie's spirits sank to a new low. She could imagine what he wanted to say and she couldn't bear it. But before she could speak, Stella had darted to the door and was tugging it open.

In a daze, Gussie heard her say, 'Mr Parr. We were just going to fetch you.'

Slowly Gussie forced herself to look at Harry, who was staring at them in bewilderment.

He said to Gussie, 'I thought you said you were in bed.'

'So I was lying!' The words came out more sharply than she had intended.

Stella said, 'Come in!' and tugged at his sleeve.

He came in, shutting the door behind him. Gussie edged away until the backs of her legs touched the bed, whereupon she sat down heavily. Stella sat on the chair, while Harry remained standing with his back to the door. He looked from Gussie to Stella and his consternation deepened.

'What's happening?' he asked.

Stella said, 'I've done it, Mr Parr. I've killed Clive, and now we have to take him to the rail and push him over.'

He held up his hand and said, 'Whoa! You've done *what*?'

She tutted impatiently. 'I've just told you. I've killed him and now we need your help to—' She seemed to sense that something was wrong. 'You said you would help me, Mr Parr.'

He stared at her, then gave Gussie a horrified look. 'Is she *serious*? Is she saying what I think she's saying?'

Gussie said, 'Stella insists that you agreed to help her.'

He gave a groan of dismay. 'I didn't say I'd help her to – God Almighty! I didn't mean . . .' He gave a silent whistle which said more than words.

Stella said, 'We must hurry before it gets dark. We don't want to be seen.' She stood up. 'We're wasting time, Mr Parr. Now that you're here we can—'

Harry took a deep breath and interrupted her. 'Mrs Nicolson, I came to talk with Mrs Malone – not to help you dispose of your husband.' He turned to Gussie. 'Is he *really* dead? What happened?'

'She says she gave him a mixture of pills in a bottle of whisky and that he collapsed and died. Do you think you could go and take a look, Harry? Just in case it's true – although I can't believe it is.' She was thinking that Harry had come to her cabin to talk to her. If Stella had stayed away, Gussie might know the worst by now. Or the best. She knew the odds were stacked against her and tried not to hope, pushing the thought to the back of her mind and concentrating on their present dilemma.

Stella said, 'I'll go with you, Mr Parr.'

She sounded almost eager, thought Gussie, and considered what awaited Stella when the murder was discovered. *If* it were a murder and not an accident. Stella Nicolson's entire future depended on what Gussie and Harry were prepared to do for her tonight. If Stella were arrested and sent for trial, she would certainly be found guilty and would hang. Her only hope would be to plead insanity, and then she would be certified and committed to an asylum. Stella would lose her daughter, Abby would be haunted by the shame of her mother's trial and subsequent death; it would be far worse for Abby than the disgrace of her father's crimes would have been.

Gussie was aware of a nagging doubt and increasing guilt. Surely somehow she should have guessed what was going through Stella's mind? There must have been clues which Gussie had missed.

Harry said, 'I'll go with her, Gussie. No point in us all going.'

'And then?' she asked.

He shrugged. 'God only knows. I don't. If a crime's been committed—'

Gussie said, 'Couldn't it have been an accident? Or suicide?'

He looked at her. 'But we know it wasn't, don't we?' Gently he took Stella's arm and said, 'We'll go and take a look, shall we?'

Gussie cried desperately, 'Harry! Wait! You're not a policeman now. You're Stella's *friend*, and you're employed by her father to *help* her. Couldn't you – couldn't we all – forget what's been *said*? Shouldn't we just think about it? What difference would it make to tell a few small lies? If the poor man's dead, we can't bring him back, so why sacrifice Stella and ruin Abby's life? We all make mistakes; God knows I have, and too many to count. You have, too. Stella's been through hell, Harry, and she's shown great courage in a way.'

Harry looked at her. 'We'd be accomplices,' he said flatly. 'A conspiracy to pervert the course of justice.'

'Jargon, Harry.' She glared at him.

'*Jargon*?' He glared back.

She ploughed on, ignoring his expression. 'Words on paper, Harry. I'm talking about a real person in deep distress and – and *confusion* of mind, to put it kindly. We both know that she is not entirely responsible. She *says* she did it, but how do we know she's telling the truth? Maybe she *wishes* that she'd done it. Now, Harry, I don't need a jury to make up my mind, I'm prepared to go for reasonable doubt.'

He smiled faintly. 'You're getting a bit mixed-up, Gussie. You'd never make a lawyer.'

She held her breath.

'But just maybe I take your point, much as I disapprove of the thinking behind it. I think I could, in the circumstances—' He stopped, shaking his head unhappily.

Gussie thought: Even now he can hardly bring himself to say it. Good old Harry. Honest as the day is long.

He said, 'I might forget the odd comment. Here and there.' He frowned. 'Then again I might not. God Almighty! Why is it always so difficult? There's right and there's wrong.'

'And there's somewhere in between,' said Gussie. 'There's mitigating circumstances, Harry.'

He laughed then. Not at her but with her, and the sound charmed her.

'Oh, Gussie,' he said, 'you know nothing about mitigating circumstances! You make it sound so simple, but the fact remains that the law is the way it is to protect the innocent. It's not there to provide excuses for the guilty ones.' He shrugged. 'First we must establish the facts. I'll take a look and then come back here. We'll think of something.' He looked at Stella and said, 'Come on, then.'

Gussie threw herself on to the bed, exhausted. She hugged Clara to her chest and allowed herself to think about Harry. He hadn't looked at her unkindly; he hadn't treated her any differently. So what did that mean – if anything? He might have been acting normally because Stella was present and because the situation was so unexpected. But what was it he had intended to say to her when he gave that first knock? He had dressed in the middle of the night – unless he hadn't even *un*dressed. Maybe he was so overwrought that he had been out pacing the deck for hours. Or maybe he intended to reject her and wanted to get it over with as quickly as possible. Gussie groaned. She longed for the smallest ray of hope, but it was dangerous to think of what might be.

'The trouble is I *love* the dear man!' she whispered. 'I could make him a good wife. He *needs* me. I can see it in his face. And his clothes need attention, and he's not eating properly.' She would give him hearty stews with dumplings and fruit pies with thick, crumbly crust. Not that she could cook, but she'd learn.

But *not* if they were all arrested on a charge of conspiracy to pervert the course of justice. Reluctantly she returned to the question of Clive Nicolson.

'The late Clive Nicolson,' she muttered. It crossed her mind that now she would never take him to bed. Not that he was any great loss, but she was always curious about men. How does such a good-looking man go to the bad, she thought, sad for him. She imagined his young mother looking at her newborn son with joy and holding such high hopes for him. When, she wondered, had he taken that first and fateful step from the straight and narrow?

She wanted to pray for help, but that would mean alerting the Holy Virgin to their plight and she rather doubted the wisdom of that. Better shared with as few people as possible. First she pondered the question of disposing of the body. A man could conceivably fall overboard in the middle of the night, but it probably didn't happen very often. There would certainly be an inquiry of some kind. She and Harry could stick to an agreed story (about the fact that Nicolson was drunk), but under pressure Stella might say all the wrong things. She was definitely the weak link.

'Oh, Stella! *Stella!*' she murmured. The quicker she could be reunited with her parents in the relative calm of the family home, the better for all of them. Stella was having a breakdown, that was obvious, and they should have recognised the fact. She needed medical care and support if she was not to slide into an irreversible mental decline.

No, Gussie decided, they must go for accidental death – remembering that there would be an inquest which would involve a post mortem. Her knowledge of the latter was hazy, but she shuddered at the very idea. Yes, it would have to be an accidental overdose of his pills which had killed Nicolson. They could say that he lost count of how many he had taken. A heart attack would have been convenient, but if they were going to look inside him they were bound to discover an undamaged heart . . . unless he had *fallen*. Maybe they could say he had tripped and split his skull open? Stella said he had collapsed so he might have hit his head on something – the edge of the bath, perhaps, and . . .

Ah! They were back. Footsteps along the corridor. Gussie slid from the bed and hurried to open the door.

She took one look and gave a loud scream. As she stumbled backwards and almost fell, Clive Nicolson lurched after her into the cabin.

Chapter Twelve

He looked ghastly, deathly pale, with a huge, deepening bruise across his forehead which oozed blood. His eyes were bloodshot; his lips were grey and his arms dangled at his sides. For a moment Gussie was too shocked to speak and then relief swept over her. He *wasn't* dead! Stella had *not* committed murder, and they would not have to conspire to protect her from the gallows.

She stammered, 'Mr Nicolson,' and was then lost for words. What do you say to someone newly risen from the dead, she wondered. 'You'd better sit down,' she said.

As though to prove the sense of her suggestion he swayed, took a step backwards and fell against the door which slammed with a crash.

Gussie crossed herself and muttered a quick prayer for help. When the others returned they would be unable to get in. Clive Nicolson's weight was pressing the door shut. She would have to move him – or persuade him to move himself.

'Would you be better on the bed?' she suggested. 'I could help you.' She held out her arms, but he stared at her dully without apparent comprehension.

She said, 'Let me help you up,' and took hold of his hands.

With a quick jerk he tugged her forward so that she overbalanced and fell on top of him. Scrambling to free herself, she caught sight of his face. His smile was twisted but it was recognisably a smile, she thought, astonished.

He said, 'We never did . . . you and I . . . great pity . . .'

Her hopes rose. If he could joke, then he was not that far gone.

And his saucy remark amused her in spite of herself. She knelt beside him and took his hand.

'Maybe some day,' she lied, 'but right now we must get you away from the door. If you can't walk you must crawl. Mr Nicolson—'

His eyes closed and slowly opened again.

She repeated, 'We've got to move you away from the door.'

'Gussie . . .'

'Now don't talk.' And for pity's sake don't call me Gussie, she thought. She stood back, her thoughts chaotic. Suppose Harry had been present? He knew, of course, but to have such proof tossed before him would be highly embarrassing. She had to get Clive Nicolson out of her room – and suddenly it came to her. She would fetch the doctor and have him admitted to the ship's infirmary. That way, if he said anything compromising they would put it down to the ramblings of a sick man, and no one would be any the wiser.

She bent over him and put her hands under his shoulders. 'Come along now, Mr Nicolson.' She would drag him if she had to. If she *could*.

He said, 'That bitch tried . . . she tried to kill me . . .'

Gussie froze. 'Now what sort of nonsense is that?' she asked. 'Nobody's tried to do any such thing!'

Horrified, she imagined the doctor's reaction if he uttered such a comment in his hearing. He would have to take it seriously. But first things first. She must clear the doorway. She gave up the struggle to move him; he was much too heavy, so she would have to persuade him to move himself – if he still had the strength. She retreated to the bed and said, 'Come over here, Mr Nicolson. You can do it if you try.'

To her surprise he grinned and crawled a few steps towards her. She kept her eyes on his face, smiling. Suddenly he stopped with a groan and shook his head. 'Can't . . . no more . . .' He looked up at her. 'She's . . . killed me, Gussie . . . the bloody . . . pills . . .'

Compassion surged through her. He might be a bad man, but she couldn't just sit back and let him die. She knelt down and put her arms round him. 'I'll go for the doctor,' she said. 'He'll help you.'

'Gussie . . .'

'Mrs Malone to you, if you please! And hush now. It's going to be all right. You'll see.'

She looked down at him. Could she leave him to die without a shred of comfort? He was one of God's creatures. Impulsively Gussie knelt down and cradled him in her arms for a long moment. Then she kissed him. She stood up and moved to the door. Glancing back she saw that, as he watched her go, his face was abruptly contorted with pain. She closed the door and ran along the deserted corridor and down the stairs. She wondered what Harry and Stella were doing. Looking for Nicolson presumably, never expecting him to be in Gussie's cabin. Thank the Lord! She began to work out the tale she would tell the doctor which would cause the least trouble.

The doctor was not too pleased at being woken from his sleep. He opened the door to her, busily tying the cord of a paisley dressing-gown.

'Doctor Rowse?'

'I'm Doctor Mawle.' He rubbed his eyes sleepily. 'Is this an emergency of some kind?'

'It most certainly is. It's Mr Clive Nicolson,' Gussie told him. 'He turned up at my cabin about five minutes ago and—'

The doctor's expression changed from irritated to positively grim. 'Mr Clive Nicolson? Ah!' He nodded. 'A very difficult man. I'm afraid I've been expecting something like this. He came to me – was very abusive, as a matter of fact – and now of course—'

Gussie said, 'He came looking for his wife. He thought we might be together—'

'At *this* time of night?' He gave her a suspicious look.

Gussie felt like shaking him. 'Stella Nicolson and I are friends. She has been rather upset herself these last few days. Family matters. He probably thought she needed someone to talk to. To unburden herself. It's quite obvious to me that poor Mr Nicolson's ill. He's rambling and very pale. And he can't stand unaided.'

The doctor pursed his lips with annoyance. 'Drunk, you mean?'

'No, no. Ill.'

'And where was his wife?'

Gussie hadn't thought of an answer for that. She said, 'I've no idea. Out looking for him, I shouldn't wonder. I think he's very ill, doctor.'

'I'll get myself dressed and—'

'You should come right away,' she insisted. 'He looks very bad. Incoherent. Groaning.'

He hesitated. 'I'll come as I am,' he said. He picked up his bag from the corner of the cabin, checked the contents quickly and followed her out.

She led the way back to her cabin and found Harry and Stella waiting anxiously outside. Gussie raised her eyebrows to Harry in a gesture of despair. He said nothing. To Stella, Gussie said loudly, 'Oh, Mrs Nicolson. I expect you've been looking for your husband.' She inserted the key in the lock. 'He was looking for you and he's not at all well, so I took the liberty . . .' As the door swung open, they all stared at Clive Nicolson who was sitting on the floor with his head against the bed.

Stella said 'How on earth did he—' She made no attempt to go to him.

Harry said quickly, 'Don't touch him, Mrs Nicolson. Let the doctor deal with it.'

The doctor knelt beside his patient. He felt his pulse, put a stethoscope to his chest and then peered into each eye. He stared at the crumpled figure in silence while Harry and Gussie exchanged nervous glances.

Stella said, 'I don't understand. He was already—'

Harry tugged at her sleeve and said, 'Perhaps we should wait outside, Mrs Nicolson. It's very upsetting for you. The doctor will do all he can.'

Stella resisted his efforts to dislodge her and said again, 'I don't see how he got here.'

The doctor stood up slowly, shaking his head. 'I can't help him, I'm afraid. I can't do anything for him.' He looked at Gussie. 'I'm afraid he's dead.'

Gussie said, '*Dead*? Oh, no! He was speaking to me – mumbling. He was definitely alive when I left him.'

'I'm afraid we've lost him. What else can I say?'

For a moment no one spoke. Gussie was wondering frantically how to get Stella out of the way before she said something that would arouse the doctor's suspicions.

At last Harry said, 'The poor chap. What on earth happened? Heart attack or something?'

To Gussie's ears this sounded very forced, but the doctor seemed not to notice. He was wiping his hands on his handkerchief and there was perspiration on his brow.

'I'll fetch a stretcher. We'll have to put him in the infirmary. Bit of a blow, really. Never happened before. Not on the *Mauretania*.'

Gussie signalled to Harry and indicated a half-bottle of brandy. Harry nodded.

'A drop of brandy, Mrs Nicolson. That always helps at times like these. Sit on the chair and I'll find a glass.'

To their relief Stella obeyed him. She said, 'Well, he's gone. I suppose it doesn't matter where.'

Gussie whispered to the doctor, 'She doesn't know what she's saying, poor soul. Jabbering away there. It takes some people that way.'

'Hmm.' Fortunately he was still staring at his erstwhile patient and paying little attention to Stella. 'I can smell drink on his breath, and he's got that nasty bruise on his forehead and a bit of a gash. Maybe he wandered around drunk and fell. Or maybe another bout of fisticuffs. Some people are too handy with their fists, I know, but we don't expect that sort of thing on this ship. I hate to say it,' he said, 'but I did warn him. He came to me with serious pains and I suspected internal bleeding. I wanted to examine him, but he was most uncooperative.' He spread his hands, palms upwards, in a gesture of helplessness. 'If a doctor doesn't have the patient's trust, these things will happen. Thank goodness there is no question of negligence of any kind.'

Fixing the blame squarely on the patient, thought Gussie, but she sympathised with the doctor. No doubt Nicolson had tested his patience and, if internal bleeding had contributed to his final collapse, the doctor was not to blame.

Dr Mawle glanced at each of them in turn. 'I wanted to have him in overnight. To keep an eye on him. Do a couple of tests—'

Harry said, 'I'm sure we all know that you did your best for him. As you say, if a patient doesn't *want* to be helped . . .' He shrugged, leaving the sentence unfinished.

Stella watched wordlessly, sipping her drink slowly. She appeared totally disinterested in the conversation.

The doctor turned to Gussie. 'You must have been the last person to see him alive,' he said. 'Did he say anything? Anything at all that you could understand?'

'He said something about some pills. That he'd taken a lot of pills. I assumed he meant for the pain. Maybe all the pills on top of the bleeding . . .' She shook her head. 'I suppose we may never know.'

'Oh, we'll know,' he said. He lowered his voice. 'There'll have to be an inquiry – I shall notify the captain immediately. The company will arrange for an inquest. A post-mortem.' His sigh was deep and ragged. 'But as you say, it may have been a fatal combination, poor fellow. And he must have been in considerable pain. A ruptured spleen or damaged kidneys. Any manner of things. He told me he'd had a severe blow to the solar plexus. Oh dear! Terrible thing. Terrible! How very sad.' He turned to Stella: 'My sincerest condolences, Mrs Nicolson.'

She looked at him over the rim of her glass and said, 'Yes!'

Harry asked, 'Is there anything I can do to help? Fetch the stretcher, for instance?'

'Oh, that would be splendid. But I'll come with you. Must get a form – cause, date, time of death, you see. All these formalities have to be observed even on board a ship.' He looked at Stella. 'I really am so sorry, Mrs Nicolson.'

She gave him a vague smile and said, 'We all have to go some time, doctor. His time had come.'

'If only he had allowed me to examine him—'

'You did your best. He was terrified of doctors. He always referred to them as—'

Gussie said hastily, 'You've been splendid, doctor. A rock of support.'

Stella finished, '—quacks.'

But the doctor was smiling at Gussie. 'A rock? Oh, how very kind.' He looked absurdly grateful. 'But now another unpleasant duty. I must wake the captain and break the bad news.' To Harry he said, 'Come with me and I'll show you where the stretcher's kept.'

They went out, leaving Gussie with Stella and her dead husband. Gussie poured herself a large brandy. 'Stella, I think you'd be better off in bed. Shall I come with you to your cabin? If Abby or the nanny needs you, they'll worry if they find you both missing.'

Unprotesting, Stella allowed herself to be taken back to her cabin. Gussie saw her into bed, where she fell asleep in the middle of a sentence. As Gussie closed the door on her way out, Mary Crisford appeared.

'Is anything wrong? We heard a crash earlier, but Mrs Nicolson said everything was all right. Just perfect, she said. But there's been people backwards and forwards and I thought—'

Gussie said, 'I'm afraid there's been an accident. Poor Mr Nicolson was taken ill suddenly. He died before we could get him to the doctor.'

Mary's face registered genuine horror. '*Died*! Mr Nicolson? He can't be dead.'

'I'm afraid he is. Mrs Nicolson is sleeping. She's had a terrible shock. Is Abby asleep?'

'Yes, but she was awake earlier.'

'In the morning, Mary, please say nothing to Abby. Her mother will break the news later. And don't disturb Mrs Nicolson. The doctor will be along in the morning to see how she is.'

At that moment Abby's face peeped out from behind the nanny. She asked, 'Who's dead?'

Mary looked stricken. 'Oh dear! She must have woken up.'

Gussie sighed. 'Let's all go into your cabin,' she said. They trooped in, Mary looking as though she might burst into tears at any moment.

Gussie, knowing that kindness would bring the tears, gave her a sharp look and said, 'Pull yourself together, Nanny! Sit on the bed while I talk to Abby.'

Abby was wearing a sprigged winceyette nightdress and her hair had been loosely braided on either side of her head. If Tess had lived to this age, she too might have worn night-time braids and – Gussie fought back reminiscences. This was not the time. She must think about what was best for Abby. The sooner she knew, the sooner she would begin to recover. It suddenly seemed unfair to leave the unhappy task to Stella, who would be in no fit state to comfort anyone.

'What did you hear?' she asked the child.

'Nanny said, "Dead? Oh no!" She *did*. I heard her. Is it Mama? Is Mama dead?' Her eyes seemed too huge for her small face.

Gussie made an instant decision. 'No, it's not your mama, Abby. It's your father.'

'Papa? O-o-ooh!' For a moment she stared at Gussie and then her face crumpled.

'He had some very bad pains, Abby, and he wasn't well at all and we sent for the doctor. By the time the doctor came, your poor dear Papa was dead.' She saw the colour drain from the child's face. 'Gone to heaven,' she added, 'to stay with God and the blessed angels.'

Two tears threatened to fall but Abby blinked them back. 'Is he in a coffin?'

'Not yet. He's nice and comfortable in a special bed in the ship's hospital.'

'Is he asleep?' Her mouth trembled.

'A sort of sleep, yes.'

'Poor Papa. He hates hospitals. Papa said that doctors kill people. Did the doctor kill him?'

'Certainly not. I told you how it happened. He had bad pains.'

'Is Mama crying?'

Gussie bent the truth. 'She was, poor Mama, but now she's asleep.'

Mary began to cry. Gussie said, 'Now don't give way, please, Mary. Abby is going to need you.'

Abby said, 'Shall I give way?'

'You can cry if you wish, dear, because he's your Papa.'

Abby was frowning. 'Why did Mama say that everything was perfect?'

Gussie thought quickly. 'She probably meant perfectly dreadful, Abby. She was very unhappy and – and worried about poor Papa, but she didn't want to worry you. In the morning I expect your Mama will come and talk to you and answer all your questions, but until she does you must be a good girl for Nanny. You understand? I think there's a fancy-hat competition for the ladies tomorrow morning. Maybe Nanny will take you to watch that? Papa wouldn't want you to be too sad, Abby. He loved you a lot.' She drew the child towards her and gave her a big smile, followed by a quick cuddle. Abby felt small and unbearably frail in her arms and reminded her painfully of Tess. Tears for her own lost child swam in her eyes, but she blinked them back. 'You pop back into your bed – or better still, maybe Nanny will make room for you in her bed. Isn't that a wonderful idea? Then if you both want to shed a few tears you can comfort each other.'

Mary climbed obediently into bed and opened her arms and Abby scuttled across the room and climbed into bed with her nanny.

Gussie left them. She had done all she could.

She hoped that by the time she returned to her own cabin, the doctor would have gone, taking Clive Nicolson's body with him. With any luck Harry might be waiting for her. Gussie dreaded what he would have to say to her, but he held her fate in his hands and she had to know.

As she had expected, Harry was still in her cabin. He was sitting beside the desk and rose to his feet as she went in. One look at his face warned her to expect the worst. His smile was forced and he looked ill at ease.

She asked, 'So what happened?'

'We've taken him to the infirmary. There's nowhere else to put him, and fortunately there's no one in there at the moment. The captain was told and is none too pleased. Not a good advertisement for the ship, you see.'

'I can see that but—' She shrugged and sat down on the edge of the bed.

'He's hoping to keep it out of the newspapers. Hoping for our cooperation.'

'Doesn't he care at all about a poor dead soul?' She knew that was a mistake as soon as the words were out.

Harry said, 'You sound as though you might regret his death.'

'Not exactly, but he's human – or was. Not a nice character, but none of us are perfect.'

Already she could see the conversation leading the wrong way. Harry was putting her on the defensive and she objected to that. She stared down at her hands, willing herself to be careful.

She said, 'I had to tell Abby. The child overheard me talking to the nanny.'

235

Harry asked, 'How well did you know him?'

Gussie almost said 'Who?' but at the last minute realised the folly of pretence. 'Not at all,' she said, avoiding his eye.

'Only he seemed to know you. That night in the Verandah Café – he put his hand on your shoulder as though . . . Well, I felt there was something between you.'

His voice was cold, she thought fearfully, but forced herself to meet his gaze. 'There might have been, but it didn't happen. Overtaken by events, you could say.'

Now, she thought wearily, it's up to him. If he follows this line, we are in for a confrontation.

He obviously realised it, too, because for a long moment he said nothing. He fiddled with the blotter on the table, his face half turned from her. His back was stiff and she knew the signs were not good. Mentally she began to prepare for the worst. She felt she should say something to help matters, but something within her – some shred of remaining pride – prevented it.

He said, 'Poor Abby.'

'Yes. I think Mary was upset, too.'

'Well, it doesn't happen every day.'

'No.'

Shadow-boxing, she thought, feeling slightly hysterical. Perhaps she should come right out and ask him: 'Does what I've been mean you don't want me?' She was tempted, but at the last moment her nerve failed. She mustn't push him away, but neither would she nudge him in her direction. If he was teetering on the brink, she must let him reach his own conclusion. He would get no help from her.

He said, 'I was grateful for your letter. It couldn't have been easy. I was full of admiration.'

'Oh, good.'

Oh, good. She almost groaned. It sounded fatuous. He had paid her a compliment of sorts and all she could say was, 'Oh, good.' She said, 'I'm glad you thought so.' That was only slightly better.

He began to fold the blotter, keeping the edges straight. 'Gussie, I want you to know that – that I wanted very much to – to . . .' He shook his head. 'To make some sort of fresh start, but when I think about everything there's this – this block. This wall between us. I need to get over or around it, but I *can't*!'

Gussie had expected it, but she felt as though he had struck her a physical blow. Deeply wounded, her natural response was to defend herself. She said, 'I doubt if you ever will,' and then felt cruel and heartless. She knew that he needed her to help him through, but she couldn't do it; she couldn't make things easy for him. He must either succeed alone or he must give her up.

'Gussie, *please*.' He was looking at her now and she saw hurt and shock in his eyes.

She drew a deep breath and let it out slowly. 'What you want to say, Harry, is that you love me but you can never marry me. Because the images of me with other men will always be between us.'

He stared at her without speaking, then shook his head unhappily.

He hadn't contradicted her.

There was a deep ache starting up within her, but Gussie went on relentlessly. 'You don't think you'll ever be able to trust me. Isn't that about it?'

'Gussie!' he whispered. His expression was agonised.

'*Isn't it*?' she demanded. She felt demeaned, *wounded*, by his acceptance of her reading of the situation and anger came to her rescue. He had made no protest; had said nothing to deny her charges. Then damn him to hell! she thought. 'I can't help you, you know that. I won't pretend I don't love you because I do, Harry. I've never loved anyone else and I never will. But other men have come and gone in my life, and I've done what I could for them. I've made them as happy as I could. I've earned my money, and if you want me to say I'm ashamed I won't – not for you or anyone else . . .'

He tried to interrupt her but she went on, 'Men are still boys inside, Harry, did you know that? They're selfish and scared and foolish and lonely, and when they needed me I felt it a privilege in a way. I was the one they turned to, you see. I had no one to love or need me – except them. I don't expect you to understand. How could you? I was stupid to write the way I did, and I can see that now. I was asking the impossible.'

He said, 'I went with a – a loose woman once. For money.'

She waited.

'It was about a year after my wife died. It was a cold and loveless business, and afterwards I felt disgusted with myself—'

'And with her.' It was an accusation.

'Yes . . . I'm sorry.'

'And ever since you've thought about *me* doing it!' Gussie took a deep breath; she was almost shouting. With an effort she lowered her voice. 'It wasn't what I wanted, you know, Harry. I wanted a husband and a family.'

He put his head in his hands and she watched him, hardening her heart. This is how it will end, she thought, but she didn't regret the letter. She couldn't be sorry that she'd tried to bring them back together. Only sorry that it had led to this sad and empty exchange which neither of them wanted.

He said, 'I blame myself for what you – for how you ended up. If I hadn't deserted you we'd have had Tess, and everything would have been different, and she would never have been in front of that horse-bus. I suppose you've thought the same thing.'

'Oh yes! So many times.' And at first she had blamed Harry. After a while she had learned more about the world and its wicked ways and had blamed fate instead. She said, 'If things had been different we'd have made each other happy.'

He was silent.

'Wouldn't we, Harry?'

He looked up. His face bore the pinched look that comes with suffering and Gussie was suddenly reminded of Tess when she had fallen over or shut her finger in the door. It is so much easier to comfort a child, she thought, because you assume you know what a child needs. She used to take Tess on to her lap and kiss the hurt better. Tears sprang into her eyes as she recalled the sweetness that comes with easing the little one's pain, knowing that with the right words you can make them happy again.

A man is different, she thought. A man like Harry could keep his soul locked away for ever, defying you to know him. Harry was afraid of surrendering his happiness into her hands.

She sighed. 'This is "goodbye" then, Harry,' she told him, 'but before we part I want you to know that it was never sordid. I called them my "gentlemen"– one was a young doctor whose wife very ill and could never be a true wife.'

'I don't want to hear it, Gussie,' he said quietly.

Gussie flared up. 'But I want to tell it!' Her voice rose. 'I need to get it all out, just this once and then never again. Because we can't be just friends, Harry. We both know that. It's either all or nothing, and it's going to be nothing. So let me say my piece . . .' She stared, eyes unfocused, into the past. 'One was an elderly man whose wife had left him for another man. Never recovered properly; needed reassurance. And the young man who – well, never mind about him; he was a sad case. And then Cecil, a fussy little body, if you'll excuse the phrase. Cecil Fiske. Poor soul. He always carried an empty briefcase because it made him feel important . . . There was a failed politician, living on his memories, alone and poor . . . And Ian, an actor. I won't tell you his other name, but he's quite well-known. He lived with his mother, adored her. Then she died. Sometimes all he did was talk about her. Poor little man. He needed someone to take an interest in him . . . They all visited on a regular basis, sometimes once a week, sometimes more or less . . . I made sure that they never met each other. They were my reason for living, sad though that may sound. After Tess died I had no one to live for. I missed all the caring . . .' She smiled at him tiredly. 'Poor Harry. A little more than you bargained for, wasn't it? Never mind. It's all said. All water under the bridge.'

He said, 'I shouldn't have come,' and walked towards the door as though a great burden had been laid across his shoulders.

Gussie said, 'Go away, Harry. Make a new life for yourself and leave me to do the same.'

He paused. 'Will you – go back to it?'

'Why should you care?' The words were out before she could stop them.

He shrugged. 'I do care.'

'Of course I shan't.' Her tone was sharper than she intended. 'I've got a job with the Nicolsons for as long as I wish. I shall see them safely back to her parents in America.' She shrugged. 'I might decide to stay on with them, or I might come back to England. But by then I shall have a good reference, Stella has promised me that. With that I can find employment anywhere. Another position as governess, or perhaps a nanny. Maybe companion to an old lady or housekeeper to a rich old gentleman. You can think of me sliding into a respectable old age, Harry. This voyage has changed my life in more ways than one. Stop worrying about me and get on with your own life.' She managed what she hoped was a bright smile. The worst had happened and she would survive.

He asked, 'Are you making the decision for me?'

'Someone had to make it.'

'Can we write to each other?'

'No, Harry, I don't think so. A clean break is best.' She knew there was no other way she could bear it.

After a moment he said, 'We can at least wish each other well. Maybe you'll meet someone else.'

'I'll never marry anyone else, Harry. If you ever change your mind – if you ever decide you can share my past as well as my future—' She shrugged. 'Come and tell me. If you can't, then do your best to forget me.'

He took her hand and his was warm and slightly rough. He's not going to kiss me, she thought, anguished. He didn't. Instead he pressed her hand to his heart and then, releasing her, stepped outside into the corridor. She longed to throw her arms around him and hug him. Just once – but it was already too late. Tears pressed against her eyelids and she wanted him to go before she broke down.

He turned. 'Tomorrow we have to speak to the police and maybe make a statement about what happened to Nicolson.'

Gussie took a long last look at him. Then she said quickly, 'Tomorrow is another day, Harry.'

And she closed the door as the tears started to fall.

The next morning Stella was awoken by a quiet but persistent knocking on her cabin door. Struggling into wakefulness, she sat up. As she did so the events of the previous night came back to her. Her husband was dead and she had killed him. She felt nothing but relief. She frowned. Had they pushed him over the side of the ship? No-o . . . Then what had happened? She slid out of bed, pulled on her wrap and crossed to the door.

'Who is it?'

'Me. Gussie Malone.'

Stella opened the door. 'Is it about Clive?'

'No.' Gussie stepped inside and said, 'I have to tell you something, Stella.' She turned to face her and Stella could see how ill at ease she was.

'Do sit down.'

'I think I should – before I *fall* down!' Gussie sat on the bedside chair and avoided Stella's eyes. 'I have something to tell you – about myself – that you won't want to hear,' she began. 'I know this is a bad time after what happened last night, but there's never going to be a good time. I've been thinking it over and – much as I want to be Abby's governess – I can only accept if—'

'I thought you'd already accepted!' Stella slipped her feet into her slippers and sat down in one of the armchairs. The thought of Gussie's companionship had given her the strength to carry on with her life, and there was no way Stella would let her go back on her promise to begin Abby's education. Not that it was a permanent arrangement – surely Gussie had agreed to give it a try for three months? Or maybe she hadn't. Stella couldn't remember. Her mind seemed to be functioning very sluggishly. Perhaps that was the sleeping draught the doctor had given her.

'The circumstances are changing,' said Gussie. 'You'll understand when I tell you – when I explain – oh, heavens! This is so difficult. I was awake all night, thinking about my life – what's gone and what's left of it. I'm not what you think, Stella.'

Watching her friend's face, Stella suddenly remembered her husband's wild accusations. But no! That was ridiculous. Mr Parr had vouched for Gussie Malone, and she trusted his word.

Gussie went on, 'You may wish to change your mind about Abby – about me being her governess.'

Stella saw desperation in her eyes. 'I doubt it,' she told her.

Gussie drew a deep breath and said, 'There's something in my past – something I feel you must know.'

A long silence followed and Stella felt a wave of faintness. This *was* what Clive had spoken about. She closed her eyes, not wanting to know. 'Please! Don't tell me! My husband said something about you – I didn't believe him.'

'It's true.' The voice was almost a whisper.

'I don't believe it! I don't *want* to know, Gussie. *Please*!'

241

Gussie's hands were clenched so tightly that the knuckles showed white. 'I have to tell you.'

Stella tried to think, forcing her mind to focus on the awful truth. If she believed it, then how could she employ Gussie to supervise her child? Better *not* to believe. She said, 'He said you were a – a street-walker. He called you a "lady of the night". I don't believe him – or you. You're a widow.'

'I'm not.'

Stella stared at her friend – her *only* friend. The friend who had helped her deal with Clive's death; who had put herself at risk to shield her from the results of her own wrongdoing.

As though reading her mind, Gussie said, 'It *is* true. I've reached a stage in my life when I'm not hiding anything from anyone. If we're to have any kind of friendship, Stella, you have to know me for what I am – *was*.'

It was impossible. Stella protested, 'But Mr Parr said he would recommend you; that he would employ you. I believed him.' Because she had *wanted* to believe. Looking at Gussie, she couldn't begin to understand what an effort this had cost her. She could only guess how much courage it had taken for her friend to confess. Admiration softened her sense of shock.

Gussie said, 'Mr Parr was lying to protect me. We were in love years ago.' Her voice shook dangerously and she blinked furiously. 'I had his child – Tess – but he didn't know.' As Stella watched, astonished, tears erupted and Gussie brushed them away with an impatient hand. 'We parted and then, later . . .' She gave a choking sob, 'Tess was *killed*.'

'Oh, my *dear*!' Stella rushed forward and knelt beside her. How could anyone live with so much grief, she wondered, taking Gussie's hands in her own. 'I'm so sorry.' As she did so, her imagination made the required leap and she could *see* Gussie waiting for a client. She imagined Gussie, haunted by the loss of her little daughter, struggling to make a living, feigning cheerfulness, trying to be all things to all men. The truth was that Stella had only a hazy idea of what such a life would entail, except that it was dangerous. She certainly didn't want or need to know more. All she wanted now was to comfort this brave, warm-hearted woman who was the only true friend she had ever had. The thought of losing Gussie was uppermost in her mind, and the prospect terrified her.

She said, 'Don't cry, Gussie,' and she offered her a clean hand-kerchief from the bedside table. 'When Clive told me,' she said, 'I thought he was lying but he wasn't. Well, what difference does it make to us?' She pushed a damp lock of red hair from Gussie's tear-stained face and suddenly saw that beneath her friend's toughness she was as vulnerable as anyone else. It came to Stella abruptly that this was her chance to repay her debt to Gussie.

'Listen to me, Gussie Malone,' she said firmly. 'I don't care what you've done. Truly I don't. They're only *men*, when all's said and done. We're *friends*.' She took the handkerchief and gently wiped Gussie's face. 'We shouldn't let a few men come between us. We can both make a new start and we can help each other.'

'Oh, Stella!'

As they hugged each other, Gussie gave a small, tremulous laugh and Stella drew back. They stared at each other, smiling with renewed hope.

Stella lifted an imaginary glass. 'Here's to us, Gussie!'

Gussie did the same and whispered, 'Here's to us!'

Chapter Thirteen

Abby stood at the ship's rail beside Uncle Jerry, who was leaning on it watching the approaching New York skyline with interest. Down below, passengers were already going ashore and the band was playing. Leaning on the lower rail, Abby clutched a blue velvet rabbit which Mrs Malone had given her for her eighth birthday a few weeks before. Six weeks had passed since Papa had died, but the time had gone quickly. She could say most of her tables now, could write her own name and was learning about t-h for thunder, c-h for church and s-h for ship. She had nearly finished her first reading book and was very proud of it. In fact she liked having a governess, even if Mrs Malone was rather strict. It was better than going to a school with rough boys and girls.

Uncle Jerry was nice. He always made her laugh, and wore a funny tie that was really a leather shoelace slotted through a blue stone. He wore a hat called a stetson, and Mama teased him about it, but he said he didn't give a damn so that was all right. He was wearing it now and peering out from under it to watch the people down below. Poor Mama was resting in her cabin while Mrs Malone unpacked for her. Later Abby would unpack her own things. At first Mama had been rather strange after Papa went to heaven; she cried a lot and said funny things. Abby had heard her telling Mrs Malone that Mr Hemmings deserved a medal, but Abby didn't know him so she wasn't sure what he had done. Probably been very brave. Probably a soldier. When she asked Mrs Malone she said that little 'pictures' had big ears, but Abby thought it must be a joke. She was glad that now Mama was getting better.

Uncle Jerry glanced down at her and smiled. 'Everything OK, honey?' he asked.

She liked the way he called her 'honey'. It made her feel rather grown-up because he called Mama 'honey', too. He had come all the way to England to look after them and Abby was glad, because she missed Papa so much and now there was nobody to call her 'little rabbit' and tweak her nose.

She sighed. Now they were back in America, they were going to stay there for ever and ever, and that meant she could never be Nanny's bridesmaid. And it wasn't fair because Nanny had gone away to live near John and had never written to her. She had broken her promise, and Abby didn't feel able to forgive her for that.

'I was going to wear little sparkly shoes,' she said aloud, 'and a blue dress.'

'U-huh?'

He wasn't really listening, she thought resignedly. Grown-ups never did – except Mrs Malone. 'I was going to be a bridesmaid.'

'U-huh?'

He was always saying that, and she didn't know what it meant. 'A bridesmaid,' she repeated, 'but now I'm not.'

'A bridesmaid, eh? That's great.'

She regarded him with sudden hope. 'Are you ever going to get married, Uncle Jerry, or are you too old?'

He turned round and she could see that at last she had caught his interest.

He said, 'Can you keep a secret, Abby? A big secret?' He held his hands wide to show how big it was.

Abby nodded solemnly

He went on, 'One day, when your Mama is better – I mean when she's good and ready – I'm going to ask her to marry me.'

She said, 'U-huh!'

He laughed. 'And your Mama will say "Yes". So I'll be your new Papa. Will that be OK with you? You can be a bridesmaid and wear that blue dress.'

Abby thought she would burst with excitement. 'That'll be OK with me,' she told him. It would be nice to have a new Papa, and she didn't think the other one would mind because he had the blessed angels to keep him company. Mrs Malone said that angels were very accommodating and that Papa would be enjoying himself in heaven.

When Abby realised that, she had stopped crying about him.

Uncle Jerry said, 'We'll buy a little spread in the country and take vacations, and we'll find you a pony. We'll get your Mama on a horse, too – damned if we don't – and then we'll all ride up into the hills and have a picnic.'

'What is a spread?'

He was just explaining that it was a 'parcel of land with a log cabin' when she interrupted him, pointing excitedly.

'Look, Uncle Jerry! There's Mr Parr, coming up the gangway. That's funny!'

'Mr Parr? I guess it is, yes. But what's so funny?'

'Mrs Malone said that we wouldn't set eyes on him again, and that if we did she'd eat her hat.'

Uncle Jerry was still laughing when Mr Parr reached them. The two men shook hands; they seemed to like each other.

Mr Parr said, 'I thought you'd like to know the verdict first hand, although the papers will be forwarded of course. I had a cable this morning from Liverpool. Accidental death.'

'Thank God for that! That's a load off my mind. Stella will be so relieved. They took their time.'

'The wheels do grind exceeding slow, I'm afraid, but they got there in the end.' To Abby he said, 'Hello, young lady. Are you pleased to be back in America?'

She said that she was and told him about the pony, but not about being a bridesmaid because that was a secret.

'I like the rabbit.' He tweaked one of the floppy ears.

'It's a present from Mrs Malone. His name's Hal.'

'Hal? That's a strange name for a rabbit.'

Uncle Jerry laughed and said, 'Abby's a strange kid! But great.'

Abby scowled. 'I'm *not* strange and I didn't call him that. Mrs Malone said that he was born with that name. Mrs Malone's ragdoll is called Clara, and Clara and the rabbit are great friends. If I've been especially good, Mrs Malone lets them sleep together in my bed.'

Mr Parr looked very surprised when he heard that and he nearly smiled, but not quite.

To Uncle Jerry he said, 'How is Mrs Nicolson bearing up?'

'Making good progress, thank God. The voyage has done her good. Mrs Malone's been a godsend: strong and caring. Stella would never have pulled through without her, that's for sure. She certainly appreciates that woman. The doc thinks there's no lasting damage done. A minor breakdown, he called it, but we'll look after her. She's going to be fine. I'll make it all up to her.'

Abby wondered if Uncle Jerry knew about Papa dying in Mrs Malone's cabin. She hadn't told him because Mrs Malone had told her not to, and because Mrs Malone had warned her that if she went on listening when she wasn't supposed to she would grow into a sneaky person and have no friends.

Mr Parr said, 'Well, I'll just go down and find Mrs Nicolson. Pass on the good news.'

Abby said, 'She's resting while Mrs Malone packs. I don't need a nanny now because I'm too grown-up. I have a governess. Shall I take you to Mama's cabin, Mr Parr?'

'Um—' He gave a little cough and said, 'I'll find it, thank you, Abby. You stay here and watch the excitement. Listen to the band.'

Abby frowned, afraid she might miss something, but Uncle Jerry said he had seen enough and was going to find a drink and did Abby want a glass of fizzy lemonade? Abby smiled at Mr Parr and took Uncle Jerry's hand firmly in her own. Mrs Malone said that of course Abby loved her real Papa and always would, but Abby thought this new one was very kind and she couldn't wait to see herself in the blue dress.

Gussie was gently closing the lid of the small trunk when the knock came on the cabin door. She glanced at Stella, who was fast asleep, then crossed quietly to the door. She expected the steward but found Harry Parr instead.

'Harry!'

He looked tired but cheerful. The sight of him so near, so unexpected, warmed her right through to the centre of her being. She couldn't take her eyes off him, loving his hair, his eyes, everything that was Harry Parr. He was wearing a grey suit, a sober tie and brown shoes. He looked vaguely prosperous.

'What are you doing here?' She stepped outside into the corridor and pulled the door partly closed behind her.

He said, 'I've brought the inquiry results. Accidental death. I thought Mrs Nicolson would like to know as soon as possible. I was keen to tell her in person before I go home. It's a very satisfactory verdict.'

'*Very* satisfactory – in the circumstances!' Gussie raised her eyebrows meaningfully 'Did you have to give evidence?' How on earth had he managed it, she wondered – hand on the Holy Bible and all that stuff?

He rolled his eyes. 'I'm trying to forget certain aspects of what happened.'

'I'm sure you are. I think we all are. And 've're all in your debt, Harry. ' She glanced behind her. 'Stella's sleeping, but I'll wake her if you—'

'No!' He drew a deep breath. 'The truth is that's just an excuse. I really wanted to see you again, to talk to you before you disembark. I thought you might disappear into the wild blue yonder.'

The surge of hope was unsettling and Gussie found herself resisting it. 'I shan't disappear, but I am looking forward to America. I have another six weeks to go, but in fact I can stay just as long as I wish.'

'You're not thinking of staying here, are you?'

'I am, actually. A new country. Maybe my luck will change.'

She tried to read his expression but failed.

He said, 'You were right, Gussie, about my father. I followed your advice. I went to see my father's grave and I took some flowers.'

'I'm glad you did, Harry.'

'I feel better about him – and rather ashamed. I was condemning him all those years while my own behaviour left much to be desired.'

'To err is human . . .' She gave a small shrug and smiled.

After a long pause he said, 'I have an offer that might interest you. I'm hoping it's one you can't refuse.'

'An offer? Well, I've no long-term plans. I'm free as the proverbial bird, Harry, and never been happier.'

You liar, she reproved herself. You're respectable, you're needed and the future's rosy enough, but there's something missing. You're living on the fringe of someone else's life and your own is slipping away.

At that moment an elderly couple came along the corridor, followed by a steward carrying their various boxes and bags. She and Harry flattened themselves against the wall to allow the flustered trio to pass.

Gussie said, 'You look tired, Harry.'

'I'm very busy. The point is that I need a partner, Gussie . . . Well, no not a partner exactly. That is—'

She smiled. 'Which is it, Harry?'

'I need someone to deal with the paperwork, answer the telephone, that sort of thing. I was hoping you'd grown tired of being a governess, and I thought you might consider the post. Do you think you could master a typewriting machine?'

She smiled. 'What you want is a secretary, Harry, not a partner. And I could learn to work the machine. There's nothing I can't learn if I put my mind to it.' She gave him a long look, wishing she could say 'Yes'. If she worked for him, she would see him every day, but it would never be enough. 'But I don't need a job, Harry, and even if I did I wouldn't accept it. I think you know why.'

'Gussie, I'm doing this all wrong,' he said, running his fingers distractedly through his hair. 'Look, let me try again. I've just bought a large house in Finchley, and the office would be in the upstairs front room. I'd live in the rest of it – but I do need some secretarial help—'

Gussie wondered what more there was to be said. As she waited, the steward dashed past in the opposite direction, pocketing his tip as discreetly as possible.

Harry said, 'It's a bit public here.'

'It's fine.' The more public the better, she thought. Less chance of her ending up in tears.

He went on, 'Actually I was planning to marry the secretary.'

Marry the secretary? She stared at him suspiciously.

'A wife *and* a secretary,' he told her. 'Two for the price of one.' When she still didn't speak, he added, 'For a while at least . . . It's a family house, Gussie. Five bedrooms.'

Now she could clearly read the longing in his eyes. A family house. *A family*? She thought of Tess, remembering the feel of those little arms around her neck, the bubbling sound of her laughter. No child could ever replace Tess, but to have a family – oh, heavens! Was it possible? Her heart began to race.

'Oh, Harry!' she whispered. 'Is this a proposal? If it is, you'd better be very sure because I'm going to say "Yes" and once we're married you'll never get rid of me.'

He was obviously nervous, she thought, surprised, but there was a certain gleam in his eyes. She thought it was hope.

He said, 'We could have another child, couldn't we, Gussie? Or two?'

Her heart was full as she nodded. 'It's not too late. Another child – now wouldn't that be wonderful?'

He was gaining confidence; beginning to believe. 'We could go to bed together,' he said with a grin. 'Just like Clara and Hal!'

Gussie's hand flew to her mouth. 'Abby! Oh, that child!' she gasped, feeling her face grow hot with embarrassment. Then they were laughing and both trying to talk at once, and somehow he found time to kiss her and she kissed him back.

Reluctantly they moved apart as a portly gentleman marched past carrying a briefcase and trying to look important. Gussie knew the type. In fact – she gave a gasp of dismay. She knew *him*! It was Mr Fiske. He must have been on board all this time and she hadn't spotted him. Fate had waited until now . . . Desperately she averted her eyes, but it was too late.

With horror she heard him say, 'Good heavens! It's Gussie Malone, isn't it?'

It was one of the few times in her life when Gussie was speechless. Desperately she glanced up at Harry. *Please, God*! Time seemed to stand still as she waited breathlessly. Then Harry took her arm firmly in his; he winked at her and smiled at Mr Fiske.

'It *was* Gussie Malone,' he said, 'but I am proud to say that she will soon be Mrs Harry Parr.'

There was a poignant silence. Gussie's heart almost stopped beating as Mr Fiske, wide-eyed, looked from Harry to Gussie and back to Harry. Then he smiled broadly, held out his hand to Harry.

'May I be the first to congratulate you, sir!' he said.